Last Judgement

Also by Richard Hugo

The Hitler Diaries

Last Judgement

Richard Hugo

MACMILLAN

ISBN 0 333 37612 9

First published 1984 by
Macmillan London Limited
London and Basingstoke

Associated companies in Auckland, Delhi, Dublin,
Gaborone, Hamburg, Harare, Hong Kong, Johannesburg,
Kuala Lumpur, Lagos, Manzini, Melbourne, Mexico City,
Nairobi, New York, Singapore and Tokyo

Typeset by Wyvern Typesetting Ltd, Bristol
Printed in Hong Kong

To my brother Denis

How can one live in the heart of a misunderstanding so total that everything which surrounds us is in reality non-real, a reflection, an illusion, a distorting mirror, a phantom? . . . For surely knowledge itself, in a world of illusions, can only be illusory?

JACQUES LACARRIÈRE, *The Gnostics*

BOOK ONE

Terror in fact is fraternity. For Terror is the guarantee that my neighbour will stay my brother; it binds my brother to me by the threat of violence it will use against him if he dares to be unbrotherly.

MAURICE CRANSTON, on Sartre

Prologue

29 September 1939

As far as he could remember, it was the first time in his life that Alois Schimmel had ever seen an erect penis that was not his own.

That it was about to be thrust into a naked female was almost more than he could bear but, though he turned away, the same scene was forced on him. On a grassy bank near a clear pool a nude pair were copulating with gusto. Behind them, top to tail, two more bodies made love in a manner that Schimmel had heard of but hitherto only imagined. Near them, three more partners, mouths and legs agape, inspected each other in a fashion that he hadn't heard of and couldn't imagine.

He looked around slowly at every wall of the room and then at the ceiling, but saw only the same repetition of sexual abandonment painted with every refinement of eighteenth-century taste and reflected from cleverly placed mirrors so that, as he walked through the bedroom, it seemed to shimmer and gyrate with hard and soft flesh, each pleasuring the other. He stood in wonder at the sight and then retreated from the place as though his sanity depended on it.

Reinhardt Egger saw the great house for the first time through a pair of Zeiss binoculars: a pink, stuccoed building, so precise and mathematical in its line and yet so delicate in the details of its carved stonework that in the shimmering autumn air it looked like a theatrical flat, the painted backdrop to an opera by Mozart.

"You wouldn't think the Poles could build a thing like that, would you?" Buchholz grumbled with grudging admiration. "It seems to be all they can do to put up a shack that keeps the rain out. That's about all they do keep out – not the bugs, that's for sure. I'm crawling with something I picked up in that place we bivouacked in last night."

Egger watched his sergeant wipe his nose on the sleeve of his battledress and pick at something – fleas or lice eggs – in the seams.

"The Poles didn't build it. We Germans did."

"In a pig's ear," Buchholz answered with cheerful scepticism. It was news to him that German kings, of the house of Saxony, had ever ruled Poland, and he was too used to Nazi propaganda to the effect that the Germans had built or invented or done everything worthwhile in the world for him to start believing it now.

Egger didn't press the point. He confined himself to marvelling at the house which Augustus of Saxony had built for one of his mistresses. Whether you called it German because of the king or Polish because it was Polish craftsmen who had created and fashioned the beauty was immaterial to him. That sort of point was only important to the Nazis. As a child living in Egypt where his father had an export business he had experienced Muslim art and knew that real culture knew no boundaries. But if the Nazis wanted to make out otherwise. . . . He had the ambition and realism to get along in the tawdry vulgarity of the Third Reich.

He cast the binoculars around again at the horizon where relics of the fighting hung as plumes of smoke over distant towns, then nearer at the surrounding expanse of birch and fir, and finally at the house again.

"The soldier boys must have checked it out," Buchholz said. He pointed to the small, bucket-shaped *Kübelwagen* parked at the head of an avenue of trees directly in front of the main building. The driver, in Wehrmacht grey, was lounging against the bonnet, smoking. The sergeant shook his dark, close-cropped head – Egger thought that no one looked so much like a reject from the master race – and added: "Still, they're taking a chance. How many in that car? Four or five? They'd be a pushover for any Polish deserters who wanted to kill a few of our side before calling it a day."

Egger agreed. In the rout and destruction of the Polish army these last four weeks there had been no lack of courage on the Polish side; and even after the disaster there was no shortage of martyrs. On the road that morning three uhlans on their tired, scraggy horses had bounded out of the trees and loosed off a volley of shots at the last of the four German cars. Two of the Poles had been quickly chopped down by gunfire, but the third still emptied the magazine of his carbine and then, with deliberate slowness, taunting them to kill him, trotted off into the forest. Egger wondered what could be done with people as incompetent and yet as inspired as the Poles.

However, for the moment there was no sign of the enemy. He let the binoculars fall and signalled the lead vehicle to go ahead and complete the reconnaissance. In the other three the crews sat at ease and broke out their cigarettes. They were a tired and filthy bunch, looking like something less than the pride of the Wehrmacht except for the determination and readiness in their faces. Egger let them take five minutes, then, when the front car gave the all-clear, gave the order to advance. "Los!" he shouted. "Let's go!"

On closer inspection the house seemed smaller, a dainty toy carved out of sugar icing. In the court directly outside the main entrance was a carp-pond with a fountain in the middle – a bit of statuary, a lusty Cupid who was evidently about to catch up with Venus. The fountain was out of order and the pool was starting to fill with leaves, but the theme of love and delight was still there, almost palpable in the air.

"What do you want here?" The shadow in the entrance-hall hid the owner of the thin voice. The driver of the *Kübelwagen* rolled his eyes and stamped out his cigarette; Egger guessed that the voice had been grating the soldier's nerves for the last two hundred miles. The driver hadn't bothered to stop Egger and his men when they arrived. He had done nothing more than cast a cursory glance over them. Same uniform – same side.

The owner of the voice emerged into the sunlight: medium height, plastered-down hair and a round face out of which peeped two weak eyes – a civilian in uniform, no insignia apart from a Party membership button, a pince-nez attached by a black ribbon to a button-down pocket.

"Who are you? What brings you here?" the civilian asked. He remembered his situation as he spoke, decided a salute was appropriate and brought his heels together with a gratifying click whilst his arm jabbed the air. "Heil Hitler!" Egger returned a conventional military salute and gave a name. He had a feeling of having met the other man before.

"Alois Schimmel."

Egger remembered. Schimmel had worked with one of the major auction-houses, Weinmüller; they had a branch in Vienna, but Egger guessed that it was at the other branch in Munich that they had met. God, but it seemed an age ago! Schimmel, however, gave no sign of recognition – an effect of uniforms, blotting out the individual. Perhaps that was why the Nazis were so fond of them, because the man inside had no responsibility; it was as if his uniform were acting.

For the rest, Egger's face was smeared with oil and dirt and he had two days' growth of beard.

"What's a civilian doing in a war zone?" he asked. "How many of you are there?" This last question was answered when two soldiers with rifles slung over their shoulders came clattering down the marble corridor at the double, having belatedly taken note of the arrival of strangers. Egger considered them with disdain: incapable even of keeping a proper guard, they were probably the dregs of some company, troublemakers got rid of on any excuse to wet-nurse a civilian art-historian who for some unfathomable reason had to be at the Front. "Only four of you?" Egger went on. "You're in luck. We had a brush with some Polish cavalry this morning and lost a man."

Schimmel blanched. He squeaked out: "I have orders to be here. It is necessary to preserve Germanic cultural treasures against destruction so that they may be saved for the Reich. I have accordingly taken possession of this house and its contents. And you, Herr Major?"

"Just looking for a billet. My men are tired and need to lie up for a few days."

Schimmel looked outside at the four cars parked in the court. Experience would have told him that ordinary troops would not be driving Mercedes staff-cars, but he lacked it and his own men didn't tell him.

"Well, you can't stay here. It must be obvious" – he meant to say "even to you", but something in Egger's bearing stopped him – "that this house is unsuitable as a lodging for troops."

"We'll just stay the night." He took his cap off – fair hair, the peak casting shadow over a pair of blue eyes. He wiped his forehead with a piece of rag. "You may appreciate our presence if there are any more stragglers in the district. And, for my part, I'd appreciate the opportunity of looking round" – he searched for an expression that would appeal to Schimmel – "this piece of German heritage."

Schimmel finally warmed to the idea of a tour. This urbane major was evidently a man of culture and not to be got rid of until he had seen the interior of the house. They went inside leaving their men to lounge and smoke and piss in the carp-pool.

On the ground floor they found themselves in a long gallery. The original decoration had been painted out and replaced by a row of uninteresting portraits.

"Exactly what is your role here, Herr Doktor Schimmel?" Egger asked, staring into the eyes of a pasty-faced, self-satisfied woman with a brood of children.

"I am the representative in Poland of Sonderauftrag Linz," said Schimmel. "Have you heard of it?"

"Something to do with collecting works of art for the Führer," Egger offered noncommittally. But he knew full well what Sonderauftrag Linz was.

"It is the Führer's intention", Schimmel expanded, "to make his home town of Linz into the cultural centre of Europe, the repository of the finest treasures of Western civilization." They passed into an elegant salon trimmed in gilt and silk. Egger paused in the doorway. The empty room, which had once been filled with light and music, gave him a sense of melancholy. Such rooms were in his dreams as he sat listening to the string quartet which his father had formed with others from the German legation in Cairo – Brahms in a small apartment where they could hear the muezzin calling the faithful to pray. "Take this," Schimmel was saying, waving an arm and pointing his pince-nez at a picture of a minstrel serenading a girl on a swing – a Fragonard, Egger suspected. "A work like this will be considered trash compared with the paintings that will be shown at Linz!"

"Astonishing," Egger murmured. He halted by one of the windows and looked out on a view of ill-kept strip fields and a Polish peasant rooting around in the furrows. He looked up again as Buchholz came bustling in, smiling through his tobacco-stained teeth and leaving a trail of mud from his boots on the drugget.

"They've got a truck at the back," Buchholz whispered. "My guess is that they intend to pick the best bits and then clear off."

"Have you selected any pieces for the Linz collection?" Egger asked Schimmel.

The civilian looked evasive. He was mentally counting the number of men the Major had brought with him. He was out of his depth in the customs of war: he had no idea whether, left to their own devices, Egger's men would loot the house or not. The aura of power in the other man's self-confidence and natural authority left him with a feeling almost of sexual nakedness. He cleared his throat and murmured: "I doubt that there is anything here that would merit inclusion."

They moved on again, this time into a library which held some porcelain in a closed cabinet: a dinner service with the electoral arms of Saxony paired with those of the dead king's paramour. The porcelain was mostly Meissen, but Egger recognized a clown figure modelled by Bustelli of Nymphenburg. He wondered what she had been like, the mistress on whom so much had been lavished.

"We have better examples in Dresden," Schimmel said. "You can be sure that none of this stuff will be of interest to Linz."

Egger looked up from the delicate modelling of Bustelli's clown. To Schimmel the porcelain and the other treasures of the house might be nothing more than commodities to be bought and sold, but to him it was quite otherwise. Stranded as his family had been in that other world of Egypt, it was only *culture*, his father impressed upon him, that kept him a European, a German. They must keep it. They must practise it, if only four middle-aged men like his father, sweating away at their fiddles, so that culture should not fail.

"Is there anything else?"

Schimmel coughed under his hand. "There is a bedroom that might . . . amuse you."

Egger smiled at the unabashed eroticism of the painted bedroom. He wondered how a lover, engaged in his own sweating exertions in the great four-poster bed, would react to the view of the well-endowed satyrs at their effortless copulations. Schimmel pretended to be unaffected and, instead, expounded platitudes about the Wehrmacht's Polish campaign, full of observations about "the valour of our troops" and "the wisdom of the Führer". It recalled to Egger that he was a German officer and that this house was a bizarre island of luxury and tranquillity in a country that was being plundered and destroyed.

"Is that everything?" he asked.

"Everything," Schimmel said. He shuffled from one foot to another and stared at his boots.

"What's through there?" Egger pointed to a door leading off the bedroom.

"A chapel, a small oratory. There are some icons and religious statues, all of Polish workmanship and quite valueless. The owners carried off the most valuable stuff before we arrived," he sneered. "No doubt they've been forced to sell them dirt-cheap to some filthy Jew."

"No doubt," Egger said. "All the same, I'll take a look." He strode across to the door, ignoring Schimmel's protests, and opened it.

The room was in darkness, and Egger was forced to light one of the alter candles, which flickered and gave off a faint light that reflected dully off rich reds and golds. There was a smell of cold incense that had impregnated the walls.

Unlike the rest of the house, which had been created all of a piece to suit the taste of the long-dead king, the oratory reflected the devotional tastes of successive generations of pious women. The image of a saint, carved in wood by the hand of a local craftsman; a gimcrack statue of the Virgin, mass-produced in plaster and painted the conventional blue and white of purity – Egger supposed that to some poor soul they had once meant something. He turned from them to the altar, and then saw the painting.

At first he noticed only the light glimmering from the gilded frame and the glow of colour dimly seen through smoke-grime. His eyes turned on the painted panel, and suddenly it was alive with action. It showed Christ, the Son of Man, sitting in splendour among the chorus of the cherubim and seraphim, judging the quick and the dead. Beneath His feet the clouds rolled and below them the damned souls were carried off to chaos and violence.

Egger stood for a moment, transfixed, and then recoiled from the power and awesomeness of the image. The damned stared out at the observer, their faces stripped bear of every hope of mercy, with every last chord of despair visible, almost audible.

"The painting is by a Polish artist in the Italian style," Schimmel said from the doorway in an attempt at being matter-of-fact.

Egger ignored the charade. He looked at the altarpiece with its fearful imagery of damnation, then through the open doorway at the elegant pornography of the bedroom and, still further, through a window out on to the real world and the haze of smoke from the distant war. He could make no sense of the several juxtapositions and his place in them. He turned and strode out of the chapel, his boots clattering across the floor. He went to the window again and waved at Buchholz.

"If you've seen everything," said Schimmel, scurrying after him, "perhaps we could discuss arrangements for billeting your men tonight."

Egger heard the rattle of small-arms fire nearby. "I don't think that will be necessary," he said.

"What was that noise?" Schimmel asked. He stepped over to the window and looked out. "There's something going on. My car, it isn't there!" More rifle shots. "I don't understand. It can't be the

Poles." He looked to Egger, who had opened his greatcoat. Yellow collar-patches were visible on the uniform jacket.

"You're not in the Army?" Schimmel said disbelievingly. Egger had taken out a pistol.

"No."

"You're going to kill me?" Schimmel was so stunned by the unaccustomed thought of his own mortality that the reflex of fear was blunted. He searched for something to say, but all he could find was "Heil Hitler. . . ." The words, squeaked out in his reedy voice, sounded like a question, the last one before Reinhardt Egger shot him four times in the head and chest.

Egger regarded the body briefly, waiting to feel a reaction. Schimmel was the first man he had killed. Contrary to the popular view, most soldiers never have the opportunity to kill a visible enemy. He examined Schimmel's bland features and noted with surprise that he felt less about the other man's death than about the painting in the chapel.

Buchholz disturbed this train of thought. He came running into the bedroom breathless and his rifle unslung. "We've got trouble!" he shouted. "The driver was only wounded. He managed to clear off in the *Kübelwagen*. Our lads are after him." He glanced at Schimmel's body and said: "I'm glad you managed to finish off that bastard."

Egger didn't wait for further explanation. With Buchholz on his tail he swept out of the house and jumped into one of the cars. With Schimmel and the rest of his escort dead, it was a matter of life and death to Egger that the driver of the *Kübelwagen* should not escape.

They came on the car only a kilometre down the road. The driver had taken the bend too fast and the vehicle was lying on its side, burning fiercely. Two of Egger's own cars were already on the scene.

Buchholz braked hard and shouted: "Where is he? In the car?" One of the soldiers shook his head and pointed across the adjacent field. In Polish fashion it was divided into strips among several crops.

"He's probably hiding in the corn," Buchholz said to Egger. "What do you want me to do?" He waited for a reply. His eyes showed some doubt that this handsome young officer, for all the firmness of his face, had the guts for the job.

"Kill him."

"Zu Befehl!" The sergeant snapped to attention. He put a finger to the wind, then barked to the others: "Bring me one of the petrol-cans!"

Egger watched Buchholz pour the contents of the can over the edge of the corn patch and then light it. Flames shot into the air and were driven by the wind across the dry, ripe heads of cereal. Egger turned from the flames to the men. They were leaning on their rifles, spectators with bets on whether the driver would escape. One of them spat out a corn stalk: "I shot the poor sod in the leg. I wouldn't give much for his chances of keeping ahead of the fire." And as if by magic there was an unearthly scream, and through the smoke a figure could be seen springing from the corn, beating the flames from its clothes. The vision lasted for a few seconds only and then Buchholz, taking his rifle, shot the man dead just as if he had been a rabbit.

They were in their cars and about to drive back when they saw the child. The line of vehicles stopped without waiting for any command.

"He was in that strip of beans," Buchholz said. "He saw everything. What do we do?" Egger noticed a tension in his voice that had not been there when Buchholz shot the driver. The child was standing in the roadway behind them, wiping the smoke from his eyes – a boy of about eight who had probably rarely seen a motor-car. Behind him the overturned *Kübelwagen* was still burning, and the corn strip smouldered and sparked.

"Leave him alone," Egger said at last. He felt the life of the child weighing on him like the souls of the damned. "No one will listen to a child."

Buchholz smiled and put his foot on the accelerator. "I hope this bloody painting is worth it," he said.

Egger didn't answer. He was still watching the child, who stood by the road, waving.

Chapter One

"SEXUAL PERVERSION consists in painting one's toes with beef extract and having them licked clean by a dog. Everything else is mere lightheartedness."

Hortense Ainsworth had always preferred even a half-decent epigram to plain, dreary truth. Her acquaintances had got used to the habit and were nowadays only good for a token smile, but at her age and on this occasion she did think she was entitled to more than a moment's pause in the conversation around the dinner-table before it resumed on the topic of some public figure or other's sexual peccadilloes. At least her squib was on the right subject. Wit tended to come harder as she grew older; she had to work at her aphorisms, and that ruined the timing. By the time she cranked out her joke, the conversation was feeding in pastures new.

It was her seventy-fifth birthday, and the small dinner-party was in her honour. A miscellany of friends, accumulated over fifty years like the bric-à-brac of her house, for the most part they shared only the fact that they had succeeded in being almost but not quite unsuccessful. It seemed unreasonable that they should get on together.

In the mirror on the opposite wall, over a heavily carved sideboard, she caught sight of her own reflection, over-made-up and skinny as a plucked chicken, her face pinched and white over a flowered-silk kimono. She had got beyond revulsion at the decrepitude of advancing age: she was prepared to face the end with perverse good-humour. She only wished that everyone – Tom Furnival, for example – would face the prospect of death in the same spirit instead of becoming more and more pompous.

The trade unionist was just then holding forth. In the forties he had been a noted Stalinist. Now he was angling for a peerage and in favour of "public morality". Hortense felt sad for him and angry, too. The passion in his voice had become simply a loud noise. The good looks of his youth had distilled into a nose thatched with hair and earlobes that were fleshy and pink like baby mice. He was a relic from Hortense Ainsworth's radical past, which included a spell of internment in 1939 for expressing unseasonable support for the Soviet Union so soon after the Nazi–Soviet Pact. It was then that she had met the young firebrand.

She noticed Sebastian nodding in agreement with Tom Furnival's last remark, holding his talcumed hands in a cat's cradle. Sleek and plump, there was something so *obvious* about him and he had never been particularly successful as a closet homosexual, she thought, but no one would have guessed that he was a closet prude. Yet there it was, and ever since his particular orientation had been made legal he had rediscovered his lost moral sentiments. Tonight his sermon was fidelity, and Hortense divined trouble between Sebastian and some younger man.

Sebastian Summer was the owner of the Summer Gallery, a small place, tucked away off Bond Street, where he chased but never quite caught the vanguard of taste. He was neither as brash and successful as the Waddington Galleries with their Cézannes and Mirós and their moderns like Patrick Caulfield, nor as established in the Mayfair psyche as Marlborough Fine Art and the Lefevre Gallery. Instead Hortense felt that she had come close to the truth when she introduced Sebastian with the words: "He has a gallery in Bond Street. That's a sort of alleyway for the artistic mugger. One can make a living by sandbagging the occasional sheikh."

The bright note to Sebastian's future was that he had brought in a younger man who seemed to have some flair and a determination to make a go of the business. John Donaldson was at the dinner-table at the request of Hortense's daughter, Helen Ainsworth, who also worked at the gallery. He was a disappointment to the old lady because he had a reserved character which she felt was impenetrable. This disturbed her since she liked to have levers to pull so that people should hop in the right direction. Donaldson seemed immune to this approach. Instead he sat there, darkly good-looking in a Celtic way, sparsely built, black-haired and with intense grey eyes. He looked slightly bored, slightly amused and, to Hortense, wholly annoying. She supposed that he was in his late thirties since he had had time to study fine art at the Slade and afterwards travel extensively in the Middle East and Russia pursuing some studies of Muslim and Orthodox art, but his claim to a sort of fame came from the fact that two years ago he had been credited with the recovery of a lost Turner.

21

Discovering Turners was not absolutely unique. There was almost a competition between the younger dealers over who could identify the painter's work among the mass of unattributed watercolours that passed through auction. Pictures of Ludlow Castle, Tamworth Castle and the fountains of Melek Mehmet Pasha had all turned up in the past few years. None the less it was still a rare achievement to have identified a watercolour of Raby Castle in the stiffening behind a framed photograph, and it marked John Donaldson as a man who knew very clearly what he was doing. Hortense Ainsworth had not been surprised when her daughter became attracted to him; and had been equally unsurprised when she dropped him. Since then she had acquired someone else.

Robert Marshall had known Helen Ainsworth a month.

"We're what you might call an old Anglo-Marxist family," she told him.

This was after a demonstration in Trafalgar Square, which had adjourned to the pubs in Soho. They found themselves jammed at a table by a crowd of LSE students baying for beer and trying to find space to stash their placards. Marshall looked at them and had a sense of *déjà vu*: he had caught the tail end of the sixties – the real thing.

"And what would an old Anglo-Marxist family be?" he asked.

She had bright brown eyes that flashed with humour and fixed his firmly and intelligently, without any sexual intent but for that reason even more attractive.

"I'm not sure I could define it. I suppose it's a sort of High Marxism, vague and rather English – like Waugh and his Anglo-Catholics – a more traditional and sonorous affair than the low non-conformity of your common-or-garden street-radical."

"And do you practise?"

She smiled: "No," then added off-handedly, "but I feel an affection for the tradition, a nagging sense of guilt and fear of damnation. Probably I shall die in the faith. Anglo-Marxists experience deathbed repentance and are given the last rites." With the same lightheartedness she went on: "If you won't believe me, you must meet my mother."

So here Robert Marshall was, meeting her mother around the dinner-table in celebration of her birthday. Helen Ainsworth did indeed come from an old Anglo-Marxist family, if one stretched the definition to take account of a campaigning interest in the abolition of

22

slavery and child-labour through the family's connections with Wilberforce and the Russells. Her great-grandfather had been an ironmaster who dabbled in experimental factory systems for the workers. Her grandfather had lived on his private income but spent a considerable period in Russia until arrested and expelled by Okhrana, the Tsar's secret police, after which he had returned to England and campaigned vigorously for socialism and women's emancipation. And there was her mother. Hortense Ainsworth had fought forcefully for the British communist party during the thirties, interspersed with periods when she flew between remote points of the globe in pursuit of obscure aviation records – Mombasa to Johannesburg, Chengtu to Canton. Naturally she had taken part in the Spanish Civil War, as had her brother Tarquin. She had one child, Helen, but had never married.

Hortense had been in her forties when her daughter was born, in 1952, in the exuberance of the New Elizabethan Age. At the time she had hoped but not been certain that Tom Furnival was the father. Nowadays she regarded the trade unionist, hunched over his port, and was more inclined to mutter darkly, "Parthenogenesis" – virgin birth – her eyes twinkling with mischief.

Robert Marshall watched the old lady now and wondered how youth, vitality and high-mindedness had been turned into this querulous eccentric, who seemed to be hunting among her guests for someone to offend. He suspected that her radical commitment had always contained an element of perversity; and as her ability to bring about the workers' revolution diminished with age so she had turned from the destruction of capitalism to the softer targets of her friends and neighbours.

There were twelve for dinner but, aside from Helen and her mother, Robert Marshall had met only Sebastian Summer and John Donaldson before, having encountered them at the gallery. Tom Furnival he recognized from occasional appearances in the news and he had also heard the name of one of the other men, an ancient, faded character who turned out to have been an MP and somebody's Parliamentary Private Secretary in the 1945 Labour government. For the rest, there was a brace of liberal clergymen; a cheerful old lesbian with brown brogues, buckled teeth and a whiff of after-shave about her, who had some unspecified claim on the socialist conscience from long-dead days; and a pair of unattributed wives whose interests seemed to have been blanched out of them by

23

long association with their husbands.

The table conversation continued on the theme of morality. Hortense Ainsworth was visibly bored by the subject and threw in only the occasional quip. With age she had rediscovered that self-conscious schoolgirlish lust for talking dirty which is acquired only in the best schools. The men, on the other hand, had become more pompous and, with predictable irony, Tom Furnival and Sebastian Summer were arguing the case for the maintenance of moral standards, whilst the forces of sin and darkness had the support of the left-wing bishop. Since he was an Oxford Union-trained speaker, the bishop was getting the better of the argument.

"I've brought you some coffee," Helen said.

Marshall had left the table, finding the hot-house atmosphere of the dinner-party more than he could take. He had come across the study on the first floor whilst searching for a bathroom. It overlooked Blackheath, the velvet curtains undrawn and a chain of lights visible – the traffic crawling along Shooters Hill Road. Hortense Ainsworth had the untidy habits of a woman brought up in a world of servants; the floor was littered with Fabian Society pamphlets and backnumbers of the *Listener*. Marshall browsed through them and then flicked through the titles of the bookshelves: a biography of Rosa Luxemburg, several books by the Webbs and two shelves of Penguins in the old orange and white covers.

"Coffee?" Helen repeated. Her head was slightly cocked with curiosity, her auburn hair falling over one shoulder. She was wearing a simple black dress set off with a plain silver brooch, but the lights of her hair and the depth of colour to her skin gave a richness of effect. Her features were strong and firm, almost mannish, but they had the accidental sort of beauty that doesn't show in a photograph but lives in the face and takes the play of humour and intelligence to bring out.

"What were you thinking about?" she asked and sat on the arm of his chair.

"My brother James is due home in three days." Marshall stubbed out a cigarette. "He'll be here until New Year."

Helen nodded. Whenever Robert's conversation could be directed to his own background, which was not often, then his brother invariably figured. She had gathered that they had been orphaned as children and brought up in various institutions, and that James, the elder, had been the force that had kept them together. "Do that mean I shall see less of you? I can see that a threesome might cause problems."

"It depends. I can't tell at the moment."

"You seem very preoccupied." His face was naturally frank and open in its expression, fresh and fair in its good-looks as if he had only just come from the cricket field. For it to show worry seemed not only odd but in some sense *wrong*. People instinctively wanted to help Robert Marshall.

In the north-west London suburb of Kenton, Marion Ross carried out the last homely checks of the evening. The television set was unplugged; the empty milk-bottles had been put out; the lights in the children's bedrooms had been switched off and the bedclothes were still in place. She took her cup of tea and the novel she was reading and went into her own bedroom.

She was a light sleeper. Her eyes were too tired at the end of the day to allow her to read for long, and she became trapped in that intermediate state where the senses are not switched off and the mind balances the external and the internal in its own synthesis. She was a woman who needed the security and animal warmth of another body beside her as a catalyst to sleep. But David was not yet home and she was left to dream and make patterns of lights projected through the window as cars spattered past in the rain.

A sound slotted into her consciousness. David come home. She could feel him in the house, drifting about the margins of her senses. Her body keyed itself to expect him. The door opened and he stood dimly silhouetted against the night-light that burned on the stairs.

"Come to bed," she murmured. Between half-closed eyelids she watched David take off his clothes and slide into bed beside her. His body pressed against hers, and she felt his hands running along her smooth flanks, his fingers insinuating themselves towards her body's magic places. A dream! she thought, just a dream, but turned into it because it was all she had when David was not there. She moaned softly as her nipple was grazed and turned over so that her body was open to him like the sun, then felt him again as he drew back the delicate folds of skin and entered her. Her eyes came awake at his force and looked straight up into his.

"Who are you?" she asked. The movement of his body against hers, to which she responded, smothered her thoughts except for her sense of his alienness. She turned again so that with each thrust he would touch her just *there*, her body's automatic response to its needs. I'm dreaming, she knew again – one of those delicious adolescent dreams that had left her weak and moist those years ago and now came back to haunt her because David wasn't there, was never there enough.

"Who are you?" she asked again, waiting for the phantasm to disappear as she shuddered and gasped with release.

Robert Marshall returned to the dinner-table. The conversation was in full spate; a sea of red, glistening faces expounded on good and evil and recompense in the after-life, while the port decanter went round in the regulation direction, the wall clock ticked heavily and the fire crackled in the hearth and cast a glow about the room. Hortense Ainsworth sat like a spider at the head of the table and brooded.

"I've never been able to believe in the final judgement, myself," said the liberal bishop, about to launch into heresy under the influence of drink. "Christ in His glory, come to judge mankind – I'm sure it can't be so *simple*. It makes Him sound like a terrorist, clobbering all the poor innocent blighters who never even had a chance to hear the Gospel in this life. What about the Hindus, for example?"

"I don't know about that," said Tom Furnival heavily.

"I once saw Leonardo's painting of the Last Judgement," Hortense Ainsworth threw in.

"You mean the Last Supper," Sebastian Summer corrected her.

"No, dear, we're *eating* the Last Supper: the painting was of the Last Judgement. It showed all the poor sinners being consigned in cartloads to the everlasting flames while God sits in his heaven with his smiling crew just as if he were an American. And, you know, Leonardo was right: Christianity is so simple and" – she addressed the bishop – "so preposterous. The problem is to reconcile the two." The rest was buried under denials.

"I must go," Marshall said to Helen. She nodded and squeezed his hand.

"Lectures tomorrow?"

"Yes." He was a lecturer at the LSE.

"I wish I could join you. We've arrived at the ridiculous stage of the proceedings. Anything said from now on will be regretted in the morning. When shall I see you again?"

"I'll call tomorrow."

"I'll come with you to the door."

At the door Marshall turned to kiss goodbye. Helen held her face forward and then drew back. Her toe tapped impatiently against the elephant's-foot umbrella-stand which cluttered the hallway along with the assegais, native shields and other debris of the Ainsworth dynasty.

"I wish you didn't have to keep vanishing so early," she said. She sounded more angry with herself than with him. "The pressures of preparing to teach come first, I suppose. Frankly it makes me feel as if I'm having to chase you."

Marshall didn't answer. She relented in a second and then kissed him with the same directness as she did everything else. *I love this woman,* he thought to himself, but the feeling only occasioned bitterness.

He journeyed across London encapsulated in the night. The traffic was light, the rain was still falling, the neon haze was reflected off the road. Marshall could not drive out of his mind the pictures of his wife, bright as he had first met her, in a printed cotton dress, her blonde hair bobbed about her face. She was fresh and cheerful and had no more ambition than to be a good wife and raise children and carry on in a way that she would have described as perfectly "normal". It was a vision of a quiet, domestic future that he had thought he shared until his boss, Calverton, had introduced him to the Lie. And now he lived the Lie because that was what his work demanded; and so he had betrayed his wife and Helen and, somewhere in the mess, himself.

His brother James might understand. There had to be somebody who would listen while his authentic self struggled to the surface of the deceit, and there was only James left. He would understand because he had dragged his younger brother out of the orphanage where they had been brought up and at every turn had pointed him in the direction he should go. And James was due home from the Gulf in three days.

The street in front of the house was quiet. Across the road a bedroom light burned dimly and a baby cried to be fed. Marshall parked the car in the garage and turned the key to the kitchen door. The cat dashed out and ran into a corner by an old toolbox, where it glowered at him. He tried "puss, puss" a few times, but the animal would not respond and he gave up. The house was full of a warm, breathing stillness, the kitchen set for breakfast, the hallway speckled with light from the stained-glass panel in the front door. He hung up his jacket, picked up some mail from the hall-table and made his way upstairs.

He pushed open the bedroom door and murmured his wife's name, not expecting any answer in the thick silence. "Thank God for that," he said to himself and undressed slowly in the darkness. He slipped between the sheets taking care not to touch or disturb her. "Only let me sleep."

In his dream Hortense Ainsworth announced the Last Judgement. God was otherwise engaged and it would therefore be conducted by Leonardo da Vinci. His representative, art-dealer John Donaldson, would assume the role of Christ. The dinner-table agreed that it was about time that morality stood up for itself.

Donaldson–Christ turned round to face him. He opened His hands to show the bullet-wounds in the palms, the marks of His stigmata, the fingers downturned so that the blood ran down them.

"This is my blood of the New Covenant," said Christ and turned His palms upward so that the blood began to puddle.

Marshall woke up abruptly. The palm of his right hand was pressed into the mattress and damp with sweat. He shuddered at the recollection of the dream and rolled over to put his arm around his wife and squeeze gently for the comfort of her breast. His lips touched the skin of her back, moist and sweet. In his half-dreaming stage his tongue licked out unconsciously for the salt. He felt the wetness and stickiness in a rim around his mouth. The hand that touched her breast was wet, the fingers sticking together. It was then that Robert Marshall began to scream.

The light was on. He supposed that he had done it but had no recollection. All he could see was Marion, a cord around her neck, her tongue thick and lolling on her left cheek and her body and the bed soaked in blood. He jumped out of the bed and glimpsed himself in the mirror, a naked spectre streaked red about the lips and hands like some figment of his own nightmare.

"No!" he shouted. In his head a quiet voice said, *I am going insane,* but his lungs could only explode the same word, "No! No! No!" as he ran out of the bedroom and burst open the doors of the other rooms.

His son Jack was dead. Pegged out on his back in the bunk bed, staring dreamily at the ceiling. There was a hole in his chest that a fist could stuff.

His daughter Alice was dead, too, curled up in a ball around her doll, with no marks or stains visible in the darkness but the presence of death so tangible that Marshall didn't need material evidence.

He staggered out of the room and on to the landing. He looked about him. The house was still his house, the walls papered in flowers, the bathroom smelling of lavender; but it seemed suddenly to have been tilted out of the ordinary world into a dark realm where dream and reality permeated each other. He opened the door to Naomi's room and saw the stranger sitting by her bedside.

"Who are you?" he asked quietly, not knowing that he was echoing his wife's words.

The stranger raised a gun and pointed it directly at Marshall.

"I am the incubus of pure terror," he said and mercifully pressed the trigger.

Chapter Two

THE NIGHT AIR felt cold as Sebastian Summer pushed his blue Porsche through the late-night traffic towards his home in Chelsea. Blowing through the open window and over the velvet collar of his coat, it cooled his face and shook the cobwebs of drink and cigars away. He felt that he needed it: the evening in the company of people with fading reputations – like, he had to admit, his own – and the banal moralizing of their conversation had left him with a lingering sense of futility. He avoided contact with people of his own generation precisely because they acted like a hormone on the ageing of his own behaviour and preferred younger men. To console himself for his annoyance he took the car for a spin along the Embankment and then into the West End, vaguely looking for some comfort out of the night.

Young men lounged by the statue of Eros in Piccadilly Circus. They reminded him of his current lover, Anthony; they had an aggressive, macho quality that had not been cultivated by his class and generation, and Anthony matched them in his tailored brown leathers, which Sebastian had paid for. He was tempted to stop and make an approach, but he meant what he had said about fidelity, his theme at the dinner-table. He did believe in it, and for people like himself, without the conventions and the ties of children that bind a man and a woman in marriage, fidelity was so much more a moral rather than a practical question. To make it work he had to believe in it. So for now he passed up the opportunity and drove home in the hope rather than the expectation that Anthony would be there.

John Donaldson drove home directly to his renovated terraced house in Islington, went to his study, poured himself a whisky and sat down to think about the events of the evening. He had a cool and ironic nature and he had observed the other guests with the detached amusement that Hortense Ainsworth had noted. The old lady, too, came under his consideration. He remembered her firmness on the question of the Leonardo painting. *The Last Judgement*? He couldn't identify the title with Leonardo da Vinci's works and the subject sounded out of character: religious and ecstatic rather than humanist and rational. Perhaps she had El Greco in mind. But, then, she was an intelligent, educated woman. He was provoked to check the point out.

In his bookcase he had a copy of Vasari's *Lives,* which contained the earliest biography of Leonardo. Donaldson took it down and, settling into his chair, read the short piece. As he expected, it contained no reference to any work on the Last Judgement theme. So far so good, but he remembered that Vasari was not exhaustive: the *Leda*, he recalled, was mentioned by Anonimo Magliabechiano but not by Vasari at all. If he were seriously interested, he would have to look further.

It was five in the morning by the time he was finished. He had been able to read Burckhardt in his account of Leonardo the "Universal Man" and Benedetto Croce's more human appreciation, and in neither of them did the Last Judgement figure. Whilst there was far more written on the same subject, it was inconceivable that anything else would throw up a reference to a painting not known to those two great critics. The conclusion must be that Hortense Ainsworth had been mistaken.

Donaldson put his books back on to the shelves and prepared to go to bed. He was turning off the study light when he caught sight of the Turner watercolour of Raby Castle, lost for seventy years until he had identified it as the backing to a photograph that he had bought simply for its frame. What if *The Last Judgement* were a lost work? Donaldson retired to bed amused by the thought.

Sebastian Summer was woken at three by the sound of Anthony moving in the next room. He got out of bed, slipped into a silk dressing-gown and went to investigate. Anthony was sitting, brooding and watching a video of *Casablanca* with the volume turned down. He was staring intently at the screen and mouthing the remembered dialogue.

"I thought you wouldn't be coming home tonight," Sebastian said. He was careful to keep any note of acerbity out of his voice.

Anthony looked round. "Did you, now? Did you, now?"

"Where have you been? Care for a cigarette? A drink? Where have you just come from?"

" 'From going to and fro in the earth, and from walking up and down in it' – I'll have the cigarette."

Sebastian lit two cigarettes and held one out to Anthony. The younger man seized his hand and kissed it. "How romantically you light a cigarette. A scene from *Now Voyager*, isn't it? We can show it on the video, if you like. Which one of us shall be Bette Davis?"

"Let go of my hand. You are being particularly trying tonight. You seem very excitable." Sebastian withdrew his hand and sat down on the edge of the table.

"Very well. Then, shall we talk to each other like an old, settled couple? Where have *you* been tonight?"

"To have dinner with Hortense Ainsworth. It was her birthday."

"Indeed? And what did you give her as a present? One of the famous pictures by Geordie Fenwick? One of the few of his masterpieces that won't have made you a tidy sum?"

Sebastian didn't rise to the bait. Anthony was always carping on this particular theme – as if he hadn't himself made money out of Geordie Fenwick. What did the boy want? Recognition? He compared Anthony's refined features, the dark hair and nervous lips, with his image of the Durham miner. What would Geordie Fenwick make of the soft and, alas, paunchy Sebastian Summer and his catamite? Sebastian had few illusions: probably the miner would get together with some of his mates and beat them up for a pair of pansies. He supposed that it was partly in defence against such treatment that Anthony and his modern friends went equipped with manufactured masculinity.

The younger man finished his cigarette and began to take off his clothes. His torso was muscled and expensively tanned. Sebastian looked away. Anthony's body had the power to fascinate him, but tonight he wanted to be self-contained: Hortense's party had made him feel old.

"Are you going to put your clothes away?" he asked without thinking.

"Why? Are we to have one of your tirades about my sluttish habits, with specific reference to the allegedly fabulous sums spent on my wardrobe?"

"Please, Anthony, not tonight. I'm in no mood to quarrel."

"Having one of our monthlies, are we?"

"I'm simply feeling my age. Be kind and let's not quarrel. You have a tendency to become shrill and then we look like a pair of slightly ridiculous queens. Hopeless for our image and not very good for our self-esteem. There's a dear."

Anthony shrugged and flexed his body. He picked up a palette of oils and, whilst Summer lit another cigarette, applied a few touches of paint to the canvas which stood on its easel by the window. Sebastian watched him work. He felt that, in an imitative way, Anthony had real ability, a sense of a striking image and a certain rude force. It was all consistent with Geordie Fenwick, the crippled painter, with his bold visions of working-class life. He wondered where, in his Home Counties and public-school background, Anthony had acquired the talent.

"Are you coming to bed?"

"No, I want to get to grips with this thing."

"The light. . . ."

"Sod the light! I can tidy up the colour in the morning when the light is better. It's the structure, the feeling of the thing, that I want to get right."

Sebastian turned away. There was no arguing with Anthony in this mood. Although his general habits were untidy, he could be obsessively methodical about those things that really possessed him. It occurred to Sebastian that, if Anthony had ever become interested in business or politics, he had the drive and singlemindedness that would have made for success. He could only have wished for more tenderness.

Later they lay awake in the darkness. Anthony had lit one of his Turkish cigarettes. Sebastian could see the glowing ember and smell the aromatic smoke.

"You seem touchy this evening," he said. "Where did you go?"

"Everywhere and nowhere. I inspected the tarts in Piccadilly."

"Oh."

"They frighten you?"

In his heart Sebastian Summer acknowledged that they did. His own experience was of a narrow world of initiates, a band of brothers of like mind and background who had kept their mysteries to themselves like some schoolboy secret society. He had once ventured into the wider male sexual world when for three years he had performed his national service. The barracks washroom with the

33

other conscripts promiscuously washing, shaving, defecating, urinating together remained his picture of the unregulated masculine universe, and it filled him with horror.

"Could I have a motorcycle?" Anthony asked suddenly.

"Why? Do you want one?"

"No – I was just testing."

"What's wrong? Aren't you happy with me? Is it something to do with the painting? You resent the recognition given to Geordie Fenwick and feel that it should properly go to you?"

"Well, I am Geordie Fenwick, aren't I?"

Sebastian made a pot of tea and brought it back into the bedroom. Anthony had turned on a side-light and was sitting up in bed.

"I have something to tell you," he said. "I'm leaving you."

"I see." Sebastian assumed an air of calmness while he poured the tea and stirred in a little sugar. "Well, we always recognized that possibility."

"There's more." Anthony's nervous lip trembled. "I want twenty thousand pounds."

"Come, now, isn't that a little immoderate?"

"It isn't a request; I'm insisting."

"Oh dear," Sebastian said softly. He sat down on the edge of the bed and stared into his hands.

Anthony became more businesslike. "We've sold upwards of a hundred 'Fenwicks', not to mention some lithographs."

"But hardly twenty thousand pounds. Not now. Not left."

"I intend to paint under my own name. I don't expect I shall do well initially and I shall need something to tide me over."

Sebastian felt thankful that at least there wasn't another man in the picture. Assuming that Anthony was telling the truth – and he fancied that he was – Anthony's naïve egoism would cause him to believe that there was some value to his paintings, more than the charming myth that they had woven about them.

"What if I can't raise the money?"

"I'm afraid that you'll have to. People have been sold paintings under false pretences. If the true story came out – well, they might send you to prison." The younger man hesitated at this. "Honestly, Sebastian, I don't want to do this to you, but I have to. You do understand, don't you?"

"Yes, dear, I understand." He understood how in some crimes the victim was a participant, conspiring with his oppressor.

Sebastian got up from the bed. He hunted around for nothing in particular. He was too stunned to know how to react. He remembered the dark days before the law was changed, when a mild indiscretion first let in the spectre of blackmail in the form of a man with a provincial accent and insinuating manners who had demanded a hundred pounds, as the lawyers say, "with menaces". It was an experience that had given him a permanent aversion to chance encounters, particularly with the beguilingly rough *gamins* who could be found loitering in certain spots with a view to a bed for the night. He had confined himself to the security of his own class of person, and the security had proven an illusion.

He drank his tea and shook his head slowly. "You are . . . a disappointment to me."

"Yes, I can see that I must be," Anthony replied. He took Sebastian's hand and kissed the fingers. "Forgive me."

"I shall try to," Sebastian agreed quietly. He put the tea-tray down on the floor, got back into bed and turned off the light. Presently he heard Anthony's regular breathing and closed his own eyes in an attempt to sleep, while, inside, his heart was breaking.

Chapter Three

JAMES ROSS arrived from Saudi Arabia to find a letter waiting at the agents he used to fix him up with apartments when in England. It was postmarked London SW16, which he guessed was Streatham, and addressed in copy-book italics like a wedding invitation. Inside the black-edged card read: "The funeral of our dearly beloved. . . ."

It was held in suburban Pinner. The cemetery flanked the highroad and was flanked in turn by low, white apartment blocks with green-shingled roofs and metal-framed windows like prison bars. It was too recent a place to have accumulated the lush decay of the Victorian commercial cemeteries. Too modest. No tilted urns or family vaults collapsing on themselves; just unpretentious marble beds in loving memory of — and only now laying down the first patina of age. An avenue of young chestnuts on either side of the main path, a stone-built gothic chapel at the high point of the ground, in front of it a circle of tarmac where the paths intersected; some benches and the corporation flowerbed. David's wife had been wedded to the idea that felicity was a large, between-the-wars semi-detached house in Kenton, where her emotional tap-root was sunk firmly in the tennis club and the light opera society and her children were sanitized at a local preparatory school. It was, David said, an indulgence towards Marion; but James Ross suspected that his brother's strong and determined spirit had sought its own anchor in the domesticity of suburban life. In the cemetery at Nower Hill it had found its final expression.

He came by taxi directly from the agency office to find the service nearly finished, the five coffins laid out by the grave and the vicar well into his stride.

"No press," a man said, gripping Ross by the sleeve of his jacket. The camera which he carried when he travelled swung by its shoulder-strap.

"I'm the brother."

"I don't care who the hell you are, I think it's bloody disgraceful," said the man. "Taking photos at a funeral – it's downright ghoulish."

"I wouldn't quarrel with that," said Ross.

The mourners were from Marion's side of the family. Dr Barnardo furnished parents to the living not to the dead. Her mother, over-fortified on sherry, was alternately theatrically grief-stricken or heroically firm in adversity; her father, a slightly built man, seemed faded like a double exposure. An uncle, fair like Marion and lithe as a whippet, slipped away from the others and accosted Ross.

"I remember you," he said confidingly. "The brother, am I right? Never forget a face." He looked down modestly and twiddled the Rotarian pin in his tie. "How much do you know about this murder business?" he asked.

"I've just got back in the country. There was a letter, from Marion's mother."

"Not much, then, eh? Alice never was one with words."

"No, not much."

"That's wrong," moralized the uncle. "People need to know the truth before they can be comforted. Otherwise they fret. They wonder what happened and they fret."

"Do they?"

"Yes." the uncle rummaged in his pockets and pulled out some newspaper clippings. "There was buckets of blood. The *Daily Express* used the words 'a bloodbath of horror'. I thought you'd like to know. Here, take these; the facts are all in here. Knowing them may give you some comfort." He pushed the pieces of paper into Ross's hand.

The coffins had been laid in the grave. The vicar was shaking dirt over them, which gave the uncle inspiration. "You're in the construction business yourself, aren't you? Good number. Home on leave?"

"Yes."

"Got a car while you're over here?"

"No."

"See me if you need one." He looked at the mother, who was at the collapsing-point in her cycle of emotion. "It's the children that get her. My sister. Didn't really like Marion. Mother and daughter, they fall out sometimes. Only natural. Took to your David, though." He had a sparrow's curiosity. "Are any of your lot here? I only ask because I thought you was orphans, but those two over there aren't none of ours." Those two. A man and a woman standing a hundred and fifty yards away, ignoring each other but intent on the burial.

The man was about fifty years of age and wearing a sand-coloured trench-coat and a brown felt hat like a racing tipster. The woman was thirty or so, the view of her face obscured by the folds of a headscarf, but her black Burberry suggesting a certain restrained chic.

"Recognize them?" asked the uncle in a speculative tone.

"Why? Do you want to sell them something?"

"Sell them . . . ? Oh, ha, good one. Yes, I'd forgotten that David had a sharp tongue in his head. Must be a family trait. Still" – he looked around – "looks like things may be finishing. Well, I'll see you later."

The knot of mourners was breaking up. The vicar helped support the grieving mother but kept glancing round wildly as if he felt it was a job for the fire brigade and was expecting their arrival. The others, too, had decided that the contemplation of death was, at best, an embarrassment and were hurrying to their cars. Ross watched them without introducing himself. The uncle brought up the rear.

"Keeping well out of it? Wise man!" he said cheerfully and then composed his face to extend a meaningful handshake. "Another one gone to join the Great Architect," he murmured solemnly and was disappointed at the lack of response. "Yes, well, see you around, eh?"

"Sure." Ross watched the man go and then looked back to see that the woman in the black raincoat was still there. Her male companion had gone.

He heard her behind him. Her breathing had that particular catch in it: the heart crying and the body trying to deny it. It was unusual for a woman: there should have been floods of tears if only because it was expected. And where were his own? Surely he had some to spare for blithe, bright Marion and the children and for the only open, welcoming arms that had ever waited behind a door.

"In the Army they teach you that death is a cause for anger, but never for tears," he heard himself say. Whoever she was, it seemed they shared something.

"Never?"

He turned round and saw a face with eyes that held his, a directness to it, handsome but not particularly beautiful. "Tears? Maybe for comrades and dogs – the Army approves of sentiment – but not for the rest. What's your excuse?"

He regretted the words as he spoke them, but she only smiled palely and answered: "Ah, you have your brother's cruel sense of humour." There was no resentment in the voice, and Ross saw why tears were not necessary: bits of grief were breaking from her and formed flotsam in every syllable she uttered. She held out a hand. "My name is Helen Ainsworth."

"Oh?"

"Your brother hadn't mentioned my name to you?"

"We never wrote."

"I see." She turned away from the open pit and together they walked in silence until she stopped on a shaded path among the lonely graves of Czech servicemen killed in the war. "Would it interest you that I was, for want of a better word, your brother's mistress? A surprise? Yes, well, I should have expected that, I suppose. Perhaps the whole business has come as a surprise to you. When did you learn that. . . .?"

"Two hours ago. I just flew in from abroad."

"Ah, that explains something."

"Does it, now?" Ross answered and then realized that he was wearing an electric-blue safari-suit and buckskin boots. The suit he had bought in a dim light from a Calcutta tailor because it could be washed in the sink and, wrinkled or pressed, looked lousy. The boots he had won from an American in a card game.

She changed the subject. "Would you like a lift? I saw you arrive by taxi. My car is just outside."

"I want to call at my brother's house."

"That's OK. I'll drop you off and wait."

Ross responded at last to her warmness. "Fine," he said. "Let's go."

Her car was an ancient Morris Minor that smelled of dog and was cluttered with a tool-kit on the passenger-seat and a pair of green wellington boots.

She cleared a space. "Where to?"

"Kenton."

"Kenton?" Half-disbelief. "Is that where Robert lived?" She put out her hand to turn the ignition, but Ross's hand was there first.

"Who is Robert?" he asked.

*

He waited until she stopped crying. The careful barrier she had erected had broken when he asked her about Robert and the tears came. They were soundless ones, hidden in her hands, unadmitted, and when she finally spoke she made no reference to them.

"You don't know Robert Marshall?" she asked. She obviously expected him to say "no", but in that "no" was something that hurt her beyond all depths. He felt that he was implicated by David in some crime. "He was your brother," she said at last.

Ross let the information sink in. "What kind of brother would that be?"

"Evidently not the one called David Ross, married with three children and living in Kenton. The one I knew was called Robert Marshall, a bachelor, a lecturer in history, living in a flat in Islington – which, I may add, I once spent the night at. Or is it," she said, "that the two are the same and that your brother was in truth a philandering travelling salesman with a bigamous wife in every city? Do you know what sort of brother you have at all?"

"Maybe you're mistaken."

"The police had no doubts. It took them only two days to make the connection, link your brother to the flat in Islington and then to me." She didn't know whether he believed her and went on: "There's a strong family resemblance. He was your greatest fan: I don't think he lied about you." She turned away because she didn't want him looking at her. Ross stared ahead, catching his own faint reflection in the windshield. The resemblance to David's clean, sporting looks was there – if you broke the pieces and glued them together.

"What did he tell you?"

She began again, her sentences out of phase with her emotion, like a comedian with bad timing. "He said that he had a brother James. That you were both orphans, brought up in a home in Manchester. You were the wilder of the two – he used to tell me stories of your scrapes, the sort that people can't make up." She paused there to capture something, but the recollection passed. "You joined the Army as soon as you could. He wanted to but you wouldn't let him – you told him he had to go to university and saved to provide him with money so that he could travel instead of spending his vacations scratching after pennies."

"I sound like a great guy."

"In David's eyes you were. That doesn't suit you?"

"No," said Ross quite simply. Then: "Is that it?"

"More or less. You tired of the Army and used your engineering training to get a job with a contracting company. . . . He was looking forward to your coming home for Christmas." Her voice fell. "It sounded as though you were all that he had."

Ross leaned over and turned the key in the ignition. "Let's go," he said. He sat back in his seat to let her drive.

"Why was he killed, James?" she asked suddenly. "And the children? Why did they have to kill the children?"

The question and the softness of the pain that was in it slipped past his guard and broke him. And for a minute or so he turned away from her, seeing only David, his brother's wife and the children. The children would always be there. The calendar would bring round the birthdays for which there would be no presents to buy; and the voice of every child in the streets would be full of ghosts.

The house in Fairfield Crescent sheltered behind its laburnum and variegated holly. The curtains were drawn behind diamond-leaded panes and the potted plants died slowly in the window. The baronial door was studded with iron nails; the coachlamps beside it still kept their polish; the stone above it still recalled the date, AD 1938, and the initials of the builder.

In the roadway under the lime-trees a police Ford Escort was parked, the driver eating his sandwiches and making up his notes. Ross and his companion took the Morris into the next street and went on foot down the narrow lane between abutting gardens until they reached the rear of the house.

The lawn was ragged from the last of the autumn's growth and bare in patches from children's feet. There was a potting-shed, a brand-new gazebo in rough-cut logs with little stained-glass windows and a thatched roof, a child's pedal-car tucked against the compost-heap, and a ginger cat that stalked up and down the kitchen window-sill wailing for food. Someone had been practising tennis with a ball strung from a pole and had abandoned the racket in the middle of the grass.

Ross found the key in its usual place in the shed and broke the police seals on the kitchen door. The kitchen smelled of disinfectant and something going slowly rotten in the refrigerator. The working-tops were cluttered with dirty Horlicks mugs from a last nightcap and the cups of tea made by the police. The table was still set for breakfast. They went through and into the front lounge.

The room was Marion's: Habitat furniture, Sanderson patterns, fingerprint powder. David's contribution was a shelf of books, unread in their crisp dust-jackets, the random result of not replying to the book club's monthly offer.

She walked towards the window. "Our friend from the police wouldn't like the idea of our being here," said Ross. He stopped her before she could be seen from the car in the street.

"I suppose not," she said. His fingers had accidentally brushed the auburn hair on the nape of her neck. Unconsciously she turned into the touch, responding to the sensuousness of memory, a faint reflex, the dying track of a song. Her eyes still examined the room as if it were wholly mysterious.

"When did the police call on you?" he brought her back.

"Yesterday. It was one detective. He came to ask about the dinner-party for my mother's birthday, the night that David was murdered."

"How did he know about you? David was using a false name and presumably he was hiding the facts from his wife. So how did the police know about you?"

"I – I hadn't thought about that. I suppose he wrote something down. Perhaps he told someone. I don't know."

"Who else did the police talk to? Your mother?"

"No, I think they intended to, but they didn't. I don't know why. None of the other people at the party has mentioned what happened, so I suppose the police haven't interviewed them. I can't be sure because I haven't talked about it to them. The police said I should speak to no one."

"And you obeyed?"

She had been facing away from him and only now turned to let him see again the pain and confusion inside her. "What was I to talk about? Can you imagine what it is to love and make love to a person who doesn't exist? Everything I gave to David is lost: everything he gave to me was an illusion. When I meet people I find myself thinking: Will they be there tomorrow? Who can I talk to and trust?"

Ross didn't try to answer. He let her find her own time and words. She began slowly, with an uncertain calmness in her voice.

"We met at a rally in Trafalgar Square. Did you hear about it?"

"No."

"I forgot: you've been out of the country."

"Go on, if it helps."

"It was a peace demonstration – against the rumours that the Americans are planning to deploy biological weapons in Europe. There's a NATO meeting in Brussels in the New Year, when everyone expects an announcement." She was trying to be matter-of-fact.

"David was at this demonstration?"

"You don't think David was opposed to this evil?" she asked; then corrected herself: "Don't answer that. It's too trite. We're all against sin and in favour of virtue. You don't think that David would have been at the demonstration?"

"Look around," said Ross as gently as he could. "The man who lived here wouldn't demonstrate against anything except the size of his taxes." He watched her again, scanning the room to reconcile it with the image of the man she knew. He began to wonder what her image of David had been like. Not like his, the bold, shrewd, danger-loving Barnardo boy. And not like the third David, the dead man's private personality: domesticity, Kenton, Marion and the kids. Shake them up and they had somehow got him killed.

"Trafalgar Square." He eased her memory along.

"I was keeping company with the Trots – the Trotskyites – Socialist Workers' Party and that crowd," said Helen. "It was a case of being with them or the Anglicans."

"So you preferred Vanessa Redgrave to the Archbishop of Canterbury."

She smiled, and he noticed how lovely her face became when animated. "My class of socialist," she admitted. She fingered the titles on the bookshelves. "And David's, too, or so it appeared. I was standing with my back to the National Gallery, listening to the speeches from Nelson's Column and hanging on to one end of a red banner. When I turned, I found David hanging on to the other end."

"He said he was a Marxist?"

"Yes, in a fairly relaxed way. Or, at any rate, so I thought. . . ." The pain again; a pause while she found herself and survived it. "But, then, whatever view I formed of David isn't necessarily true. Maybe even the contrary as if I were seeing a mirror-image. Does that make sense to you?"

Ross didn't answer.

They went upstairs. The master bedroom, where David and Marion had slept, was in chaos where the police had pulled it apart in their search. The bed had been moved and the carpet rolled back so that the bullet could be levered out of the floor. Gaping holes in the plaster where two more had been removed from the wall. There was a fine coat of plaster dust on the white bedroom furnishings.

They went into the eldest child's room, pushing open the door bearing an enamelled plaque labelled "Naomi" and set with painted sprigs of flowers. Faint light from the window over the garden. More dust, more holes in the plaster. Specks of blood on the wall. A teddy-bear that the child had covered herself with. Helen picked it up and hugged it while the stuffing crumbled from the hole in its chest and sprinkled her dress. She cried softly and then asked calmly: "Can we leave, please?"

On the landing they found the chalk outline that had been described around David's body as it lay on the floor. The police had photographed the corpse and taken it away, leaving its shadow in chalk to be walked over and obliterated. Helen and Ross glanced at it and went downstairs. It seemed as insubstantial as any of the images of the David that they knew.

Chapter Four

SEBASTIAN SUMMER took a sleeping-pill, and when he woke late the following morning Anthony had left his house. As a mute note of apology he had tidied the place up and, next to the lengthy letter left at the bedside, which set out a sentimental account of their relationship terminating with an address to which the money could be sent, Sebastian found a present of a carved ivory figure of the Buddha and a card that said: *Existence is suffering – love, Anthony.* He got up slowly and opened the windows to clear the smell of Turkish cigarettes and aftershave, fragrances of the other man.

For two days he stayed at home, having no other contact with the outside world than the daily newspapers. Next to the story of the moment, the persistant rumour of American intentions towards the stationing of chemical and biological weapons in Europe, he saw the piece on the murder of David Ross but did not associate it with the man he knew as Robert Marshall. On the third day he called John Donaldson and asked him to come over with the accounts relating to the sale of the Geordie Fenwick paintings.

Donaldson arrived at 10 a.m., bringing the books with him. Summer had dressed himself carefully in slacks, a pale-green shirt and a neatly tied cravat, and was trying to appear calm.

"Anything wrong?" Donaldson asked. "Why have you been staying away from the gallery?" He put down the books and took a seat. His dark, intense eyes could see that Sebastian's clattering about in the kitchen under the pretence of making some coffee was nothing but a distraction.

"I've had . . . a shock. Something personal," said Sebastian at last. He found it difficult to confide in Donaldson. The other man seemed so self-contained. Anthony, for all his weaknesses, was at least accessible; it was the flaws in the personality, the chinks of need, that allowed people to get a grip on each other. Donaldson was aware of Sebastian's homosexuality but treated it as a neutral fact, dispassionately, slightly ironically. Even so, there was no one else for Sebastian to turn to: his gay friends of his own age had always been jealous of Anthony's beauty, and their sympathy was likely to be barbed with secret smugness. And, in any case, whom could he tell about Geordie Fenwick?

"Anthony has left me at last," he said.

Donaldson nodded. "That leaves you with a problem over the Fenwicks."

"You know?"

"They're not in Anthony's usual style, but I saw something similar, years ago. What will you do now?"

"He wants twenty thousand pounds. He fancies that he's a great painter and maintains that he needs the money to set himself up. Frankly," Sebastian admitted, "I don't have that amount, paltry though it seems. To tell you the truth, I've been speculating in gold stocks and commodity futures and lost rather heavily." He felt ashamed in front of the other man.

"I shouldn't worry," said Donaldson. "It's just one of Anthony's passing moods. I'll speak to him." The assurance in his voice put the other man at rest. Donaldson picked up one of the ivories that Sebastian collected and examined the carving as he went on: "There was something else I wanted to talk to you about."

"Oh?"

"Do you recall any of Hortense's absurd conversation at dinner the other evening?"

Sebastian remembered only the oppressive sense of growing old that he had felt. "The woman is losing her mind," he said snappishly. "She has the conversation of a social gargoyle. Was there anything in particular you had in mind?"

"She mentioned a painting of the Last Judgement," said Donaldson. "She claimed it was by Leonardo. I've spent the last two days trying to find a record of such a painting and found nothing."

"I'm not surprised. I told her so at the time. She probably had in mind *The Last Supper* and confused it with something she had seen by El Greco or Bosch. She spent a lot of time in Spain in the thirties and may well have remembered a work she saw at the Prado."

"Perhaps. But she's nobody's fool."

"An unknown Leonardo? It's hardly likely, John."

"Not likely, but not impossible," said Donaldson. "It's happened before, with Leonardo da Vinci, with the *Leda*. Everyone accepts that Leonardo painted a *Leda*, but when you go to a primary source like Vasari there's no mention of it. We have a copy of the painting, but where's the original and why did Vasari miss it when he wrote his biography?"

"You are talking about an exceptional case."

"Not so exceptional, Sebastian. Think of all the wars and disruptions that have occurred in Europe in the last five hundred years, when a painting might have gone missing. You only have to think of Cromwell's dispersal of Charles I's collection."

"Or the sack of Rome," Sebastian said thoughtfully. He mulled the idea over. "I suppose it isn't quite as unlikely as I thought. I was remembering my history. The Emperor Charles V let his army loose on Rome some time in the 1520s, I can't recall why. But let's suppose there were an unknown Leonardo there at that time, which seems not unreasonable – eh?" He found himself amused by the idea. "Shades of your missing Turner. But to find a Leonardo da Vinci! It would be like finding the Holy Grail. How on earth would one start?"

Donaldson allowed himself a smile. "I have a few weeks' holiday coming up. I was planning on a holiday in Greece but could be persuaded to change my mind. But I suggest we start with something modest and simply go to see Hortense and ask her some questions. You need some exercise and fresh air. Have some lunch with me and come along."

They drove to Blackheath and found Hortense at home in the gloomy Victorian villa that overlooked the heath. At the rear of the house was a broken-down conservatory filled with pots of withered herbs and strings of dried onions, a token gesture at self-sufficiency. Wrapped in a floral peignoir and wearing a pair of wellington boots, Hortense Ainsworth was holding an old *Observer* supplement open at the gardening page and fiddling among the shrivelled stems with a pair of secateurs. Her ancient face with its pixie eyes brightened up to see them.

"Sebastian, John, how wonderful to see you! Let's have a cup of tea and you can tell me what brings you here." She cast a distasteful look into the garden, at the mounds of compost and the shreds of decayed lupins, and added: "I can't seem to get the hang of this gardening thing. Whenever I touch a plant it seems to die on the spot. Do you have any better luck? I'm sure that you, Sebastian, must have lots of neat little window-boxes and potted plants –

you're so tidy." It sounded like a reproach.

"Anthony has a way with plants."

"Anthony – ah, yes! How is he? You should have brought him to dinner the other night."

Sebastian wondered if she knew. With Hortense it was impossible to say: her conversation was always full of innuendo. The two men followed her into a dirty kitchen. The remains of breakfast. Innumerable yoghurt cartons standing on damp newspapers; seedlings dying in them. She made the tea, kicked off the wellington boots, slipped into a pair of mules and, carrying the tray, shuffled into a room at the front of the house where the winter sunshine caught the dust in the air and bathed everywhere in a warm light.

"John wanted to ask you about something you mentioned the other evening," Sebastian began. Hortense had closed the door and wedged it with a copy of *Crockford's Clerical Directory* and was now fluttering over the tea-tray.

"Really?" she said over her shoulder. "I had the impression that no one was listening to a word I said. Sugar or lemon?" She passed out the cups. "I'm afraid this tea is filthy stuff. I do all my shopping in Lewisham Co-op and this is the best I can do. Still, one has to support socialism – though it does make it extraordinarily difficult to buy aubergines. I'm trying to grow them: that's what I was doing when you arrived." She sipped at her tea. "Well, what did I say that was interesting enough to bring you out here?"

"Do you remember talking about a painting – *The Last Judgement*?" said Donaldson.

"Oh, that old thing!" She sounded disappointed. "I've been telling that story for a positive *age* and no one ever listens to a blind word."

"You said it was by Leonardo da Vinci."

"Yes, and Sebastian pooh-poohed the notion, accused me of confusing it with *The Last Supper,* implying that I was as ignorant of art as some common *Reader's Digest* subscriber. I was offended, even if I didn't show it. And what now? You've discovered I'm right. So?"

"Perhaps," Sebastian answered. He felt embarrassed. If he hadn't known Hortense so well, he would have dismissed the whole idea as absurd. He wondered whether losing Anthony was making him unbalanced.

Donaldson finished his tea. "We wondered if you could help us," he said. His eyes looked beyond Hortense at a photograph on the wall. It showed her as a young woman in a leather flying-helmet, set against a background of an ancient biplane and a desert scene of sand and grinning Arabs. The pigments were fading into sepia.

"Ha! I see," said Hortense. "You still don't believe me, but you're not so sure that I've entirely lost my marbles and you want me to tell you all about it. Oh, don't worry. I don't mind." She poured another cup of tea for herself and muttered darkly: "They laughed at Velikovsky, and now where is he?

"Have you ever heard of Katerina Wolska?" she began. "No, I can see you haven't. Well, she was one of history's great mistresses in an age – I speak now of the eighteenth century – which was particularly rich in them."

"Whose mistress?" asked Donaldson.

"Augustus I – II – III – whatever," she said impatiently, "Elector of Saxony and King of Poland, a man who was very free with his seed and seems to have fathered half the bastards in Europe. At all events, he fathered several on Katerina Wolska and was reputedly so besotted by her charms that he gave her large estates in Poland and built the Bereznica Palace for her as a sort of love-nest, which – by the by – is said to have the most obscene frescos of any building of the period. But I digress.

"Her grandson or great-grandson – I forget which – was Marshal Prince Stanislaw Wolski, one of those romantic Poles who look around for a suitably doomed cause and proceed to lay down their lives for it. You must have seen a portrait of him. No? *David*," she said with emphatic French pronunciation, "painted one, all thunderous skies, rearing white charger, brave Polish warrior and so forth, all very tedious."

"He was a contemporary of Napoleon, then?" Donaldson interrupted.

"You have it. He was one of Bonaparte's generals. You may remember how Bonaparte was going to liberate the Poles from the Russian yoke, etcetera, and they, naturally, flocked in droves to join him."

"And?"

"I come to the point. Prince Wolski, it goes without saying, was terribly brave and at the first opportunity he put his finger in the dike, held the bridge against the Etruscans and generally saved Bonaparte's bacon, thereby earning the Little Corporal's undying gratitude. In evidence of which, Napoleon made him a gift of the Leonardo."

"Very generous," said Donaldson. "But where did Napoleon come by it?"

Hortense Ainsworth paused and regarded Donaldson coolly. So good-looking and so unsympathetic unless one liked men with a ruthless streak. His manner seemed to give nothing away of his state of mind. She put aside the distraction and went on.

"To be truthful, it wasn't exactly Napoleon's to give, but he was a little lax about that sort of thing. A few years before Prince Wolski's act of bravery, Bonaparte had been roaring up and down Italy with fire and sword, fighting the Austrians and the Neopolitan Bourbons and the rest, and he had picked up *The Last Judgement* along with the *Mona Lisa* and the rest of the booty."

"But where from exactly?

She threw up her hands. "Well, there you have it. God alone knows! The Medici, the Sforza, the Aldobrandini – any one of a dozen Italian families might have had it and never told. They're all *banditti* at heart, waylaying travellers and retiring to their castles to share the spoils with their friends – the Christian Democrats seem to have kept the habit – so who can say? Or maybe the painting was looted from some church. It still happens today; there are hundreds of little parish churches with their cinquecento treasures tucked away in the vestry along with the whist-tables and the bingo-cards or whatever it is that they *do* keep in Italian church vestries. But you know what I mean: they're always being robbed." She paused and said brightly: "And I'm afraid that's all that I can tell you."

Sebastian Summer put down his cup and stared about him, astonished that he could know this bizarre little woman who could blithely tell such a tale about a great lost masterpiece.

"But, my dear," he said, "how can we believe such a fantastic story? How do you know yourself that it's true?"

"What possible interest could I have in telling a lie?" Hortense retorted. "Besides, I have it on the best authority."

"You've seen the painting?"

"Not exactly that, but I did talk to its owner.

"It was in 1937," Hortense went on. "I was in Paris doing something or other for Spain – my brother Tarquin had been killed by Franco and I was feeling a bit miffed with fascism – and I was sharing an apartment with another girl who was working for the Republican cause. She was Princess Helena Wolska."

"A princess supported the Republicans?"

"Dear Sebastian, you must remember", she said, maliciously hinting at his age, "all the best people were communists in those days. Helena was a positive firebrand – her mother was related to Felix Dzerzhinsky, the founder of the Soviet secret police – and very acceptable in Moscow. Her husband, Prince Jerzy Wolski, was one of the foremost art experts of the period – I speak of before your time, John – and a very charming man in that ingratiating *mitteleuropäische* way, and he became a sort of convert by marriage.

"Of course they soon discovered that they couldn't continue to live in Poland. The place was being run by that reptile Pilsudski and communism was out of fashion, what with the war with the Soviets back in 1920 and all that. And, in addition, Pilsudski at this time was cuddling up to Hitler – not that it did the Poles any good in the long run – and that made Poland a very uncomfortable place. I must say that I have always thought that the Poles between the wars were every bit as unpleasant as the Germans; but, being Poles, they weren't as good at it."

"What happened?" Donaldson asked.

Hortense was growing tired with the story: she preferred acquiring secrets to divulging them and suspected that there was more to the present enquiries than met the eye.

"Oh, one night some tiresome men in shabby raincoats came to arrest them and they had to escape down the drainpipe wearing just their pyjamas and the sort of diamond tiara one wears around the house. They got away to Russia, but shortly afterwards Stalin was in one of his xenophobic moods and it seemed advisable to move again; so they went to Paris and started involving themselves with Spain. That's when I met Helena."

The conversation fell. Hortense suggested some more tea and enquired about Anthony. Feeling resistance to the question, she pressed it more forcefully, and Sebastian was compelled to admit that Anthony had left him. Hortense affected to be sympathetic.

"I'm sure that you're better off without him, Sebastian," she said "I never really felt that Anthony was your style." She examined the art-dealer's dress, with its understated hint of effeminacy, and said: "It seems to me that legalizing the *act* marked a break between generations. Those who were gay before don't seem to be able to get over being slightly *furtive*, and the modern generation seem to have become vulgar. I'm sure you should be looking for someone comfortable of your own age – a civil servant or somebody like that. I do hope I'm not prying."

She want away to make the tea. Sebastian Summer stood by the window, watching the heath through the fly-specks on the unwashed panes.

"Do you believe her?" he asked. He found it difficult to sort out his own thoughts from his sense of humiliation.

"I'm inclined to," Donaldson said. "She finds the story too tedious to be making it up."

"But an unknown Leonardo! It would be the greatest discovery in a hundred years."

"It happens. Wars and revolutions, the relegation of a painting to the back of beyond like Poland. That's how things get lost. Think of all the works of art unaccounted for since the last war."

Hortense came back with the tea.

"What happened to the Wolskis?" Sebastian asked as they settled over another cup.

"Ah, well, this is particularly romantic. Once they were in Paris, Jerzy used his knowledge of art to set up as a dealer. No offence, but art-dealers don't meet the right sort of people, and Jerzy found himself selling pictures to some rather low characters – old nobility and right-wing politicians. Then it occurred to him that he could serve the Party by working his way into those circles. When the Germans invaded France, the Wolskis stayed behind to work for the Party. Helena made out that she found the response of the socialists to the war rather flabby and that she was annoyed with Stalin rather than with Hitler for what happened to Poland. It was superb cover and positively heroic. But, of course, it couldn't last."

"How did it end?" Donaldson asked.

"Tragedy! How else? And shrouded in mystery. They just disappeared off the face of the earth! One assumes that the Gestapo discovered that they were spying for the Russians and hauled them off to one of their unspeakable camps where they died. But, frankly, one will never know."

The subject languished again at that point. Hortense felt that she had done more than enough and felt that she was entitled to some small consideration; so she changed the subject to present politics and held forth until she thought they had agreed with her enough. John Donaldson brought the subject round to the painting again.

"From what you just told us, you never saw the actual painting.

But the other night you were able to describe it."

"That's true. I never saw the original," Hortense said, "but Helena had a miniature of it – I'm not sure what you would call it – a sort of portable shrine that she made her devotions to. She was still a Catholic, would you believe?"

"And where do you think the original is?"

The light dawned on Hortense Ainsworth. "My dear John!" she said with sudden warmth. "You're going to look for it!"

"Perhaps. But I need somewhere to start."

"In Poland of course," said Hortense. "As far as I'm aware, it must still be in Poland."

Chapter Five

THE AGENCY had fixed up James Ross with a flat in one of the large houses built in the final decade of the last century at the end of Eton Avenue nearest to the Swiss Cottage Underground station. It was an affair of hard red brick with Dutch gables and strapwork mouldings which was crowded off the street by the overgrown trees in the front garden. A garage built out of prefabricated asbestos sections had at some time been squeezed by the side, but gradually the house had been overwhelmed by cars and these were now parked bumper to bumper outside with "for sale" signs tucked under the windscreen-wipers.

Helen Ainsworth gave Ross a lift from the house in Kenton. Their conversation was limited to mundane enquiries about Ross's intended stay in London until the car pulled up in Eton Avenue. Then as he was about to get out she announced: "I'd like to keep in touch if possible." She fumbled in her bag for a card and wrote her home address and telephone number on the back.

"Why?" asked Ross.

"I'm not sure. Does there have to be a reason?" She ran her fingers over the lobe of one ear and stared down the street. "I know that, in a sense, David betrayed me," she said in a flat, neutral voice, "but, for all that, I think there was a part of him that loved me." She looked now at Ross, and he wondered whom she was seeing. "Even betrayal isn't final. It's just a new sort of relationship. I just can't feel that everything is over. . . ." Her voice ran down as she leaned over to open the door and let Ross into the street. Then she put the car into gear and drove off without looking back.

Ross found the door of his flat open and the light switched on against the fading daylight. Calverton was sitting in a threadbare armchair, still wearing the military raincoat Ross had noticed at the cemetery; the brown felt hat was perched on the back of the chair.

"Didn't want to frighten you, James, my boy," Calverton said affably. "Wouldn't do to test the old reflexes. A fellow could get his neck broken that way."

Ross noted that nothing had changed in Calverton's style. The voice was the remembered slightly breathless tenor, stuffed with the good-quality vowels that Fortnum & Mason sell. The tone was of supercilious banter: Ross suspected that Calverton was basically a shy man and that this was all he could manage. The man was wearing a suit with a sporting check, a lovat tie over a plain shirt, and a pair of handmade brogues – an officer's weekend uniform. His face put him in his indeterminate fifties: greying hair that had once been reddish-brown, a pale skin that lit up with small veins over the cheekbones, a thin ginger moustache over a rat-trap mouth. He looked and sounded like an old-style officer and gentleman who had been recycled and put to something slightly disreputable.

"I was expecting you," said Ross. He looked around for the kitchen, found it and the standard box of groceries left by arrangement with the agents. "Tea?"

"Not for me, old man." Calverton paused until Ross was back in the room. "I hope I wasn't too intrusive at the funeral. Didn't want to poke into private grief."

"Were you with the girl?" asked Ross.

"The girl? Ah, David's girlfriend! What a suspicious mind you have. No, I haven't had the pleasure; her presence was purest coincidence. The fact is," Calverton added more diffidently, "I wanted to have a few words with you."

"What could we have to talk about?" Ross asked.

Calverton came from a long-dead past. There had come a time when James Ross the Barnardo boy had got to turn himself into something else and go out into the world; and, since the only world he knew was that of institutions, then, if Barnardos would no longer have him, the Army could. He had joined the Army to become an engineer and had trained for the job. But the Army discovered that he had other skills that he himself didn't know of. They led him to the Special Air Service.

In 1970 the SAS had become involved in one of those wars in a place no one had heard of and for a cause no one understood, except – the wits said – God, and He wasn't too sure. It was a date when Britain was sloughing its imperial role and trying to support friendly

55

local regimes and create the illusion of stability and security.

In Oman there was a sultan who was as frightened of his own bodyguard as he was of his enemies. Since they had both tried to kill him, he was in a position to know. His country faced a left-wing guerilla backed by neighbouring South Yemen, and Britain sent in the SAS as part of its effort to defeat the threat. They also employed a local, irregular, counter-guerilla force, the *firqa*.

In January 1975, James Ross found himself leading a *firqa* unit against a group of Dhofar rebels holed up in a catacomb of caves scoured out of a bare hillside near the Yemeni border. They launched a night attack that took the rebels by surprise; their pickets were caught napping and the main group was captured still asleep in one of the caves and forced to surrender.

So far so good. It was a classic example of the expertise for which the SAS was noted, and all would have been well but for one thing. Before they could be finally disarmed, one of the rebels pulled a knife and lunged at Ross, taking a piece out of his side. The other rebels jumped on their own comrade, realizing that their position was hopeless and fearful of antagonizing the *firqa*, but it was too late. Ross, nearly passing out with pain and dizzy from loss of blood, lay in the shadows of the cave, his eyes swimming with dim movements and flickers of steel and his ears dulled by screams; and when it was all over there were no prisoners, just ten dismembered bodies scattered in the dirt.

No one blamed Ross. He had been in no fit state to stop the massacre. And yet, though he was not responsible for the killings, a corrosive sense of guilt became associated with the incident. For five long years it lingered in his memory and figured in his dreams, until at length he realized what it was that troubled him. If the circumstances were right, he could enjoy seeing men die.

At that point James Ross left the Army.

And Calverton? He first came into the picture in 1978 when Ross was at the SAS home-base of Hereford between spells in Northern Ireland. It was at times like this that Whitehall sent its minions to look over the Sasmen for any who might like to apply their skills in other directions: it might be as instructors for some foreign potentate's palace guard, or to join or train one of the specialized branches of the police. Or it might not. It was called the Beauty Parade.

"And in your case", said Ross's commander, "you have what they would consider the equivalent of big tits. I suggest you watch out for that one" – he indicated Calverton among the small panel of unassuming judges – "an emissary of the Powers of Darkness if ever I saw one."

On this occasion Calverton spoke of the other opportunities that were open to Sasmen. He said that Britain had need of their services. He spoke as if there were a special and deep meaning to that abstraction. Ross didn't take the bait.

When, in 1980, James Ross finally took his discharge, he met Calverton again when the latter popped up in a West Country pub without warning.

"I heard you'd left the service," he said, insinuating himself on the oak settle next to Ross, where the pair could stare across the public bar at the horse brasses and at the logs smouldering in the hearth. Uninvited he had brought across a half of bitter, while for his part he dipped his lips into a small dry sherry. "You must be looking for a job."

"I have a job," said Ross.

"Turning your engineering knowledge to good account, joining a contracting company – yes, I know. Very laudable." Calverton had earnest blue eyes which he turned on Ross as if he were advising a daughter against a bad marriage. His sense of people's need for space was poor: he tended to crowd in on them. "Of course, it won't work. I wish you well, but it won't work."

"Why not?"

"It's been tried before, simple as that. Men leave the service – your service – for civilian life, but they miss the excitement. They take to drink and fighting strangers in public houses." He waited, but Ross saw no reason to respond. Then: "Why did you join the Army, James?"

"A roof over my head and food in my belly."

Calverton must have guessed the same answer from Ross's personal file but he still treated it as a joke, a glib throwaway. He couldn't comprehend what a bed and a meal might mean to an orphan. "I'm sure that there were other reasons," he said. "Hasn't it occurred to you that in civilian life the values are all wrong: selfishness instead of self-reliance, the company instead of the country? What will you do when the joys of the contracting industry begin to pall? Of course," he went on, "you could always join one of those freelance outfits – guns for hire to take over Angola for the South Africans or some West Indian island on behalf of the Mafia. Believe me, it's not the same. Such enterprises are a counterfeit of the service, a home for egotists and misfits. They fall apart under the contradictions of their own aggression. And where's the *moral* satisfaction? It isn't the same as doing it for Britain." That word again, full of the same moist sentiment.

Ross drank the beer and left Calverton sitting at the bar, smiling politely at the customers.

Calverton hadn't changed. His voice was still alternately arch or full of oppressive sincerity.

"I thought we might talk about your brother David," he said. Ross detected an insinuation he didn't want to hear.

"Get out!" he snapped.

"Come, now, aren't you interested in his murder?"

"Not to hear about it from you. I want the real police, the ones who help old ladies across roads, not the kind who push them under buses in the national interest!"

"The real police?" the visitor repeated ironically. "Do you really believe they can help you? The *real* police, as you nicely put it, are turning over the burgling fraternity of north London in the hope that one of them will admit to committing five expert killings in the panic of the moment when disturbed about his work. Is that a solution which appeals to you as the truth?"

"Who called on Helen Ainsworth?"

"Special Branch – a little misunderstanding between ourselves and them, a little tiff that will no doubt sort itself out. We put a stop to that line of enquiry, reserved it to ourselves. Now do you understand, James?"

Ross understood: no one other than Calverton was going to do anything for his brother. "You bastard!" he muttered.

"I don't suppose", Calverton went on, "that David ever told you that he worked for me? What was it – a Civil Service job, Department of the Environment? It all went with his house and wife and all that *traditional* side of David's character. David had so much energy and daring, and yet was so conservative and loyal that – well – he fitted us like a glove."

Ross caught the word "loyal" and thought of Helen Ainsworth, who had loved and been loved by a man who didn't exist. Calverton probably had a scale of loyalty that extended to higher things and excluded purely domestic treason.

"He admired you terribly."

"I've heard that once already today," said Ross.

"It bears repeating. After all, consider how David imitated you. Remember that he wanted to join the Army but you insisted that he should go to university. He complied, but once he had graduated and you had, so to speak, no further rights over him, then he did volunteer for the Army."

"And when I left, he left."

"Only, in his case, it was to join me," said Calverton.

"I don't think you understand. We *cared* for David." Calverton's tone had changed. It was sincerity sounding like sentimentality. Ross was even prepared to believe that the other man was sincere. It didn't help him like Calverton. As a child he had known too many people who sincerely cared. They had taken him and David out for weekends – uncles and aunts with too many sweets, who were anxious to push them on swings and play hide and seek, and whose caring eyes bored holes in their backs whenever they were turned. Caring people could get you sincerely killed for your own good.

"Who killed him?"

Calverton looked away to admire the unadmirable decoration. He asked airily: "Have you heard of the NATO meeting called for January or didn't this piece of news penetrate to Saudi Arabia?"

"I've heard. A minsters' meeting in Brussels. Something to do with biological weapons. It used to be Cruise missiles, now it's lethal bugs."

"There are fashions in these things. The point is that the Americans will be passing through the UK on their way to Brussels. We have a major security exercise on our hands. Feelings on this matter run very high."

"Then, send the Americans direct to Brussels. Where's your problem?"

"We couldn't do that. We have a Special Relationship with Washington. It has to be cultivated."

"Special Relationship? It sounds like an old man's sex life."

"Meaning?"

"Who cares anymore?"

There was a click and the light went out. It was dark and the room was cold. Ross struck a match, found the meter and fed it some coins. Back in the room, Calverton was waiting with some final proposition.

Ross was struck by the alienness of the place. The walls were white emulsion, relieved only by dirt and cracks and a Dylan poster tacked up by some desperate soul. The furniture was a job-lot of bentwood chairs, a mahogany-stained table with varnish like tar, a melamine bookcase and a sofa in worn moquette. He had seen none of it before. In the matter of possessions, he was not David. If David chose to imitate him in other respects, that was David's business: there was no inevitable umbilical link.

"What was David doing?" he asked.

"He was looking for a terrorist, a threat to this current operation. But before I tell you more, James, are you with us? Will you join us?"

"Why do you want me? What do I have that you need?"

Calverton didn't answer. Instead he said: "For what it's worth, the man that your brother was investigating is called 'Kaster' – not his real name, we suppose, but all we have. English, somewhere in his late thirties and allegedly Soviet-trained, though none of this is confirmed."

"And how was David supposed to find him?"

"Oh, through the highways and byways, through people we know. Indeed, through people *you* know from your days in Belfast." He raised an eyebrow. "Your old IRA friend, Gerald Patrick Kelly, alias Riordan, is in London."

Ross was silent for a moment and then laughed bitterly. "Gerry Kelly in London," he murmured.

"You can help us to find him, help us to pick up where David left off!" Calverton urged.

Ross shook his head. "Get out!" he whispered.

"You should think about what I've said."

"Get out!" Ross felt the chill of anger and grief welling up inside him, for David, for Marion and the kids, for all the pasts that would never now be understood and the futures that would never be lived. He felt his hands shake and then steadied them. He looked away, at anything except Calverton, who was still sitting there with his caring expression floating on his face. "There was a man at the funeral today," he said quietly. "He tried to sell me a used car."

Calverton was genuinely shocked. "At a funeral? That must have been very distressing."

Ross looked up at him. "At least it was an honest deal," he said.

Chapter Six

GERALD PATRICK KELLY was the bright, sparkling broth of a boy, the stand-up, Guinness-in-hand, sing-out-his-heart-for-Ould-Ireland boy, the man on whom there were no flies, the hero of every woman who looked on his red hair and big, jovial face. He was the weekend cowboy of every bar and country gig. The Big Man. Himself.

Kelly had roared his way around Belfast from the age of twelve in light-hearted, boisterous criminality. Arrested, in care, arrested, in Borstal, arrested, in prison, he was cheerful about the whole proceeding – a poet, not without wit. There was only one road to take for a Catholic boy of his talents who wanted the light and the admiration, who wanted the reputation. And Gerald Patrick Kelly eventually took it.

Kelly had relatives in South Armagh, the wildest bandit country of any in Ulster. On the run from a robbery, he took shelter with a cousin in Crossmáglen. This was in August 1975 when the extremists on both sides were engaged in a tit-for-tat war of murder and Kelly's relative was hit by a Protestant death-squad. It pushed him over the edge into murder.

Those next twelve months were to be the peak of Kelly's career as an IRA gunman. Border-hopping between South Armagh and the Republic, he robbed post offices, ran guns and explosives and participated in the murder of three Royal Fusiliers in an army outpost in November 1975.

In January 1976 the British Prime Minister, Harold Wilson, formally committed the SAS to Ulster. At that date James Ross was at the tail end of the campaign against the Dhofar rebels, and it was not until the beginning of the following year that he was posted to Ulster. For the Provos, 1976 was not a good year. The SAS seized two of their leaders, Peter Joseph Cleary and Sean McKenna, amidst speculation as to which side of the border they had been caught on; two more men were arrested by the authorities of the Republic and a further six had retired south. On 19 January 1977 the SAS ambushed and killed Seamus Harvey – a judgement, it was said, on the IRA murder of a soldier on 2 January. Gerald Kelly now discovered that he had lost his taste for South Armagh.

He returned to Belfast and submerged himself in the Catholic community of the Lower Falls, concentrating his attention on fund-raising, hitting soft targets like post offices and illegal drinking-clubs. On the way he collected a mistress and two children and discovered a talent as a nightclub singer, which he pursued openly since, by luck, he was no longer on the RUC's wanted list. Then, in March 1978, he was recalled to South Armagh. Attrition was taking its toll of men with stomach for running the SAS gauntlet and an experienced hand was wanted for running a consignment of arms into Crossmaglen. Kelly was picked for the job.

As he later admitted: "The operation was a balls-up from beginning to end." The weak link was a sixteen-year-old whose own ambition was to be the man-with-the-power, which had led him to talk about the mission in clubs on the Republican side of the border, where the story was picked up by an RUC informer. As they were making the transfer from their car to a waiting tractor trailer that moonless March night, the SAS struck.

The IRA team consisted of three. Kelly and the boy headed through the hedgerows for a ruined barn standing among the sodden fields. The third man ran off in another direction and got away. Kelly reckoned that he might have got away himself, but the boy had turned into a berserker and was blazing away at shadows with his Armalite and leading the soldiers on by the gunflashes. In the event it seemed like a miracle that they made it as far as the barn, where they holed up among the straw and the cowpats and prayed for deliverance.

Outside the soft rain had started to fall. Kelly tried to calm the boy down in the hope that they could play possum and escape in the encircling mist. But the boy had his eyes on the crown of martyrdom and kept up a stream of fire at any fancied movement in the hedges and scrub, all the while shouting to Kelly: "Come on, Paddy, be a man! Do you want to live for ever?" Kelly looked at the boy; he was sixteen, beardless and eager. Kelly was thirty-five and didn't need to look at himself to know that the brightness had gone out of his eyes and that middle-age with the comforts of his family was staring at him through the years. It was then that he decided that he had had enough. He reached inside his jacket for the pistol he kept there and shot the boy once, calmly, through the head. Then he surrendered.

James Ross was first in the SAS "stick" that caught Gerald Kelly. When they entered the barn they found the big man squatting on the ground, rocking gently, his head in his hands, sobbing. The boy was spreadeagled on the ground in a pool of blood and the powder burns on the side of his face told immediately what had happened.

Ross knew straight away that Kelly was no ordinary find, to be turned inside-out by the Royal Ulster Constabulary and then locked up for ever in the Maze. Kelly was committed by his own act in killing the boy. He was utterly exposed both to the IRA and to the British, infinitely pliable. With care he could be refurbished, turned round and used against the Provos.

Turning the man against his beliefs was not easy, even a man as doomed as Kelly. The guilt of betrayal could as easily have become a search for an act of self-redemption; and for six months, even after Kelly had become operational, there were bets that he would kill himself or turn himself in to the Provos with the same result.

Converting the former gunman into an informer was also hindered by the operational mess that the British intelligence services had got themselves into in Ulster. For the careers of those involved it was the best game in town, and DI5, DI6, RUC Special Branch and the Army's own intelligence people were all fighting for a piece of the action. It took an unholy row and Kelly's own insistence before James Ross became the Irishman's case-officer. He had won over Kelly and worn down his resistance because it was easier for Kelly to bear the betrayal of the Provos than the death of the boy; and Ross was able to persuade him that it was the Provos themselves who were responsible for the killing when they put an inexperienced boy on such a dangerous mission.

Ross worked Kelly for a year before quitting the Army. Seeing the big, bluff Irishman destroy himself with guilt was one of the reasons for his decision.

James Ross had no illusions that Calverton was other than a mean, calculating bastard He had hammered at the theme of brotherly – what was it? – love? – dependence? – a vague web of guilt and responsibility. The Bible asked: Am I my brother's keeper? For some reason the answer was always: Yes. Big brother, little brother: the years ought to have, but hadn't, made a difference. Ross felt his life being driven by the engine of David's admiration and dependence. When they were children, David had physically held on to his shirt tail while he had fought against a world that threatened to split and destroy them. Ross didn't know how, but the psychological relationship between them had become fixed in the same pattern. Calverton had identified and exploited that weakness. David's death had become a wound and, with the name of Gerald Patrick Kelly, Calverton had injected the speck of infection.

Ross guessed that Calverton's vagueness as to Kelly's whereabouts in London was put on not simply to excite his interest but because Calverton genuinely didn't know. Kelly hadn't stayed alive so long without some cunning. Back in the early seventies the Military Reconnaissance Force had run a bunch of recycled Provos, nominally called the Special Detachment, but known as the "Freds". Like Kelly they had operated on the streets of Belfast, but unlike him they hadn't lasted long. The fact that Kelly was a survivor made him a one-man miracle.

Knowing Kelly's history, Ross was fairly certain that Calverton would expect the Irishman to be lying low in some out-of-the-way place. Logic said that was how you stayed alive. But there was an alternative approach. If you were thrown into the lions' cage, you didn't have to climb out: you could always say your prayers and growl with the lions. And just maybe, if you were very good. . . .

Ross knew that Kelly had never been fully turned round. Sure, his feet had been turned in the right direction, but his heart was never in it. The old myths, the IRA, one of the Boys – they were Kelly's meat and drink. Without the feeling that he was in some sense still with them, he would have been a useless husk. Somewhere on the fringe of London's Irish community Kelly could still be found, stilling his soul with the balm of the old ways and the old songs.

On the night following his meeting with Calverton, Ross went searching for his man amongst the Irish clubs and pubs. On the second night he went out again. He had no luck on either occasion.

The day following their visit to Blackheath to see Hortense Ainsworth, John Donaldson made a call at Sebastian Summer's house in Chelsea. He had a parcel to collect, the house was supposedly empty and Sebastian had given him a key. He found Anthony there.

"I thought you'd left," Donaldson said. The other man had been surprised naked coming out of the bathroom. He stood now staring at Donaldson with a look of jaunty insolence, unconsciously twiddling a curl of pubic hair.

"I'm a little stuck for accommodation. I thought I had certain . . . rights."

There was a noise from the adjacent bedroom. Donaldson opened the door and looked in. There was a girl on the double bed, lying where Sebastian ordinarily lay to judge from the toiletries and the half-read book on the bedside table. She had blonde, short-cropped hair and a strong, athletic style of beauty. Her blue eyes had a darting quality as if whatever she was looking at was disappointing and she wanted to look around and beyond it at the next horizon. She had a brown mole on her cheek near the left side of her mouth.

"Annaliese Schreiber, John Donaldson – John Donaldson, Annaliese Schreiber. We met in Hamburg," Anthony explained. Donaldson understood. Anthony had once done the left-wing Grand Tour, cadging his way through the network of radical communes and squatters that had sprung up among German youth as it tried to adjust to the seventies. He had kept himself by sponging and by selling dope or his body, whichever commodity was in demand. Hamburg was a market for both.

Anthony put on a dressing-gown and the girl one of Sebastian's shirts. They adjourned to the kitchen and sat around the table drinking coffee.

"Sebastian tells me that you asked him for money," said Donaldson.

Anthony brightened up. "All a mistake. A misunderstanding," he said. "I thought he might want to help me to make a start in my profession as painter." He was eager to placate. "However, it doesn't look as though any of that will be necessary." He leaned over to the girl and squeezed her breast. She reacted as though nothing had happened, as if it were a preliminary to something else that never came. "I've found true love. Ta-ran-ta-ra!" A hand out towards Annaliese.

Later he slipped into some all-leather gear that Sebastian had bought him. The girl was getting dressed in the bedroom.

"Fact is," said Anthony, "her father is extremely wealthy. Industrial electronics. Made his pile out of the 'economic miracle' and feels inclined to spend it on his daughter. And she would like to spend it on my career as a painter."

"Why?" asked Donaldson.

"Who knows? Who knows? She doesn't have a life of her own so she decided to borrow mine." Anthony looked into Donaldson's eyes – looking for approval. He turned away, glimpsed Annaliese in the next room. She was wearing designer jeans and a loose blouse. "We met in her slumming phase," Anthony went on. "Dragging her arse around Hamburg. Into Marxist heavy petting and hoping that it didn't make you pregnant. Cock and cunt; dialectical materialism in a nutshell." He spoke disdainfully. It was all part of his love–hate relationship with both men and women.

Donaldson nodded but didn't try to understand. He kept his mind away from the irrational whereas Anthony basked in his sub-conscious.

The girl joined them. Her eyes had the same offset look, directed at Anthony, watching Donaldson.

"I want you to move out of here and stay away from Sebastian," Donaldson said.

Anthony shrugged his shoulders. "Don't I always do what you say?"

The morning after his second excursion round London's Irish pubs, James Ross received a telephone call from Helen Ainsworth. She was at home. Would he like to meet her and have lunch?

Ross's stripped-down life didn't include a car. He took the train to Blackheath and walked up the hill and on to the heath. The day was one of winter's cold, bright lapses, the sun shining over an open landscape of grass and the houses around the heath edge glittering white.

Helen received him at the door. Without her raincoat and scarf and the drama of grief, her features looked plainer.

"Please," she said, "come in. Would you mind entertaining my mother for a minute while I get ready? Curiosity is one of the few satisfactions she has at her age."

She showed him the study where Hortense Ainsworth was sitting by the window. She was reading the Book of Mormon.

"Mother, may I introduce Robert's brother, James?"

Hortense put down her book and eyed Ross coldly. "Bit chilly for that sort of clothing, isn't it?" Ross was wearing the lightweight clothes he had brought back from Saudi Arabia.

"I've just returned from the Gulf."

"H'm. I was out in the Middle East in '35. Flying from nowhere to nowhere. It was full of Arabs killing each other. It doesn't appear to have changed." She reached for her book. "Have you read this?"

"I'm not a Mormon."

"Me neither. But I can't help thinking that if so many people believe in it there must be a core of truth there somewhere." She subsided into silence.

Helen Ainsworth returned to find Ross examining the photographs on the wall. She stared over his shoulder at a picture of a small stone-built cottage: from the photograph she stared confidently back, one hand holding the arm of John Donaldson. "We have a cottage near Hexham, in Northumberland," she explained. Then: "Shall we go?"

They took a dog with them. It was a cheerful old Labrador, wall-eyed and ripe-smelling but lively enough. It's name was Hardie – after Keir Hardie, the Labour leader, Helen said. Their walk took them across Blackheath and into the royal park where Hardie treed a squirrel in one of the sweet chestnuts. He could only be deflected by Helen's throwing a stick for him to retrieve. Ross noticed the girlish gangliness behind the throw. He wondered whether her restraint was a conscious reaction against the feyness of her mother.

"Why does your mother read the Book of Mormon?" he asked.

"The pursuit of *gnosis*," Helen answered. She was trying to get the stick back from the dog. "Down, Hardie, down! How am I supposed to keep throwing the stick if you won't give it back? There! Good boy! Good dog!" She threw the stick again and turned to Ross. "You don't follow *gnosis*?"

"No."

"Well, it's simple enough. Mormonism, Velikovsky, Horbiger, homeopathy, whatever you like. . . ."

"Marxism?"

"That, too, They're all the same to my mother. They offer secret knowledge, a simple explanation of the world which is intelligible only to the initiates. It gives a wonderful sense of well being, knowing that you know the meaning of life and the rest of humanity doesn't. That's why my mother wants, *gnosis,* secret knowledge." The dog returned with the stick and had to be fought with again before he would give it up. Helen threw it into the distance and dusted her hands of the dirt and fragments of bark. She looked at Ross. "I suspect that you're too direct for *gnosis* to have any appeal," she said, "unlike David, who succeeded in possessing secret knowledge only too well."

Ross nodded. Maybe that was what Calverton and the MI5 apparatus offered to David: secret knowledge, the opportunity to radiate illusion and alone to know the truth.

They walked on slowly towards Greenwich and the river. Behind them the Royal Observatory was picked out on the skyline. Ahead St Alfege's church glowed warmly in the low winter sun. They stopped for a snack at the Cutty Sark pub where the dog curled itself under the table while Ross brought the drinks.

"Your mother still doesn't know about David? You haven't told her?" he asked. She fingered her glass and shook her head.

"No."

"Aren't you surprised that the police haven't spoken to her?"

"No. I suppose you want to know why not?"

"If you want to tell me."

"Because there is something secret about David's death. Perhaps he was a policeman himself – even a secret policeman. I suppose we do have secret policemen in some peculiar British way, all pipes and tweeds and terribly decent? So why should I tell my mother or my friends? Why involve them when the police themselves haven't done so? What possible good would it do them?"

Ross didn't answer. For a few minutes they sat in silence or occasionally glanced out of the window, over the river to the Isle of Dogs.

"Would you give me the names?" Ross said at last. "I've got a right to them as his brother. I can't sit back while the police do nothing." He found himself saying "I'm the only person David ever had to rely on."

She considered for a moment and then told him. The names meant nothing. Perhaps they were irrelevant? Perhaps Helen herself was the key? Why had David got to know her?

"What did you and David talk about?" he asked.

"We were still getting to know each other – or at least I thought I was getting to know him. We talked about people and ideas, who we were and where we had come from. David talked a lot about you – it seems he couldn't lie about that. He was very convincing as a lecturer in history."

"He had a degree in history."

"Oh." She looked away and tried to make light of the fact. "It's rare that degrees in humanities have any direct relevance to one's work. David seems to have managed it."

"Didn't David force your conversations into any particular directions? Wasn't he interested in your friends, or maybe in organizations you were a member of?"

She smiled. "He was a much subtler man than you. Perhaps he was leading me towards some particular goal, but if he was, then it never showed. I'm sorry, but I was naïve enough to think that he was trying to find out about *me*."

Ross listened thoughtfully. He wasn't David; he wasn't starting from the same place; he didn't know what David knew. Even if he could reconstruct his dead brother's relationship with this woman, where would it take him? How would he know what it signified?

"Did David ever mention a man named Gerald Patrick Kelly?" he asked. "He might have called him Gerry Riordan." He took the only clue that Calverton had left him.

"No," she said. And that was that.

They walked back through the park.

"Why did you call me?" Ross asked.

"Oh, I had a reason but, in the way of things, it probably wasn't the main reason. I wondered if you could help a friend, John Donaldson; he wants to visit Poland. I gather there are some problems with tourist visas. I wondered if you could help get him a business visa." She told Ross about the Last Judgement painting and of Donaldson's plans to spend his holiday searching for it. "David said you had worked in Poland, that your company built plants in Poland."

Ross nodded. "This Donaldson – a 'friend' as in 'we're just good friends'?"

"Yes . . . at one time."

"Like David?"

"Was he like David? Is it important to know?"

"Maybe I shouldn't say 'like David', since we're not sure what David was like. No, it's not important."

"No, he isn't like David."

"Nor like me?"

Helen smiled. "John is tall, very handsome in a saturnine way, urbane, cultivated. . . ."

"Christ!"

"Shall I go on?" She was laughing, but it was with Ross not at him, and he found that he liked it, and her.

"You work at the gallery with this Donaldson?"

"Yes. Am I not what you would expect? You were looking for some Sloane Ranger type with a Courtauld degree?"

"I don't know. It depends on what a Sloane Ranger is."

She was ready to laugh again but stopped herself and regarded him closely. "You really don't know what a Sloane Ranger is, do you?"

"Not a clue," said Ross; then changed the subject. "Where does your high-class friend want to go?"

"He thinks the painting may be at a place called Bereznica. It's near Lodz."

Ross knew Lodz from working there in the heyday before the Polish crash of 1981. The company still had a half-finished project there, not in Lodz but close enough in a town named Budla. "I may be able to help. I could even fix up some accommodation. It all depends on whether there's any call for men to go out there."

"Doesn't that happen all the time?"

Ross smiled to himself. He would do what he could. The company wouldn't like it. In fact they'd go crazy. Their policy towards Poland was strictly one of honest dealing. On the other hand, the company didn't have to know. It was just a case of sticking an additional name on an application for visa support.

"What was the real reason you asked me out here?" he asked.

For a moment she avoided an answer and, instead, called the dog and made a fuss of it. At last she faced him. "I suppose I just wanted to know what had happened to me."

Chapter Seven

HELEN AINSWORTH had misunderstood one thing about the plant construction at Budla in Poland. There wasn't any site team, hadn't been since the Poles had finally run out of money twelve months before. There was only Jack Henshaw, an old hand in Poland, who had personal reasons for being prepared to stay out as a permanent resident site manager, watching the silent plant in the hope that money would be found and the work would start up again. Unless Henshaw had other plans, no one would be applying for visas for Poland.

Ross was back at his flat in Swiss Cottage by four and put a call through to the office. The project manager on the Budla job owed him a favour. Was any application being made for visa support for Poland? Ross was told he must be telepathic: Jack Henshaw was insisting on taking his Polish mistress to spend Christmas on the Black Sea and wanted a stand-in; a slate of volunteers had been conscripted, the lucky man to draw the short straw in a couple of weeks' time, but meantime an application for visa support was being made. John Donaldson's name was added to the end of the telex.

He scraped a meal together out of eggs and some scraps of ham and ate the result while watching the television news and staring at the blank walls. There was a film report of the latest demonstration and fracas outside the American embassy.

At eight o'clock he stirred from his chair and went into the kitchen. The day before he had found a two-pound hammer in the cupboard under the sink amongst the clutter of moulding detergent-packets and dirty rags tied to stop a leak in the S-bend. Now he slipped it into his belt and pulled on a blue parka to hide the result. If he ever succeeded in finding Gerry Kelly, he didn't know what reception he would get.

The Parnell was the third pub he tried. It was stuck on a corner site in a side-street off Kilburn High Street, linked on one side to a row of mean houses with sagging roofs and on the other flanked by an alleyway between the public house and a small timber-yard. The main door to the public bar was on the corner, with a door to the lounge bar facing on to the street. Down the alleyway there were two windows with frosted panes where the toilets would be and a third door half-blocked by crates and aluminium beer-kegs. Ross moved one of the crates aside, tested the door and went in.

It was ten o'clock and the evening was in full swing. In the public bar a crowd of Irish labourers were set on a good time, while a few old Londoners sulked at a corner table over pints of flat beer and complained that someone had stuck pages from the newspapers on the walls to celebrate the last IRA success. There was a small apron, scarcely a stage, squat against one wall. It was trimmed with broken mirror-tiles and held a microphone and a Japanese electric organ, and on it a big, red-faced man with veins like hawsers was belting out a sentimental ballad against an organ that was locked on a Latin American beat. "Will you listen to that, Wally!" someone yelled. "He thinks he's a bloody Irish matador!"

Ross slipped into the bar from the passage which led to the toilets and leaned against a wooden partition scanning the faces through the cigarette smoke. Gerald Patrick Kelly alias Riordan was sitting on his own by the door to the lounge.

Kelly had changed since Ross last saw him. The red hair was dyed brown, he had grown a beard and had a nose-job. But he hadn't dyed his eyebrows or the hairs on the back of his hands, and Ross had spent too many months nursing Kelly through his personal hell not to recognize him anywhere. The Irishman was taking an enormous risk in a place like this, but Ross had expected no different: the big man needed his fix of Irishness to keep himself alive. All Kelly could do was look the part and take precautions: from his table he could see the main door and the passage to the rear, and a mirror on the opposite wall gave him a view of the lounge. Unless all three exits were covered, he was in a position to make a break through any one of them. It was no more than luck that he hadn't spotted Ross.

Ross pulled back from the partition and retired down the passage to the gents' toilet. It was a dirty, tiled affair that stank like a monkey-house, and one of the customers was throwing up his guts into the urinal. The water closet with its missing seat stood in a flimsy cubicle with the window directly behind it, and on the opposite wall a mirror was fixed next to a broken Durex-dispenser.

Ross looked at the drunk, but the latter was absorbed in his own misery. He took the hammer from his belt and, masking the mirror with his coat, smashed the glass and took out a large sliver. This he placed against the wall, angled to reflect anyone coming in at the door. Then he waited, hidden from the doorway by the screen that masked the urinal.

The options were three and they panned out OK. Kelly might leave the pub without visiting the gents': that was no problem since Ross could catch him another night. There might be others in the toilet when Kelly came in: in this case Ross would have to turn his face to the wall and piss quietly until the place cleared. The third possibility gave him Kelly to himself, and he had plans for that.

A few customers came in. They ignored Ross except for one who asked for a light and fumbled with his cigarette until he dropped it into the urinal. Ross began to wonder whether Kelly had left. He waited half an hour and then saw the big man's reflection in the piece of broken glass.

Kelly came strolling through the door with the same swagger he had had when he was king of the world. Ross hit him with a slam in the abdomen as he turned to face the urinal; the Irishman folded up, took a punch on the jaw and was bundled back into the open WC and jammed on to the pan before he knew what was happening to him. Ross bolted the door and took out the hammer.

"Holy Mother of God," Kelly groaned as he slowly regained his grip on the world. His heavy-lidded eyes opened gradually and he looked up at Ross.

"Hello, Paddy."

"Hello yourself." The voice was a soft brogue with a glimmer of humour. "Can I get off this thing? There's no seat and my arse is getting awful wet." He registered the hammer. "I'll stay put if you insist, but it's a hell of a way to welcome an old friend."

"How's life treating you?"

"Fucking terrible, much as always. I should never have listened to your silver tongue when I could have got my brains blown out like an honest man. And you? Are you sure I can't get up? Sitting here makes me feel like I've pissed myself."

"My brother David is dead."

Kelly shook his head. "I know – a crying shame. But you, I thought you were out of the game, got religion or something. Or is this personal – big brother looking after little brother?

David was always your chief fan."

"You were dealing with David?" Calverton had been equivocal on the point.

A sharp laugh. "What the hell else would I be doing? Socializing?" Kelly let his head fall into his hands and his voice lowered. "You shouldn't have dropped me, Jim, not fucked off out of the service and dropped me just like that. It wasn't friendly. Who was I to trust if it wasn't you? Sod all the professionalism; treachery is a *personal* business, and it wasn't right to pass me on like a secondhand suit."

"You were given to Figgis, one of the best."

"Figgis was a wanker! I wanted you, Jimmy, someone who cared about Maureen and the kids."

Maureen and the kids. Ross had half-forgotten them; names flooded back – Damien and Patrick? Had he bought them Christmas presents one year or was his memory playing tricks? Now Kelly was telling him that his leaving the service had been as much a betrayal of Kelly as the big man's betrayal of his Provo colleagues.

"What about David?"

"I told you, Figgis was no good for me. He was gung-ho for glory. He wanted me out on the street, flashing my wares like a tart. The Boys would have got me in a week. So I cleared off out of it to London."

"And?"

"Six months ago David sussed me out. He said you had told him about me – that was wrong, Jimmy, you shouldn't have done that."

"I didn't," said Ross. It was one of David's lies, an attempt to trade on the past relationship.

"Maybe not, maybe not. Maybe David lied to me. He was a tough, ruthless bastard. Not like you. I always knew that even when you were kicking the shit out of me you still *cared*." Kelly's voice fell there. They could hear someone come into the toilet. There was a sound of whistling and an intermittent splashing in the urinal. The two men paused until they were alone again. They were left examining each other's face. "David brought up the old story," Kelly began, "about the boy. He said he'd tell, well, you know who – and he meant it, Jimmy. Jesus, what was I supposed to do?"

"What did he want?

Another pause while someone came into the toilet. Kelly looked about to explode with something, but was bottling it up until it was clear.

"What the hell *do* you know, Jimmy?" The words came out in a rush of air. Kelly started to get to his feet, but Ross pushed him firmly back into the toilet pan. "You don't know that David was working me, you don't know what he was working me for. . . . Why, for Christ's sake, did you come looking for me at all? Who put you up to it?"

Ross shook his head. He didn't know himself what Calverton's motive was except to flush out Kelly when he had lost him. Perhaps Calverton was only guessing where David had got to.

"The problem with being a turncoat", said Kelly more philosophically, "is that you get bought and sold like a commodity and you can't help wanting to know who your current owner is – you follow me? It's a case of capitalism applied to human relationships." He raised an eyebrow. "Oh, yes, we've heard of capitalism and Karl Marx in the Provos; nowadays we're a pretty fancy bunch. Did you ever hear tell of Desmond McKilroy?"

"Another South Armagh cowboy, good for knocking over those little country piggy banks – yes, I've heard of him."

"Well, let me bring you up to date," said Kelly. "Denny – that's what everyone calls him – Denny and me were friends back in Belfast. He was one of the Boys, but nothing too heavy, no killings and stuff; he was more interested in the money end of the business, screwing post offices, running drinking-clubs, you know the sort of thing. He had a string of taxis operating in Belfast, which was very profitable, what with everyone being nervous of the buses and all."

"Go on."

"OK, so five years ago things got too hot for Denny and he came over to England," Kelly went on. By then McKilroy had got a taste for the high life and learned the trade of robbing banks and strong-arming people. "So he decided to set up on his own account; he took a few banks and bought his way into the porno business."

"Did he drop the Provo connection?"

Kelly gave a wan smile. "How do you drop the Boys? You might as well ask to stop being Jewish. OK, he wasn't as closely involved; he chipped in with money on flag days and kept himself to himself, but he wasn't absolutely out."

"But that changed," Ross said.

Kelly asked for a cigarette. He lit it, drew on it a couple of times and stubbed it out. "You know how it is," he said. "The Boys have always had problems in keeping the war going over here – I mean in

75

London. But this is where the real decision is: nobody gives a fuck how many people are killed in Belfast, but start blowing up Harrods and everyone starts saying 'Isn't it about time we got rid of these bloody Irish?' "

"Denny was pressured to mount a campaign?"

"A Christmas present for the Government, that was the idea. But that put Denny in a spot; his organization is geared to muscling in on nightclubs, not to slipping bombs into Wimpey bars; and, in any case, as Christmas comes the likes of Denny and me can hardly move for the Special Branch hanging round the clubs and boozers buying drinks for all and anybody in the hope of a tip-off. In the end he farmed the deal out. He put out some feelers and found someone who was long on being crazy but short of funds."

"One man?"

"How many does it take to plant a bomb? Maybe it was one, maybe it was more. The only name I heard was 'Kaster'." Kelly paused there and looked at Ross curiously. "Do you really know nothing of all this?"

"I've heard the name Kaster before, that's all."

"Well, you can take private enterprise too far, Jimmy," said Kelly. "My advice to you would be to lay off this one, even if it was David."

"Why?" asked Ross.

Kelly shook his head. "Look, nobody can give you chapter and verse on these things. I can tell you David was every excited when I turned up this Kaster. It seems he's some sort of superman, Soviet-trained, contacts with the PLO, the whole works. And maybe he is – you know what happened to David."

"Kaster killed him."

"That seems reasonable."

"Then, why didn't he kill you? He got wind of David, so why didn't he get wind of you?" Ross gripped the hammer and waited for the answer.

"God knows," said Kelly. He saw the hammer but didn't care much. "I was following one lead. Maybe David was following another. There was a girl he was seeing. No names, no details, I know nothing more than that."

"I believe you," said Ross and let the hammer relax. "Who paid for the nose-job?"

Kelly rubbed his nose. "David. It was done on the cheap. The fucking thing went septic." He lifted himself from the toilet bowl. "Are you finished with me, Jimmy? I want to get out of this place."

"Just one thing," said Ross. "How do I get in touch with Denny?"

Kelly looked at him sadly. "You really are heading for trouble. Still, that's your business. I'll see what I can do. Denny doesn't live in London; he's got some place out in the country, but sometimes he comes down to make his own collections from the shops. Where can I get in touch?"

Ross gave him a company number. "Leave a message where I can reach you." He held out his free hand and pulled Kelly out of his seat. The Irishman brushed down his clothes and scrambled his face into a jaunty grin. "God save us all from treachery," he said. "It's almost as binding as friendship."

Chapter Eight

IN THE early seventies Warsaw had been Babylon, the whorehouse of Eastern Europe, awash with borrowed dollars. Then, like at the end of any determined party, came the hangover. Warsaw had spent ten years living a fantasy life, a frenetic imitation of Western consumerism, and then returned to a grim, drab reality of shortages and Soviet pressure that were more normal than the West gave credit for.

John Donaldson flew in on the LOT flight from London, having obtained a visa with James Ross's indirect help. There was no alcohol served on the plane, and the genuine contract crew, identifiable by an approximate uniform of parkas and pigskin shoes, were visibly missing it. For the rest, the passengers were a collection of Poles burdened with carrier bags full of canned meat and a bunch of bankers who pored over their schedules of defaulted loans and yet contrived to look cheerful.

Warsaw was in chilly sunshine. The airport held the usual collection of outdated Tupolevs in the LOT blue and white livery; perspex bomb-aimer's canopy in the nose and a bulge that suggested they carried enough radar to knock a fly off a lampshade, they were built to an old Soviet military design. Now they were grounded for lack of spares, fuel and customers.

There was a standard reception committee of conscripts in khaki greatcoats and caps with the green hatbands of frontier service, who looked bug-eyed at the passengers and examined all the outside surfaces of the plane as though after a flight at 30,000 feet someone might still be hanging on. Donaldson passed them, made his compulsory currency change at the Orbis desk, cleared Customs and took a taxi to the city.

He went to the Warszawa Zentrale railway station through grey streets of uniformly high buildings. The pavements were broken, and lined up against them were rows of Polski Fiats, out of fuel, stored under green weatherproof sheets like an encamped army. Like a monument to the past, the still-unfinished LOT building looked down on the city-centre and was dominated itself by the idle jib of a crane, the cross on a grave.

Budla was little more than a village, but the planners had decided to bless it with a chemical plant. The stopping train to Lodz dropped Donaldson off on a broken platform overhung by the bare branches of some birch-trees. The main street held a Catholic church, a dull public building identified by a red-enamelled name-plate bearing a white Polish eagle, and a few shops mostly closed for stocktaking – the Poles had discovered that it was most efficient to count stock when the shops had run out of any. Behind the main street ran a few rows of houses of the old type; then these gave out and the skyline was marked by blocks of workers' flats new-built for the chemical complex but managing to look old.

"Jack Henshaw?"

The man at the door was aged about forty, with a build that was determinedly unathletic. A bust zip on the fly of his trousers, an old cardigan and a pair of slippers indicated that he had adjusted to Poland as if it were an old, ill-regarded wife.

"Who are you?"

"Donaldson – John Donaldson. You got the telex?"

"Oh, don't worry about that," Henshaw said in a cheerful Brummy voice. "I got the message from Jimmy Ross all right: could I put you up for a couple of nights as necessary, since there's no hotel worth the name in this godforsaken hole? No problem. Come on in and make yourself at home. Have a drink and, later, we'll check you in with the local militia – that's the police – so that the buggers have nothing to complain about."

Henshaw was a gregarious type, stranded in Poland at the tail end of a construction contract when the rest of the crew had gone home, and glad for the sound of an English voice. As he took Donaldson's bags he rambled on, not particularly caring whether the other man listened or not: ". . . so when the money ran out they pulled all our lads off, but someone had to watch the plant so the Poles wouldn't steal the sodding thing, and I had this Polish bint, Wanda, and a wife in Solihull, so I volunteered. And, what with the tax relief for being abroad, the pay's bloody marvellous; except that there's nothing to spend it on." Then, as they reached the living-room: "This is

79

Andrzej and Jerzy" – two men in dungarees and calf-length boots sitting round a table dealing cards into the space between a litre of Wyborowa vodka and a six-pack of American beer. "They're the opposition," Henshaw went on breezily. "I keep them boozing with me so they can't swipe all the plant spares." Big toothy smiles from the Poles. "You got here quick, though. How did you manage it?"

"I went to the visa office in Weymouth Street and sat there until they handed one over the counter."

"I've done that before now: it wears the arse off your pants. See" – he addressed the two Poles – "you buggers can get a move on when you want to. Do you play cards?" he asked Donaldson. "No? Well, never mind. Just help yourself to some beer, as much as you like. We get it from the Pewex hard-currency shops so there's no shortage." Then, feeling he had done his duty as host, he settled at the table with his two friends and resumed his game of cards.

Donaldson looked for somewhere to dump his bags. He found a bedroom, bare and functional as the rest of the apartment. Henshaw had customized it with a *Playboy* centrefold, heavily pockmarked with dart-holes, and a photograph of the Aston Villa first team. There was a sour smell of laundry that has been hastily hand-washed and left to dry. He dropped the bags and went hunting for the bathroom.

He was tired from the flight and the long train-journey across the Polish plain. He missed the bathroom at his first try and found Henshaw's bedroom. It was dark and musty with animal warmth. A woman, presumably the Wanda who kept Henshaw away from the erotic delights of Solihull, was asleep in the bed. Donaldson tried the next door, which proved to be the bathroom. Inside, a man brandishing a knife turned round to face him. The man was naked and covered in blood.

"I should have mentioned that," Henshaw said. He had been about to laugh with the two Poles at Donaldson's discomfiture. Then he saw that Donaldson was not discomfited. Instead the other man radiated an unearthly chill. "You're not the upper-class ponce I thought you were," Henshaw said to himself. He scratched his backside vigorously and turned back to his game. It had occurred to him that he knew next to nothing about his visitor.

Donaldson could still see the naked man and the part-grown pig, strung by its heels from the shower-rail, its throat cut and the blood draining into a bowl that had been placed in the bath. The man, knife in hand, had looked at Donaldson, his teeth bared in a grin that was half fury and his eyes exultant. He saw the Englishman and then his own nakedness mirrored over the washbasin, his chest running with blood.

"We raise a few pigs around the plant," Henshaw was saying, "particularly while things are slack, there's not much going on and there's not a lot of meat around. It's a sort of club. All the Poles do it." He felt the explanation was lame. "Our old sow had a large litter. We didn't have enough space or feed for the lot; so we thought we'd half-rear one and pop him in the pot in time for Christmas. We don't normally slaughter them here," he added.

The bathroom door opened and the other man came out carrying the pig across his shoulders. He was still naked, but the demonic quality had gone. Now he was no more than a pasty-faced welder from the plant, bronchitic and running to fat.

"Dump it here," said Henshaw, clearing the table and laying it with newspaper. He looked around the circle. "Anybody know how to cut up a pig?"

"I'll do it."

Henshaw stared at Donaldson and handed across a knife. Donaldson took it and with one flowing movement laid open the carcass from pelvis to breastbone and scooped the lights out of the abdominal cavity.

"Somebody's been teaching you anatomy," said Henshaw. He was impressed and a little fearful, though he couldn't have said why.

Later that night Donaldson dreamed of the naked figure bathed in blood and of the pig's head sitting in the middle of the table while the men played cards. Blood of the Pig: a perversion of Blood of the Lamb. It was a tableau of Hell from the unseen painting of the Last Judgement.

The British Council library in Al. Jerozolimskie, Warsaw, had turned up a guidebook with an entry for the house at Bereznica and directions for the walk from the station two stops up the line from Budla on the local train. The rest of the entry was uninformative beyond the advice that the house had been built for Princess Katerina Wolska and that its famous erotic murals were no longer on public view.

The guide didn't say that the house would be closed for lunch. John

81

Donaldson was left in the winter chill, stamping his feet for warmth and pacing the gravelled path around the dried-out fountain. The house and park were silent except for the distant crows and the snap of burning leaves from some workman's bonfire. The peeling stucco walls, pink and white in the sunlight, were imbued with a melancholy charm.

At two-thirty the main door opened. A fat woman was sitting at a card-table in the hallway. She put aside her knitting to take a handful of zlotys and issue a ticket and a two-page guide in Russian, German and English, printed on recycled paper. Behind her the interior was dimly lit by daylight filtering through the windows. Donaldson thanked her and went inside.

Hortense Ainsworth had told the tale of the beautiful Katerina Wolska, the princess who became a king's mistress. The Bereznica Palace had been his gift to her. What had it been like? Donaldson looked around the empty rooms. The treasures were gone. Crossing the floor, his feet made holes in the echoing stillness, but in a way the vast spaces were more evocative than if the jumble and trappings of the place had been there, as if the emptiness cleared the stage for the ghosts. Suggestions of lightness, music and merriment clung to the air. But the question remained. What had happened to everything?

He reached the upper floor. By some bureaucratic perversity each empty chamber was watched over by a curator in a canvas chair. The painted bedroom referred to in the guidebook had its murals masked by hessian drapes. Instead of a great bed, there was a photomontage displayed on screens around the walls. It showed the destruction of Warsaw by the Nazis. To the Poles there was apparently no incongruity in such an exhibition in such a place. To Donaldson it underlined only a growing certainty.

There was no Leonardo painting in the Bereznica Palace.

Professor Wojciech Karpinski noticed the foreigner examining some of the photographs and plans of the house that hung on the walls by the staircase. Kowalski had first claim on the foreigner. Kowalski was in charge of all the petty rackets run by the staff such as fiddling the returns from admissions and he was not going to pass up the chance of a black-market currency deal. Foreigners at Bereznica were about as rare as honesty.

"Change money?" Kowalski said. The Professor was fairly certain that one phrase and a knowledge of numbers were all the English that Kowalski commanded.

The Englishman, a man in his late thirties with dark, intense, elegant good-looks, shook his head and changed the subject to point at one of the photographs and ask a question. As he had supposed. Kowalski was stumped for an answer. He turned his ugly head, round and folded over with skin like a cabbage, in Karpinski's direction and noticed him at the head of the staris.

"Hey, you! Toe-rag!" Kowalski snapped. "You may as well be useful for once. This one wants to know something about the house. Tell him what you can and get a few dollars out of him."

Karpinski smiled inwardly with satisfaction. He had remarked the Englishman going through the rooms, clearly searching for some particular thing, and he had longed to speak to him. His own equivocal position, an intellectual relegated to the job of museum guard, made such an approach too dangerous. Yet here was the Cabbage handing it to him on a plate!

"Nie mowiem po Polsku," the foreigner said in phrase-book Polish.

"English?" asked Karpinski. Having made the approach, it occurred to him that this was going to more difficult than he had imagined: the stranger's manner was inaccessible. Karpinski felt suddenly ashamed of his shabby uniform and pulled the front of his jacket together as though that remedied something.

"You speak English?" the stranger asked.

"A little."

Donaldson pointed at a photograph on the wall, framed between an architect's elevation of the house and a small print. "This," he asked. "What is it?"

Karpkinski turned from studying the Englishman to look at the photograph. He identified it at once as a snapshot of the oratory attached to the main bedroom. It must have been taken before the war since it showed a priest giving confirmation to a small boy. The communists would never have permitted such a thing. Karpinski surmised that the child was Prince Jerzy Wolski, the last private owner of the house.

"It is a . . . church." He hesitated, not knowing the correct English for "oratory". For clarity he explained: "Here . . . in the house."

"And the painting?"

Karpinski did not follow until he saw that Donaldson was picking out the fragment of the altarpiece dimly visible behind the priest's head.

"Does the painting have a name?" Donaldson asked.

Karpinski looked again but already knew it. He had seen it himself in better days, long ago, as a child. His limited English defeated him.

"It is 'sąd ostateczny'."

"I'm sorry. I don't speak Polish. Nie mowiem. . . ."

Karpinski caught the other man's hand as he riffled through the phrase-book.

"Not in book. . . . 'Sąd ostateczny' not in book. . . ." He struggled over the words. "It means 'final court'? You understand? God – everything destroyed – world end. . . ."

"The Last Judgement?" the Englishman said.

"Yes."

They stood in silence for a moment. Then Karpinski caught a glimpse of the Cabbage watching him from the landing above. He knew that there was only one way to be safe, and to do that his abasement would have to be complete.

"Please," he said, "give me ten dollars." He heard the dry rattle of Kowalski's cough. The Englishman's eyes flickered but he showed no surprise. "Ten dollars. Then I meet you in Budla, at Ruch kiosk near station, five o'clock. I explain everything."

The Englishman having gone, Professor Wojciech Karpinski stared at the ten-dollar bill clutched in his hand and then dragged his way over to Kowalski and handed it over for a few unusable zlotys. Then for the remaining hours of the day he performed his menial duties. He asked himself continually: What have I done? Why have I done it? He had committed himself to a clandestine meeting with a man who was a perfect stranger to him, and for what purpose? To answer the stranger's questions at no possible benefit to himself. For a man in his exposed position it was insanely dangerous. But it was because of that danger that he was going to do it. It was not the content of the act that was important: it was the fact that it was prohibited; and to do what was prohibited by a tyranny was the act of a free man. For the first time since the disaster of December 1981, Wojciech Karpinski felt alive.

He took the local train to Budla and stood all the way, jostled by the crowd, next to Kowalski, who was smiling like a contented cat, the ten dollars tucked into his wallet like a talisman. At the station he fell behind the other passengers. He was filled with an incoherent guilt as if he had committed some nameless crime, and the paranoia that went with it made him look around to see if he were being followed but he lacked the skill to know one way or the other.

The Ruch kiosk was visible by its red fascia. A queue had gathered outside it, shuffling forward slowly to purchase cigarettes and newspapers. On the other side of the road more people had collected outside a grocery store. Its windows were filled with bottled redcurrants, which never seemed to be out of stock; but there were also some goods in brown paper sacks, a delivery of . . . what? Reflectively he started to cross the road to join the queue in the hope that the paper bags represented something worthwhile. Then he remembered the Englishman and saw him slouched and blending into the crowd by the kiosk. Two militiamen in their grey-blue jackets and black trousers pulled an old man out of the line and demanded his paper. Wojciech Karpinski remarked with admiration that the stranger regarded the scene indifferently and moved forward in the queue as if nothing were happening. Karpinski felt a flush of confidence that the Englishman knew what he was doing.

John Donaldson recognized the museum guard in the figure swathed in an overcoat and dragging his down-at-heel boots along the pavement. At a guess he was fifty years old, with high cheekbones and thin, pointy features and a straggle of hair that was on the way to grey but was halted at the colour of weak tea. The Pole had been anxious to speak to him: Donaldson had noticed him bob up in his chair the first time he had entered that particular room of the house, but at that time had thought nothing of it. What did he want? The Pole glanced in his direction, and he noted that the expression in the older man's eyes was determination, not fear, and that was good. Donaldson reached the head of the line, pointed to a newspaper and walked off with a copy of *Zycie Warszawie*. The other man was fifty yards ahead and walking slowly.

Their route left the main street. It went into a maze of grey apartment blocks that led to a railway cutting and a view over smouldering spoil-heaps and pithead winding-gear. Between the tenements was a railed-in garden with a few trees stencilled sparsely against the concrete walls. The Pole opened the gate and went in. Apparently he was a regular visitor, for, the moment he showed up, a pair of squirrels dashed out of the trees and began to dance in front of him for breadcrumbs.

*

85

"I was once a professor of history – at Lodz," Karpinski said in a calm, low voice. His back was turned to the Englishman as he fed the squirrels, but he had heard the footsteps.

"Once?"

"Yes. . . ." Karpinski's tongue fumbled over unfamiliar words to express the pain behind that "once", finally stumbling inadequately on "All past. Now, as you can see, I am humble – guard? – at museum." An explanation occurred to him and he lifted the lapel of his overcoat, disclosing a Solidarity button pinned to the underside. "Solidarnosc," he said with the flicker of a smile suggesting his embarrassment since, after all, Solidarity had failed and, with it, marked him as a failure. "Not popular with regime," he said, pointing at himself, "so. . . ." He gestured and made the sound of having his throat cut. "But why worry?" he added more cheerfully. "Now I am an honest man. And you?"

"I?" The Englishman was reticent, but Karpinski had expected diffidence from the English, particularly an urbane type such as this one. By contrast he felt himself a gibbering Man Friday, his thoughts hopelessly lost in the limitations of his schoolboy English. "I work for a man who buys and sells paintings," Donaldson said.

"Aah! I understand." Zarpinski nodded and shook his fingers free of crumbs. "That is why you want to know about 'sąd ostateczny'."

"Yes. Where is the painting? Still at the house?"

"No. Gone."

"Destroyed?"

"Destroyed, no. Well, maybe destroyed, who can say?" Karpinski felt his courage draining away. The other man remained unresponsive even when he had revealed, if imperfectly, that he was a man who had been ruined by his commitment to truth. There was something frightening about that degree of detachment. Karpinski turned away, bent down and chucked one of the squirrels under the chin, murmuring to it in Polish. "Is forbidden to give bread to animals," he remarked to the stranger. "But who cares?"

"If you keep feeding them, they may hibernate too late, in which case they'll die," said Donaldson.

Karpinski's smile died on his lips and he quickly threw the rest of the bread away so that the squirrels scattered. He had been indulging in an act of personal sentimentality: he hadn't expected to be demolished with such cruel rationalism.

"The painting," Donaldson reminded him. "What happened to it?"

"Stolen by Nazis. Everything, all stolen. That is why house is empty."

"Everything?"

"Stolen. All for Hitler. Who knows where now?" Karpinski reached into his deep pockets and produced a bottle of diluted Spiritus, the solace of his bitter memories. "Drink?" The other man shook his head. He took a pull for himself. "I was there," he said finally.

"It was beginning of war," he resumed after a fit of coughing at the fire of the spirits. "I was – eight? – eight years old. My father have farm near Bereznica and my brothers are soldiers."

"What happened?"

Karpinski shrugged his shoulders, not out of ignorance but because of the abyss between the words he could formulate and his images of childhood in that sunny autumn of 1939.

"German soldiers come to house in car." That much was tangible. "Not many. Man with them is . . . not soldier?"

"Civilian?"

"Yes. . . ." Karpinski tasted the new word and applied it to his memory of the prissy little man with the pince-nez that dangled from a black ribbon. "Civilian. They have wagon and put in paintings, furnitures – all treasures – in wagon. Then more soldiers come. Different ones."

"Not Germans?"

"Yes, Germans. But . . . different." He couldn't explain further because he understood neither then nor now. "More of them. They have officer. Tall. Gold hair." Again an image came back like a snapshot: the burning field, the German soldiers driving away in the cars, the handsome officer with his sad eyes, and himself, little Wojciech, jumping up and down and waving at the brave show. "He wear a uniform with . . ." – he indicated his lapel – "yellow."

"Yellow?"

"Yellow, yellow, yellow – badges? All yellow . . . on here. . . ." He pointed to his lapels again. He could not tell whether his description of the yellow collar-patches was getting through or signified anything to the other man. He felt deflated. "I was once a professor of history – at Lodz. . . ." He tried to pull the conversation round to something else, and then realized that there was nowhere else for it to go. In turning over this meeting in his mind while he travelled on the train with the Cabbage smirking next to him, he had never once thought of what they would talk about, merely of the fact of his having a person to talk to.

"What happened next?" Donaldson asked.

Karpinski turned out his pockets for more crumbs and threw some on the ground, but the squirrels had retired to their tree. "The soldiers quarrel," he said, returning to the subject. "New soldiers shoot the others. I see with my own eyes new soldiers shoot others, shoot driver of car then take wagon and all things from house." He could have added that he had also been with his father when they had seen the body of the murdered civilian lying in the painted bedroom. His father, more shocked by the sexual licence of the frescos than by the violence, had forced the child to look away and stare instead at the corpse lying in its pool of blood, the face surprised by death. He put away the memories and pointed at a small stone tablet lying in the grass. Withered flowers half-covered the names: Stanislaw Szezeblewski – Miroslav Kawlowski – Andrzej Kawelski – Karol Karpinski. "Later," he said, "Nazis say people of Budla have killed soldiers. So they shoot four Polish men – here." He looked around him at the faded garden still hung with the dry shreds of autumn. "My father is Karol Karpinski. They shoot him. But I know the truth. It is Nazis kill each other."

There was nothing more to say. Wojciech Karpinski reached into his pocket and offered the handful of zlotys he had received in exchange for the ten dollars. He had intended to say by this gesture that his information had been given freely and not for the dollars. But he was not able to make his point. The Englishman thought he was trying to change more money and pressed another ten dollars into his hand with a fleeting look that might almost have been sympathy. And on this note of misunderstanding the meeting ended.

Chapter Nine

THE MORNING after his meeting with Kelly, James Ross gave Calverton a call. The latter was full of the same specious *bonhomie* as before, enquiring after Ross's health, the weather and the joys of London.

"I want to know where I can find a man named Desmond McKilroy," Ross asked.

"Now, there's a name to conjure with – Denny McKilroy. May I ask where we picked it up? Been talking to our friend Kelly, have we?"

"Drop the banter," said Ross. "You lost him and I found him. No doubt as you intended."

"A little acerbic this morning, aren't we?"

"What about McKilroy? Where can I find him?"

"Not so impatient, please. What did our Gerald have to say about him? Mark Denny's card for your brother's murder, did he? Well, I can guess about that. But before I can help you I need to know whether you intend to take up my offer and join us."

With the last request, Calverton's voice had changed to a cold, business tone. Ross wasn't surprised by the question but his answer didn't change. "Not on your terms. As far as I'm concerned, this is a one-off, a personal matter."

There was silence at the other end of the phone and then a sigh. "Sorry to hear that, James. We operate a strictly regular business: nine-to-five and no moonlighting."

"And McKilroy?"

"A trade secret. Couldn't possibly tell you."

Ross called his office to find out whether any messages had been left. He gave them Kelly's name and asked them to call him immediately if Kelly tried to get in touch. Next he got on to the Summer Gallery and from Helen Ainsworth obtained a list of the guests at dinner on the night of his brother's death. He set about tracing them.

He managed to speak to the first person that same day. She was Letitia Corbett-Strong, described by Helen Ainsworth as a "friendly old dyke", an acquaintance from her mother's Stalinist days. Ross found her living in a bedsitting-room in Leytonstone, where she collected and smoked old pipes; they were housed in racks on the wall by the hundred. Robert Marshall? She remembered the name from Hortense's dinner-party but that was the first and only time she had heard it. On that occasion, too, she had not spoken to him: "After all, what on earth should I have to say to a handsome young man?" She had indeed been a member of the Communist Party, from some date before the war until 1956 when Khruschev's speech denouncing Stalin had left her in a state of political confusion. She had retired to think about the matter but had never come to any firm conclusion. Nowadays she made a precarious living writing pulp Westerns under a male pseudonym.

That evening he returned briefly to the Parnell, but Gerry Kelly was not there.

Two days later Kelly still had not called. Ross had made an appointment to see Tom Furnival. The trade unionist lived in a detached bungalow in Watford, where, when not working, he grew alpines in a series of elaborate rockeries. His manner with Ross was one of suspicion. He preferred to talk in the garden, where he scratched all the while in the thin soil between lumps of Dolomitic limestone.

"So you're the brother of this – whathisname – Robert Marshall, if I'm to believe you."

Ross guessed that Furnival was in his early sixties, which made him ten or fifteen years younger than Hortense Ainsworth. He looked for resemblances to Helen, but, if she were his daughter, he had bequeathed her nothing in appearance.

"I've already had the police to see me," said the older man, "asking me what I knew about this Robert Marshall, which is precisely nowt, except that he was Helen's boyfriend. I'm telling you the same. I'd never met him or heard of him before that night. I didn't know him from Adam. You can try all you like to link me with him, but you'll get precisely nowhere, and I've got an alibi for the night that will satisfy anybody, because it just so happens as it's true." He ignored Ross's questions and went off instead into a eulogy of the regular police, which was obviously something that he had rehearsed: "Uncle Tom desperately wants to be a peer," Helen Ainsworth had said.

"What I have no time for", said Furnival, "is spies, counter-intelligence agents, secret police or whatever you call them. Is that what your brother was at?"

"What makes you think that?" Ross asked.

"Don't come it with me, laddie! I had one of them round, said he was CID, but I know a spy when I see one. You're forgetting that I'm the boy who went to gaol for his socialist principles." He hacked furiously at a stubborn weed that was rooted firmly under one of the stones. He turned to Ross and gestured with the hand-trowel. "You don't live that sort of thing down. You can slog your guts out for public causes, but you can never make them forget, even your own bloody party!" He shook his head. "Clement Attlee, there was a Labour Party purist: I could have got into Parliament in 1950 if he hadn't been Prime Minister. But I was tainted, do you see? An old Red."

Ross listened to more of the same. It was political archaeology, all of it. Hortense Ainsworth and her friends had become frozen in the politics of the past. What, then, had been David's interest in that circle?

The call came through that evening. Ross picked up the receiver and heard the pips of a call-box.

"Hello, is that Mr Ross?"

"Who wants him?"

"Mr James Ross?"

"OK."

"This is a friend of Gerry Riordan. The name's Rafferty, Eddie Rafferty."

The arrangement was to meet in an hour outside the Odeon cinema in Leicester Square. Rafferty, when he arrived, was a small man with a port-wine birthmark that covered one side of his face from a half-closed eye to the skin of his throat. As he spoke, he shied and shuffled and turned his good side towards the listener. It was no great improvement. He came sidling out of the evening crowd and touched Ross on the arm.

"Ross, eh? Ross – knew you would be – knew it." The words ducked and weaved like his body, expressions repeating themselves like a boxer's feints.

"Where's Gerry?" Ross asked.

"Oh, around – around – but you scared the shit out of him good and proper, you did, finding him out like that at the Parnell and him thinking himself safe." The little man tried a smile that came out as a leer. "He won't be going back there in a hurry, no, not in a hurry. But he has friends to help him."

"He's safe?"

"Safe? Why not? If he wasn't safe, how would I have your number, eh? Gerry gave me the name of your company and they gave me your number."

Ross reminded himself to put somebody through the mill for that lapse. "So what now?" he asked.

"You like the . . . uh . . . cinema?" Rafferty queried. He glanced over his shoulder at the Odeon and gave another of his grotesque gestures, a wink that would have done justice to a pantomime dame. "I can show you stronger stuff. Make your hair curl – make some of the other bits straighten out, though, eh?" He scuttled off up the street without giving Ross any chance to argue.

Ross followed as Rafferty made for Charing Cross Road and caught him amongst the crowd by the Underground station. One or two people were carrying placards tucked under their arms, wondering what to do with them. There had been another demonstration near the American embassy, this time peacefully, and the demonstrators were now looking for a drink and the train home.

"I want to find Denny McKilroy," Ross said.

Rafferty bobbed out from behind a placard. "Gerry told me." He pointed down a side-street at a Porsche that was parked on the pavement. "One of Denny's clubs." The building was labelled "The Blue Vision Adult Cinema Centre" and a pair of heavies were outside it, pimping for custom and keeping an eye on the car. "Denny is inside making a collection. You want to see him, eh?"

"Are you volunteering to come with me?"

Rafferty laughed. "Me? Not me! Gerry told me to show you where Denny was and then piss off. The rest is up to you." Rafferty threw another wink and then vanished around the street corner.

The club was a regular porn-house complete with billboard giving the film titles and the usual come-on photographs. On the left-hand side was a bookshop and on the right a fast-food franchise. Next to the fast-food franchise an alleyway blocked by dustbins led to the rear

92

of the block. Ross felt for the hammer in his belt and went down it.

Behind the shops was a small courtyard with empty vegetable-crates; a cook from the fast-food place was lounging by an open door, smoking and sharpening a carving-knife on the wall. The cinema-club sported a fire-exit into the yard; the fire-door was half-open and breathed out mist and condensation with snatches of Swedish dialogue and some disco mood-music. Ross took in as much as was visible through the doorway and then went inside.

He found himself in a passage lit by a dim red bulb. It led to the front of the house, with a door on the right labelled "Projectionist" and, on the left, a staircase to the first-floor office. Ross went the whole length and into the auditorium.

The house lights were down, and on the screen a naked couple were grunting and making Scandinavian liltings to twelve rows of seats and a scattering of men hunched like pigeons in the rain. A curtain led out to the ticket office and what passed for a foyer. Ross tapped at the ticket-office door.

"It's McKilroy," he said in a passable Belfast accent and waited whilst the key turned in the lock.

"Who the hell are you?" The owner of the voice was a young, stocky type, with ginger hair, a moustache rimmed with cigarette ash and a throw-out tuxedo from a dress-hire firm. Ross caught him with a blow to the throat that confined his objections to a few gargles, pushed him back into his seat and pulled down the blind on the ticket-office window.

"I'm the man you were expecting," Ross said. "You were expecting me, weren't you?"

"Oh, fuck," groaned the other man.

"Where's the welcoming party?" said Ross.

The manager pointed at the ceiling. "Office . . . " he gasped.

"How many?"

"Two with Denny and two more out front."

"With hospitality like that, he should register with the Irish Tourist Board." Ross looked around the cramped room. The ginger-haired man had been making up the week's takings – the ones McKilroy had come to collect. There was cash stacked on a side-table along with the ticket stubs, and the carpet had been rolled back to reveal a floor-safe.

"How is the collection made? Do you go up or does someone come down?" Ross asked.

"Denny comes down," said the other man.

"In that case we'd better settle and wait for him," said Ross. He pushed a chair into a corner where he couldn't be seen from the window and then released the blind. "You just deal with the customers." It was midnight.

John Donaldson arrived back in London by an evening flight. It was midnight by the time he had cleared Customs and got from Heathrow to Sebastian Summer's house in Chelsea. He routed the older man out of his bed in silk dressing-gown and his hair still awry from sleeping.

"John, dear boy, what a surprise! I thought that your little trip was going to take up the whole of your holiday, and now here you are. Have you just got back?" Summer was wide-eyed and disoriented and let the other man pour two stiff shots of brandy before protesting: "I think I'd rather have tea."

"And I think you'll need this." Donaldson pushed the glass into the other man's hand, then sat down and stared at Summer through his intense eyes. "The painting exists."

"But that's wonderful," Summer murmured when the implications had sunk in. He sipped at his drink and added: "I'd still prefer the tea." From the kitchen he asked: "How on earth did you find it? Surely it's impossible that you might actually have it."

"No, I don't have it. And I don't know for certain that it's by Leonardo. But that *The Last Judgement* exists is a fact."

Summer returned with some tea brewed in a large mug stamped with a heart and labelled "Valentine". He glanced at the cup and murmured: "I keep it for sentimental reasons. Silly, isn't it?" He thought he saw a flash of sympathy in Donaldson's otherwise impassive face. Then: "Well, dear boy, *do* tell me all!"

Donaldson did just that, giving his account of the journey to the house, the finding of the photograph of the chapel showing the altarpiece, and his meeting with Wojciech Karpinski.

"Tantalizing, isn't it?" Summer sighed. "Just a piece of background in an old snapshot. I don't suppose you have even a copy of the photograph? No? It really isn't a lot to go on, is it? What, one asks, are we to do next?"

Donaldson had held back Karpinski's story of the shoot-out between the two parties of Germans. Now he told it.

"Good Lord," said Summer. "What an extraordinary circumstance! Why should they do that? I suppose some of them may have been looters, but it does seem a remarkable risk to take. Are you sure that this Karpinski wasn't mistaken?"

"He was there."

"But the merest child, you tell me."

"I believe him."

Summer shook his head. "My, my, so the Nazis took the painting. I wonder what they did with it? It rather looks as though it got lost at the end of the war."

"What happened to all the Nazi art-collections at the end of the war?" asked Donaldson. "Who might know?"

Summer thought for a moment. "I suppose you could try Aaron Eichbaum," he said doubtfully. "Before the war he used to work for one of the German auction-houses. Although they locked him up in the end for being Jewish, he got to know some of the Nazi bigwigs and their little tricks where paintings were concerned. You might ask him." He checked his watch; Donaldson's story had taken a couple of hours in the telling. "But now, dear boy, if you don't mind – it is two in the morning."

At two in the morning the Blue Vision closed. The ginger-haired manager pulled down the blind on the ticket office and turned to Ross. "What now?"

"When will Denny come down?"

"Five, maybe ten minutes. He'll give me time to balance the last takings and clear the punters out."

"Then we'll just wait."

"It's your funeral."

The exact time was seven minutes. There was a rap at the door and a voice said: "It's me, Micky. Open up." Ross turned the key and flattened himself against the wall.

McKilroy came breezing in. "That bastard Ross didn't show," he said. He may have wanted to say more but Ross chopped him in the neck, bundled him against the wall and locked the door.

"Surprise, surprise," Ross murmured.

He took his first look at Denny McKilroy – at the real McKilroy. There was another one on record; Gerry Kelly had pointed him out when he was reciting his catechism for his new British masters at the time of his conversion in Ulster – at the time when he was called upon to renounce the Devil and all his works and, incidentally, finger one of the lesser demons. It was a prison shot, and with their bleak incompetence the prison photographers had unintentionally endowed the subject with preternatural, mythic menace. The McKilroy of the photograph was one hundred per cent the hard man. And, hence, had probably never existed.

The present McKilroy was soft with good living, dapper in his light-fawn Savile Row suit and hand-made shoes, his pale hands chunky to the knuckles with gold rings. His face still betrayed his past, the features looking as though they had been cannibalized from spare parts and pounded until they fit, but even here there were signs that he was planning on replacing it with a custom-built job, small scars and tucks in the skin showing the outline of the work. His appearance and voice all suggested that he was in the middle of a refit. His hair-replacement course still had a few instalments to run and, for the moment, was a carpet of sparse, regular tufts of brown hair. His accent had been stranded midway on his social climb. He spoke Bog Etonian.

"Good Lord!" McKilroy gasped. "What the hell did you do that for? I have a weak heart." He slipped gingerly into a chair and tried to recode his face into an affable grin. "They always said you SAS buggers could break a man's neck while disguised as a bottle of stout."

"I'm not SAS."

"Well, not any more. But I always found, for myself, that killing was like riding a bike. You never forget how to." McKilroy's lip curled, but his sardonic smile could not disguise the fact that his injured neck was giving him pain.

"The gun," said Ross. He held out his palm. McKilroy gave a what-do-I-care shrug and removed his hand from his pocket, holding a revolver by its barrel. It was a dinky little gun, silver-plated, with a mother-of-pearl butt. Ross collected it and dropped it into his own pocket.

In the corridor outside, two of McKilroy's henchmen had got it into their heads that something was wrong and started to pound at the door.

"Tell them you're not coming out to play," said Ross. McKilroy thought about that one, sizing the odds. A foot kicked through the flimsy plywood panel. Ross hit the exposed ankle with two pounds of steel-headed hammer. There was a scream from the other side of the door.

"Stay out of this, chaps," said McKilroy in a passable imitation of an Irish brigadier-general – one who had just lost a battle.

"Jesus Christ, he's broke my fucking leg!" said one of the troops.

"Just thank your stars that it wasn't your head through the door."

The noise outside subsided.

"All right," said McKilroy at length. "What do you want?"

"Let's start with an easy one," said Ross. "Where's Gerry Kelly?"

"Mother of God!" McKilroy laughed. "Gerry always said you were the sentimental type, too sentimental for the rough stuff with the big boys. Why should you care? Feeling guilty about leaving him out in the cold?"

"Where is he?"

"Where do you think?"

"I could kill you just for that," said Ross calmly, but asking himself all the while: why? Why should he feel responsible for Gerry Kelly – or for David?

"Let's try not to get excited," said McKilroy. Then it occurred to him that his problem was that James Ross wasn't excited but deadly still. He tried another tack. "Who do you think told me where to find you? Who do you think was working for me?"

"I'm out of thoughts, tell me."

"Did you ever believe that Gerry would be able to break with the Provos? You must have seen the withdrawal symptoms yourself. Gerry could no more get Ireland from under his skin than cut off his own bollocks."

"I'm listening."

"After you dropped him, Gerry was taken up by a cunt called Figgis – I see you met him. So Figgis nearly got him killed and Gerry came to London to get out of the firing-line. That's when your brother found him. OK, so all this you know." McKilroy paused and ran his fingers through the greasy ringlets on his neck. He looked up at Ross. "What can I say about your brother that doesn't get my neck broken? He was a tough, ruthless bastard – rougher on Gerry even than you." He waited for a violent reaction but didn't get one. "Living up to your image, says Gerry, after your brother has been knocking seven bells out of him, *except,* says Gerry, that your brother never got the point."

"What point?"

"The trick, *your* trick," said McKilroy. "He could kick the hell out of Gerry, but he could never make him *love* it. That's powerful magic, Jimmy – can I call you Jimmy?" By now McKilroy had lapsed into a soft brogue. "Gerry was a guilt-ridden man," he went on, "and what you did to him was a penance. You've got to be a Catholic to understand that."

"So?"

"So – " McKilroy smiled – "Gerry was cut off from the bosom of Mother Ireland, cut off from Parnell, de Valera and all the Saints, and your brother was riding him too hard. And Gerry came to me – doing penance, you might say. And, for our own reasons, your brother and I played the poor sod between us."

"Until you decided to do Gerry a favour and kill David."

McKilroy looked annoyed. "Why in God's name should I do that? I can hardly go for a piss without Special Branch popping out of the drains; so what do I need with all the trouble that comes from killing your brother? Listen to what I'm trying to tell you. It was Gerry who set your brother up to be killed. I knew nothing about it."

"He said you did."

"Of course he did. Treachery gets to be habit-forming. Gerry sold the Provos to you, he sold David to me and now he sells me to you. He was a weak man, and betraying people got to be the solution to all his problems."

Ross listened to Denny McKilroy and believed him. He had always known the vulnerability of Gerald Kelly, and in turn Kelly had played on Ross's own weakness: he persisted in living in a world of human beings, the lowest of whom deserved – well, something better than they got. He closed his eyes a second to lament the dead past and opened them to face a gun.

"I take back what I said earlier," grinned McKilroy. "You just fell off your bike." He took the gun from the third man, the ginger-haired manager in the faded tuxedo.

"Out of practice," said Ross without any anger. "You had a gun in the cash-drawer?"

The manager threw in his own smile, lots of pink gum and teeth like ranks of turnstiles. "You should have done more than just search me."

"Drop the hammer," McKilroy snapped. Then: "Did I ever tell you that Micky here used to be in the Paras? Not in the same class as the SAS, but with the gun I think it gives him the edge."

Ross dropped the hammer and kicked it across the room. McKilroy picked it up by the head and with a swing of his arm brought the wooden handle down on Ross's skull.

Chapter Ten

ACCORDING TO Sebastian Summer, who had first mentioned the name, Aaron Eichbaum was by now nearly eighty. Before the war he had been with the Lange auction-house in Berlin. His knowledge of fine art was second to none, and it was this knowledge and some influential Nazi patrons – Summer didn't know whom – that had kept him free through the gathering shadows of the Third Reich until in 1943 he had disappeared into the camps to emerge two years later with his wife, his children and his past all gone. Now he had premises in Great Russell Street above an occult bookshop. From the window of his upstairs rooms he had a view of the British Museum and here he traded in watercolours.

"Herr Eichbaum?"

The door had opened to the tinkling of a brass bell, and an old man looked up from his work. He had been examining the foxing dotted on the sky of a small landscape. He was a frail, gentlemanly figure in a cardigan and the sort of suit that lasts for ever. The hair was thin and white, the skin a waxy yellow and spotted brown, and the eyes turning milky but with only that first hint of cloudiness that gives them a look of transcendence. He turned at the sound of the newcomer and gave him the warmly innocent smile of a man who was old enough not to care about anything overmuch.

"I'm sorry – I don't think I've had the pleasure. . . ."

"The name is John Donaldson," said the stranger, and quickly he explained his connection with Sebastian Summer. In fact Aaron Eichbaum had heard of Donaldson, just as the younger man had vaguely known of the old Jewish dealer before Sebastian had spoken of him. The world of art was small enough.

"So what brings you here?" asked the old man. "Watercolours? I heard about your find of the Turner – Raby Castle, was it? You should be so lucky here. I know. I have looked. How is Sebastian by the way?"

So the usual preliminaries of strangers with acquaintances in common and business to transact. They exchanged a few commonplaces. Donaldson had an opportunity to look about the old man's small room. The wallpaper was faded and every corner seemed to be stacked with pictures in crumbling gesso frames, but what was on view was of recognizable quality. The old dealer took a seat by a table which held a silver-plated samovar, a bottle of kosher rum and a plate of water-biscuits.

"Have you come to sell me one of your Fenwicks?" asked Eichbaum.

"I didn't know you were interested in oils." Donaldson wondered whether Sebastian had told the old man about the Fenwick paintings and their origins, but thought it unlikely. In which case Aaron Eichbaum was exceptionally shrewd.

"I am interested in *paintings* – but not in your Fenwicks. They have the wrong feel. Oh, they are strong, masculine celebrations of the working man! But the emotions behind them are not *echt*. A boy like you should stay away from them."

"Maybe I will."

"Very wise, I'm certain."

They came to the point.

"What do you want from me?" asked Eichbaum. "Or is it Sebastian? What does he want of me?"

"I want to ask you about art thefts," said Donaldson. "About Nazi art thefts."

Aaron Eichbaum had got to the stage of life where his answer to almost any question was autobiographical and where he had ceased to believe in easy solutions. It was impossible for him to answer John Donaldson's question without explaining his whole life.

"I was born in Berlin . . ." he began after a few excuses for addressing the problem in this way. Then he told his story by small accretions of detail, struggling through the lumber-room of his memory, bumping into recollections as if they were solid objects and pausing in his narrative to discourse and negotiate a way around them.

He had been born in Berlin during the last flourish and bombast of the Wilhelmine Empire, when he had actually seen the Kaiser, withered arm held to his breast, riding down the Unter den Linden amidst the clash and glitter of his white-clad cuirassiers. The Great

War came. He served in the last days and thus survived, and disaster was to come later when his family's modest fortune was swept away in the great inflation of 1923. Even so, other relatives rallied round and sent him to university during that period of specious prosperity which preceded the economic crash of 1929. All of this with careful attention to names, dates, descriptions.

They paused for tea from the ancient samovar. The old man served it out in china cups and then, producing a paper bag, took out some tea-cakes and toasted them against the bars of an electric fire.

In 1931, Aaron Eichbaum continued, he had obtained a position at the Lange auction-house. From a professional point of view he was to enjoy ten years of success as an acknowledged expert in fine paintings. But this was just the highlight. The reality was, as he put it, *chiaroscuro*. The background to his success was the gathering darkness as the power and malice of the Nazis grew. He secured safety by the bargains and favours he provided to Party notables as they dismembered and pawed over the treasures of fleeing Jewish families. He was, he said with an appreciation of the irony, a victim of his own skill: with his knowledge and love of art, he was too valuable to the men he served; difficulties were raised when he tried to pay the *Fluchtsteuer,* the cash price of freedom, so that he might escape with his family. And the Holocaust drew nearer.

At this point the old man changed his style and, avoiding the meticulous detail of the early part of his story, he described the last period of his old life – the increasing harassment and danger until his eventual arrest – briefly and impressionistically. Donaldson could not decide whether the change was because the old man had blotted out the unbearable recollections of that time or whether in fact it was an artistic device in the telling: the hearer would dramatize the unexpressed in his own imagination. It occurred to Donaldson that Aaron Eichbaum had converted his life into a story. Most people did not live stories.

Outside the early winter's evening drew in and the car lights swept shadows across the walls of the small shop. Eichbaum lifted his tired body from the seat and pulled the curtains closed. A customer came in and pottered among the paintings, but the two men pulled their chairs more closely around the samovar and the conversation continued in low voices.

*

"Now you know of my connections with the Nazis."

"Who was selling them art works?" asked Donaldson.

"Everybody who could." The old man saw that this would not do and amplified. "The profits were fabulous, and the Nazis were so ignorant that one could sell them anything. Lange, Weinmüller, the Dorotheum, the Hotel Drouot, they were all involved in it." He paused. "Let me tell you how it worked.

"Hitler, you may remember, came from Linz in Austria. His father was a Customs official; it was a petty background – *kleinbürgerlich*. So what should he want when he became the great man but to show off to the people of Linz that they were wrong to reject and despise him? Out of generosity, he would give them the greatest art collection that the world had ever seen!

"To do this Hitler set up an organization: Sonderauftrag Linz. It was to scour Europe for works of art for the collection. Its chief was a man called Posse – Heinz Posse. So, they establish a clearing-house in Munich. Everything photographed and catalogued. They plunder Germany, the properties of the great Jewish families – I know because I am helping them. Next Czechoslovakia after Hitler occupies it in 1939. Afterwards they have the Low Countries and France." Here he laughed. "But in France Goering was too sharp for the Führer."

"How so?"

"He had a deal with Rosenberg's Einsatzstab – Gestapo. They gathered all the spoil together at the Jeu de Paume clearing-house in Paris before cataloguing and shipping out to Hitler. Goering had an arrangement to have the pick of the pieces before this was done."

Donaldson now pressed the aspect which most interested him.

"What about Poland?"

"Poland?" Aaron Eichbaum showed no flicker of interest. "The Nazis scarcely concerned themselves with it. It was axiomatic with the Nazis that the Poles could produce nothing of value."

"So they were left alone?"

"No, but it was a small affair! The Nazis took a few things, like the Veit Stoss altarpiece, which could be attributed to German artists – rightly or wrongly – but very little was taken for the Linz collection. Why are you interested in Poland?"

"Please, go on."

"What can I say? I know very little because it was not important to the Germans. An SS colonel was put in charge of the business, name of" – he ransacked his memory – "Muehlemann. That was in October 1939. There was another man involved, I think it was earlier: he was called Alois Schimmel; I knew him slightly; he was killed by Polish partisans. Maybe others were brought in later. I don't know. I do know that everything of significance that was taken was collected and catalogued at the National Museum and the Wilanow Palace in Warsaw, or else at the Jagellon Library in Cracow. The Germans always seem to prepare catalogues of their crimes."

More details as, by degrees, Aaron Eichbaum described the paintings that he had handled in these years, the deals he had fixed, the Nazis he had sold to and their particular idiosyncrasies. The room grew dark except for the glow of the fire. The old man pulled his cardigan around him and suggested suddenly that they should eat. "What would you say to a Chinese take-away?" he asked. "I'm an old man," he explained with a chuckle that rattled around his throat, "and I never learned to cook. You can get used to any sort of food in time."

"I'll get something," said Donaldson.

He left the shop and spent half an hour finding somewhere that sold Chinese food and returned carrying the meal in foil containers. Grease spots punctuated the cardboard tops and a trickle of juice stained his hand. In the upstairs room Eichbaum cleared the table and set it with what looked like an old prayer-shawl. He opened a bottle of wine. They ate in silence. Donaldson was absorbed with the information he already had. Eichbaum had largely ceased to be curious about the tittle-tattle of the world; what Donaldson wanted the information for was his business; Eichbaum had become a teller of his story, not a listener to other people's.

"What happened to the things that were taken?" Donaldson asked at last.

"To all of them? Who can say? Do you mean were they recovered?"

"Tell me about the Linz collection."

The old man wiped a dribble of sauce from his chin. It was apparent that he had suffered a mild stroke sometime before, and the right side of his lip hung slackly.

"Everything was stored," he said, "in Munich, at the Führerbau. But by 1944 there wasn't enough space. The Linz collection had spread and was occupying two castles and a monastery. Then Hitler got worried. What happened if the Allies bombed these places? Poof! Smoke and then – nothing! The great treasures of European culture, all gone. Another home had to be found. A bomb-proof one."

"Where was that?"

"There were some salt mines near Bad Ischl in Austria. Alt Aussee was the name of the place. In late '44 it was decided to move everything there." Here he paused. "This, you understand, I don't know for myself. I had been arrested." He said no more about his life in the camps but resumed his story. "You may imagine, it was a colossal task, but the Germans more or less managed it entirely. The Americans found virtually the whole collection there."

"But not everything," said Donaldson.

The old man became testy at the interruption. "Of course not everything! How can you have disruption and destruction on such a scale and not lose something? Works were lost, even great works. I remember the *Portrait of a Man in a Black Cap* by Memling. I saw it before the war. But where is it now? Other things, too. Some were destroyed in the bombing; others were stolen. When the Americans entered Munich, a small part of the Linz collection was still at the Führerbau awaiting transport to Alt Aussee. German civilians broke into the building and stole everything that was left."

They finished the wine, sitting in front of the electric fire, peeking through the red liquid at the glowing bars.

"You are interested in a specific painting?" Eichbaum asked. "Something that was lost?"

"A Leonardo."

"Please?" The dealer's eyes filled with curiosity. "I never heard of such a thing. Not lost. What was it called?"

Donaldson shook his head.

"You won't say? But what do you know?"

"It was stolen by the Nazis. I thought perhaps for the Linz collection."

The old man smiled. "I should be angry with you. You come here under false pretences, not telling me what you want. So you think you know of an undiscovered da Vinci, but you don't want to broadcast the information in case you are wrong or someone finds the painting first – am I right?"

"Yes," Donaldson admitted.

"Well, you are right in one thing. If the painting was taken by the Nazis, and if it was by Leonardo da Vinci, there can be no question that it would have been in the Linz collection. Goering acquired the Spiridon *Leda*, which is almost certainly only a copy and not by Leonardo, but Hitler forced him to give it up for the Linz collection."

"But?"

"But the Linz collection is fully documented. From the start to the very end it was meticulously catalogued and the American OSS have the catalogues. If your Leonardo was ever in the Linz collection, then it would be already known. So it seems obvious, does it not, that your painting does not exist."

The subject drifted. Aaron Eichbaum asked the other man his opinion on some of the watercolours. Donaldson felt reluctant to bring the topic back, but there was more he wanted to know.

"Did you ever hear of a dealer by the name of Prince Jerzy Wolski?" he asked. He still remembered Hortense Ainsworth's words: "one of the foremost art experts of the period".

"Wolski," said Eichbaum in a knowing manner. "Oh, yes, I remember Prince Wolski."

"I gather that he had a considerable reputation in the thirties."

"A reputation certainly – but not, I feel, in the way you believe. Let me tell you, I know this Wolski. Everyone who is dealing on the international art market, sooner or later I am bound to come across them through my work for the Lange auction-house. So, I repeat, I know this Wolski." He broke off to suggest another bottle of wine. He took one out of a cupboard, still in the off-licence tissue-paper wrapper, and poured two glasses.

"Before – let me see – 1936", he went on, "nobody had ever heard of this Wolski. Then suddenly he appeared in Paris, absolutely penniless. 'I am a Polish prince,' he says. Perhaps he is, but nobody is very interested because Polish and Russian princes are much the same, and every restaurant in Paris has a waiter who is a Russian prince.

"So, according to him, he has just come from Russia, driven out by Stalin. He says he is not a communist, just a Polish patriot, which is why Stalin will not have him. People in general, however, are suspicious, but he has a beautiful wife – I forget her name – and people are sorry for her and make sure that the Wolskis do not starve." Eichbaum halted to explain, "You follow me: during this period there is no talk of Prince Wolski the great art expert."

They sipped their wine. The old man went on. "One day Prince

Wolski has money. He has managed to get his funds in Poland released, he tells everyone. He buys a small shop, very nice, near the Champs Elysées and starts to sell paintings, sculpture, furniture, whatever; it does not matter, because the man is an ignoramus – no, a crook, because he sells rubbish."

"Did he deal with the Nazis?"

"What would you expect? Hitler had buying agents everywhere, but one of his particular favourites was a woman named Maria Dietrich, though God knows why, because she was a fool who could be taken in by anything. Wolski made her acquaintance and in this way sold a few small things to Hitler. Probably he was selling other things to Goering, too, since Paris was Goering's artistic home. In the way of such a man he was very successful. And then. . . ."

"What?"

"Poof! Disappeared. Some say that Hitler had him killed; others that it was Goering. Whatever the truth, something happened to one of his deals."

Chapter Eleven

James Ross came to nursing the effects of Denny McKilroy's blow to the head. He was in a room washed with the rainy half-tones of dawn light. Whose room, he didn't know, but it had lace curtains tied back with bows and the chintzy feel of retired ladies and country vicarages and the sugar and spice and all things nice that little boys like Denny McKilroy are not made of. The growing daylight filled out the image of a child's bedroom, with neat flowered counterpane over the bed, a chest of drawers all tucked up with tidy lavender-bags and, on the walls, a pair of Beshley Heron prints showing hedgehog, rabbit and the rest. Eddie Rafferty was squatting on a chair like a leprechaun with a shotgun.

"Awake, then, eh? Awake at last, aren't we?" Rafferty bobbed his head in Ross's direction, toasting him with the port-wine stain on his face. "Did you come unstuck – ho! ho! – come unstuck?"

Ross ignored the other man: in anybody's plot – McKilroy's included – Rafferty was only good for a walk-on part; Ross wasn't obliged to talk to him. He felt instead at his wrists and found himself professionally strapped to a chair. With that and Rafferty's nervousness with the shotgun, which threatened to blow either or both of them into the hereafter, it wasn't a very promising breakfast.

Ross looked out of the window. The sun was up and a grey bank of rain was driving in from the east across a flat landscape. In the foreground a stretch of lawn suggested that the house was a large one; the clipped grass extended for two hundred yards to a line of willows and a suggestion of water. A lake? The edge of a fen? The view was packed with trees but, here and there, patches of open water glinted greyly in the pale light. Norfolk? Lincolnshire? Assuming it was now about eight o'clock and he had been unconscious since three, either was possible in the time. They had had all the time they wanted: the ache in his arm told Ross that the knock on the head had been supplemented by something delivered by needle.

A tap on the door and a woman came in carrying a breakfast-tray. She was a blonde, of uncertain age, ladled into a dressing-gown and spilling out at the edges. It might be early, but she had made up her face and wore her hair lacquered into a helmet. She placed the tray by Ross's side and pulled up a chair.

"You've made a bloody nuisance of yourself, haven't you?" she said in cheerful cockney. "Denny doesn't seem to know what to do with you. Have you got good connections, love?" She cut up a piece of bacon and offered it. Ross shook his head. "Suit yourself."

"Where is this place?"

"Denny rents it. He's got a couple of other big places. Proper little gent."

"He has kids?"

She looked around the room and laughed. "Him! No chance. It takes him all his time to get it up. This is just one of his fantasies – imagines he has a little daughter. He has lots of little fantasies, does Denny." She was wistful. She had few fantasies of her own left. Her hand drifted to the side of her face and Ross saw the bruising visible beneath the make-up.

"Is that one of Denny's fantasies?"

"In a manner of speaking," she said slowly, then brightened up. "But it cuts both ways: he does it to me and I do it to him, if you get my meaning. A bit of strict discipline. Shall I leave the food?" Ross nodded and she placed the plate by the side of his chair.

She quit the room leaving Ross alone with Rafferty. Ross examined the little man and weighed his chances. He judged that Rafferty was a spectator not a doer, and that he probably knew no more about firearms than which was the business end. But a shotgun in a confined space allowed a lot of room for mistakes, even for a rank amateur. Ross began to wonder where Denny had got to in his deliberations.

McKilroy was in no obvious hurry. Ross was left to watch his fate ticking away to the sound of a Mickey Mouse clock and the click of Rafferty cracking his knuckles and occasionally the other man's giggles at his own private jokes. It was ten-thirty by the time McKilroy put in an appearance.

He came in looking blown with exertion, the recycled flesh of his face red and sweating, the small scars from surgery looking yellowly pale. He was wearing hunting pink and a pair of black varnished boots which he smacked with a riding-crop as he spoke. Ross recognized the crop for what it was: like the dinky pearl-handled revolver, Denny's personal fetish of power.

"How do you like my place?" McKilroy said for an opening. His voice this morning was the best product of his elocution lessons.

"You need my approval?" Ross suspected that in some bizarre fashion McKilroy did. The boy from the Belfast slums needed to know that he was buying the right things. "What can I say? I love it." The other man seemed pleased.

McKilroy relaxed a little and took a chair. "Believe me, old man, I don't have anything against you," he said.

"I know that I'm still alive."

"See what I mean? It was the same with your brother. As far as I'm concerned, he could live for ever."

"I believe you," Ross said. He did. The problem was to persuade the other.

"Was it just your own idea to come after me about your brother's death?"

"Or do I have any influential chums who'll miss me when I'm gone?" said Ross. He guessed that McKilroy was struggling to discover how secure his position was if he killed the Englishman. Denny was a businessman: he was as economical of violence as he was of any other resource. "You don't fancy the likes of Figgis after your blood," Ross voiced his concern. "If you cut me loose and tell me what you know, we can still kiss and be friends."

McKilroy toyed with this last idea. "Ah, but there'd still be Gerry Kelly between us," he said. "Another man would say, 'To hell with Kelly; he was a grassing bastard who got what was coming to him.' But you? I don't know. Gerry got to like you – he told me so – and you liked him."

"Tell me how he set my brother up. Convince me."

"Maybe I will. Maybe it will get you off my back."

"Were you ever in Libya?" Denny McKilroy asked.

"No."

"Well, don't bother; it's a bastard place. I was there once, it'd be five years ago. Does that surprise you?"

"I'm surprised," said Ross. "Go on."

"Well, I guess you know I was never into the heavy stuff."

"This isn't heavy stuff?"

"I'm talking about political murders, killing soldiers and the like. You can get your arse shot off like that. Blagging banks and scaring the shit out of club-owners, on the other hand, is just the rough end of legitimate business. It's halfway to being respectable." McKilroy looked as though he believed it.

"So? Tell me more."

"OK, so it's no secret that Gaddafi is in the business of training and supporting liberation movements and, like it or not, the Provos come into that category, huh? So there I am, sent out to Tripoli to fix a consignment of arms for the Boys, and hanging around for weeks in some fucking hotel because the Libyans can't get it together and because, the guns being 'free' and all, no one in Belfast thinks to give me the money to bribe the bastards into completing the deal.

"After a week I start to get nervous. The hotel is full of riggers and construction men and some American petroleum crew, all pissed on smuggled booze. But there's one bloke who looks to me like CIA, and I get worried because no one believes my story that I'm just a regular businessman. I mean, what the hell have the Irish got to sell to Libya? In the end I kick up a fuss and they move me out to some camp in the middle of the desert."

The camp, said McKilroy, was one of Gaddafi's terrorist training-grounds. It was run by the Libyan army but most of the training was done by Palestinian Arabs.

"It was a mixed bunch of people. Mostly PLO or other Arabs, all split into factions and fighting like hell among themselves when the Libyans weren't keeping an eye on them; but there were some Japanese and a lot of Europeans. The only Americans were two men who said they were ex-CIA and working freelance – I guess that's capitalism for you."

Basque separatists, the remnants of the Baader-Meinhof Gang, the Italian Red Brigades – McKilroy didn't have much time for them.

"The Basques I could get along with: they were after kicking the Spaniards out of their country, just like we want to kick the Brits out of Ireland. But the rest were a bunch of head-bangers; spouting bloody Marxism and the rights of the working class till I wanted to throw up – and none of them that had done a day's work in their lives."

There was more of the same. Denny had a deep and bitter envy of wealth and privilege. He couldn't understand why anyone would want to give it up. Ross let him vent his hatred until it was

111

spent and he could pick up the theme.

"You'll know all about this," McKilroy ended. "You'll *understand*. Gerry told me that you and your brother were brought up in an orphanage. Is that right?"

"That's right."

"Underneath we're two of a kind, Jimmy."

"Sure."

McKilroy got off his chair, went over to the window and stared out over the bleak, grey countryside, stripped down for winter.

"There was this Englishman," he said. "His name was 'Kaster' – 'Kasta' – something like that – don't ask me how to spell it. That's it, just one name – Kaster."

"What was he like?"

"To look at? Age thirty or maybe a bit older – mind, this was five years ago. Dark hair, good-looking. Pretty upper-crust I'd say – but, then, I wouldn't know much about that, would I?" McKilroy looked at his captive again.

"It's just a matter of training and upbringing. With a bit of determination anybody can be like that."

McKilroy nodded. "Anyway, this Kaster was one of the instructors, not one of the customers."

"Where did he learn his trade?"

"He didn't say. In fact he didn't say anything about himself. It was all rumour. The story was that he had done a stint at some place in Russia called Sok . . . ? Sok . . . ? Shit!"

"Sokhodnaya?"

"You've heard of it?"

Ross nodded. It was a place near Moscow where the Soviets had their own terrorist school; there was another one near Simferapol on the Black Sea. If Kaster had graduated from Sokhodnaya, then he was something quite other than a bourgeois psychopath looking for a cause. He was a product of the KGB machine: rational and deadly.

McKilroy was still talking: " . . . so that made him cock of the walk as far as the rest were concerned. You should understand, Jimmy, what these places are like: playing soldiers all day and tossing off at night because the Libyans won't let you near their women – it addles the brain. So whatever anyone said about Kaster, it wouldn't necessarily be true. Anyway, for what it's worth, everyone in the camp – apart from Kaster – used to gossip like schoolgirls about all the big hits they'd been involved in, and they used to tell tales about Kaster.

112

Everyone said he was a big mate of Carlos – you know, 'the Jackal'; worked with him here, there and everywhere, particularly on the kidnapping of the OPEC oil ministers back in '75. The PLO said he had done some of the planning and training for the Lod airport massacre. The Libyans said they used him as link-man with the group of fascists who did the bombing at Bologna railway station. In anybody's Good Terrorist Guide, Jimmy, these were four-star jobs with a couple of rosettes thrown in."

Ross nodded. To anybody with Kaster's credentials, murdering his brother must have been a walk in the park.

"When I'd finished my business," McKilroy continued, "I was left with a contact in London – a Libyan working at the local embassy, People's Bureau, or whatever it is they call it. We had a working relationship, saw each other a few times, did a few deals. Then I dropped out of active operations and went into business for myself."

"Until last year."

McKilroy was thoughtful. "I suppose Gerry told you that. The Boys wanted a Christmas campaign in London, but the local organization was paralysed and in a bloody mess because of Special Branch. So I got in touch with my contact, and he produced Kaster, who was back in England. I think you know the rest."

Ross did: the explosions in Oxford Street, the Aldershot bombings – all with no warnings given. He remembered the television coverage showing the crowds of shoppers fleeing out of the West End and the ambulances carrying away the injured.

"You're saying Gerry knew about all this."

"He must have, and he used Kaster against your brother. Tell me, was he on to Kaster's tail?"

"I don't know," Ross said. No one – not even Calverton, he suspected – knew just how close David had been. Ross wondered why his brother had been so secretive. Did he need the kudos of a big *coup* to lay at James Ross's doorstep? Was that where love and admiration led to?

"He must have been," said McKilroy. "He must have been so close that he could smell Kaster sweat."

Suddenly Desmond McKilroy stopped the conversation and left, as if the strain were harder on him than on Ross. Five minutes later James Ross heard the sound of a horse plodding across the damp turf outside his window. He looked out and saw the other man sitting uncertainly on a large bay gelding. Stationary, he was surveying his possessions from the vantage-point of the saddle. Then he glanced up at the window and his eyes caught Ross's. They looked melancholy and doubtful. McKilroy touched the horse with his crop and the gelding cantered off, wreathing the rider in the mist of its warm breath.

"You got Denny worried there," Eddie Rafferty said with amusement. Throughout the preceding conversation he had kept his place, nursing the shotgun and chuckling quietly at the jokes only he saw. "My money says he decides to kill you."

"Five pounds says he doesn't."

"Done!" Half an hour later Rafferty asked: "How would I collect if I won?"

Ross passed the time watching the slow changes of the day marking the sky. He had decided that the house was definitely by the side of a stretch of fen. He had picked out the boathouse built of tarred boards laid horizontally. He was still identifying detail when he saw a movement that his training had made him recognize.

"Come over here," he said to his guard. "I think Denny is signalling something but I can't see clearly."

Rafferty moved closer and stared across the lawn. "Where do you say he is?" he asked and turned round too late to see Ross balanced on the balls of his feet, the chair tilted forward towards him. "Holy mother of God!" he yelled and twisted the gun in the Englishman's direction, but Ross's charge caught him under the ribs before he could level the barrel. The two men careered into the window, which burst open with a shattering of glass and splintering of glazing-bars. Ross was held back by the weight and bulk of the chair, but Rafferty was not so lucky. The shotgun, deflected by his surprise, went off, blew a hole in the ceiling and propelled him with the recoil through the broken remnants of the window. Ross looked down on the little man. Rafferty had landed in a bush and was strung up on some thorns, cursing his head off. Ross left him to it and got down to the business of severing the cords binding his hands, using the shards of glass in the window-frame. He was still cutting his legs free when there was a sound of splintering wood and Figgis burst into the room like a one-man killing machine.

"Good work, Batman," said Ross. He knew that David had worked with Figgis. The thought made him feel sick.

*

114

Figgis was a big, square character with a moon-shaped face, a tangle of brown curls and the frank and friendly smile of everybody's favourite croupier. He had been a marine before serving ten years in the SAS, variously in Oman and Ulster. Calverton had picked him out of the Beauty Parade at the regiment's Hereford base and Figgis had jumped at the chance. By one of those curious juxtapositions of character traits, Figgis was a man who could track across any wilderness relying on his skills for food and shelter and one who could kill another human being with or without any weapon you cared to name; but the thought of planning his own life scared him witless. He wanted pensionable employment. He was the combat wing of the Civil Service.

He stood in the doorway for a moment, a bulky figure in a black leather jacket and striped sweatshirt, trailing a machine-gun in one hand. Then he approached the window and looked out on Rafferty still hung up like a marionette.

"Denny was going to let me go," said Ross. He caught a glimpse of Figgis's eyes sizing up what he had done. The other man was interested in the technique; it was only technique that interested him. "Do you follow what I'm saying? Your little piece of heroics nearly caused Rafferty to blow my head off."

Figgis was unimpressed. "It's a risk business."

Ross kicked off the last of the rope around his feet. "How did you get in without any fireworks? Or did I miss something?"

"I knocked on the door. And when somebody answered I said I was in the SAS and waved my Hockler at them." "Hockler" was SAS slang for the Heckler and Koch MP-5 submachine-gun. Figgis brandished the weapon. Ross touched the barrel.

"It's made of plastic."

"So I lied. There was so much bloody paperwork every time I wanted the real thing that I made myself one. Bought a kit at Hamley's toyshop. Like it?" He gave a boyish grin. "A quick flash of this and a mention of the SAS – people are only too glad to co-operate." He looked out of the window, saw someone and signalled by whistling on two fingers.

"Who did you bring with you?" asked Ross.

"Two regular coppers – a pair of woodentops I borrowed from CID in King's Lynn. I've got to take them home by bedtime or their mother will say I made them pregnant." He paused. "You sound as though you were expecting me."

"I spotted you in Charing Cross Road when Rafferty collected me last night."

Figgis sighed. "I told Calverton that would happen. I'd have been here sooner, but they had to have a whip-round in King's Lynn before they could find two coppers capable of holding a gun. That's why I pulled my little stunt." He tapped the machine-gun made from a child's toy. "It seemed safer than having my bollocks shot off by my own side." Before he could say any more, one of the two policemen came crashing into the room out of breath and waving a standard police .38 Smith & Wesson.

"Put that bloody thing away," groaned Figgis.

The policeman blurted out in a Norfolk burr: "McKilroy has got away!"

"I knew I should have shot that bastard," Figgis complained.

"I need him alive and co-operative," said Ross.

From the veranda of the house he caught sight of a figure down by the boathouse. McKilroy was untying the painter that held a flat-bottomed punt to the landing-stage. The Irishman looked up at the shape sprinting across the lawn and loosed off a couple of shots before clambering into the boat and poling off the bank. He headed for the shadow of trees growing on a mudbank in the shallows.

Ross reached the landing-stage. There was another punt tied to it, half-derelict, its bottom filled with dead leaves and the broken remains of a wicker picnic-basket. Denny had slung the pole into the water and put a few badly aimed shots into the boat, but they had only chipped the gunwhales. The bubbles of marsh-gas said the water was shallow. Ross waded out and retrieved the pole, but by then McKilroy was no longer in view.

From the window of the house, Ross had guessed the nature of the terrain. The willows and the dying rushes masked a maze of shallow water-courses threading their way between a chain of islets and sandbars, the open stretches being nowhere more than a hundred yards across and like as not blocked by hidden obstructions of mud and fallen trees. If Denny knew the fen, he could dodge from cover to cover or lie in wait behind any turn of ground.

Ross waited and listened. The air was still except for the complaining of some crows in the distance. There was silence from the house, which was now visible: tiled façade, white paintwork and a red-shingled roof, all set off with chestnut-trees. The water lapped gently around the boat. He stood at the rear of the punt and poled a couple of strokes in the direction he had last seen McKilroy, towards a bend around the nearest of the islands. In the small bays scooped out of the mud, the water lay motionless, gathering weed and fallen twigs. Elsewhere it seemed to breathe with the sky, rising and falling like the chest of a sleeping man. But here and there Ross saw in the mud-clouded reflections and the trails of gas bubbling up from the disturbed bottom signs that his quarry had passed that way.

He reached the tapering point of the nearest island and doubled back along its further shore. He saw the wake of something that had, only shortly before, crossed the open stretch to the next mudbank. He slackened on the pole and tensed his body in readiness. A duck bobbed out from the sedge, took fright and flew off over the trees. Ross poled on and followed the next twist of the water.

A narrow channel gave on to an open stretch, still as a millpond and grey with clouds. On the left a line of willows, truncated and spiky with new growth from their coppiced tops, bordered the water. Ross guessed that, if they were easily accessible to be cropped for basket-making, they probably marked the true shoreline and not just another island. The stand of tall trees on the right suggested the same. In each case the inlets going in those directions were probably backwaters heading nowhere, and Denny was not likely to have abandoned the water when still so close to the house. Ross pointed the nose of the punt towards a promising-looking island. It was then that he beached on a hidden bar of mud and McKilroy's craft slid into view.

At fifty yards the Irishman was a bizarre figure, balanced uncertainly at the stern of the punt, still dressed in his hunting pink, struggling to control the vessel with one hand, pivoting the pole on his hip against the slow current, and the other hand holding a silver-barrelled revolver. Then he managed to get the hang of both and, with seemingly infinitesimal slowness, glided towards Ross.

Ross threw his weight on to the sternmost edge of his punt, rammed the pole into the mudbank and, painfully, levered the boat off. In the silent seconds it took to do this, McKilroy had closed to ten yards.

Ross shouted across to him. "I don't have a gun, Denny. We can do a deal if you want to." The words were flat and empty under the open winter sky.

"No gun? Whose the trusting sentimental bastard, then?" McKilroy's face was a mask of hatred. He raised the gun and fired two shots, but the movement of the punt and his balancing act with the pole caused him to miss. A flight of ducks broke from the trees and skidded across the fen. He pressed the trigger a third time but got only the click of empty chambers revolving. McKilroy swore and threw the gun at Ross; then turned the punt on its axis and poled away into a dark channel between the nearest island and the shore. Ross followed, only five yards in his wake.

The water snaked in a narrow path between rotting stands of reeds overhung by scrub and undergrowth from the island and the shore. Each man laboured till he felt he would break from the strain, but the only noise was their breathing and the almost inaudible splash of the poles slotting into the water; their progress was a creep between the crowding banks. They broke into another open pool which was bathed in light through a gap in the clouds. The sun was pale and wintry. McKilroy swung his punt around and dived into another channel that slipped away between mudbanks. The speed of the manoeuvre took Ross by surprise, and McKilroy gained twenty yards. The Irishman's lips opened in a grunt of satisfaction. But the sound came instead from below the boat. It was the grinding of the punt against the bottom as it came to a dead stop.

McKilroy looked behind him. Within seconds Ross's punt was nudging the stern of his own. He raised the unwieldy pole and, holding it in both hands, jabbed it in Ross's direction, catching him straight in the chest before he could recover his own pole from the water. Ross keeled over into the water. McKilroy leapt into the other punt to finish him off.

Ross got to his feet knee-deep in water, still holding on to the punt-pole. He parried McKilroy's next strike and jabbed back but missed. The weight and leverage of their weapons against the muscles of their arms made movement slow and painful, but, like medieval knights, they traded cumbersome blows that would have broken either man in half had they connected.

Ross felt a stabbing and burning sensation growing in his chest and guessed that the other man's first blow had broken a rib. He could breathe only shallowly, and the lack of oxygen for his exertions was making him feel dizzy. On the other side McKilroy looked no better. His scrambled face was swollen purple with blood being pumped into it and his eyes protruded blank and lifeless in their expression as if they would suddenly burst and spray blood from the pressure. Ross steeled himself for one more effort. Then, suddenly, without warn-

118

ing, McKilroy dropped his bamboo pole and held up his hands.

"Ah . . . sod this . . . for a game!" he gasped. Hs hands massaged his chest and his legs sagged until he was sitting in the punt bottom. "If you don't kill me, my bloody heart will." He sat back resigned, whilst Ross climbed back in the boat.

"What do you want with me now?" McKilroy asked as they coasted slowly back towards the landing-stage. His store-bought accent had worn out and the soft brogue was back in use. "I've told you the tale. What more can you ask?"

"You're going to talk to your Libyan friend," said Ross.

"What for? To fix up a meeting so that you can kill Kaster? Come on, Jimmy, don't be a bloody romantic! You and David, you both had the same training. Kaster got to David. Why should it be any different for you? He'll eat you for breakfast." He glanced at Ross and saw only the chill in the other man's soul reflected through his eyes.

"It's still a long way to the bank."

"So it is." McKilroy dipped a hand into the water, took out a palmful and sprinkled it over his face. "Well, maybe I've misjudged you. Maybe you're the hard man after all."

"You should meet my friends."

"Back at the house?" asked McKilroy, then understood. "Ah, Figgis. Now there's the boy who'd like to tear my head off and whistle down the hole."

Calverton was at the house. He had rushed up from London at the word of James's predicament as relayed by Figgis "in the wee small hours of the morning. I wouldn't propose that we hold too detailed an inquest into how you got yourself into this mess," he added, "though I gather that you had gone a fair distance towards extricating yourself before that unlikely knight in shining armour, Figgis, came to the rescue. By the way, I hope you were duly thankful."

"He gets a half of my kingdom and my hand in marriage. Thanks for your concern. What else brings you here?"

"Don't be too despondent, James. Here, have a drink of this." Calverton had made himself at home in the large, airy room at the front of the house, which opened on to the veranda and a view of the water. Among the chintz, the Sanderson prints and the consumer durables from Harrods, which had been props to McKilroy's fantasy of gentility, he had discovered a black Spanish bull, souvenir of

119

Malaga, which opened to disclose a decanter and six whisky-tumblers. "A touch of the old, authentic Denny." He put his nose to the decanter. "Do I detect a drop of Bushmills? Ah! my mistake – not the old Denny, but the new – South African sherry if my tastebuds do not deceive me." He poured two glasses none the less.

"Where were we? Your performance last night. It showed that the spirit it still there, even if the technique is a little rusty. And the latter is excusable for want of practice."

"You knew what was happening and left me on my own," said Ross.

Calverton leaned over, nursing the glass of sherry in his hand. His face was earnest. The shy inner man was trying to reach out, make contact. Why does everyone think I'll understand? thought Ross.

"I had to demonstrate to you the futility of thinking that in this matter you can go it alone," said Calverton, "while somehow testing your *commitment*." He smiled blandly. "There were some – not merely Figgis – who said that you were a broken reed. I assure you, I was not one of them – quite the contrary. It was – is – my theory that a service manned exclusively by the likes of Figgis would lack *balance*. There is room for a certain tenderness of spirit provided that the resolve is firm. You have that quality. It showed in your handling of Gerald Patrick Kelly – in Figgis's hands the man simply fell apart. What I'm saying, James, is: do join us!"

Ross glimpsed in Calverton's words a picture of the service as the other man saw it. Figgis, smirking behind Calverton's chair, represented the reality. "Believe me," said Ross. "It wouldn't work."

"Try us!" said Calverton.

Ross didn't answer. He knew that he was in and there was no way out.

Chapter Twelve

"GAME PLAYERS" was the name of a small shop in Air Street, just off Regent Street on the north side of Piccadilly Circus. It had been in business a week. Its predecessor had been a souvenir shop that had traded for twelve months and gone bust, and the litter of its demise was still lying around: the company plate still screwed to the door, the remnants of picture postcards and tartan-clad dolls trampled into corners. The shopfitters had only just got out, the floor was covered in woodshavings like a Western saloon and the stock was piled in boxes.

A lacklustre girl was in the process of selling an Avalon-Hill boxed wargame to a wispy-faced student in jeans and anorak. "What can I do for you?" she asked John Donaldson, and to emphasize the point that she would rather be doing anything else than selling the goods added wearily: "If *he'd* only given us another week, we'd have all this stuff out and on the shelves and they'd know what we have in stock."

"Where's Armitage?" asked Donaldson.

"Oh, *him*." She jerked her thumb. "Upstairs. Thinks he's Napoleon. You want to see him? You'll have to take yourself up: I can't leave the shop." She looked Donaldson up and down. "You don't look like a wargamer."

"I'm not."

"Good for you," she said cheerlessly.

Armitage was in high good humour, manoeuvring his bulk between boxes, skipping around a table in the centre of the room: a young man, physically middle-aged and spiritually ever-boyish.

"What ho, Jack D.! Terrific, eh?" He ran his hand through Brylcreemed hair, wiped it on his V-necked pullover and thrust out a hot palm like a weapon. "Must be years. Five years, eh? Never thought I'd. . . . Take a seat. Sorry there's no space, but we have to get rid of that thing." He pointed to an ancient Chubb safe, painted green, with a big, shiny medallion advertising the Victorian virtues of security and reliability. There was another man in the room, aged about twenty, in Levis and check shirt. Armitage spoke to him. "Go mind the store, Dave. I won't touch anything."

"OK," said Dave. "But I'll kill you if you move my bloody artillery."

"Scout's honour."

When the other had gone, Armitage and Donaldson sat down, facing each other across a table set with a terrain of plasticine and sand and ranks of model soldiers. Armitage's brown eyes were bright with the recollection of times past. "Well . . . " he said, and abbreviated the years since they were at university together with a long sigh.

"You have problems?" Donaldson asked.

Armitage missed the point. "Cuirassiers," he said brightly, pleased to be drawn back to his game. He pointed at some cavalry. "This squadron of cuirassiers – no, don't touch – has forced this infantry battalion into square. If they have to stay there, then Dave's horse-artillery will shell the pants off them." He looked up. "I don't suppose you have any suggestions?"

"Surrender?"

"There's a thought. But cheating was more what I had in mind. What can I do for you? Social call? Buy something? I had to sell my house in Wapping to take out a lease on this place. Linda was furious. That's her downstairs. So I could do with the custom." Armitage's words formed a bulk with his body.

"I want some information on uniforms," said Donaldson.

"Oh? Taken up the sport of kings? What sort of uniform?"

"German."

"Second World War?"

"Yes."

Armitage sucked his teeth. "Not my period. Napoleonics is more my game." He waved a hand at the table. "Still, we ought to be able to do something, eh? Anything more specific?"

"A yellow collar on the jacket." Donaldson was repeating the description of the German officer that Wojciech Karpinski had seen at the Bereznica Palace. But Karpinski had been a child of eight.

"H'm – yellow collar?" Armitage confirmed his suspicions. "Doesn't sound likely, does it? Too flamboyant for the Hun."

"What about . . .?"

122

"Collar-patches? Little thingumajigs stitched on to the whatnot? Could be. Sounds much more plausible." Armitage danced around the table and over the clutter of cardboard boxes to the head of the stairs, and yelled: "Dave, fish out one of the Blandford books on WWII uniforms, will you? Jerries in particular."

"You should be so lucky in this mess," said Dave.

While they waited, Armitage asked: "What do you think of all this – the shop and everything?" He looked about him as if his question were making him see it himself for the first time. The room was tatty with neglect. There were white, efflorescent crystals on one wall where a leaking gutter allowed rain in. A mop stood in a bucket, going rotten with mildew. It was the sort of room that generations of owners always intended to clean out. "Of course," Armitage said largely, "it's in the mind's eye at the moment – a bit."

"I hope the place makes money for you."

"Oh, it will!" Armitage affirmed with a condemned man's conviction in the afterlife. "Positive goldmine. Wargames, boardgames. Selling like hot cakes." Distractedly he licked the palm of his hand and slicked down a tuft of hair sticking out from his crown. "Linda hates it, though. Won't forgive me for selling that dump in Wapping. Got to make a success of it. Tried everything else – the old man's stockbroking firm and whatnot – so got to make a go of this." He looked away at the table laid out with the make-believe battle and added: "You made a go of it, though, eh? Found yourself a Turner. I read about it in one of the Sunday comics. Terrific! Funny, though: I never thought this art-dealing was in your line. Too bourgeois. Pandering to the acquisitive instincts of the possessing classes – witness the old dad with his seascapes cluttering up the house. You always used to be the radical firebrand."

"Left infantilism," said Donaldson.

Armitage looked stumped, then laughed. "Oh, yes! Good one, that. Lenin said it, didn't he?"

"I wouldn't know. I gave it up years ago."

"Good thing, too. The important thing is to find your *métier* and stick at it, I say."

Dave came up with the book. Armitage took it, gave his thumb a hearty lick and turned over the pages of colour prints. "Look here, what a beauty!" He pointed at a figure in black with a black fez and death's-head insignia. "Bosnian Muslims in the SS. Who'd have thought it? Doesn't say much for the old blond giants of the master race, eh?" He riffled through a few more pages and stopped at a block of plates. "Here we are."

"You have it?" asked Donaldson.

"More or less. See, these are Luftwaffe uniforms and, look" – a dirty finger stabbed at the page – "this one and this one. Yellow collar-patches." He turned quickly to some pages of army uniforms. "I thought so. None of the Wehrmacht stuff has them, not so as you'd notice; and you can forget about the navy and the SS. Yellow collar-patches are obviously an arm-of-service badge, you know, like wings for the RAF."

"So?"

"So whoever was sporting your particular uniform was in the Luftwaffe. Guaranteed."

Two days after the arrest of Desmond McKilroy, there was a meeting of the Operations Liaison Committee which had been set up to cover the security aspects of the American visit. For historical reasons – which was an explanation for an arrangement that was inconvenient and inexplicable – these took place in the Admiralty building in Whitehall. It was there that, half an hour before the meeting, Norman Calverton encountered his superior, Lionel Sholto, as they stood at adjacent urinals in the men's toilet.

"Glad to run into you before the meeting," said Lionel Sholto lustily. He was a barrel-chested man whose face had generous features folded over like dough and set off with a crust of brown hair. Ex-Cambridge, ex-Guards, ex-barrister; he had a judge for a cousin and a courtroom voice that boomed at juries and pinned them by the ears. "Sorry we haven't had time for our usual pre-meeting fireside chat, Norman," he apologized, "but, with one thing and another, not the least being that business of yours up in Norfolk, I haven't had the opportunity."

Calverton nodded understandingly. Sholto ran his empire from a redbrick building in Curzon Street, Mayfair. As one of the lesser satraps, Calverton had recently been allocated a bleak office-block in Battersea High Street which had been borrowed from the Department of Trade so that its costs might be hidden conveniently in the parliamentary estimates. Between Curzon Street, with its Oxbridge graduates and cerebral pursuit of intelligence, and Battersea High Street, staffed by the likes of Figgis, there was a certain tension.

"Molly is in the chair today," Sholto announced. His voice ricocheted off the walls.

"Gervase Molineux from the Foreign Office?"

"The self-same Molly. He wasn't on the rota for today – in fact I was – but since he has observed that the FO will be paying the bill for this jaunt by the Americans he wants to be the big chief. So I let him." He gave a large wink. "You have to let people play their games, Norman, you know that."

Calverton agreed. He was all in favour of games. He loved the formal properties of games. They had rules. It was informal, human contact that seemed to cause all the trouble.

Sholto leaned over the partition as he fastened his flies and went on confidentially: "I should have thought you knew all about Molly's being in the hot seat; in fact you probably did. But you wouldn't let on, would you? Frankly, it's Molly's position that troubles me. He's not in the profession." He added in a stage whisper: "*And the Americans will be there.*" This last was a caution against exposing any dissensions there might be between MI5 and any other branches of the intelligence services, such as Special Branch. There was no particular love lost between them, but the etiquette of the profession was like that of a floundering marriage in respectable circles. The motto was "Not in front of the Americans", as if the CIA were especially delicate children.

"In this connection," said Sholto, "I've come to a little arrangement with Williams of Special Branch." Williams was a fiery Welsh Baptist who had a policeman's dislike for the irregular methods of MI5.

"And what would that be?"

"I only wished we could have talked about it before, but pressure of business, etcetera. Fact is, there's a feeling going round", explained Sholto airily as he washed his hands at an ancient basin which stood on a cast-iron pedestal, "that the balance of this operation is becoming distorted; that, when the business of cleaning our house before the Americans pass through for the New Year talks results in a punt-chase across the wilds of Norfolk, there's something frankly wrong. How shall I put it? That this business is turning into a vendetta against whoever it was that killed your man."

"So is there a new party line?" Calverton asked. Sholto had paused in front of a rust-speckled mirror where he trimmed the hairs in his nostrils.

"I've agreed with Williams that the murder of David Ross looks

125

more and more like a killing by the IRA, and nothing to do with our present operation. In such a scenario, we could have no interest in Desmond McKilroy and, since he was arrested by the King's Lynn CID – I speak technically now, Norman, and no disparagement to your fine chaps – he falls neatly as a matter for the police. The Anti-Terrorist Squad will involve themselves as appropriate. We – meaning you – drop gracefully out of the picture."

"I see," said Calverton calmly. "You obviously had a very fruitful meeting with our Welsh colleague."

"Now now, not too severe, Norman. You make it sound like someone moved the chessmen while you were out of the room."

"What did Williams have to say about Kaster?"

"Ah, yes," said Sholto. "About that. Well, Special Branch say that they have never been convinced about Kaster, even that he exists. The super-duper terrorist of the Western world, involved in every major incident since Lord knows when, cunning, professional, dangerous – it all sounds too good to be true. They say you've been listening to too many dirty stories and that Kaster is just a fiction on which to hang unexplained mysteries, a sort of Abominable Snowman of the intelligence industry. As for Denny McKilroy's story of meeting Kaster – well, you have to admit Denny would have shopped Hansel and Gretel if he thought it would save him from the hands of your man Figgis."

At the door of the conference-room Sholto took Calverton aside again. "I know that this is a great disappointment to you, Norman," he said, "but I have to impress upon you that no mention is to be made of David Ross's death within earshot of the Americans. I can count on you, can't I?"

"Of course," said Calverton loyally.

"Good show. I can't tell you how that helps. The trouble with these Liaison meetings is that, whenever one goes to one, the whole business seems to fall apart. And I always understood the intention was the reverse."

The Committee had appropriated a large salon in imperial baroque style – coffered ceiling, marble half-columns dividing the walls, sundry portraits of British admirals: Nelson, Anson, Howe. The windows looked over Whitehall. Aside from the minions who were packing their tool-kits after a routine search for bugs, there were thirteen present. No one commented on the resemblance to a coven.

126

Molineux of the Foreign Office took the chair. Old Etonian and ex-diplomat, he was a ponderous character with a monumental turn of speech, words laid like foundation stones and cemented by dramatic silences. To his right were representatives of the Home Office and the Treasury, similar types to Molineux but looking less robust through in-breeding. Next to them, Williams of Special Branch, a tense man in a ready-to-wear suit, who continually rubbed the point of an over-shaved chin. He was shadowed by the Scotland Yard second team, three men representing the Anti-Terrorist Squad, the Diplomatic Protection Group and the Metropolitan Police. Together Home Office, Treasury and Police were united on a programme of the rule of law and honest accounting and in a belief that MI5 didn't subscribe to either.

On the other side of the table, Lionel Sholto sat on the chairman's left: "the *sinister* side," he observed with satisfaction. Below him were Atherton of the Ministry of Defence, a soft-spoken, diffident man in military tweeds, and Rogers of the Cabinet Office, who would report back to the Prime Minister. These three also were roughly in agreement, Sholto for obvious reasons, Atherton because he despised civilians, and Rogers because, after the latest round of leaks, the Cabinet Office believed in spying on everybody. Calverton sat behind rather than with Lionel Sholto out of deference to Williams, who preferred to think that the business run from Battersea High Street did not exist.

The remaining places at the bottom of the table were occupied by the two Americans. They were Grover Wagner, the CIA Head of London Station, a relaxed, outward-going, reach-me-down agent, and another, just in from the States, with bulky jacket and gimlet eyes who was clearly custom-built for somebody's protection.

Molineux suggested coffee and, while this was drunk, started the proceedings. This was the first sitting of the Operations Liaison Committee, he said, and proceeded to open the meeting as if he were inaugurating a substantial public building, with effusive references to "kith and kin across the Atlantic" and the "joint leaders of the democratic world". Next he abandoned the agenda and threw the meeting open to the Americans.

Wagner had an easy manner. He had meaty features and Holly-wood teeth, and he gave a neat thank-you before riffling through his papers and beginning a slow exposition of the American visit with dates, times, places, routes, numbers of support staff and a punch-list of questions on British support.

"Sounds like all he's interested in are the catering arrangements" was Lionel Sholto's conclusion, which he whispered to Calverton with satisfaction.

Williams picked up the ball on the British side and, fed with details by his aides, covered similar ground in his lilting Welsh voice.

Two hours ticked away and there was a general feeling of a morning's work well done.

"Your turn now, Lionel," said Molineux. As a diplomat he prided himself on catching the tone of the American's informality and so used first names. "Tell them the tale."

"May I interrupt?" said Calverton. "Just checking the first item on the agenda before we move on. Have we made a decision on the gun issue?" He looked around him innocently.

"Nothing to decide," said Williams with force. "It is clearly established that no one carries guns except for our own men."

"Now, hold on a minute," said the second American, but Williams was not to be held.

"This is a matter of principle."

"You're damn right."

"Can I suggest a compromise?" said Calverton. "What if the American side promises not to carry guns?"

"I don't follow," said Grover Wagner. "What's the compromise?"

"We'll promise to believe you."

"Clever idea that, Norman," said Lionel Sholto later. "Very unwise of Williams to annoy the Americans, though."

Gervase Molineux brought the meeting to order with: "As we were. Lionel, time for your report, I think. Tell us all what the status is on possible subversives."

"Oh, we're keeping an eye on all the likely characters who might want to rock the boat."

"I say, Lionel. Come on, now; there's more than that. Your people are sufficiently close to the opposition that they've suffered casualties."

There was a silence broken by a Welsh groan from Williams; then Grover Wagner spoke. "So some of your guys have been hit?"

"Only one actually," conceded Sholto.

"Tell me more. Have you girls been keeping secrets from me?"

128

Williams jumped in testily. "Point of order, Mr Chairman. This killing is strictly in respect of an off-balance-sheet item."

"What on earth is an 'off-balance-sheet item'?" enquired Molineux.

"Something that's not on the list, not in the equation."

"Oh?"

"Our friends from the United States and ourselves had a preliminary meeting some weeks ago," explained Williams as to a child. "We drew up a list of subversives, both individuals and organizations. Anything not on that list is officially not a threat. It's an off-balance-sheet item."

"And our American colleagues are agreeable to that treatment, are they?" asked Molineux.

Grover Wagner shook himself slowly into action, eyeing the Welshman suspiciously. "Uh, well, we agreed a list, sure. But it isn't the Bible. As for any item being off-balance-sheet, well, I went to Harvard Business School and they taught me there that whether an item is on- or off-balance-sheet depends on the way the accountants want to cut it. I'm not so sure now. . . ."

Williams, with a show of reasonableness, said: "There's absolutely no secrecy to this matter, gentlemen. One of Lionel's men was killed by the IRA. That's all there is to it. The IRA aren't interested in killing Americans: they want the support of American public opinion."

"One of your guys, Lionel?" asked Wagner. "Was he working on this operation?"

"As a matter of fact he was," said Sholto; then added smoothly: "but before that he had been running an IRA turncoat." He smiled in Williams's direction: he was still supporting Special Branch's position as agreed in their arrangement.

"Even so, it's a hell of a coincidence that he gets himself killed just now," said Wagner.

"Coincidences do happen," opined Gervase Molineux.

"Yeah, yeah, but I want to know more. Who was he chasing?"

Williams stared across the table, but Lionel Sholto gave a resigned response.

"He was tracing a potential terrorist. I believe the name is 'Kaster', or according to some sources 'Castro' – you follow, I'm sure: Fidel, Cuba, *viva la revolucion* and so forth."

There was silence around the table as if everyone had suddenly

129

been discovered in a collective act of adultery. Calverton waited for the American reply, but Grover Wagner was still briefing his partner in whispers. Kaster was not a new subject between Calverton and the American Head of Station. Swopping shop-talk over a number of years, the question of Kaster – existence or not – had cropped up like a garden weed, to be hacked at and survive.

"Who is this Kaster?" asked Molineux innocently.

"Norman?" suggested Lionel Sholto.

"An Englishman in his thirties," Calverton said diffidently. "Not a lot known. Reputedly KGB-trained. From time to time an associate of Carlos 'the Jackal' Ramirez, but essentially freelance. Implicated in the planning of the Lod airport massacre, the kidnapping of the OPEC oil ministers in '75, the Regent's Park bomb incident in '82 and the London bombings last Christmas, to name but a few. With those credentials and a base in this country, he could pose a hazard to this operation."

"Will-o'-the-wisp," snorted Williams. "The view from this side of the table is that there is no such person."

"What about our American friends?"

"Kaster. Sure, we've heard of that one," said Wagner as if Kaster were a proposition of logic. "I've read the file, the sightings, the attributed hits, all the scuttlebut. The Company's position is officially agnostic: we don't know whether there's such a terrorist or not."

"Agnostic! There's the word that hits it on the head!" was the exasperated cry from Williams, who on this point, however, was an atheist. "It's become a theological dispute. It's like Voltaire said: 'If there were no Kaster, we should have to invent him.' "

"Who the hell is Voltaire?" asked the second American.

"Whereas I prefer to apply Occam's Razor," Williams went on. He quoted Occam: "Entities should not be multiplied unnecessarily."

"Jesus!" said Wagner under his breath.

"Amen to that," thought Calverton.

The meeting spluttered on in a degree of confusion after this last exchange except for a general feeling on the British side that something had to be done to placate the Americans. Wagner was heard to say: "They lost a man chasing *something*. Whatever it was, someone should still be chasing it."

Whilst the parties retired to their respective corners to recover,

Gervase Molineux took Calverton aside. "A word in your ear, Norman," he said, red-faced and flustered.

"Certainly, sir."

"Look, someone has made me look a bloody fool and I can't decide whether the cause is you or that Celtic idiot Williams. Why wasn't I told that the Americans hadn't been informed of your fellow David Ross's death? It was in your briefing-note and I assumed that anything in there was known to the Yanks."

"I just stated the current situation. You understand: I wasn't party to this so-called balance-sheet that Williams drew up with the Americans. It was Special Branch who insisted on suppressing the Kaster enquiry."

"So I bloody well saw!" said Molineux.

"Meet you in my club at one-thirty," said Lionel Sholto after the meeting had struggled through to any-other-business. "Wig and Pen. In the Strand." He glanced at Williams. "I've got to do five rounds with this lot to thrash out the new line following this morning's fiasco."

"Ask them if Denny McKilroy's contact, the Libyan, is fair game."

Calverton took a taxi to the Strand and hung around in the downstairs bar of the Wig and Pen, examining the "Spy" caricatures of Edwardian celebrities which plastered the outside windows and excluded the prying eyes of passers-by. As a lunch-spot it was inconvenient for Sholto's office, but the Law Courts were just across the road and it gave him a chance to meet his legal confrères away from the Whitehall hot-house.

Sholto was jovial. "Well, Norman, quite a triumph for you!" They had laboured to the uppermost room and were ensconced among the dark wainscoting with their meat and two veg and bottle of Beaujolais. "If you hadn't sat so mum, I'd have said that you set old Molly up to drop this morning's bombshell."

"I don't follow," enquired Calverton mildly.

"Ho, ho, you don't!" boomed Sholto and gave the other an affectionate punch on the arm. He leaned across the table. "Molly gave our Welsh brother a first-class roasting. 'So!' quoth Molly, 'A threat to the operation in the shape of one dead agent is withheld from our American cousins! And not in the name of security, but on a point of – what did you call it? – theology!' " Sholto's impression of

Gervase Molineux was professionally lifelike. " 'As one would expect,' Molly goes on, and beams at me, 'Lionel and Norman loyally defer to your view, but this one can't be laid at their door.' "

"And?"

"And the upshot is: total surrender by the Welsh!"

Calverton considered his victory slowly. "What about your agreement with Williams that Ross's death had nothing to do with the current operation?"

"You have a cruel memory, Norman. It was the merest ploy, a move in the game between our two admired branches of the service. But", said Sholto more brightly, "Munich and the days of appeasement are over. We have a New Deal, as the Americans would say. Aren't you pleased?"

Calverton stabbed at an overboiled Brussels sprout. "Naturally I'm delighted," he said. "I take it that the search for Kaster is live again?"

"More or less. Of course I had to throw Special Branch a bone – maintaining good relations and all that."

"Oh?"

"Now, now. This is the new line. First, the murder enquiry."

"Yes?"

"The Yard get that, but only in the narrow sense – a sort of Agatha Christie drawing-room murder: which guest at the fatal dinner-party did the dastardly deed, and all that."

Calverton considered that one. "What about Denny McKilroy?"

"I was coming to that." Sholto's smile unwrapped the present. "You get him back to play with. But strictly on a loan basis: date-stamped and they want a receipt, preferably signed in blood." His eyes darkened and he sounded a cautionary note. "Mind, you're not to break him like you did the last one – Kelly, wasn't it?"

Calverton nodded and came by degrees to the main point at issue: McKilroy's contact with Kaster, the Libyan diplomat, Khoder Saleh.

Sholto wiped the wine from his lips and grinned from ear to ear. "It's Christmas, dear chap! Though I don't suppose the Muslims celebrate Christmas. At all events, Saleh is yours, subject only to the usual rules about not killing diplomats, even wogs."

"Thank you, Lionel. Very grateful," said Calverton. And he was. First James Ross and now this. It was a week of triumph over adversity.

Chapter Thirteen

DONALDSON'S second visit to the small gallery above the occult bookshop in Bloomsbury found Aaron Eichbaum in a wry, cheerful mood. They shook hands. The old dealer squeezed the last dregs of tea out of the samovar and enquired warmly after Sebastian Summer's health and the progress of Donaldson's investigations.

"Before you tell me, come, there is something I want to show you." The old man crossed to a corner of the room and hunted a picture from a stack that was gathering dust. He regarded it with amusement. "Last time, when you came here, I was of a mind to show this to you. But . . . it was something I bought perhaps five years ago, an act of charity, not to resell, you understand. And here it has been. I gave it no further thought, until. . . ." He passed the picture over. "What do you think?"

Donaldson took the object and held it to the window. It was a Fenwick, a gouache showing a group of sullen coal-miners showering in a pithead baths. The only differences from the product sold at the Summer Gallery were that the latter were in oil and nowadays didn't carry Anthony's signature.

"Not my taste in pictures," Aaron Eichbaum said, taking this one back, "but the artist was obviously in need. I think he had been taking drugs; his health was broken down. It seemed a service on my part. And, then, his manners were so engaging. All in all, it is not bad, is it? It has often reminded me of your Geordie Fenwicks. But it couldn't be, could it?" He read the look of impassivity on the younger man's face and the moment passed away. "However, that is all by the by. I'm sure you didn't come here to discuss that. What can I help you with?"

Donaldson sought for a way to begin. He remembered what his old friend Armitage had told him: the officer seen by Karpinski as a child on the day that the Bereznica Palace was looted was in the Luftwaffe.

"We talked last time about Hermann Goering, do you remember?

Who was he dealing with? How did he acquire his pictures?"

"Such persistence!" Eichbaum said and raised an eyebrow; but the curiosity was subdued by an old man's need to tell stories. "What more can I say that you don't know? I told you about Goering's deal with Rosenberg to get the pick of the French paintings."

"Yes, but he must have had agents working for him."

Eichbaum was dismissive. "Of course. Two I remember. One was a clever, talkative fellow by the name of Walter Hofer. The other was called Lohse, Dr Bruno Lohse. He was a young art-historian. Between them they advised and handled Goering's dealings in Paris."

"What about Poland?"

"What is this interest in Poland?" the old man asked testily. "You raised the same thing last time. It was Muehlemann, Frank and Posse who ransacked Poland. . . ."

"And Alois Schimmel," Donaldson said. He remembered Alois Schimmel. The man who had been murdered by Polish partisans. Wojciech Karpinski's father had been shot as a partisan. And the truth? Had there been any partisans? Not according to the recollection of Karpinski the boy. Only an officer in a uniform with yellow collar-patches. Luftwaffe. Intangible. The picture changing according to one's point of view.

"Yes, and Alois Schimmel, too," said Eichbaum. "The point is that they were acting for Hitler. Goering had no interest in Poland." He paused. "No, that's not absolutely true. There were some pictures by Dürer. Hitler forced him to hand them over. Like the *Leda*." He was musing now. "Hitler forced Goering to hand over two things. Some works acquired in Poland – the Dürers. And a Leonardo – the *Leda* – even if the last was a fake. Does that signify anything, I wonder?"

Donaldson did not know. He could only guess dimly. "Let us assume", he said, "that Goering knew of a painting in Poland – something unique, a Leonardo that no one had ever before heard of. He would want to whisk it away before Hitler could get his hands on it. We know that because that was how Goering behaved in Paris. But who would he use? The two agents you just mentioned, Hofer and Lohse?"

"No. But this is all fanciful!" the old man protested.

"Not fanciful. I have an eyewitness account of a Luftwaffe officer searching for works of art in Poland within days at most of the

134

German invasion. If Alois Schimmel was there working for Hitler, who could my man have been working for if it wasn't Goering?"

Aaron Eichbaum absorbed the point only slowly. He went over to the window and peeked out at the British Museum squatting greyly in the rain. He wrapped himself more thoroughly in his knitted cardigan and stared at the electric fire as if he wished he could poke it to raise a flame.

"There was someone," the old man began slowly and, in the fussy, almost literary style of an intelligent man who had learned his English rather late in life from books, he told his story. "My friend was a serving officer, but I first knew him because he was one of my contemporaries at Lange. His family came from Egypt – Germans, you understand, but with some sort of business interests out there – but this isolation made them . . . culturally aware . . . sensitive . . . humane. He was interested in art because, out there" – Eichbaum waved a hand to suggest a country unintelligibly alien and distant – "his heritage was so precious."

Donaldson realized that he was listening to a morality tale. The old man was creating a picture of the Garden of Eden before the Fall; it was painted by Hieronymous Bosch. The serpent was entwined about the Tree of Knowledge.

"My friend was very ambitious and, being so, he realized that the path to success lay in associating himself with the Nazis." There was the betrayal. "He was of an active, athletic disposition and, already when I met him, a member of one of those quasi-military flying clubs that the Germans had set up between the wars when they were not permitted an air force. So it was not unnatural that, when the opportunity arose, he should join the Luftwaffe. Nor that he should have attracted the interest of Hermann Goering."

"You sound. . . ."

"Sad?" Eichbaum looked up. The other man was apparently not entirely without feeling. But this strange coldness about him: it seemed so unlikely in someone who was, by reputation, so sensitive to paintings. Somewhere in him there must be a well of feeling, which was tapped sparingly and directed with intensity towards one source of release in the paintings. It seemed to Aaron Eichbaum a dangerous way to conduct one's life. His old friend, too, had courted that danger. He thought about him and answered: "It is merely that I should like to forget. We were friends but, of course, when he became a Nazi that was all over."

"He sacrificed you to his career."

Eichbaum shook his head. "No. He protected me. Do you understand? He protected me because he needed a good deed."

"A good deed?"

"Yes! He wanted to touch pitch and not be defiled! He wanted to
work with the Nazis and not be one!" The old man stared wildly
around the room looking for anything that would help him to express
the old anger and sadness. He gripped his knees with both hands and
held his body rigid while he spoke more calmly. "He wanted to wake
up every morning and know that, because of him, Aaron Eichbaum
would live another day. And that fact told him that he was not an evil
man."

The conversation seeped away into the dusty melancholy of the
small room. Donaldson was overcome by a sense that *The Last
Judgement* existed in a purely abstract way, as the object of stories.
Hortense Ainsworth's, Wojciech Karpinski's, Aaron Eichbaum's.
Stories within stories: Hortense Ainsworth repeating Prince Jerzy
Wolski repeating his family story of the picture – all stacked together
like Russian dolls. And the dolls themselves made by different
craftsmen so that their fit was eccentric, each the solution to a
different puzzle.

The old man was standing by one of his beloved watercolours
remembering the last time that he had seen the once proud Luftwaffe
officer. Ironically it had been in England – in 1947 – at a camp in some
sodden corner of Wales where the British had interned prisoners
after the war. The German, after years as a staff officer, had actually
flown a mission in March or April 1945 and got himself shot down and
captured. Where? Was it in East Anglia? At all events, he was nearly
killed and suffered imprisonment within weeks, if not days, of the
Nazi surrender. One of fate's twists. And so they had met again.
Eichbaum had gone to visit him. It was in the freezing winter of 1947
when the whole world seemed buried in snow. They met in a Nissen
hut, sitting across a bare table, frozen to the bone, scarcely seeing
each other because some hessian curtains had been drawn across the
window to keep in the heat and the window itself was opaque with
frost.

He couldn't remember what they had talked about. Clearly something had been said about the circumstances of the air crash but
otherwise Eichbaum came away only with snatched impressions of
the other man: a way of holding a cigarette which suggested an

invisible but almost tangible holder dangling elegantly between his fingers; the fingering of creases in his trousers; a look of irony. They were small strokes on the canvas of the other's personality. Eichbaum remembered that he had been struck at the time by the thought of *The Picture of Dorian Gray*.

Standing in front of the picture he found himself looking into it, not at it. It showed upturned boats and nets drying on a beach. He was looking at the dust and flecks on the glass. He realized that he had pronounced the story of the last meeting aloud and that Donaldson had been listening.

"But are you sure that your friend was ever in Poland?" he asked.

"Yes. He was involved in the taking of the Dürers." The old man turned round. "But your painting? Who can say, when it may not even exist?" The answer seemed inadequate. "You are looking for a Luftwaffe officer with a knowledge of art and close to Goering – someone who would be brave enough to steal a painting from under the noses of Hitler's agents. Those are rare qualities. My friend had them."

"What was his name?" asked Donaldson.

"Egger," said the old man. "Reinhardt Egger."

Chapter Fourteen

IT WAS only after a meeting of the Operations Liaison Committee had sanctioned the operation in principle that Lionel Sholto released the full file on the Libyan diplomat, Khoder Saleh, to Calverton. "The usual matter of protocol between ourselves and the FO," said Sholto. "Molly administered heavy reminders that the Foreign Office doesn't want us pestering diplomats unduly. Spy on them, by all means, but no rough stuff. You might look up what the Rules of Engagement say on the subject."

Calverton agreed to. "The Rules of Engagement" was an expression borrowed from the Ministry of Defence: they represented the political constraints on a field-commander's use of force.

"Here it all is, then," said Sholto, handing the material over. "Fascinating reading; and no doubt you'll tuck up in bed with it while dreaming your nefarious dreams, eh, Norman?"

"Very decent of you," said Calverton and took the file away.

The material on Khoder Saleh was not altogether new to him. When the Libyan had first surfaced in London back in 1977 he had been studied routinely, with a view to assessing whether he was what he seemed. With the Libyans, MI5 had worked out a routine. They procured an invitation for the newcomer to attend a function in his particular field of interest, trade or cultural as the case might be, and stipulated in the invitation that lounge-suits should be worn. It had been discovered that the more lowly the Libyan official, the more likely he was to comply. Despite his nominally low-grade position, Saleh turned up in tee-shirt and jeans: anything else would be unsocialist.

Having deduced from this contradiction that Saleh had to be an intelligence officer, consideration was given as to how he might be suborned. It was quickly established that he had left his dowdy wife back in Tripoli, and, with a sense even at that time that this was all too easy, he was lured into a trap baited with an attractive blonde. There was a general feeling of disappointment when the target did not respond. The only result was an interdepartmental wrangle over the cost of the operation.

It was then suggested that Saleh might be homosexual. This fitted with an unconscious Foreign Office prejudice about Arabs, and it was decided to test the theory out. At this time Lionel Sholto wrote to Calverton: "Can you furnish us with a bugger? I leave the exact specification to you but would prefer something not too exotic." Calverton provided the necessary assistance, but the experiment was a failure. Sholto wrote again: "Thank you for your promptness in fulfilling my earlier request. I could, however, have wished that you were not quite so quick off the mark. It gives the unfortunate impression that the department is full of them."

The next step had been to test Saleh's interest in gambling. There was a flutter of excitement when the Libyan was seen going into one of the Mayfair gaming-clubs, but it proved premature: Saleh was running a low-level agent in the Saudi embassy, and it was the latter who had acquired the taste from watching visiting royal princes.

At this point there had been serious concern. A minority in the department thought that Saleh might actually be virtuous. This assumption ran counter to first principles but had always been admitted as a theoretical possibility. Even more dispiriting was the view that Saleh might only be interested in money; for, while there were sufficient funds available to suborn some lowly Soviet functionary, there was not enough to bribe a diplomat of oil-rich Libya – certainly not enough to do it as a matter of routine out of the mere desire to have a ready-to-wear spy in the London embassy against a possible rainy day. In the prevailing cuts in government expenditure, and with the break in relations with Libya after the 1984 Embassy siege, the project for recruiting Khoder Saleh was dropped.

Rereading the papers Calverton felt that not enough effort had been applied to cracking the problem. He noted two facts from the Libyan's work-pattern. The first was that he was not an out-of-doors operator: his meetings were invariably arranged indoors and largely in hotels. This could be a mere point of technique, and agents had prejudices one way or the other. The second point of interest was, however, more unusual. Whenever Saleh made a rendezvous there would be twenty-four hours before he was seen again. What was he doing with the time? Contrary to earlier indications, was it possible that he had a mistress?

"Are we still keeping an eye on him?" he asked Lionel Sholto.

"On and off. Mostly off."

"What about the Americans? Libya is the country they love to hate; perhaps Grover Wagner has been keeping his hand in by watching Saleh."

"You want to ask the CIA?"

"Purely a friendly exchange of information."

Grover Wagner was glad to oblige. London Station had plenty of data but few theories. He produced a report containing the new fact that, even in London, whenever Saleh fixed a hotel meeting he would book a single room for the night despite the fact that he had an excellent apartment in the embassy colony in St John's Wood. In witness, the hotel bills. Calverton examined them. He was struck by the fact that in every case the cost of the room was exceeded by the size of the bar-tab. Could it be . . . ? On analysis no other explanation offered itself. In short, away from the puritanical constraints of embassy life and the teetotal injunctions of the Koran, it appeared that the Libyan diplomat was a drunk.

On this basis Calverton set about preparing his plans.

John Donaldson meanwhile was following a new lead, the name of Reinhardt Egger, though for the moment he had no proof that the former Luftwaffe major had been involved in the theft of the painting or any knowledge of his present whereabouts, assuming he were still alive. The only immediate clue to further information was the fact that Egger had been made a prisoner of the British in April 1945.

With this in mind, he went to the Public Record Office in Kew, a modern building in pink concrete layers, sitting in its patch of gardens, a suburban version of the Ministry of Truth. The staff were helpful.

They told Donaldson, first, that there was no nominal roll of German prisoners of war on record; so there was no immediate way of confirming that Reinhardt Egger had ever been a POW. Second, they told him that the interrogations of captured German aircrew, which were in the files of the Directorate of Intelligence, were still classified. In the ordinary way they would have been released under the thirty-year rule but their release might embarrass people who were still alive. In short his line of enquiry led to an apparent dead-end. Donaldson wasn't prepared to accept that.

140

In the reference-room he started to take down the Foreign Office and Air Ministry class-lists. These were volumes simply listing the files and books held in archive by source, title and reference number. While there was no single list of German POWs, Donaldson calculated that there would be partial lists or individual names on file for other purposes. It was a case of using inspiration and common sense in deciding which files to select.

His first choice wasn't too lucky. Under the entry FO 939/40 he called up a file on German officer POWs, but on examination it was nothing more than a series of memoranda on the problems of housing officers with other ranks: the officers were still Nazis and the other ranks couldn't stand them. He had hoped for a list of captured officers, but it wasn't there.

The next choice did produce a list. Under FO 939/201 Donaldson found a nominal roll of prisoners who were members of Nazi organizations banned as criminal under a system known as the Heymann categories. These prisoners were still being held under "freezing orders" as late as December 1947 when the list in FO 939/201 was prepared. The names were split between several classes, in each case with the rank and serial number and the camp where the prisoner was held, but nothing more. Category I prisoners were members of criminal organizations: in most cases this meant the SS, as was evident from the ranks held by the individuals, though the specific organizations were not stated. Category II consisted of men regarded as dangerous to security in Germany. A third class was composed of accused persons and witnesses in specific war-crimes cases. The fourth class, listed in Appendix F, was a miscellany: the names in it were of people being detained for reasons no one was prepared to mention. It held the name of Reinhardt Egger.

Donaldson stared at the page, but there was nothing more: a bare name which confirmed that at some point Egger had been in British custody. But in itself it raised a question: what had Egger done that they were still holding him at the end of 1947 with a bunch of war criminals and misfits?

He broke for lunch, having left the PRO staff to hunt out a Foreign Office file containing correspondence on individual German officers. It was a long shot that it might hold something relevant. After a quick bite in the downstairs restaurant, he made a telephone call to the number that Anthony had last given him and asked to speak to Anthony's girlfriend, the German girl, Annaliese Schreiber.

"I need some help," he told her. She was anxious to please: even on the telephone he detected that way she had of looking from the present at the horizon in expectation of – what? For the moment, he guessed that he provided a diversion from Anthony.

"I'm trying to trace the whereabouts of an old man, a German. . . ." He gave her quickly as much as was necessary of the story of Reinhardt Egger. It had occurred to him that if Egger were alive he would be drawing a war pension; the Germans were generous in that regard. Through the pension system or through the various old-comrades associations – hadn't Annaliese's father been a soldier? – there ought to be a fairly easy way of finding the old man's address. All he needed was a contact in Germany who could do the legwork. Annaliese was glad to help.

When he went back upstairs to the Langdale Room he found that his material was ready for him. It turned out to be an undistinguished buff folder with the reference FO 939/359 gummed on the outside and the name of the Control Commission for Germany and Austria printed as a heading. Inside was a file of correspondence between the Control Commission based at Bush House in the Aldwych and a department of the War Office operating out of the unlikely address of the Hotel Victoria in Northumberland Avenue. It dealt with the topic of release-dates for individual German officers. Donaldson read it and quickly got the drift.

The British had adopted an ABC system of classifying prisoners according to their political views. The ranking affected the individual's release-date. Those with "A" classification, the "whites" in the jargon of the Foreign Office, were targeted for early release. The "greys" were for later and the "blacks" came nowhere. Attempts were made by the POWs and their friends to influence their classification, and FO 939/359 set out the interdepartmental discussion on these attempts. It was straightforward stuff and the only point of interest was the name of Aaron Eichbaum.

Donaldson thumbed back through the pages looking for a reference to Reinhardt Egger, but it didn't appear. The memorandum with Eichbaum's name in it referred to a letter written by the old dealer, but that wasn't on file, either. Instead there was one sheet from a longer message and everything else was missing. Donaldson read it.

According to the writer, Aaron Eichbaum, a Jew who had suffered under the Nazis, had appealed for a reclassification and early release for his friend – here a serial number was given – who had never been a Nazi and who had given him assistance when he most needed it. The comment was terse:

I can hardly believe that this man, Eichbaum, is talking about the same character as the prisoner. The latter is an out-and-out Black, the worst type of Nazi, arrogant, ambitious and a consummate hypocrite. There is no question of reviewing his Freeze Order until the mystery attached to his mission to England had been explained.

Donaldson folded the file. He was tired with staring at papers, piecing their message as much out of what was left unsaid as what was said. He thought of Aaron Eichbaum, whose modesty had prevented him from telling that he had tried to help Reinhardt Egger, the man who had betrayed the values of humanity and culture which the old Jew loved. When he had written the letter, Eichbaum must have known that Egger no longer resembled the man he had once been, but he had done so out of old affection and to repay a debt.

For the moment Donaldson didn't think of what the mystery attached to Egger's mission to England might mean.

Chapter Fifteen

KHODER SALEH agreed to meet McKilroy in Hyde Park near one of the entrances by Lancaster Gate. It was a precautionary measure by the Libyan so that he could establish that he was free of any tail before heading for whatever hotel he had in mind.

From his position by the newspaper-kiosk outside the Underground station, Ross spotted him walking west along Bayswater Road from Marble Arch. With him was a second man. Saleh was a pale-skinned, neat type in a tan safari-suit and a light-coloured mackintosh. His face had a dark, Napoleonic sort of beauty, curve-nosed and full-lipped. It gave him a faintly sinister air and wasn't improved by a pair of tired eyes, their whites turned yellow and waxy, and socketed in dark folds.

The second man was taller and darker. He was built into a sports jacket and slacks as if there were two of him. His name was Malik. His presence was not unexpected. Saleh's file showed, and McKilroy confirmed, that he took the big Berber with him as insurance. It also showed that he had had occasion to call on the policy. This time his job was to watch his master's rear.

"If he runs true to form," said Figgis, "then as soon as Saleh and Denny have snuggled up together, he'll clear off to do a spot of shopping." There was a plastic bag in the big man's pocket to prove the point.

Attention turned to McKilroy. There had been nervousness in using him in case the Irishman panicked; but on balance there were more risks in using look-alikes. In fact McKilroy was slowly turning into his own imperfect look-alike as he made his gradual change into butterfly. Since Ross had last seen him, he had had his earlobes surgically removed, to give him small, neat ears that lay flat against the head, instead of the large pair with teeth-marks which had been his recent possession. He had also added an inch to his height with lifts in his shoes. Now he was standing nervously by the park railings, looking as though he were chained to them, and stamping his feet against the cold.

"Give him another month," said Figgis, "and his own mother wouldn't know him. Why did he pick that suit?" – referring to a sober blue pinstripe – "He looks like he's going to a bloody funeral."

Ross nodded but kept his eyes on the target and watched the contact being made; it was complete with all the cues for safety just as McKilroy had described them. Ross had been curious as to McKilroy's response to betrayal. He had become a connoisseur of treason from seeing too much too close. He remembered the late, unlamented Gerry Kelly, whose heart was never in treachery and who had to be alternately wooed and blackmailed according to season. Not so Denny McKilroy, who, having been broken, hardly needed reminding of the fact. "A gentleman has to be a good loser," he said smoothly and in best voice.

"They're under starter's orders." Figgis was watching as Saleh turned into the park, followed by McKilroy at a decent interval and then the hatchetman, Malik. "And they're off!" Figgis added as their own car, which had been snoozing among the pillared fronts of the houses in nearby Sussex Gardens, collected them off the pavement.

Unless he intended to double back to one of the cheap hotels around Paddington, logic suggested that Saleh's goal was either Knightsbridge on the south side of the royal parks or Mayfair on the east. With Malik riding shotgun for his master, it was unsafe to put a moving tail on the three men, even with the trimmings of relays, substitutions and all the other tricks of the game, and Calverton had confined himself to a few static posts. So Saleh would find himself strolling past old ladies feeding ducks on the Serpentine and mothers wheeling prams. Calverton wouldn't admit it, but he liked the technique because it was corny. It was real spy stuff.

By the Peter Pan statue in Kensington Gardens one of the posts picked up the group ambling slowly down Lancaster Walk. When the message was relayed to Ross and Figgis, they were still boxed in the traffic backing out of Oxford Street and into the Bayswater Road under the pressure of Christmas shoppers.

"Sod it," muttered Figgis. "That means Knightsbridge. Probably the Sheraton. Saleh's used it twice just so that bastard Malik can go stealing in Harrods."

"Maybe," said Ross. "On the other hand, it could be that Saleh simply enjoys the walk." He watched for the other man's reaction. The idea that Saleh could want anything as normal as a pleasant walk on a crisp sunny day struck Figgis as perverse.

The next sighting had the Libyans turning towards the Serpentine. Saleh stopped by the water to light a cigarette. Sheepishly Malik pulled a bag of breadcrumbs from his coat and threw them mechanically towards the birds, but his eyes were elsewhere. Two minutes of this would have been enough to embarrass even the most inventive moving tail. Denny had reported a similar ploy on earlier occasions when he had met Saleh.

His cigarette finished, Saleh resumed his movement east. "Thank God for that, he's heading towards us," was Figgis's reaction. Park Lane had been relatively clear, but there were vehicles jamming Knightsbridge. They abandoned the car at Hyde Park Corner with a "Thank you bloody much!" from the driver and took up a pitch in the entrance of Apsley House.

In Rotten Row, Saleh stopped on account of the horses. A party of Household Cavalry, swathed in grey capes, with horsehair plumes bobbing on their helmets, went jangling past at a trot. The Libyan evidently admired them.

Saleh was now satisfied that his meeting was secure, and his remaining moves were direct. He came out of the parks by Hyde Park Corner, through the pedestrian subway and directly in front of Apsley House where Ross and Figgis were waiting. Denny McKilroy saw them, too, but had the presence of mind to do no more than throw them a glance. He, Saleh and the big Berber went under the next subway into Piccadilly and at last reached Half Moon Street, a small lane leading into Curzon Street, where MI5 had its main offices.

Figgis watched them enter Flemings Hotel and shook his head. "Cheeky sod! What's the point of giving us all this run-around and then showing up on our front doorstep?"

Flemings Hotel was a small, pleasant place; but Ross could have wished it bigger, with a crowded lobby and room for an observer to breathe while the two Libyans and their guest checked in. Next they passed out of sight.

In Calverton's office they had gone over the game-plan – Calverton liked game-plans – and identified this as the most vulnerable moment. For five minutes or so, until they could next make contact with him, McKilroy would be on his own while Saleh and Malik frisked and grilled him in the privacy of their room. At this point they would find nothing; but, as Figgis observed, "They could tear his head off and stuff it down the sink and we wouldn't even know." They said their prayers that McKilroy's nerves were good.

A third man joined them. He had been introduced to Ross as a Glaswegian named Bliss, and he brought a black box of tricks with him to monitor the conversation in the bedroom once they had McKilroy wired for sound. He was an uneven man, built in a loose, lumpy way like an athlete running to seed. His nose and cheeks were mottled with red veins and he had a cold which he endeavoured to staunch with a green paisley handkerchief.

From his bag Bliss took a pack of cigarettes and handed them to Ross. "Salem Lights, just as ordered. What sort of smokes are they, for God's sake?" Ross didn't answer; but the answer was that they were a brand that Saleh was unlikely to have about him when Denny McKilroy ran out of cigarettes.

Bliss settled in the washroom with his gadgetry. Figgis pulled Saleh's room number from reception and gave it to Ross. A minute later Ross was on his way to the second floor, changing his jacket for a porter's green ducktail in the lift.

In the bedroom Khoder Saleh, his face smiling but wary, offered Denny McKilroy a drink from a bottle of J. & B. Rare which the Libyan had brought with him.

"No, thanks," said McKilroy, and he treated the other man to the sort of smile that used to slay the girls back in Killarney in the days before he became a big-shot. "I'll just have a smoke."

"Have one of mine." Saleh threw across a pack. McKilroy prayed they weren't Salem Lights.

"I only smoke Salem Lights," said McKilroy. He reached into his pocket and pulled an empty pack out. "Christ wouldn't you know it?" More smiles back and forth. "I'll get some from room service."

"Malik can get you some," Saleh proposed.

"Why put him to the trouble?" McKilroy held his hand out to the phone as if he expected it to be lopped off, faked a call and replaced the handset. "They're bringing some up," he said and the smiles went round again as though brotherly love were back in fashion.

Ross counted the minutes. According to the plan, McKilroy had

had time to find an excuse and place a call for some cigarettes. Ross knocked on the door and was invited in. He took in the room while enquiring who wanted the cigarettes and passing them over to McKilroy on a small salver. At the best of times it was a small, narrow place. With a bathroom stolen from it and the rest packed with two single beds and a television set, movement was very restricted. If it came to a fight, there would be no space for finesse.

"Give the man a tip," said Saleh and snapped his fingers at Malik. The big man struggled from the bed where he had been lying, fished some change from the pocket of his cheap jacket and handed it across with a grunt. Ross guessed that Malik would never graduate to a speaking part. He took the tip and left. Two minutes later Malik followed.

Bliss had installed himself in one of the cubicles in the men's room and was cursing in unintelligible Glaswegian.

"What's wrong?" asked Ross.

"I don't like improvising a bug. You get no chance to test it out. I'm getting some bloody taxi firm in Streatham butting in." He grimaced. "Here we are, got it! Malik's on his way down: Saleh's told him to go and play for an hour." He passed the headset across to Ross. "Care to listen to the main programme?"

In the bedroom Saleh put away two stiff scotches in swift succession and began to unwind. He stretched out on one of the beds and opened his first question.

"Why do you want to see Kaster?" He spoke with an American accent which he had picked up working with one of the oil companies. The sharpness in his tone was unintentional: acquired from the same American oilmen in the days when they could treat a young Libyan like dirt.

"I have a job for him," said McKilroy noncommittally.

"Now? Before Christmas?"

"Why not?"

A shrug. Saleh sat up and poured himself another shot. "It is only a short while until Christmas. How can anything be arranged in such a short time? Last time. . . . "

This objection had been anticipated in the game-plan and the scriptwriters had come up with a riposte.

"We want to make a single hit – after Christmas." Denny added with all the Irish bluffness he could muster: "Those British bastards will be off their guard."

Down in the men's room James Ross listened in. He looked at Bliss. "When Denny said 'British bastards' – for once he sounded sincere."

Figgis picked up the shape of the bodyguard squeezing his way through the hotel doors like a loaded beer-truck.

"Off the leash and gambolling like a bloody spring lamb," he muttered between his teeth as Malik walked down Half Moon Street with a bounce in his step and whistled for a taxi. Figgis picked up the next one, courtesy of his employers. "A pound to a penny says it's Brompton Road," he said to the driver as they followed the first cab. The prophecy was accurate. The taxi dropped Malik outside Harrods, the Libyan paid it off and went into the store with Figgis figuratively on his heels.

This scenario, too, had been played out in Calverton's game-session.

"Now, let us assume", Calverton had said in his most arch tone, "that, true to form, Saleh has dropped his bodyguard: so to speak, packed him off on his own with an injunction not to accept sweets from strange men. What are we to do?"

"Leave Malik to get on with it whilst we give Saleh the business," was Figgis's suggestion.

"What? Leave this large gentleman – no doubt tailored with all sorts of interesting hardware – to come back at some uncertain time and possibly surprise us about our activities?"

"We could pick him up as he returns to the rendezvous," Ross proposed.

"Too coincidental: he would immediately suppose that we had followed him the first time round and then the whole meeting would be compromised. I think you will agree that Malik has to be detained long enough elsewhere so as to give friend McKilroy opportunity to talk to Saleh and get clear. Suggestions, please."

Now this little scene in the overall game was to be played for real; and the reality turned out to be Malik wandering around the tiled extravaganza of the food-hall, head and shoulders above the other shoppers as they carted away the Christmas hampers. He lingered over the charcuterie so that Figgis began to wonder whether somewhere in that bovine head the Muslim was dreaming of forbidden pork.

This turned out to be just an appetizer for the other man's imagination. Malik left the food-hall without buying anything and, with a sense of purpose, took the lift and headed straight for the ladies' lingerie department. Again Figgis followed.

In the new location Malik was once more the coy tourist, the little boy told not to touch. Figgis watched his dark shape circling the plaster mannequins, examining intently their smooth legs and plaster smiles. The Berber's bright pink tongue flickered around his lips; he put a hand to his brown skin and felt the open pores that mottled his cheeks then studied the lighter brown of his palms. He looked at the life-size dolls again and Figgis recognized that look. It was awe.

The Libyan stood – it seemed for minutes – fixed in this position, and when he moved the movement was so deft that Figgis scarcely saw it and waited to see if it would be repeated. Another minute passed. Again the same gesture: a hand snaking out and pocketing a pair of female briefs from the display.

Jesus wept! thought Figgis to himself. The file showed Malik with no wife or reputed girlfriends.

Ross and the sour-faced Scot, Bliss, found themselves closeted cheek by jowl in a cubicle of the gents' toilet growing hotter by the minute. Bliss was wearing a car-coat in brown imitation leather, belted in the middle and trimmed with nylon fur. He smelled faintly of beer.

"Why doesn't the bastard get down to business," he asked of Saleh. The Libyan seemed to have taken to the Christmas spirit. He had poured himself a fourth drink and begun to talk about the differences in religious customs between Britain and his homeland and to complain of the burdens imposed on him by the Koran in the matter of alcohol.

Ross didn't answer. In between the drunken maunderings Saleh was feeling his way towards the right questions. "The problem with a diplomat like friend Saleh", Calverton had said, "is that his status gives him immunity. *Noli me tangere* is his motto: 'I'm a diplomat; keep your hands off me.' And very soon his technique starts to slip and he gets to thinking that he can walk on water. Very good, I hear you say. Couldn't be better. It makes it that much easier for us." Calverton looked around at them all. "And there's the trap. Because every once in a while the fucker will do something *professional*!" He beamed because he relished saying "fucker" like a precocious child.

"He's wary of Denny's sudden need for hired-in terror," Ross said to Bliss. "Last time it wasn't like this. There were months of notice."

"It could be that he's just bloody suspicious, full stop," Bliss said neutrally. "I can see his point of view: I'd be suspicious of yon McKilroy. But, then, I'm prejudiced – I just hate the Irish."

"Why are you still interested in" – Saleh waved his glass about, searching for the term – "the liberation struggle?"

McKilroy's mind ran on direct lines. He was nonplussed by the question. "I've told you. I've been asked to arrange a hit."

Saleh laughed and took a friendly jab at the Irishman's shoulder. Words spilled out again in his uncanny American accent. Mission – sense of purpose – goal of the struggle.

"Oh, that. I'm still a patriot," McKilroy said with conviction. "Ould Ireland for ever, eh?" He felt he could use that drink. Please God this Libyan bastard would get it over with and tell him where and when he was to meet Kaster.

"And how's Liam?" Saleh changed the subject.

God help the poor sod, thought Ross: Saleh is going to take him on a trip down Memory Lane. How's old so-and-so? Many's the happy bomb we've planted together. Since he had dropped out of mainstream Provo activity, Denny's knowledge of who's who in the terrorist world had got out of date. Saleh might have other IRA contacts. A slip in the answer could tell the Libyan that McKilroy had no current business with the Provos; tell him that he didn't need Kaster. McKilroy fielded the questions and the Libyan lost interest as the drink went to his head. Suddenly he seemed to have had enough of the whole game. Perhaps he wanted to be alone with the bottle and thoughts of home. Ross sensed a crisis passing.

"I've been in contact with Kaster – hey, there's a great guy!" said Saleh. His conversation was starting to spring leaks with clichés from every American film he had ever seen. "And I can tell you – *shi-it*, sure you won't have a drink? – I can tell you he has the hots to do another job for you."

"That's great news," Denny said hollowly.

"I thought you'd want to know."

"I did. But you didn't say when I get to meet him."

"Boy, are you impatient! You ought to learn to unwind. Take a slug of this. I thought you Irish were all great drinkers."

"Not on business," Denny said. The words were freezing on his lips.

151

"Not on business!" Saleh burst out laughing. "It's the way you tell them." He was making up his own jokes as he went along. Denny joined him, laughing uncontrollably till he collapsed back in his chair, deflated of emotion. Ross listened and for once felt sympathy with McKilroy, but blotted it out.

The laughter faded. Saleh took a pen from his coat and a sheet of hotel stationery.

"This is the where and when," he said and handed the paper across.

That's it! thought Ross to himself. Now get the hell out of there!

Two pairs of ladies' briefs tucked into his pocket, Malik had lost interest in Harrods. Figgis followed him slowly against the flow of shoppers. He checked his watch. If the other man had in mind to return to his master at Flemings Hotel, then he was going to make it back before Denny, according to the game-plan, would have time to be clear. Figgis felt for the warrant-card in his pocket. This was going to be like shooting fish in a barrel. He would go into his police routine, stall Malik for a quarter of an hour with a few questions about certain stolen goods and allow himself to understand that Malik was a diplomat; at which point Figgis would dip out with a few words of apology and no harm done, sir. Our policeman was going to be wonderful.

Malik made it into the street, under the store awning, looking for a taxi in the flow along Brompton Road. Fat chance, thought Figgis as he struggled out of the door. What he hadn't reckoned on was the Libyan holding up a ten-pound note between his fingers and whistling loud enough to crack glass. It magicked up a taxi out of Hans Crescent in two seconds flat, and Malik had the door open and one foot inside before Figgis could catch up with him and put a hand on his shoulder.

"Excuse me, sir," he said in his best policeman's accents. "I have reason to believe that you have some ladies' garments in your possession which you have not paid for." Malik turned and stared at him with a look of blank incomprehension. Figgis faltered but mustered a smile intended to be firm but fair. "I wonder if you would care to step aside while I examine the contents of your pockets?" He was still smiling, firm but fair, when Malik butted him in the face.

So much for the sodding game-plan! Figgis said to himself as he sat on his backside and the passers-by decided they had other things to do. What did the cunt do that for? he asked; but he was on his feet and in pursuit.

The taxi with Malik in it had done a U-turn and was facing east along Brompton Road by the German foodshop, blocked by the traffic trying to filter into Knightsbridge. Figgis ran across the road, dodging between the cars, and tried to catch the taxi while it was stationary in the queue. His nose was starting to fill with blood and people were beginning to stare.

The lights changed and the vehicles crawled forward then picked up speed across the junction. Figgis glimpsed Malik's face through the cab rear window. The Libyan looked calm but curious as though he no more understood what was happening than the Englishman did. Figgis put on a burst of speed and, joining the stream of cars, ran across the intersection and into Knightsbridge. The pedestrians on the pavement stopped to look at the strange figure, blood spattered across his face, running among the cars, overtaking some of them.

The traffic ground to a halt again. Figgis gained on a bus and passed a sleek Rolls-Royce with bronzed windows and embassy plates. He caught up with the taxi just as the cars began to move again.

More speed, driving his body in a destruction test, his breath bubbling through the blood which was trickling into his throat. He drew level with the cabbie's door and hammered on it; he waved the driver to stop. The window remained firmly up and the door closed, but the cabbie could be heard shouting: "You're a fucking loonie, that's what you are, mate!"

Too bloody true, thought Figgis. Please God everything was going OK at the other end.

Denny McKilroy cleared his throat and made I'll-be-on-my-way noises to a Saleh who was becoming increasingly indifferent.

"We're home and dry," said Bliss laconically.

"Maybe," said Ross.

"Bankable certainty."

"Thanks for the help, then," said McKilroy.

"Sure . . . thing." From the bed Saleh waved a hand. Then as a parting shot: "Hey buddy, got a smoke?" Two fingers to his dark lips and his breath blowing imaginary smoke.

"I'm out, sorry."

"C'mon, you got a pack from the bell-hop."

"Didn't I, though?" McKilroy felt his face weary with smiles. The fine stitches that held his restructured features in place were going to clatter on the floor like small change. He took out the cigarettes that Ross had given him and felt the pack deftly for the genuine ones. "I hope the bloody things blow up on you," he murmured under his breath.

He was about to throw a cigarette across when the other man leaned over and grabbed at the pack. McKilroy made the mistake of trying to hold on. As Saleh gripped a corner of the wrapping, the foil and paper began to fall apart at the seams and the contents spilled on to the floor. McKilroy stared down at the cigarettes and the bug sitting in the middle of them. Saleh laughed again, still amused by the slapstick humour. He bent down, picked up a cigarette and only then did he see.

"What in hell's name is this?" he asked, holding the bug. His dark face had the dead quality of someone who was sober by an act of will.

"If we don't move, we're going to have one murdered Irishman on our hands," said Ross.

Figgis lost his grip on the cab door and the vehicle pulled away, still heading east towards the underpass by Hyde Park Corner. He knew that, if he followed, the traffic would kill him if his heart didn't give out first. Instead he cut out of the roadway and back on to the Knightsbridge pavement in a blast of carhorns and screeching brakes. The taxi disappeared from view.

The pavement was crowded with shoppers. Figgis kept up his run, shouldering into pedestrians, sending parcels flying, ignoring the curses. He crossed Park Lane by the subway, sprinting past Apsley House where he had earlier picked up Saleh's trail, and reached Piccadilly to see the taxi crawling out of the underpass and Malik's swart faced pressed against the window, the nose flat and pale, and his expression of wrath and puzzlement.

The traffic stream unblocked itself again and the taxi put on a burst of speed over the last few yards to Half Moon Street, where it turned left, Figgis following, his chest heaving and pain-racked as if it would explode.

As he turned left he saw the cab parked outside Flemings Hotel. Malik was still in the back of the vehicle but the driver was talking to a regular London bobby in raincoat and pointed helmet and gesticulating in Figgis's direction. Figgis tidied himself up, zipped up the front of his plaid windcheater and smoothed down his brown curls. He slowed to a walk: Malik obviously wasn't going anywhere, though he couldn't figure why.

The policeman approached cautiously and paused, ready for anything. Figgis remembered his warrant-card and hoped the ink wasn't still wet. He reached for it as the policeman came closer.

"Pardon me, sir," said the latter slowly, "but the driver there tells me that you have been trying to molest his passenger."

"That . . . man . . . is a shoplifter," Figgis gasped out the words and produced the warrant-card. "I was simply trying to arrest him." So much for the game-plan, he was thinking to himself. I try to arrest him and he sets the police on me. Somewhere a piece of the puzzle was missing.

The officer looked at the card. "There seems to have been a misunderstanding, sir."

"Too bloody right. I'd only like to know what."

"Well, I'd say that it's probably because this dark gentleman doesn't speak a word of English."

Ross and Bliss came out of the toilet cubicle under the stare of another customer who was standing at the urinals and hastily buttoned his trousers up. They walked out through the lounge and the lobby towards the stairs, not risking a wait for the lift and not wanting to draw attention by running. It was a calculated risk with Denny McKilroy's life.

Ross had the gun, Bliss carried his bag of tricks. They reached the bedroom. As Denny had been instructed, he had contrived to keep the door closed but unlocked. Ross paused: behind the door it was out of his control; success or a bullet in the guts were both possible.

The door slammed open. Saleh was by the window holding a gun on McKilroy. As the Libyan turned in his direction, Ross dropped to the floor, aimed his own gun and said: "Police!"

Saleh hesitated, let his gun fall and, with an expression near to a grin, answered: "Diplomat." He was stone cold sober now but he reached for his glass and tossed back a drink. Then he turned to McKilroy. "They may have saved your hide, mister, but you can forget about Kaster."

McKilroy was in the bathroom standing against the washbasin, holding himself up with two shaking hands on the pedestal. He paused between retching and said: "Jesus, I'm standing here with my pants full of shit and he thinks I'm worried about Kaster!"

155

"Saleh has a point," Ross said to McKilroy. Then, without warning, he struck the diplomat a blow to the abdomen. Saleh collapsed on the floor, his mouth open and gasping for breath. Bliss eyed the result, poured himself a shot from one of the other bottles, drank it off and wiped the glass. "You clear off," he said. "I'll tidy up and take care of sonny here. Now, me," he added without focusing on Ross in particular. "I wouldna just have punched him in the guts. I'd have murdered yon bastard if he'd killed my brother." He looked up at Ross, who was cleaning the place up. "Aye, you look a hard man, I'll grant you that," Bliss opined. "But underneath you still look like a bloody humanitarian to me. And that sort of attitude will always let you down at the last."

Ross left the hotel with McKilroy. Outside they came across the spectacle of a policeman with two pairs of knickers over his arm, arguing with Malik and a taxi-driver, while Figgis lounged against the cab, observing the scene with calm satisfaction. As the two men appeared he ambled towards them.

"No prizes for guessing that my end was damn near a fiasco," he said. "Where's Saleh?"

"Out cold," said Ross.

"You mean another bleeding farce." Figgis wiped his nose on his sleeve. "Or, to take Calverton's way of looking at it, both ends of the operation happened within foreseeable limits and we have a meeting fixed at which we can do for Kaster." He stared around him and noticed the policeman taking careful notes of the taxi-driver's statement. "Woodentop!" He farted and shook a leg in the policeman's direction. To Ross he said with the same jaunty grin: "All in all, the game-plan was a hundred-per-cent success."

Ross stared back. "If that's success, you can tell Calverton to stuff it."

"Tell him yourself," said Figgis.

"I won't be around."

Chapter Sixteen

ON THE morning following the incident with Saleh, the Operations Liaison Committee was scheduled to meet in the Admiralty building as usual; but, before that, Norman Calverton found himself invited to an early breakfast meeting in the station buffet at Victoria where Sir Lionel Sholto's train brought him in daily from his rural idyll. They stood in the queue behind the dossers buying their early-morning cups of tea.

"Sorry to drag you out," Sholto began, trying at the same time to hold his umbrella and balance a tray. "Here, get yourself a piece of this. My treat and we'll stick it on the Department of Transport, a sort of poetic justice."

"I'm not sure if the Department of Transport carries any responsibility for British Rail's catering."

"No need to be pedantic, Norman. Eat up all the same." Sholto pushed across a plate of glistening sausages and an egg standing in a pool of fat. Calverton was reminded of the overboiled sprouts which the other had tackled on the last occasion they had eaten together. He seemed to take a delight in the excesses of English cooking.

"No, thanks." He looked away. An old woman was nibbling toothlessly at a sausage roll which she periodically dunked in her coffee.

"Fact is," Sholto went on in his Etonian boom, "fact is, I find these places completely anonymous. Nowhere else seems to be quite so *reliable*, particularly *you know where*" – alluding to MI5's offices in Curzon Street. "Not so much the Russians, you know, more a case of the Foreign Office. They seem to have us infiltrated. Truth is, I'm damned if they're not better at you know what than we are. There are times", he added wistfully, "when I wish, Norman, that the whole show could be like your lot, the blue-collar workers."

"Oh?"

"All those working-class accents – stymie the Foreign Office no

157

end. They're quite good at the hieratic, but hopeless at the demotic."

"My commiserations."

"Quite."

Calverton wondered when Sholto would get to the point.

"Molly called me yesterday. Sources had informed him that a certain diplomat of our acquaintance had disappeared."

"Sources? Not the Libyans?"

"Not the Libyans. Where was I? Ah, yes, Molly was anxious to know whether the incident was entirely unconnected with our dealings with the gentleman in question. If he were dead, that would naturally be a serious matter. If, on the other hand, he had defected, then initially he would be Foreign Office property."

"But, then again," said Calverton, "he might be undecided about defecting: he might be having a Crisis of Conscience."

"Ah! I take your point. The Foreign Office are not the keepers of his conscience."

"Is any complaint expected from the Libyans?"

"I gather not. Since friend Saleh is as clear a hood as Al Capone, their only surprise is that we have never killed him. They have a different etiquette in these things, as witness their slaughter of the policewoman during the 1984 Embassy business. Do you think Saleh will defect?"

"Certain to. Once the Libyans know that he has been in our hands for a period of time, they could never trust him, and Saleh knows it."

Sholto broke off the conversation to go back to the counter and dicker with the staff over the particular doughnut he wished to buy. He returned and sat down heavily, then resumed: "I gather that your fellow Ross has deserted you since this operation."

"He isn't used to our ways," said Calverton shortly.

"I've never understood your liking for the working classes. Still, it's your affair." A sigh. "Well, Norman, you seem to have established your point as to the existence of Kaster and fairly set him up to be taken."

"Does Williams agree?"

"Williams? Of course not. I had him on the phone last night, burning my ear with his acid Welsh voice: 'Well, Lionel, it seems that I've lapsed into heresy on this Kaster matter, but I still hold to the Docetic view.' The 'Docetic view' being, as I understand it, that Kaster is a phantom. However, that is not the point: he has fought the battle and lost. The thing is, what do you propose to do now?"

"I was going to report our success to the Committee. It would please the Americans, set their minds at rest." Calverton paused to spoon sugar into his cold coffee. "Then I thought I might invite Special Branch to participate in the taking of Kaster. After the recent friction with Williams, it occurred to me that to invite them to what may literally be the kill would be only the Christian thing to do." He looked up.

"No, I wouldn't do that. Better to let sleeping dogs lie. You would prefer to handle Kaster's capture on your own, wouldn't you, Norman?"

Calverton sipped at his cup and removed a film of milk-skin from his mouth with finger and thumb and deposited it in the saucer. "Well, naturally one likes to keep one's business to one's self. But I should hate it to be thought that I had manipulated things that way. Played games, so to speak."

Later that same morning, John Donaldson returned to the Public Record Office. His earlier foray into the Foreign Office files had confirmed that Reinhardt Egger had been a POW in British hands, but nothing in the Control Commission papers linked him with the missing painting. And yet there was "the mystery attached to his mission to England" lying unexplained in a routine memorandum. What had the writer meant? Just what had an officer on Goering's staff been doing flying an operational mission in the closing days of the war?

After his groundwork during the last visit, Donaldson had some ideas on how to dig out the facts surrounding the German raid. He called up the Air Ministry Weekly Intelligence Summaries for the period March to June 1945, which covered the date he wanted. The summaries came in magazine form in red covers for fairly wide circulation and covered events in the week before the week of issue plus a few general articles without particular topicality. The main thing was that they contained a digest of any air activity by the Germans.

The reports turned out to be thin. The Germans were within weeks of defeat and the Luftwaffe had almost ceased to exist as an organized force. Even so, they had managed some activity against the United Kingdom. On the night of 4 March an estimated seventy Germans followed a returning English raid and tried to attack the airfields. A repeat performance was tried on the night of the seventeenth, this time with twenty planes – a measure of the decline in German strength. Donaldson guessed that Egger had been on one of these raids: there was nothing else. Aaron Eichbaum must have been mistaken when he mentioned April.

The weekly reports narrowed the field without adding much detail: their circulation was too wide for anything of major sensitivity. Donaldson went through the Air Ministry class-lists again, looking for narrower material. In AIR 22/141 and 142 he found the daily reports for the same period. This time he had the confidential data.

He went through the reports for March. The format was in general the same, a résumé at the front and then an account by sections: European theatre, Mediterranean theatre, Pacific theatre, Bomber Command, SHAEF, Fighter Command, Coastal Command and down the chain. The guts was in the résumé, which mentioned any German activity. The details were given under Fighter Command.

The story from the weekly summaries was fleshed out here. The German raids of 4 and 17 March surfaced with more detail: times, places, units, casualties; all pretty much as expected, and yet Donaldson couldn't help thinking that there was more. "The mystery attached to this mission to England." The words had acquired an insistency that couldn't be explained by a German raid against British airfields. He moved on to the reports for April.

According to the weekly summaries there had been no enemy action against the British mainland during this final month of the war. As Donaldson turned the typed foolscap sheets of the daily reports, they confirmed the same picture with an insignificant exception of a reconnaissance aircraft plotted ninety miles east of Cromer between 1914 and 1940 hours on the evening of the ninth; no action taken. He noted it and turned over the page. More accounts of the dying days of the Luftwaffe with a bored note to the story of German inactivity and the sweeps by Fighter Command over an empty sky. He reached 22 April. A lone German raider was shot down over Suffolk.

The words were as bland as the rest of the reports. There was no intimation of purpose or significance behind the bald narrative. Donaldson hesitated over it while the question formed in his mind. Why wasn't the raider mentioned elsewhere? Because the weekly intelligence summaries were too unrestricted?

There was nothing more on the file, just the hanging question which suggested only more searches through the Air Ministry records in the hope of finding a crash report: just maybe somebody had investigated the wreckage. He turned to the class-lists again.

The result was patchy, an uneven record of the examination of the remains of German aircraft. Probably the system had been efficient enough, but only its ruins were left in the archives like the ruins of the planes that were gone over.

Fortunately what there was covered the critical period: a battered blue folder held together with white cross-tapes and labelled AIR 40/45.

When Donaldson opened it, he found a series of typed reports in serial order. There were two formats: lists of aircraft brought down in France and Belgium with a few sparse details, often because the wrecks had been looted; and, on the other hand, lengthy reports, normally concerning single aircraft, where these had been shot down over Britain. It didn't take long to trace the results of the raid on 4 March as reported in the weekly and daily intelligence bulletins: three enemy aeroplanes destroyed over Lincolnshire and East Anglia. There were descriptions of the aircraft types, markings, colourings, engines, weaponry and internal fittings and a note of number of crew, dead or alive, but with no names. There was no report on the raid of 17 March; but there wouldn't be unless there was wreckage on land. And the single raider brought down on 22 April? There was a one-page report dated 25 April 1945 with the serial number 270.

Donaldson read it – the same crisp, technical phrases as the others. The plane was a Ju 88 G-6, the same type as used in the 4 March raid. It had been shot down by a fighter from RAF Disenham and made a good landing on water in Disenham Mere where it was presently under the surface. Despite the good landing, four of the crew of five had been unable to get clear of the wreckage in time and had drowned. As with the earlier planes, there was a modest curiosity about the radio and radar equipment of the G-6, since the raid of 4 March was the first time that this Ju 88 subtype had been seen over Britain. Investigation was hampered by location and the fact that the bomb-load was believed still to be on board.

He put the file down and went for a cup of coffee to clear his thoughts. At first sight there was no way of telling whether Reinhardt Egger had been in the earlier or the later raid and no indication of mystery attached to either. The purpose of the seventy-bomber raid of 4 March was obvious enough. And the single raider of 22 April? Was there anything more than the fact of its being alone?

The break finished, he returned to his papers and had copies taken of the daily intelligence sheets and the crash reports on both raids. Maybe there was something in them, but he suspected that this line of enquiry led into a dead-end. There was no way of proving a connection between Egger and the painting unless he could find the man himself.

Back at his house in Islington there was a call waiting on the recorder. It was Annaliese Schreiber, her unfamiliar voice made stranger by the restraint of talking to a machine. Donaldson fixed himself a drink and played it several times. She hadn't known how intimately to pitch her message and had somehow got lost in what she really wanted to say so that the meaning leaked away into a complaint about Anthony. "Who does he think he is?" the tape ended. With Anthony that was always a good question. Donaldson found himself curious about her: he had met her once and spoken to her once, and together that amounted to nothing under the rules of these particular mathematics. The recording machine and the echoes of her own voice on the line must have been the person she talked to and better known to her than John Donaldson. So he listened to the tape a few times for the things she wouldn't have told him and then called her back.

She was glad to hear from him. What did she want? Her friends in Germany had found the whereabouts of Reinhardt Egger: the place to which his pension was sent. She was bored and wanted to go there with Donaldson.

He thought about this for only a moment. If it was the price to be paid to reach the end of his search, he was prepared to pay it.

"Where is he?" he asked.

"Egypt, would you believe!"

Donaldson remembered what Aaron Eichbaum had said about the origins of his old friend in the German community in Egypt. So Reinhardt Egger had gone back to his roots.

He went out for dinner, eating alone in an Italian restaurant, and when he returned he looked again at the papers he had obtained from the Public Record Office. There had to be something there, some fraction of the truth refracted through the words, an unseeing vision of it. He let the recitation of the technical jargon beat on his mind. Identification marks: C9 + RR. Call sign: TA + JJ. Works number: 620398. Maker: jgq; Inscription: "Auftrag Jüngster Tag" stencilled below canopy on port side. . . . Engines: Jumo 213 A-1. . . .

162

Armaments: 4 × MG 151/20 fixed. . . . The repetition blurred the differences between the different aircraft. Identification marks: C9 + RR. Call sign. . . . Works number. . . . "Auftrag Jüngster Tag" stencilled. . . . Engines. . . .

He gave up on the reading and hunted around for a dictionary to translate the occasional German words in the text: "Schräge Musik", "Geschoss", "Auftrag Jüngster Tag". Only "Geschoss" made sense: it meant "shell" in the explosive sense. "Schräge Musik" taken literally seemed to mean "slope music" but from the context was some sort of weapon. "Auftrag Jüngster Tag" was the same sort of gibberish: it was painted on the side on the lone aircraft shot down in the 22 April raid. Donaldson threw the dictionary down. He was angry with himself for letting the painting become an obsession.

For a while he played some music and picked over a novel. He had another drink, felt a little more relaxed and decided to clear one last point before calling a close to the whole business for the night. He called Annaliese.

She was already in bed but pleased to hear his voice.

"What do you want, John? Something I can help with?"

"Some German, a few words that I can't translate. What does 'Auftrag Jüngster Tag' mean?"

"What an odd expression. 'Auftrag' – that is a 'mission' – what would you say? – an 'operation'?"

"And 'Jüngster Tag?' "

" 'Jüngster Tag'. It means 'the End of the World', do you understand?"

" 'The Last Judgement'?"

"Yes, exactly, 'the Last Judgement'. Is that all right? . . . Hello, John, are you still there?"

Donaldson was still there but his mind could scarcely focus on the question he wanted to ask:

What was Operation Last Judgement and why had it brought Reinhardt Egger to England?

Chapter Seventeen

OXFORD STREET two days before Christmas, chaotic with shoppers at the frantic end of the hunt for gifts. Every shop and store crowded; people milling in the street, bulky with parcels and heavy coats, hunched against the cold London drizzle, dull figures that absorbed the light from the overhead illuminations.

Desmond McKilroy stood nervously outside Selfridges department store, staked out like a tethered goat waiting for the tiger to strike. His appearance continued to change: the hairline a little lower and the thatch more luxuriant; his nose straighter in alignment. From his vantage-point by the British Airways office, Ross watched the other man and wondered whether the inner chameleon would ever reveal itself and McKilroy would turn green and catch flies with his tongue.

Ross felt a professional admiration for Kaster's choice of place. The crowd offered cover both for observation and escape, the exits were virtually limitless and the same passers-by who formed the backdrop meant that the hostile field of fire was effectively nil. It was as neat a way of keeping the play in Kaster's own hands as he could have devised.

He wondered where Calverton's men were. Like fleas he could feel them even if he couldn't scratch them. Calverton was playing a hands-off game, using him as an expendable stalking-horse. If Figgis and friends were there, it wasn't as the US Cavalry ready to come into action as soon as the going got tough. Figgis would as soon see him dead as long as he got what Calverton wanted. In fact he'd probably prefer it that way.

And Kaster? Ross guessed he was probably there already. Echoes of the past came back to him; David and he learning religion at the orphanage. "*For where two or three are gathered together in my name, there am I in the midst of them.*" And perhaps he was – Kaster, David, even Christ.

McKilroy had recognized his mental leash. As he waited, he paced the pavement, never more than six steps in any direction. Ross could see that the man was so wound up with tension that he was liable to spring up and run off down the street. First Saleh and now this: McKilroy couldn't take much more. Ross knew only too well the inherent limits of a man motivated by fear. Each action he was required to take against his former friends increased his exposure to their terror; and on each occasion the countervailing threat had to be stepped up by his manipulators. And, since a man can only be scared so far, there would come a point at which the fear of both sides would be in the balance. And at that point he would break because there was no other logical thing to do; and he would run away with his feet or with his mind.

Ross surveyed the street again. The traders were administering Christmas like it was a drug to which the customers had built up a tolerance. He counted the Santa Claus figures visible in this section. On the north side of the street one who seemed to be associated with the store. Another carrying a sandwich board advertising tours in the sun. And on the south side a third sat in a doorway and handed leaflets from his sack. Some day the people were going to overdose on season's greetings and goodwill.

He checked his watch. Four-thirty. Kaster was already there, unrevealed but palpable. The delay put a strain on the watchers. No one can stay put indefinitely, vans have to move, people have to start walking. If a meeting is too long delayed, the structure of a surveillance operation starts to crack apart and an informed eye can identify the bits as they break off. If Kaster was prepared to wait it out, he would eventually know for sure whether Denny McKilroy was being watched.

Ross moved off his pitch outside the store and crossed the road. Kaster might or might not know that he was there, but he had already scored a point by forcing Ross to open up the distance between himself and McKilroy. Ross watched the Irishman from the opposite pavement across a stream of traffic that hissed past in a veil of headlights and rain. He started to hail taxis on the safe assumption that he was unlikely to be embarrassed by one actually stopping. Meantime it looked good and took his mind from the extra seconds it would take him to cross the road again.

He felt a nudge at his elbow.

"Peace be with you. Take this sample of the word of God." A

hand held out a religious tract printed on cheap paper. "Do you suppose yon bastard is no going to show up?"

He recognized Bliss. The Scot was wearing a threadbare suit and a black, sleeveless plastic overjacket carrying a slogan in white. "Christ said 'No man cometh to the Father but by me.' John 14:6."

"Is that true?"

Bliss looked down at his chest. "I wouldn't know, laddie, I'm Jewish. Now will you take the bloody pamphlet? It looks good for both our covers."

"What does Calverton want?"

"Kaster. Alive. Me and Figgis called on your place last night to persuade you to stay away today, but you weren't at home." He blew into his handkerchief and muttered about his cold, then continued: "Looks like we needn't have bothered. He isn't going to show. He was probably expecting some final check-in from Saleh; and when he didn't get it he called the whole business off."

There was logic in that. Saleh was acting the role of "cut-out" and in theory was a shield between Kaster and any other party.

"Maybe," said Ross. He doubted that Saleh would have stood for the painstaking detail, the mindless routines that that implied. "If I were Kaster—"

"Don't tell me," Bliss cut him short in his cheerless Glaswegian. "If you were Kaster, you'd leave Denny McKilroy standing around until his bum froze, just to see what happened. See whether the watchers got bored and started to fidget. Put a bit of pressure on and see what gives; and go in only when you're one hundred per cent happy." He gave a sigh that tried to squeeze twenty years of experience into it, then cleared his throat. "Well, maybe he should. But that's textbook stuff. The real world is never that professional. We all piss about like amateurs and the man who cocks it up least is the winner." He looked across the street, then checked his watch. "Looks like this is the end of the shift." He made the sign of the cross over Ross. "Peace be with you, brother."

Ross looked to where the other man had been looking. At Denny McKilroy, standing by the store, checking his own watch and waiting for the sign. He glanced back to Bliss. The Scot was shambling away in search of a pub. They were going to abort the operation. It had been decided that Kaster wasn't going to show. "Tant pis," as Calverton would doubtless say.

Across the road a car moved slowly, pulled against the pavement and opened a door. Santa Claus of the sunshine tours stepped up to McKilroy and ushered him towards the vehicle. And then it happened. Two shots rang out. Santa Claus took one in the chest and went flying into the roadway, brakes squealing, horns blasting. The second shattered both windows in the rear of the car. Rain dripped off it and revealed its colours: Prussian blue, spangled with reflected light, a Rover. Someone reached out and pulled McKilroy in and the car shot off with the sound of a horn that cut the traffic in half.

Ross was already midway across the street as the second shot was fired. He saw the trousers and heels of the second Santa Claus disappearing into the store through the main entrance under the bronze clock and the twin Christmas-trees. The crowd behaved as crowds do: screamed murder, looked to the victim not the perpetrator, spilled out into the street, blocked the doors. Ross forced his way through and into the ground-floor shopping-hall.

People were still flooding towards the main doors. Children stabbed at their mothers' hands and pulled them in the direction of the exit. Department supervisors in neat dresses and floorwalkers in banker's suits formed little knots in the aisles and issued calming noises. There was no sign of Kaster.

An assistant in the cosmetics department came running along, waving a bundle of scarlet cloth. The Santa Claus costume was a simple full-length robe, open down the whole of one side and fixed with a Velcro fastener. It could be taken off in the space and time it took to go through a swing door. The robe and beard were a magician's props and the whole trick was invisible precisely because it was done in a crowd. Kaster had pulled it off like a piece of grand stage illusion and was free and clear somewhere within the store.

The news of the killing was still sucking people out. Ross fought his way through the cosmetics department, a one-man counter-current. Hundreds of faces. Dozens of them might be Kaster's. Ross was acting with an instinctive sense of the other man's plan, assuming automatically that the terrorist would make for the nearest clear exit. From the fact that Kaster had taken the right-hand one of the three central doors, Ross guessed that he would pick the way out into Duke Street. If his quarry chose any of the other alternatives, then Calverton's men ought to have moved to cover them – assuming that they had kept their heads.

Ross brushed his way past handbags and umbrellas. Since Kaster's appearance was an unknown, searching for him was trying to detect an emanation. The man was in some way marked out. His very absence was as tangible as the wake of a ship. He had charisma, aura, presence – whatever the name was. He should be branded with the mark of the beast. Or with a halo like a saint in a painting.

At the Duke Street exit old ladies like hens squeezing into a coop pushed and struggled to get out of the door. This side of the store dealt in women's shoes and accessories, and there were no men there except one who was so securely middle-aged and in the possession of his wife that his chance of being Kaster was nil. The killer had beaten Ross to the door or had chosen another exit or had another plan altogether. Ross couldn't know which. He beat a path back in the direction he had come. Had Kaster decided to stay in the store? – hang around moving from department to department, turning into white flesh as colours blend to form white light, undifferentiated in the mass of shoppers? Did the man have the nerve for that?

By the main door there was chaos. People drawn to the macabre spectacle. People repelled by it. Management trying to draw up a cordon to hold people back but simply blocking the aisles and adding to the confusion. Ross slipped among them and made his way out on to the Oxford Street pavement. More chaos there. The road blocked with stationary cars. Milling people. And somewhere, above the cacophony of horns, the impotent wailing of an ambulance trying to get through. He looked around for Calverton's man.

He found him still in the Santa Claus costume, lying on a bed of flattened cardboard boxes where he had been moved. Ross couldn't recognize him under the beard; maybe had never even met him. A circle of pedestrians stood around, women clutching their handbags, children shouting that they wanted to see. A man in a poplin raincoat and a tweed hat with a feather in the side patrolled a small circuit around the body announcing: "There is no cause for alarm, the Saint John's Ambulance Brigade are here. Please do not panic. I am in the Saint John's Ambulance Brigade and have the situation completely under control."

Bliss, sombre in his rain-spattered suit, was kneeling over the lying figure and using one of his religious tracts to wipe away the water from the injured man's face. Bliss's own face was moisture-streaked. To Ross it looked like tears but he couldn't be sure. The other man was murmuring: "Oh fuck, oh fuck, oh fuck, oh fuck."

The man in the poplin raincoat looked down at the body clinically. "He's a goner for sure," he said to Bliss. "You're the padre. It's up to you to do the right thing, say the words or what have you."

Bliss looked at Ross in wordless anguish, nervously scratched his backside then put one hand under the dying man's head and raised it so that the pale face and the blood on the white beard were visible. "Oh fuck," he mouthed again silently, "and me Jewish." But his manner was reverent and, after murmuring the words of the Shema, just in case, he began falteringly: "Do you believe in God the Father, God the Son and God the Holy Ghost?"

Ross turned back into the store. A measure of order was creeping in. People were standing in silence while Bliss improvised his prayers. Management was reasserting its control. Even so no one questioned Ross's right to come and go as he chose. His face said that he had that right, and no one gainsaid it. Suddenly, on this point he knew his enemy. Kaster was an illusionist. He had drawn the attention of his pursuers to the other exits from the store. So he would leave by the one he had used to enter. Ross felt with certainty that Kaster was waiting in the crowd mixing in the cosmetics department until he could go out by the main doors. His problem still was to find him.

Back in the store Ross scanned the faces and clothes of men in the likely age-bracket – thirty to forty – to be Kaster. Damn it, the man wasn't invisible! He had done things, worn things – fired a gun, put on a Santa Claus robe and white beard. The illusion itself had to carry its after-image, some trace of its having happened. Ross tried to fix what he had seen. The glimpse of the other man's trousers – a neutral blue – maybe. The man's shoes – brown, but no indication of style. Height? So-so: the costume had a hood with a rising point that hid things like that. All of it dots of colour filling out a vague shape.

Men in their thirties came and went. They approached the main entrance, saw that it was crowded and went to one of the other ones. Ross ignored them. They were not Kaster. He felt the other man somewhere at the periphery, watching the crowd but not of it, an inconspicuous shopper buying perfume for his girlfriend, a husband buying make-up for his wife. Ross filtered through the management cordon and strolled down one of the aisles with the same assumed indifference. He took a plastic shopping-bag from his pocket. It was empty, except for a barbecue skewer.

In the Army, Ross had once been taught to play Chess-*Kriegspiel*. The rules were the same as for chess save for one. Each player could see only his own pieces. The enemy was unknown. It tied the logic of chess to the feel and instinct of the hunt, and the consequence of a

169

mistake could be swift and destructive. Now Kaster had converted the situation into a deadlier version of the game – except, perhaps, for one twist. Just because Ross did not know Kaster, it did not follow that Kaster could not identify him.

Men in nondescript blue trousers and brown shoes wore them like a uniform. Ross counted half a dozen in little more than a minute. Single men. Men with their wives. A man aged thirty-five or so, dark-haired and strikingly good-looking in an almost feminine way, followed on the heels of his spouse or girlfriend, stopping when she stopped, admiring the lipsticks she admired and testing the perfume-samplers. Was Kaster necessarily alone? Or was he so elusive that no part of any description of him was *necessarily* true? Some things, like Nirvana, were capable of being defined only by what they were not. The notion that that might be true of a person held an element of horror.

Near to Ross the woman stopped. She held up a lipstick to the light to judge its colours. Brown eyes and bronze shadow. She caught the note of Ross's interest and treated him to an uncertain smile, the smallest glimpse of her teeth. She gave the same smile to her husband except that her husband would never get that particular smile. Ross glanced at him and continued walking in the direction he was going without breaking his pace. He knew that he had seen Kaster.

The other man detached himself from the woman with the bronze eyeshadow and deftly attached himself to another without her knowing: suggesting, with wordless gestures and nuances like the distance he kept from her, a relationship. Ross watched and admired. In other circumstances he would have applauded.

He insinuated himself into the stream of people moving behind his quarry, observing the other man closely. He had to be sure for what he was going to do. Kaster continued his performance, apparently oblivious of Ross's presence. Ross suddenly realized that that was no more than the truth. The other man was obsessed with the detail of his own pose. He didn't know, he didn't *care* whether Ross could see him. Kaster had fallen into the fundamental narcissism of terrorism that makes the terrorist's view of the world more important than the views or even the lives of others. "Qu'importent les gens si le geste est beau?" said Calverton, quoting somebody-or-other. The revolutionary act was more truly a revolutionary performance – a piece of theatre and no more substantial.

Kaster now seemed real in Ross's eyes, a man with a faintly ironic smile and epicenely handsome. He was wearing a brown leather jacket and on the shoulders scarlet fibres from the Santa Claus robe were dimly visible. He seemed diminished, an actor without his buskins. Ross approached him from behind and said the one word, "Kaster", loud enough only so that the other man should hear. The terrorist turned, but like an actor staring across the footlights in reality saw nothing. Ross gripped the skewer inside the bag and drove it into his enemy's abdomen, then forced the bag into the other's hands. Kaster gripped the point with one hand whilst his whole body swung round and his free hand swept across the nearest counter and scattered the sprays and jars and lotions across the floor. His mouth opened but words could not come out and slowly his knees began to buckle until he finally collapsed, turned away and fell with his features buried in the drift of face-powder that lay about him on the ground.

"This man's had a heart-attack. I suggest you get a doctor." Ross addressed the nearest assistant, who was standing with her lips open and maybe screaming, Ross couldn't tell because his own senses were focused like a laser on what he had done and had to do. He glanced at the body. It was face down on the floor, the small puncture-wound would scarcely bleed and would likely be covered by the folds of the dead man's clothes and the bag which he was holding in his frozen fist. Ross had retrieved the skewer as he stabbed the other man and it was safely in his sleeve, to be wiped and ditched within a matter of seconds. There was nothing else. It was over.

"Have I done enough at last?" he asked his dead brother.

Chapter Eighteen

THE ARRIVAL at Cairo involved the usual airport hassle, the obligatory changing of hard currency for Egyptian pounds, the visa check, the baggage recovery and the eventual wait for a taxi in the dark chill of the evening under the eye of Horus, the hawks-head symbol of Egyptian Airways.

The billboards along the road to town insisted that Coca-Cola was the real thing; but somehow Cairo wasn't. The city was striving to become Marlboro country, pulled between its past and its present, the tension between the two visible in the creeping collapse of the old and the unfinished construction of the new. It looked as if the place had been abandoned and then reoccupied by nomads, who were camping on the ruins and throwing up buildings that were every bit as impermanent as their tents.

The Ramses Hilton was shiny new. It looked out over the Nile to the island of Zamalik. There stood the embassy quarter and the homes of the wealthy. The Ghezira and the National Sporting Clubs suggested a fading imperialism. Donaldson paid off the cab and checked in at the hotel. There were separate rooms for himself and the girl.

On the plane she had talked about Anthony. Within a couple of days of their encounter at Sebastian Summer's home, she and Anthony had quarrelled. He was too unstable, she said. "More to the point, he wasn't *going* anywhere." Her lips flickered uncertainly as she said this and, avoiding his eyes, she ordered something from the air hostess.

Now she was cheerful. They had changed and gone together into one of the restaurants. She was wearing a dress that set off the blue of her eyes and the sapphire studs in her ears. She was relaxed. She was somewhere new. They dined with the other well-heeled clients and she rolled out stories of her recent trip to Ceylon. *Theravada* Buddhism, as practised in Ceylon, she said, was *the* thing. They were right: existence *was* suffering. Donaldson remembered that Anthony had made the same point to Sebastian Summer when he had left his farewell note and the ivory figure of the Buddha. It was the small change of oriental religion.

She ordered something that required the attentions of the waiter. He arrived pushing a carriage that held a silver chafing-dish and a spirit-stove which flamed blue in the subdued light. He poured brandy into the dish and let it flash, and all the while he smiled a tense, conjuror's smile. Then, when the pyrotechnics were finished, he served the food and stood back for the applause he only ever heard in his head. Annaliese ignored him.

"We have to strive for the extinction of desire, the extinction of self," she said. She cut a piece of meat, tasted it and pushed the food aside. "Do you agree?" she asked and then interjected: "I'm not sure that I do. There are times when I feel as though the whole world is myself. At other times I feel as though I have no self at all – but it doesn't feel like Enlightenment." She shrugged her shoulders, asked for some ice-cream and while she ate it stared past Donaldson at something beyond him.

The subject changed.

"What is this man Egger like?" she asked.

Donaldson wasn't sure of the answer. He knew and didn't know the man. He had two pictures, portraits by different artists. Somewhere between the description of Egger by the old dealer, Aaron Eichbaum, and the account revealed in the records of the German's post-war imprisonment by the British the man had changed. The humane, cultivated man who had tried to save a Jewish friend from the camps had become absorbed by the dark world of Hermann Goering. The man questioned by the British showed the animal caution he had learned from the workings of the Nazi leaders; alternately arrogant or ingratiating with his captors as served him best. Egger's make-up showed that drop of fundamental corruption, like Original Sin.

"He sold himself out to his ambition," Donaldson said and left it at that.

After dinner they went to their own rooms. Donaldson had brought a book with him on the subject of Leonardo, and for an hour he sat at the table turning over the colour plates, trying to see with his mind's eye how Leonardo would have painted the Last Judgement. In the end he gave up: Leonardo was a genius precisely because of the

173

uniqueness of his vision. Donaldson showered for the second time and slipped into bed.

The sound of Annaliese tapping on the door woke him. He found her in the corridor, shivering from the air-conditioned chill. She had been to bed and then dressed again hurriedly: her feet were bare beneath her trousers and her breasts pressed softly against the cotton panels of her shirt.

"I didn't want to be alone," she said.

Donaldson fixed them both a drink from the mini-bar. She sat on the edge of the bed, her hands cupped and her toes grazing the carpet. She drank the whisky in one mouthful then took off her clothes, folded them carefully over a chair and lay down on the bed staring blankly at her own reflection in the opposing mirror.

Donaldson finished his own drink and turned off the reading-lamp, leaving only the faint glow of the city lights. He looked at the girl. Her eyes were closed, the mole on her cheek was a dark spot and her short fair hair shimmered palely. He put his lips to her breasts and touched the nipples into life. Her eyes opened. His hands quivered over the line of down in the hollow of her recumbent belly and touched her gently, uncertainly. He was in fact uncertain about her. He sensed that same quality that Anthony possessed: a personality that was collapsing under the mass of its own delusions and ceasing to give off light; a personality that had the gravity to drag others down with it. His fingers reached for the moist folds between her legs. Her own hand was there.

Annaliese's eyes still looked at his. They held a glimpse of humour. Donaldson's hand lay on her wrist and he felt her fingers working towards her own climax. He tried to draw back but her other hand held him there in complicity. Her eyes displayed the same bleakly ironic look and her lips gradually withdrew into a tight grimace of thrill until suddenly both eyes and mouth vacated their expression and with a moan and an exhalation of breath she was released.

Afterwards she let go of Donaldson's hand and lay back, holding her hands to the pale light from the window and forming a vaginal cat's cradle with her fingers. "I'm sorry," she said at last. "But my way" – she paused over the words – "the *pictures* are better."

The Pension El Ezbekiyah had been the Pension Ferdinand de Lesseps until the old colonial reminders fell out of favour; but in the brash new Cairo it still stood in a side-street off the Shari Sherif, a piece of Catholic France moved out of time and space to slot next to a religious-supplies shop that served the needs of the parishioners of nearby St Joseph's. The façade was of barred windows on the ground floor then balconies of wrought iron and blind shutters, the crumbling stucco adding its portion of dust to the dust of the street.

Donaldson and Annaliese found the entrance to the street blocked against the traffic by sections of concrete storm-drain standing in wait for the day when they would be laid. There was a deep trench scored into the grey sandy subsoil and running the length of the street, but the connection with the storm-drain was like as not accidental, and the piles of cement and loose scaffolding bore no evident relationship to anything that was going on.

In the shadow of the hotel doorway a group of men were playing *basra* in a litter of 7-Up bottles and cigarettes, slapping down the greasy cards and scooping up fistfuls of five-piastre notes. Donaldson pushed past them and routed the concierge out of his booth.

The old man grinned with a mouth of burned-out teeth, straightened his turban and pulled his jellaba around him to keep his secrets. Yes, Monsieur Egger was a guest, he managed to say in broken French; he had been a guest for many, many years – here he shook his head and laughed to suggest that Egger was somehow the resident freak – he and his wife had a "suite" of rooms on the second floor from which they ran their import–export business; he would be glad to show them up.

They struggled up the battered staircase, hindered by their guide, who paused every few steps to wink and beckon them to see his prize exhibit. Finally they reached a landing and a door bearing a bakelite plaque with an inscription in Arabic and below it: "Egger et Cie. – Agents de Commerce Internationale." The old man knocked at the door and then stood behind Annaliese to peek over her shoulder.

The woman addressed them at first in Arabic. Then she saw them more clearly and asked in English: "Who are you? What do you want?" Her voice was nervous, the door was open on a security chain, and her pale face, lined with a suspicion that didn't belong there naturally, peered round the edge. She caught sight of the concierge and began to abuse him in his own tongue until he scurried off cackling to himself and disappeared down the stairs.

"We should like to see Herr Egger," Donaldson said.

"Why? What about? Herr Egger sees no one." Behind her words

she needed the company, wanted to be persuaded that there was nothing to fear.

"We want to talk to him about the Last Judgement."

"Ah!" she murmured as if the request were a revelation. "At last!"

At first the room seemed in darkness. A few slats of daylight, sliced up by the closed shutters, caught up the motes of dust in the blue haze. Then they saw that the gloom was underpainted with the glow and flicker of candles. They stood in ranks on a marble-topped washstand and illuminated the painting on the wall above them and a few nearby brass objects.

"Would you like some coffee?" Frau Egger asked. She appeared more clearly now, a small, frail woman, her grey hair in pin curls over little-girl features. She wore a washed-out frock in indigo cotton printed with cabbage roses in cream and pink. Donaldson declined the coffee. "Something else?" she enquired. He followed her eyes to the corner. Next to a bank of filing-cabinets and a clapped-out roll-top desk, a pile of empty bottles mouldered.

"My husband is out," she said. She had settled into a chair, her hands folded on her lap, apparently prepared to sit in silence. Habits of conversation had been leached out of her in long isolation and she was content to watch the play of emotions on her guests' faces and speculate as to their meaning.

"When will he be back?" asked Annaliese.

"Half an hour, an hour." Then, urgently: "Please, stay, wait for him."

"I think I should like that coffee," said Donaldson. Then, while she stepped outside and found the boy who slept under the stairs, he looked around the room. He wanted to know what had happened to Reinhardt Egger in his thirty-five-year exile.

The room was both office and living-space. Grey cabinets, a desk, files piled on the floor in a scattering of papers going brown and faded, with age. Cane furniture, a table holding a bottle of Johnnie Walker Red Label and a dirty glass, an ancient radiogramophone with its speaker covered by a fretwork of flying birds. It all said that the business existed only as a ghost of the imagination and the reality was a life eked out in poverty on remittances from Germany.

Donaldson turned to the washstand with its display of candles. It had been roughly coated with gold paint. The pieces of brass were a crucifix, a chalice and a platter for holding the Host, and the painting was of Christ Pantocrator. It was a Russian icon and its price would buy and sell the Pension El Ezbekiyah five times over.

"Come here," said Annaliese in a hushed voice. "Look at this." She had opened the door into a second room.

Even the bizarre altar with its priceless icon did not prepare Donaldson for this other room. The first impression was of gold and scarlet, raw sensations of colour that at first seemed incapable of resolution into objects. There was too much light. It was poured out of candles by the hundred, caught by surfaces of gold and glass and thrown back and forward in a crossfire of mirrors so that the shrine of altars and images was locked in a prism, the effect of a kaleidoscope.

Egger had turned everything to his purpose. The baroque surface of things was an illusion imposed on a miscellany of junk that had been taken and cunningly worked into the chapel's scheme. Bottles, wire coat-hangers, plastic cartons, a motor-car radiator-grille: the trappings of modernity had been taken, twisted, gilded and tricked out with bits of broken glass and then put together and their ephemeral existence suffused with meaning, obscure though that meaning might be. The superficial gorgeousness suggested mockery; but whether the junk was mocking religion or religion was mocking modern trash, it was impossible to say. The mockery was locked like the reflections of opposed mirrors, each inseparably repeating the other's image into infinity.

Within all this, Christ in every painted mood and facet judged the observer from a hundred pictures hung on the walls of the shrine.

"Nice, isn't it?" said Frau Egger. She had come back into the main room and resumed her place with same placidness as before. An Egyptian boy had come in with her and he now applied himself to pouring out the measures of sweet coffee from the small copper jugs.

"Has your husband always been . . . like this?" Donaldson asked. He wasn't sure what "like this" covered. Egger had gone through another of his changes. Donaldson knew the civilized liberal of Egger's youth and the arrogant Nazi that the British had caught. He even empathized. But who was the other man in this new avatar?

"Like this?" Frau Egger's voice floated over the words as she repeated them. Donaldson decided the question wasn't worth pursuing. He went to the window and peered through the shutter into the street. It was difficult to believe that the seething, dusty babble of Cairo was still there. The Eggers had abstracted themselves and created their private, symbol-obsessed world.

From the corner by the Shari Sherif a figure appeared, an old man, struggling over the potholes and debris with the aid of a stick and using the same instrument to shake off a tail of ragged children who danced at his heels. He wore a baggy suit in blue and white seersucker and a straw panama. Under one arm he clutched a parcel. Donaldson returned to his chair and waited for the tap-tap of the cane and the knock at the door when it came. Frau Egger admitted her husband and shooed away the broken-toothed concierge.

"Reinhardt," she said. She took the hat and cane and poured a shot of whisky out of habit. "We have visitors."

"Who?" The voice was faintly husky. Without looking at Donaldson or Annaliese he unwrapped a parcel of candles and began to replace the spent stubs on the washstand altar. "What do they want?"

"They want to talk to you about the Last Judgement," she said and added again, "at last."

Now he turned. Two pale-blue eyes peered from the sockets of a face that was shrivelled with age and sun. The remnants of his fair hair clung to a scalp that was burned to peeling and flecked with liver spots. He deposited himself heavily in one of the cane chairs and out of his pocket took a set of beads; they were the Muslim kind, used in cycles of thirty-three to tell off the names of Allah.

"I knew you would come," he said without any enquiry as to their identity. Out of the image-charged atmosphere pictures of past encounters tumbled into Donaldson's sight: Faust and Mephistopheles; Mohammed and the Angel Gabriel; the Annunciation – Leonardo had painted the Annunciation.

"Why?"

Egger poured out the dregs of Red Label and slung the bottle to lodge with the pile in the corner.

"I am suffering from cancer. This" – he flicked a hand across his chest – "is just a remission. Today, tomorrow, some time soon, I shall be dead. So it had to be now, don't you see?"

Donaldson did see. He saw where so much youthful promise, hope and ambition had led to: an old man hesitating on the brink of sanity, waiting for his personal apocalypse.

"Where to begin?" Egger asked.

"With the painting of the Last Judgement," Donaldson suggested.

"Yes, there – why not there? Beginnings and endings – there's a certain symmetry, don't you think?"

178

Donaldson agreed. He agreed to anything that kept the old man talking.

"In a sense that's where it starts, there. Every idea has its germ, so why not in the painting?" Egger wagged a finger at his visitors. "You're too clever for me. I knew you would be. Ever so clever. Get to the essence of things, the idea behind the idea. Where do we begin in all the beginnings? You must tell me." For all the clouded implications in his speech, Egger's voice was firm.

"Let's start with Prince Jerzy Wolski," said Donaldson.

Egger's tone was biblical. There came a man, he said. From Poland. His name was Prince Jerzy Wolski, scion of a famous house, whose founder, the scarlet woman Katerina, begat Andrzej who begat Stanislaw who begat etcetera to the sixth generation.

This Prince Wolski, he confirmed, had fled Poland to escape the clutches of the dictator, Marshal Pilsudski.

"Because he was a communist," said Donaldson, remembering the account of Hortense Ainsworth. Reinhardt Egger laughed.

"Because he was a criminal!" he said.

This criminal, Prince Wolski, he went on, escaped to Paris with his beautiful wife Helena. Both of them being of the conservative aristocracy and anti-Semitic by hallowed Polish tradition, they were readily agreeable to working for the Sixth Bureau of RSHA, the Nazi foreign intelligence service. Princess Helena Wolska infiltrated those Parisian circles who sympathized with the Spanish Republican cause in the Civil War; Prince Jerzy, meanwhile, cultivated friends in the French political establishment, using as his cover an art business funded by the Gestapo.

Egger halted there. He snapped his fingers and his wife filled his glass again with whisky. He threw the drink back in one and then rambled on.

"We – the Nazis – were actively buying works of art in Paris. Hitler, Goering, and all the smaller fry. Wolski began selling things to them. He started to take his own cover seriously. In his limited way he became quite knowledgeable about paintings. And that set him thinking about his ancestral home."

"And *The Last Judgement*."

"Exactly!" Another pause. More drink, but Egger seemed unaffected. "There was a family story", he resumed, "about the altarpiece that hung in the chapel. The Emperor Napoleon had given

179

it to the family hero, Marshal-Prince Stanisław Wolski, for saving the Emperor's life in the 1812 campaign, or some such. It was by Leonardo da Vinci, there was never any doubt, but the Wolskis had never excited themselves about the fact. It was taken for granted in the way that the very rich can be careless about their inherited wealth."

With his uncertain future as an alien in Nazi Europe and with his new-found knowledge of art, Wolski had begun to see possibilities in the painting. He found to his surprise that *The Last Judgement* was an unknown work, liable to be overlooked unless one knew of it. And with that he realized that, while he did not have the picture, he had knowledge; and, in the right circumstances that could be equally valuable.

He decided to sell the information; but, being essentially unprincipled, he tried to deal with both Hitler and Goering, to sell to the higher bidder.

He compounded this error by actually selling to both men.

"I was sent by Goering to seize the picture from the Bereznica Palace before it was removed by the Poles or looted. The mission was a secret because Goering knew that, if he ever found out, Hitler would force the Reichsmarschall to give it to him."

"But you were too late."

"Yes." Egger shook his head in bitter recollection. "Hitler's agent, a man named Schimmel, who worked for Sonderauftrag Linz, was already at the house with a party of soldiers when we arrived. I had . . . to make a decision." Donaldson knew what that decision was, but the old man went on: "I saw the painting. It. . . ." He struggled over the feeling that possessed him, mumbling inadequate words that were inaudible to Donaldson. Then he lifted his head so that his eyes shone clearly and said: "It opened a window into the depths of my own soul."

With that the old man fell silent. He had made his choice and chosen evil. He had killed Schimmel and the others and possessed himself of the painting. And in the process he had broken with the past. Before he had cherished the belief that he could work with the Nazis and remain immaculate. There in Bereznica he made his commitment. Like the Ancient Mariner, he slew the albatross.

He shook himself and grimaced with pain. His wife jerked out of her chair and began to busy herself frantically with the contents of a small drawer in the desk. For the moment Donaldson ignored her.

He still needed to know. What had Egger done with the painting? where was it now? Had he really flown it out of Germany in those last days using the aircraft that been commandeered under Operation Jüngster Tag?

Busy as a squirrel, Frau Egger came over to her husband's chair, holding an enamelled kidney-bowl. It contained a syringe and an ampoule of liquid. Donaldson guessed at morphine to still the pain that was killing the other man. She filled the hypodermic, careless as to the exact amount, and squirted out a mist of droplets that hung in the air. Egger rolled up his sleeve and bared the prominent veins of his forearm.

Annaliese moved from her place and Frau Egger, in her quiet, knowing way, stepped aside. The girl took the syringe and the old man allowed her to pinch up a vein and slide the needle through the skin. She pressed the plunger and was about to remove the instrument when Egger's free hand gripped her wrist and his pale eyes looked up into her face. Seconds passed, he took the syringe from her and drew the plunger back to draw a mixture of blood and morphine into the clear vial. He repeated the process of injecting and withdrawing the drug several times with a sigh and then leaned back with his eyes closed and the needle hanging from his arm. The girl removed the syringe and replaced it in the bowl.

"Wait!" Frau Egger said. "He won't go to sleep. The pain is too strong." And as if to confirm that statement Egger shuddered and his eyes half-opened.

"What more?" he asked.

"Where is the painting now?" said Donaldson.

"Here." He gestured faintly with his right hand. "Here. This is my Last Judgement."

Donaldson couldn't tell whether this was meant literally or not. In his world of guilt and dreams, clouded by alcohol and morphine, the old man must perceive him as a phantom, barely real at all.

"In the other room!" urged Frau Egger, tugging eagerly at Donaldson's sleeve. He looked at her disbelievingly, then turned on his heels quickly and went into Egger's private shrine.

His sight adjusted slowly to the chaos of gold, light and mirrors and to the eyes of Christ staring down in a hundred forms from the walls. The high altar was an old refrigerator, gilded and stuck with fragments of glass and railed off by the grille and bumper off a 1950s Chevrolet glittering with chrome. Above the altar the icon was covered by a crimson curtain. Donaldson drew it back.

The painting blazed at him in the richness of its colours. He staggered back stunned with its awesome grandeur, his mind recoiling from the images of despair, from the faces of the damned to whom torture itself would have been a release from the terror of their isolation and abandonment by God. He stood there for some minutes and then felt rather than saw his way back into the shadows of the other room.

BOOK TWO

If there were a God, how could I
bear not to be God?

NIETZSCHE

Chapter Nineteen

JAMES ROSS pushed his way through the crowd of people who were rushing to slake their curiosity on the spectacle in Oxford Street. It was now fully dark, the rain was falling harder, and with the hood on his parka pulled up he walked the glistening streets south towards the river.

As far as he knew, Kaster was dead, but he felt no satisfaction in the fact. Just the bleak knowledge that he had been compelled to do something that he did not want to do. He felt only anger towards Calverton and towards his dead brother who had fallen for the spy's myth of patriotism, power and professionalism.

By walking and catching a bus he made his way to the dreary offices mirrored in the pavement of Battersea High Street. The girl behind the desk started to give her stock patter to redirect customers to the Department of Trade in Victoria Street.

"I want to see Calverton," he interrupted.

She was visibly shocked. "I'm afraid you must be mistaken. We have no Mr Calverton here."

"Let's find out, shall we?" Ross pointed to the bell-push by her toes. "Hit the panic-button and we'll see what sort of gorilla falls out of the trees."

She hit it.

The gorillas were two in number, piling down the stairs, straightening out their ties without spilling their drinks. One had a paper hat straight out of a cracker and the other a light-up bow-tie. They both looked as though they had nasty ideas about the appropriate Season's Greetings.

"It's OK; we know him," the taller one said curtly to the receptionist. He gave her a receipt for Ross's body and handed a visitor's pass to Ross.

"Have I interrupted something?" Ross asked as he was escorted upstairs. "Maybe the spies' Christmas party?"

"That's it," said the talkative one. "We just got our presents; that's why we're so cheerful."

"Don't tell me – the KGB desk-diaries?"

"That was last year. Wait here." He pushed open the door into the room where the party was going on.

It was an open-plan office with the stock Ministry furnishings and the usual tasteful grey and green paint-job. A Christmas-tree with lights winked from a table in the centre among a pile of parcels and sherry-bottles. Someone had improvised paper streamers out of declassified reports that were waiting for the shredder. A dozen or so dancers were creeping a waltz to the tune of "Moon River": typists in their late thirties, wearing their daughters' cast-off ra-ra skirts; men in their late thirties, in shirt-sleeves and shoulder-holsters.

Bliss, the Glaswegian Jew, had beaten Ross there. He was still wearing his black tabard with its biblical quotations and was maudlin drunk. He broke away from the group he was leaning on and came over to Ross, booming as he went: "Tell them, Jimmy!" To the others: "This is the man! He was there if you don't believe me. C'mon, Jimmy, tell them. Hear this and see if it doesn't make you laugh."

"What do you want?"

"Tell these buggers what Figgis's last words were." He lowered his voice and pleaded: "You must have heard them, Jimmy. Tell this bunch of cunts what he said."

"I didn't hear."

Bliss paused then turned to the others and in a loud voice said: "See, I told you he'd confirm what I said. I asked Figgis, 'Did he believe in God the Father, God the Son and God the Holy Spirit?' and he said . . . he said . . . he said, 'Of course I do, you stupid sod, I'm bloody Father Christmas!' "

Calverton had added homely touches to his office: his personal electric kettle and coffee-set, his framed photographs of steam locomotives in Great Western livery, an out-of-date *Wisden* holding down the contents of his in-tray. The man himself was in residence, sitting in a button-backed chair with a melancholy, self-absorbed air. He looked like a man who had suffered a loss.

"You can go," he said to Ross's escort. While the room cleared, he studied a book on his desk then closed it and laid it carefully to one side. "Why did you want to see me?" he asked.

"To close accounts, call off the dogs, get you off my back – however you want to call it. I want to go back to the life I thought I had without worrying every day that someone is going to come after me. It's enough that I killed Kaster for you."

"Kaster isn't dead," said Calverton as if he didn't care. "Critically ill and likely to die but, strictly speaking, alive."

"Put it down to my lack of practice," said Ross.

"It wasn't supposed to work out like this," Calverton continued in his sombre, distracted mood. "We had intended – thought we had – a meticulous plan. It was all worked out in detail in the games-room: everyone playing a part, each taking turns at every role. Do you follow? We had full input, all the variations. Figgis was particularly good as Kaster."

Ross followed, but not in the sense that Calverton meant. The SAS had flirted with the game-play approach. Get under the skin of your opponent; develop the alternative perceptions of the situations, the alternative lines of action; act out the enemy's part. The CIA, with their instinct for the perverse, had taken the American obsession with self-improvement and self-awareness and converted the techniques of encounter-groups into a weapon. Now it had a stale ring like the optimism of the sixties, but Calverton had picked up the idea somewhere – Langley on open-day when he was trailed around as the token Brit? – and, in the way of someone who at heart was deeply conservative, he had kept the idea as a talisman of his modernity. Ross guessed that the CIA had meanwhile passed him by. By now they had probably invented whole-food espionage.

"But plans don't work out like that," he said at last. "Bliss, out there pissed to the eyeballs, got it right: we all go from foul-up to foul-up. Professionalism is just advertising copy, something to tell the punters so that they can sleep at night."

"Do you think so?" Calverton asked. "Well, maybe. But don't you see that we have *got* to make plans, got to try to control things, to keep the whole show on a rational basis? That's the difference between us and the terrorists: they face us from the other side, from chaos and unreason. Even with the best of plans, the state of order in the world is so . . . frail."

Calverton looked away and stroked the tips of his ginger moustache. "Did you know," he resumed brokenly, "that Kaster killed Figgis?"

Ross saw the picture of Santa Claus lying on the pavement, his white beard splashed with blood.

"Bliss told me," he said. He examined the book lying on the other man's desk, the one that Calverton had been reading for solace. It was a story for schoolboys by G. A. Henty, a tale from many years ago, how golden-haired youths had saved the British Empire. Ross suddenly realized that that was what Calverton had seen in his brother David and in Figgis, too. Figgis was not the psychopath in harness that Ross remembered; he had been transfigured into the high-spirited public-school hero of juvenile fiction – perhaps, in Calverton's imagination, had always been that. And now, somewhere inside the older man, tears were welling up for poor dead Figgis, former sadist and present martyr.

Chapter Twenty

"THE painting is yours," said Reinhardt Egger.

"Yes, of course." Donaldson's voice was empty of his spent emotions. Naturally the painting would be his. His mind had slipped into the old man's logic: they had drifted through the gallery of metaphors and found Wagner – it was the pursuit of the Holy Grail and he had fulfilled the terms of the Quest. No, this was crazy!

He looked about him. Frau Egger sat calmly by, her idiot's grin wiping out the features of her face. Egger racked his body with coughing and signalled for some water. He stilled a pain and waited. The two men watched each other. Donaldson felt that he was being invited to think with new patterns of thought – to follow a dark, visceral logic instead of his clear, cold reason – and he resisted it. His mind scrabbled around for questions in the loose shale of impressions.

"How did you manage to keep the picture? You stole it? Why? What did you tell Goering?"

Egger folded in on himself again. "I saw the picture," he said simply. "And I had to have it." Donaldson didn't need more; he had seen the painting and felt its power, and nothing Egger could add would make any more sense of it all.

"Goering", he went on, "didn't know. I told him that Schimmel and his men had got there first. Later the story was put out that Schimmel had been killed by Polish partisans."

"And some innocent Poles were shot for the crime."

"Yes, yes! And I suppose you've come to sit in judgement on me for that as well as for everything else. Well, go on, do it, do it!" Egger waited expectantly, and then, in his distracted mind, fresh recollections pushed out the present and he began on a new theme. "Hitler guessed."

"Guessed how much?"

"Some but not all." Egger was amused. "He thought that Goering had cheated him of *The Last Judgement*, but he couldn't prove it; so he looked for a more subtle form of revenge."

"Like what?"

"Oh, Goering acquired another Leonardo, the Spiridon *Leda*. Hitler made him hand it over. Compensation, if you like. You follow the irony of course? The Spiridon *Leda* was not an original: it was a copy. So Hitler was compensated with the gift of a fake!"

And that was it. The pursuit of Leonardo's *Last Judgement* ended here in the fractured visions of a madman. Yet Egger maintained the same brooding expectation, as if what he had told so far was a prelude and the words "Last Judgement" mere passwords. Even now he was waiting for Donaldson to go on. What was it? What spectre had Egger been appeasing with bell, book and candle in his private shrine for nearly forty years?

Annaliese, listening quietly and intently, found the key.

"What was Operation Last Judgement?" she asked. Except that she used the words "Jüngster Tag" as Donaldson remembered them from the British records. Instantly the old man became alive.

"The plane?" asked Donaldson. The record implied that Egger had commandeered an aircraft for Operation Last Judgement. What for? To fly a stolen painting out of the country? That couldn't be the reason. Egger had clearly been involved in something else more important than the theft of a work of art, something so terrible that, both at the time and now, he had compounded the two events into one great crime and called it his Last Judgement. And for God knew how many years he had been making conjurations in front of the golden refrigerator in the next room and the ever-haunting painting in the hope that the memory would go away.

"I will tell you about the plane," Egger said at last. "I will tell you a story about Hitler."

It was 20 April 1945 – the Führer's fifty-sixth birthday. The battle for Berlin was four days old, the Russians having nearly surrounded the city, but for this occasion Hitler emerged briefly from his bunker. It was a lacklustre celebration – no champagne – held in the Ehrenhof, the Court of Honour, of the Chancellery. At the end of an hour the newsreel photographers were sent packing and the Nazi bigwigs retired to the bunker for a dismal briefing on the military situation.

For many of the Führer's closest associates it would be the last time that they would see him. Most of the ministers were planning to leave

190

the capital. Heinrich Himmler would be heading north. Hermann Goering would go south after personally dynamiting the house that he had built on his fabulous estate at Karinhall. Neither man would see Hitler again.

Major Reinhardt Egger spent the day waiting on the instructions of his chief, kicking his heels on the fringes of the Führer's reception. He was expecting no orders. It was a duty-call for Goering, and he would be glad if he could get away without being criticized in front of the other top Nazis for the failures of the Luftwaffe. He was more interested in learning whether Hitler was himself planning on leaving for Bavaria. If not, then he was doomed to die in Berlin and Goering would become Führer by virtue of the decree of 29 June 1941. It was with a mixture of fear and ambition that the fat Reichsmarschall danced attendance on his leader.

The bunker beneath the Reichschancellery was divided into two. The upper bunker was the older part. The lower bunker had been built deeper as protection against heavier bombs. The briefing on the military situation took place in the lower bunker while Reinhardt Egger and the other aides waited in the communal dining-room in the upper area. It seemed a long wait, but the self-contained world of the Führer's entourage worked to its own time-zone, a Führer-Time geared to the drugged rhythms of Hitler's body. In reality he did not know whether he had been waiting five minutes or an hour when Martin Bormann pulled him out of the group of younger officers and ordered him to follow.

Bormann held the rank of *Reichsleiter,* which made him nominally no more than Hitler's secretary, but he had cocooned his master from the outside world and in virtually anything not in the military sphere he was the power in the Reich. He could afford to look at Goering with contempt.

Egger found Goering waiting in the conference-room, staring at the maps. His idea of the positions of the respective armies was hazy. He had long since lost faith in a victorious outcome to the war and, like Nero fiddling while Rome burned, had retired to his lavish estate and whiled away his time hunting and in contemplation of his art collection.

"The Führer will see you now," Bormann announced. He felt at the collar that pinched the flesh of his bull-neck. "Don't occupy him too long," he added. "He has lots of things to do; his health is not too good, and he hasn't the time to see people just for old time's sake."

"I understand," said Goering. He was subdued in the other man's presence, not knowing what was in store for him. More fury? More denigration? As if words would somehow resurrect the air force.

Hitler's study opened directly into the corridor which served as conference-room. The man himself was sitting at the desk that fitted tightly into the study's narrow confines. He was wearing a pair of spectacles never seen in public and in front of him had an open copy of Carlyle's biography of Frederick the Great. With the imminent collapse of his own ambitions, the successful efforts of the Prussian king against his own coalition of enemies had become the object of the Führer's admiration; and even now he tried to raise that spark of mystical certainty that sooner or later history would repeat itself and he would be saved.

Goering waited to be acknowledged and, while he waited, felt his inner will seeping away, the way it always did in Hitler's presence. He knew in advance that, whatever the other man said, he would agree; whatever the other man ordered, he would do. He could only relish the guilt and luxury of giving his will and destiny wholly over to another.

"Hermann," Hitler said warmly. He removed his spectacles and focused his frightening eyes on his visitor. He got unsteadily to his feet – for some months he had felt his sense of balance going and he had a tendency to lurch to the right – and he extended a hand. Goering took it and pressed it to his cheek.

"Mein Führer!"

"So! Let me look at you. In all the crowd I wasn't able to take good notice." Hitler stood back. "Both of us none too good, eh? Neither likely to make old bones." He looked around, nodded curtly at Reinhardt Egger, and took his seat again. "How is Emmy?"

Goering said his wife was in good health; she would be better for knowing that the Führer had seen him once more. Egger, experienced and ambitious, unlike the young man that Aaron Eichbaum the art expert had known years before, listened to his master fumble over the words. Like a whipped dog, Goering was responding to a friendly pat on the head by abasing himself.

"A good woman," Hitler said and then in his abrupt manner changed the subject. "What do you think of the military situation?" he asked.

Goering blanched, sensing a trap. He was none too sure of the exact military situation. He waited for the usual tirade about the performance of the Luftwaffe.

"Not beyond remedy," he ventured, "if the Army can be persuaded to adhere to National Socialist principles."

Hitler beamed. "My sentiments exactly!" More darkly he added; "But not too good, eh? We must be prepared for . . . eventualities?"

"Undoubtedly."

"It is inconceivable, intolerable, that we should not have the last word in this business. Some final retribution."

Goering did not follow. Hitler chuckled good-humouredly.

"Have you heard of Pingfan? No? It's in Manchuria. The Japanese army has a research establishment there."

"What for?"

"Oh, work on disease, on the transmission of disease – weapons testing." Hitler paused and his eyes were bright with their peculiar light.

Reinhardt Egger paused in the telling. Something in the tale had caused his disordered mind to drift obliquely across the surface of the remembered images. He resumed in the same low voice, which caused Donaldson and the girl to lean over him to catch the words in his sweet, warm breath. "A lot has been said about Hitler's eyes," he said. "They have been described as 'mad' eyes, as if that explained something instead of placing it beyond our understanding. Mad eyes – *quatsch*! That is nonsense from Hollywood: it is Boris Karloff not Adolf Hitler that people are seeing." No more for the moment. The chime of the copper coffee-cannisters as Frau Egger moved them away. Then: "The same is true of 'hypnotic' eyes. Have you ever seen hypnotic eyes?"

The question was directed at Annaliese. She shook her head.

"Neither have I. They don't exist." He fell to silence again, his recollections crowded with visions of the Führer's eyes and their terrible sexual power. For that was what it was, and Egger knew what that entailed. Swept by that power, men and women alike had stooped to be the Führer's magdalenes, and wipe his feet with their unworthy hair.

"When we looked into those eyes," Egger said at last, "what we felt was not madness or hypnosis, but love."

"You are talking about waging war with diseases?"

Hitler nodded. "The Japanese have been working on this matter for more than a decade. In this field there is no question that our knowledge is ahead of the British and Americans."

Goering was astonished. He looked to Egger with a query. The Major told him what he would have known already if he had not lapsed into indolence.

"I know nothing of Pingfan or Manchuria," he said, "but the Forschungsamt became aware two years ago that the SS had opened an establishment at Posen supposedly for research into this area. According to unconfirmed rumour there were consultations with a Japanese military delegation which brought with it a piece of equipment codenamed 'Uji'. Conjecture says that the Uji was a bomb, but we have never received details of its exact contents or power."

"Excellent!" Hitler was delighted. "Now perhaps you can guess. We have a weapon; we have had it for some time. However, I am a humane man and I have not wanted to use it before now. But there comes a time. . . ." Hitler's voice rose and his eyes became duller and more distant. "We must rob our enemies of the fruits of victory! We must make the *Götterdämmerung* a reality for them, too! Destiny will pass its verdict on them, on all their lies and filth!" He stared about for a moment as if he were somewhere else and then sat back exhausted by the brief outburst.

"Whatever you demand of me, mein Führer," said Goering. He had a chilling certainty of what that request would be.

"There will be only one attack," Hitler explained. "The payload will be 900 kilograms, not more. What is required is a single aircraft that will sneak past British air defences and deliver the attack on London. Can you do it?"

Egger waited for Goering's reply. He knew that what Hitler wanted was beyond the capacity of the Luftwaffe to accomplish. But what would Goering say? The Reichsmarschall wasn't long in giving his answer. He pulled himself together, knowing that he was going to say what he had said so many times before, and that the promises he would make were hollow. But what else could he do before this man?

"I give you my personal guarantee of success, mein Führer!" he said.

Hitler turned now to Reinhardt Egger. "You will understand now, Herr Major, why you have been invited to this conference. You will have the staffwork to do to organize this operation. What name shall we give it? It must impress the justice and the finality of the punishment we inflict."

194

Egger was stunned. He had not expected to be addressed. From out of his subconscious, primed by the Führer's speech, the words formed and he heard them pronounced in a voice he scarce believed was his own. "Last Judgement . . .," he said. "Operation Last Judgement."

Hitler was delighted.

Donaldson listened in silence to the dying crepitations of the old man's voice. In the shuttered darkness the invalid was barely visible. The candles on the golden washstand had not all been replaced, and one by one they went out, leaving a solitary flame burning like a sanctuary lamp. Outside were the faint sounds of the Cairo traffic and the wailing of a muezzin calling the faithful to pray.

Donaldson thought of the painting of the Last Judgement in the next room and the story of the Last Judgement in this one. They were each different and unexpected and each a form of illusion that was plausible only in the world of myth. Except, he thought, that even in this world there were those rare moments, such as with Hitler, when myth breaks through into history and for a time reality and illusion run together.

"What happened?" he asked at last.

"We did as Hitler ordered – though, after the meeting, Goering admitted that, at heart, he was opposed to the idea. But what could we do?"

His visitor didn't answer. Egger had just described his final moral collapse, which all his years of atonement could not wash away in his own eyes.

"It took us two days to find and equip an aircraft," the old man went on. "Goering insisted that I should command it."

"Why? You weren't an operational flyer."

"No." The old man shook his head and, leaning forward, whispered: "It was a punishment."

"I don't understand."

"*Ach*, do you understand nothing? By punishing me, Goering was punishing himself for giving in to this piece of madness." He repeated "this piece of madness" and then fell silent. His wife began to chuckle.

When the conversation resumed, Egger described the doomed mission. At that stage of the war, the Junkers 88 aircraft which he had flown never had a chance of evading British air defences. In the hope of meeting less resistance the Germans had swung out over the North Sea and over East Anglia to approach London from the north, but no sooner had they crossed the Suffolk coast than the bomber was shot down by British fighters. It had crashed in a small lake near a Suffolk village. Except for Reinhardt Egger, the aircrew had died.

"I was caught and interrogated."

Donaldson nodded to indicate that he was aware of the fact.

"I would not tell, *could* not tell, you understand. The Last Judgement, it was too much . . . too much. Even so, they guessed."

"The British found out what was in the bombs?"

"Found out? Perhaps not found out. But guessed. During my imprisonment they would ask me, 'Is it safe to blow the bombs up?' – you follow, they were still intact, lying with the wreckage at the bottom of the lake. 'Why ask me?' I said. You see? They *knew*. Maybe not all, but they *knew*! And that is why the bombs are still there maybe, even now, because they are frightened to move them."

Donaldson leaned forward, and his cold eyes caught the old man's. "What exactly is in the bombs?" he asked. "You didn't say."

The old man shook his head, not wanting to speak, and then with a cry that picked up the echo of the muezzin's call he exclaimed: "Plague! The bombs contain plague!"

Chapter Twenty-One

IN THE bright days of the 1960s, there was a button with the catchy phrase: "Today is the Beginning of the Rest of Your Life." James Ross knew that this could be a very pessimistic idea.

He lay in bed shaking off the recollections of the past. David, Calverton, the terrorist Kaster whom he never knew – he wanted to blank them out and persuade himself that the emptiness they left behind could pass for normality. And now that David was dead he had no place or purpose in England.

He called the office to see whether they had anything that would take him away – he didn't care where to. "Sorry, mate," was the answer. "Where were you six weeks ago, when I was asking for volunteers to do a stint at Christmas? I could have fixed you a real beauty, freezing your bum in Alaska. Tell you what: leave me your number and if some stupid sod has too much of the festive spirit and cocks something up, then I'll bear you in mind." There was a parting shot. "Don't you blokes have families to go to?"

He shook himself into action. There was no point in waiting for someone to bail him out of his problems. He had seen too much of that in the orphanage and in the Army. Institutions had a way of turning people into spectators of their own lives. Give in and you became someone who waited for authority to direct and provide; as if authority actually knew what was going on. In this respect the SAS was no different, just more subtle. It made you self-reliant because it *told* you to be self-reliant.

Ross assumed that the company wasn't going to help him out with a Christmas posting, with a quiet place at the end of the earth in which to drink and find oblivion. He set out to make his own life again with a check of the kitchen and a list of groceries he would need for the holiday and went out to buy them from the shops along Finchley Road. On the way he picked up a newspaper from the booth by the Underground station.

He came back to find Helen Ainsworth's blue Morris Minor parked outside the flat with Helen sitting in the driving-seat. She saw Ross and her warm brown eyes showed sadness.

"I'm going away for the holiday," she said. "I wanted to see you before I left." It sounded like an introduction or a poor translation of something else she wanted to say.

"Come on inside." He opened the car door and allowed her to lead the way through the red-brick porch and into the house. He noticed the unaffected poise in the way she walked and found himself seeing mystery in what to her was only natural. Had she been to ballet classes as a girl? Or would her mother, Hortense Ainsworth, have considered ballet classes too *petit bourgeois*? Or maybe there were ideologically sound ballet schools in Hampstead for the children of the Anglo-Marxist gentry. Ross didn't know: there was a side to Helen Ainsworth that would always be unknowable because the knowledge could only be obtained by living it. What had she called secret knowledge? Helen possessed it and didn't know it.

They were in the flat. Ross turned on the electric fire to take the chill from the bare room. Helen floated off the walls, unable to settle. She made tea. Ross was reminded of a cat, which, under stress, will suddenly start to groom itself.

"I've decided I need a break for Christmas," she began. "Away from London. I thought I'd stay at the cottage, the one in Northumberland; I may have mentioned it."

"Yes."

"It will give me the chance to think things over."

"I hope it helps."

"Let's hope so," she said with the trace of a smile.

They drank tea and talked deliberately about unimportant things. She was ready to go, looking round with that instinctive have-I-left-anything look even though they knew she had brought nothing in with her.

"Is that why you came?" Ross asked. "To explain about Christmas?"

"I suppose it seems an odd way of passing a fairly simple message."

"The man who killed David is dead," Ross said. He corrected himself: "Dying."

She nodded; whether because she knew already or not, Ross couldn't tell.

"It doesn't matter to me. The man I thought was in love with me was never there in the first place." She considered that answer and thought it sounded too harsh. "But you were tied to David; I suppose it must give you some satisfaction."

"No. None at all."

She looked up from studying her hands and shook her head to flick a wayward strand of hair out of her eyes before focusing them on his. "I also wanted to say that I hoped . . . that I should like to see you again when I get back."

"As David's shadow?" Ross asked, not bitterly but for the sake of the truth.

"No, for yourself," she answered and left the conversation there.

John Donaldson passed the night badly, his sleep riven with dreams lifted from the painting. He woke in the the night to a small sound and found Annaliese squatting on the corner of his bed. For once her eyes were focusing on him and not on that indefinable something beyond, as if whatever she was seeking was beginning to crystallize visibly in him.

At breakfast she seemed as usual but announced off-hand: "I've decided to return with you to London."

"Why?" He meant that his search was over. The painting was a small canvas rolled in his bag and what was left of that other Last Judgement was lying at the bottom of a small Suffolk lake.

"Because I've nothing better to do – and, in any case, my father will be paying."

They caught the Lufthansa flight out of Cairo. It was a determined affair of businessmen and contract-crew trying to get home for the holiday. There was a stop at Athens and a change of flights at Vienna, and for most of the time Donaldson and the girl travelled in silence, caught in their own thoughts. Suddenly it seemed incredible to him how he had forced the pace of his research. He saw now that there had been an irrational urgency as if the Last Judgement had been not a painting but the event itself, and imminent. Without knowing it, he had fallen into the same trap as Egger and allowed the vast power of the myth to dictate his life; and now – now he was oppressed by the burden of horror locked into the painting and a subliminal dread of what the old German had told him: of that other Last Judgement lying quiescent but potent under unknown waters, suppressed like

199

some violence within the subconscious.

Annaliese glanced at him and they exchanged brief smiles that were the nearest they could get to being close to each other; and together they looked forward to arriving in London as a return to normality, a release.

After Helen had gone, James Ross dreamed away the afternoon in a waking torpor. The death of David had left him no time for mourning. He had substituted action, the pursuit of Kaster; and now that that was exhausted there was nothing left but to get blind drunk or live through the emotional cold turkey until the past and its dead worked their way out of his bloodstream. He asked himself whether he had got it wrong: had David been dependent on him or had it all along been the other way round? It was a matter of how you looked at it.

Evening came. He picked up the paper he had bought and saw that the shooting in Oxford Street had finally made the main story. It was complete with a photograph of the wounded terrorist. A lucky shopper, Thomas Hanson, aged twelve, had snapped the scene with the camera that his father had bought him last Christmas. The newspaper succeeded in giving even mayhem a seasonal flavour.

Ross stared at the picture, trying to penetrate its surface, reconcile its stillness with the movement and gesture of the man he had tried to kill. Before, he had had a sense of the other man as a force, something to be hated. Only now did he see him as an object. He had a sense of *déjà vu*. Another man, seen in another photograph. Who and where?

He reached for the phone and made a call.

The Vienna–London flight arrived on time. The passengers had the tired, disoriented air of people who, after a long trial, have been convicted of some nameless crime. They hung around the baggage carousel: discharged prisoners, waiting for their papers.

Donaldson and the girl picked up their cases, braved passport-control and spilled out into the Heathrow Terminal 2 concourse. They found a taxi and Donaldson gave instructions for his address in Islington.

Stillness. He felt the still tenseness inside her. She radiated a sense of expectation, the same that had been growing in her since their interview with Reinhardt Egger. Somehow her distracted vision was cohering, collecting the spectrum of colour back through the prism of her personality and focusing it at a pure light directed at something he couldn't see. All this in the blackness of the cab, with night-time London laid out like a basket of jewels.

He found a newspaper on the seat. He picked it up and turned on the courtesy light. The picture of the wounded terrorist stared out from the page. He stopped the cab outside the nearest public house, went inside and made a telephone call.

On the telephone Hortense Ainsworth told Ross that her daughter was not at home. Helen was out, but could be reached at an address in Woolwich where she was initiating a bunch of foreigners into the mysteries of an English Christmas.

The place was a run-down Victorian villa. A wall built of frost-shattered bricks leaned out at a crazy angle and collapsed at the corners. The front garden was full of gloomy yew-trees dripping water like poison on to a patch of stamped earth. The placard nailed to the gate said the house was an "education centre" and in some ways maybe it was. A spangle of fairylights showed at a downstairs window, and someone was having a shot at a carol and missing.

He found Helen in a large, draughty salon with grey emulsioned walls, a cheerful copy of the fire regulations and an engraving of *The Fighting Téméraire* draped in tinsel. Helen was squatting in a circle of brown faces around the local-authority Christmas-tree.

"Come to join us?" she asked uncertainly. She got up and brushed imagined flecks from her dress. A young American with a guitar stepped into the breach. "That's it, Alan, keep the party going." She turned to Ross. Bright eyes. Smiles. "What do you want, James? Obviously this isn't of interest to you." She indicated the ring of faces struggling over the words on the blackboard. "Is it so urgent that it couldn't wait until I got back from holiday?"

Was it urgent? All the way in the taxi Ross had wondered if he was mistaken. The newspaper photograph of Kaster didn't square with the man he had tried to kill. Not that they weren't the same man, but Kaster in the flesh had been a live presence, while the photograph showed dead meat. It was only in the deadness of the photograph that he could compare Kaster with another man he had seen.

The cast-iron radiators in the room began to rattle in competition with the singing, and one by one the voices failed. "Excuse me," said Helen, "but if we lose the momentum, then they'll all clam up – and then we'll all look pretty stupid."

"Come outside. I need to talk to you."

"No doubt, but first things first." She took an Indian woman by the hand and drew her to the middle of the floor. "Now, Lakshmi, you must show us how it's all done. You know your English is good enough." The woman looked reluctant but not intimidated, and, holding her sari to her, at the first note of the guitar struck up a high, wailing version of "Away in a Manger". Helen grinned at Ross. Now it was his turn.

They went outside. At the back of the house the garden had been hard-topped and handed over to the motor-car apart from some broken cucumber-frames that suggested a different past. The rain had started up again, and Helen wore a scarf and the green wellington boots which she kept in her car. Now she paced the yard with Ross and they kicked litter across the tarmac while they talked.

"When I came to your house you told me something about a photograph," said Ross.

"Did I? I'm sorry, I forget which one: we're rather a family for photographs. Can I guess at the one of my mother and a bunch of Arabs on the occasion when she tried to fly to Mecca?" She spoke with a voice that was too light. She didn't want to talk about anything serious. She would have preferred it if Ross hadn't come.

"It was a shot of your cottage."

"Oh?"

"You were in the picture, standing with a man. Who was he?"

"Why do you need to know?"

"Because yesterday I tried to kill him."

She stared at Ross, seeing that he was serious, but unable to prevent a slight laugh. "I'm sorry," she corrected herself quickly. He was looking for an explanation. "It just can't be true, that's all."

"How do you know? Who is he?"

"He's the man you helped to get a visa for. His name is John Donaldson and, as far as I know, he's at this very moment in Cairo."

"Then, who is this?" asked Ross. He produced the newspaper clip.

She looked at it and then said quietly: "It has to be Anthony Donaldson. He's John's brother."

Donaldson's call found Sebastian Summer at home. The dealer was full of goodwill-to-all-men and surprised to get the call.

"John, how wonderful to hear your voice. Where are you calling from? Are you still on holiday? How are your researches going?"

"I'm still in Cairo," Donaldson lied. "I don't know when I'll be home."

"Then I'd better wish you a Merry Christmas now. It does seem a shame that you won't be here, but it was thoughtful of you to call. Was there anything else? Forgive me but you sound a little strained."

"I was wondering whether you had heard from Anthony."

There was silence at the other end. Questions raced through Donaldson's mind. What did the police know? Had they questioned Anthony? What had Anthony told them about his brother? What in hell's name was he to do? It occurred to him that Summer was stalling to give time for a trace on the line, but the gap was in fact no longer than the emotional hesitation in the other man's voice.

"Anthony isn't about to do something wildly imprudent, is he?" Sebastian asked at last.

Donaldson put the phone down. He was satisfied from the tone of Sebastian's answers that the police had not contacted him; which could only mean that they hadn't yet identified Anthony by name. The mystery remained: what had Anthony been doing in Oxford Street? Why was he suddenly acting independently? Donaldson had the uncanny feeling of an actor who walks on stage to find an understudy repeating his well-remembered lines. But when would Anthony act independently? – except, maybe, to save his brother.

He turned to leave the booth and found Annaliese there. She was holding the newspaper open at the photograph and her face said that she had recognized everything and more: it said that Anthony had told her both about himself and about his brother. And now he knew why her eyes held that expectant look. It was as if he suddenly had the gift of the Holy Gost. God help her if that was what she saw.

Helen Ainsworth had a key to the caretaker's office. A large girlie calendar was stuck on the wall opposite the door and the place smelled of damp socks drying slowly over a radiator. Ross found the telephone and dialled Calverton on his private number.

"James, dear chap, what can I do for you?" said the voice on the other end of the line. Calverton had recovered his aplomb after the shock of Figgis's death.

"Have you managed to identify Kaster yet?"

A pause. "Not so far. But twenty-four hours is only a brief

203

opportunity. Do you think you have an answer where older and wiser heads have failed? If so, then please enlighten me."

"The name is Anthony Donaldson."

"Ah!" Calverton breathed out long and slowly. Then: "Do you have any conclusions from this interesting piece of information?"

"Only that we're dealing with two men rather than one."

"What makes you think that?"

"My brother David was investigating John Donaldson when he got himself killed. That was why he got to know the Ainsworth girl." Ross watched Helen as he was speaking. He felt sorry for her, but at some point there had to be an end to the deception. He spoke to both of them: "You knew David: it wasn't love that motivated him. The Ainsworth girl was working at the same gallery as John Donaldson; so he deliberately set out to use her. He was at her house that night because John Donaldson was a guest at dinner. Afterwards someone killed him – my guess would be Anthony Donaldson."

There was nothing else to tell. Ross replaced the receiver, all the while feeling Helen's presence as a prickling of his neck.

"I'm sorry," he said.

"I'll get over it."

He believed her. She had the guts to.

"None of this – I mean since David was killed – none of this is the real me," she said. "Well, I suppose that's not quite true: it's just that you're getting a very partial view." She was looking away. Her voice was painfully blithe. "In fact, I'm not really cut out to be Our Lady of Sorrows. It's something to do with my sense of humour." Ross remembered them laughing together as they walked in Greenwich Park, playing with the dog, and the smiles as she tried to teach her students.

"'*I am half sick of shadows*', *said the Lady of Shalott*.'" He caught the look of surprise. "Tennyson."

"You like poetry?"

"Hate it."

"Then why did you learn it?"

"I was given a book of verse as a birthday present. It was in the orphanage. That's what happens to orphans. You want a box of soldiers and they give you a book of poems. No one ever knows you. Did Donaldson like poetry?"

"Yes."

"I always suspected he was a bastard."

He let her laugh until her eyes were bright with the doing of it.

Calverton broke the news to Sir Lionel Sholto.

"Ah," boomed Sholto, but somewhat thoughtfully. "You don't suppose that this Ainsworth woman knew all along, do you – that she was, so to speak, in on it? She was his mistress and yet there he apparently was, tripping around Europe, shooting people and whatnot. For that matter, what did his employer think was going on?"

"I doubt they suspected a thing," said Calverton. "It's funny how one doesn't. One wonders how many families harbour mass-murderers all unwittingly. It's probably a failure of imagination. In Donaldson's case, he allegedly has a private income. Perhaps it gave him some freedom in his work. The art world is full of dilettantes as well as people one wouldn't buy a car from. Or so I'm told." Sholto was no longer listening.

"Of course! Norman, I do believe that we have been deluding ourselves. The fellow's name was never *Kaster*, it was *Castor*! Don't you see? They were twins!" he said. "I should have known. The children of Zeus and Leda, the Dioscuri – our Kaster is something of a classicist."

"Yes." Calverton nodded. In ancient Greek myth, Castor had a brother, Pollux, and together they formed the twins, the Dioscuri or Gemini. It was surprising really that they had never thought of it before. A failure of imagination.

"The trouble is", Sholto went on, "that I fancy that we have caught ourselves only the lesser of the twins and that an altogether more dangerous proposition is still at large."

Chapter Twenty-Two

THEY abandoned the pub, Donaldson and the girl, and bribed their way into a taxi that was dropping off the walking wounded after an office party. There was a risk that the driver would remember them but that wouldn't matter so long as they kept one step ahead in the game; and for the moment, while the police hadn't identified the Oxford Street gunman, that seemed to be the case. But what game had Anthony started? All the way in the cab to Euston and while pounding the dull streets looking for a vacant room in the terraces of anonymous hotels, Donaldson wanted to question the girl, but he needed time to think, to analyse.

They found a hotel – the Balmoral, the Sandringham, something like that – three town houses knocked together: steps to the basements and railed off at street level; over the windows, plastic awnings with scalloped edges and vermouth advertisements; a desk-clerk who looked as though he would charge extra if you embarrassed him with your real name. Donaldson booked a room.

"*What was Anthony doing?*"

For half an hour the question kept coming round to that, and he couldn't get it into her head that he didn't know the answer already. She answered obliquely, and her eyes held the serene slyness of someone who knows that she is merely being tested, and who has faith. Donaldson sat with her on the bed, holding her hands on his lap and taking her through her story like some catachumen, trying to squeeze some meaning out of the formulae.

"He was trying to help you."

"How?"

"You are joking with me?"

"Annaliese, how can I make you believe that I am not?"

She stared at him. He knew that in her way she was trying to help. Perhaps she was also trying to protect Anthony. She could sense his anger at his brother.

"What did he do to help me?"

"He killed a man."

"Who?"

"His name was Ross – I think it was Ross."

The name meant nothing to Donaldson except for a James Ross he had never met, who had helped him with his Polish visa.

"You knew him," she said. "He called himself Marshall."

That was it – Robert Marshall. He remembered the name from conversations with Helen and from the dinner-party on Hortense Ainsworth's birthday. A false name; so, presumably, he had been working for the security services. Marshall could only have come so close if he had broken into one of their connections – the Irish maybe, who stank of blarney and betrayal – and Anthony must have found out. Then what? Anthony had protected his brother by killing an enemy. The explanation wasn't enough. Why hadn't Anthony warned him? Then he remembered that there had been more. Anthony had killed Marshall's wife and family, too.

His brother had known that Donaldson would not go along with that part. It was the thing they could never agree on. Even now he could hear Anthony's insistent voice: "Fear is accentuated by the irrationality, the unpredictability, the excess of violence. We should seek to fasten on to their sleepless nights and be the incubus of pure terror."

Anthony had rejoiced in the thought, but Donaldson had resisted. He had tried to believe what their Soviet teachers had told them: that terror was either a controlled and rational instrument of policy or useless self-indulgence. It was a technique, not a sacrament.

Thinking about what Anthony might have done to Robert Marshall's family wasn't going to help. He needed to know what danger he was in and for certain how his brother had been betrayed. He picked up the newspaper again and read what little explanation it gave. The wounded terrorist was rumoured to be IRA; reference was made to an IRA Christmas bombing campaign with a casualness which made it sound like a seasonal tradition that, sadly, was becoming more commercial each year. What else could have pulled Anthony out?

There was no telephone in the hotel room. Donaldson went to the booth in the lobby and dialled a number that he carried in his head. Khoder Saleh had once given it to him for use in emergencies. It could only have been through the Libyan that anything had been arranged.

"Hello, is Mr Ismail there?" Donaldson recited the opening words of the introductory formula. He didn't need the rest. A taped voice in broken English answered.

"This is a recorded message. Mr Ismail has ceased business. His representative will contact former customers in due course."

Donaldson slammed the phone down. At the very least the line was insecure. At worst Saleh was out of action and possibly dead. Someone had exposed his IRA–Libyan connection and used it to try to kill him.

From his meeting with Helen, Ross went straight to the building in Battersea High Street. The place was in darkness, but there was a night-bell and a porter to answer it who was thirty years too young to be the real thing. Calverton was expecting him.

The regular offices were empty. They smelled of stale drink and the floors were crunchy with peanuts. In a locked room a telex machine was chuckling over the incoming messages as if it could decode them itself. A young man by the name of Elphinstone, with wavy hair and the air of a first-year undergraduate, was trying to organize two registry clerks into dealing with the emergency traffic that Calverton was generating.

Calverton received Ross off-handedly between throwing more messages at Elphinstone. "You know how it is," he apologized. "We're always a little short-staffed over the holiday."

"Sure. There's never a spy when you need one."

"Quite. My felicitations to you on the season, James, and my congratulations on ruining my own plans." He offered a chair. The heating had been turned off and they sat in their coats.

"Any news?"

"Come, now, I've only had an hour when all's said and done; and that has only served to establish from Sebastian Summer that Donaldson called him this evening to tell him that for the time being he was in Cairo. I've got the embassy checking that one out."

"And if he was lying?"

"I'm running checks on incoming flights for the last two days."

"What about Donaldson himself? What do we know about him?" Ross asked. The man was a blank to him – someone who only existed in Helen Ainsworth's conversation.

"Bit of a problem, that. We have nothing on him here or in Curzon

Street. Special Branch claim they have nothing, either, which they wouldn't have advised to us already as a matter of routine co-operation – cross their hearts and hope to die – but they're checking to make sure." He paused for a second and, thinking his answer sounded thin, added: "Elphinstone has loyally forgone the evening's festivities to assist me with our European enquiries. He claims to speak German and to be able to work the computer terminal – both of which accomplishments seem unlikely for an Oxford man – but," he went on more hopefully, "if he's right on both counts, I have high hopes of something useful from that quarter. The Germans can be very thorough. Yes, I think we may expect something from Wiesbaden."

"Wiesbaden?"

"Apologies. I forget you don't know about these things." Calverton twiddled with the regulator on the office radiator in the hope that the heating might respond. "The Bundeskriminalamt maintains a computer at Wiesbaden, a wonderful machine stuffed with valves by the million. The West European anti-terrorist forces all have access to it." He thought about this doubtfully, then asked: "Have you heard of TREVI?"

"No."

"Terror, Radicalism and Violence International. Terrible name, isn't it? Like something out of pulp fiction. But I'm told it's on our side. It's a little thing that the EEC police forces have put together on the old-boy network as a way to pool information and tactical knowledge. Our own dear Special Branch is a member through its European Liaison Section." Calverton left the topic there without its apparently leading anywhere. He suggested a drink and then found a bottle of tonic wine in a cupboard. He needed to talk. He had recovered from Figgis's death but was still affected by the melancholy of lonely Christmases warmed only by insincere goodwill. Williams of Special Branch had sent him a UNESCO charity card with a picture of three possibly wise men and a message in French, German and Chinese referring neutrally to the greetings of "the season". The Welshman hadn't used his first name, and Calverton couldn't remember off-hand what it was. "Of course", he resumed as they toasted each other, "MI5 has no role in TREVI. Social distinctions must be maintained. The clandestine services meet instead in the 'Club of Berne'. All except the Irish, that is; though whether that is because they don't subscribe to the Convention of the Suppression of

Terrorism or because they've been blackballed by their betters has never been entirely clear."

An hour passed. Elphinstone knocked at the door and came in with a readout from the German computer laboriously decoded and translated. Calverton held it under the anglepoise lamp and read it over to himself, moving his lips as he struggled over the younger man's writing.

"Sorry about the fist, sir," said Elphinstone. "Would have typed it, but couldn't get the hang—"

"That's all right," Calverton said comfortingly. A brief look passed between himself and his junior as if not typing was a secret vice they shared. To Ross he said: "What do make of this, James? Donaldson placed a call a week or so ago to Hamburg, to a number lodged as a terrorist-number-at-one-remove."

"What's that?"

Elphinstone answered, quoting some lesson or other: "If a known terrorist calls his tailor once, it's interesting. If he calls him twice, it's suspicious. If he calls him three times, then it's evidence of the tailor's guilt."

"Perhaps he just wants a suit?"

"Very probably," said Calverton, "but I'm sure you get the general idea. Now, to go on: it seems that GS9 have a tap on a low-grade line which picked up a call from John Donaldson to a lady name of Annaliese Schreiber, who is considered by our German colleagues to be – wait for it – a Suspicious Person. He asked her to discover the present whereabouts of an elderly ex-Nazi, one Reinhardt Egger. It will come as no surprise to learn that Egger is in Egypt."

"Donaldson was looking for a painting. Helen Ainsworth told me something about a Nazi being involved in taking it. It was an innocent explanation, and I believed it. Why shouldn't it be true? Terrorism isn't a seven-day-a-week job."

"We're not allowed to believe in innocent explanations," said Calverton. "We're talking about Kaster, James! About the man who caused your brother's death!"

Ross shook his head. "Kaster didn't cause David's death. It was looking for Kaster that caused it. I'm not sure it's the same thing."

Calverton didn't answer that one. Perhaps he didn't hear. Kaster was a private obsession with him. Elphinstone, who had been out, came back into the room waving another note.

"Report from Lufthansa, sir! Target and associate were booked through from Cairo via Vienna today. Passenger manifest for both flights shows both subjects on board. There's no doubt, sir: Kaster is back in the country!''

Ross listened to Elphinstone's eagerness and felt sorry for him. He was a virgin in love and would soon find out he had only discovered sex. Ross spoke to Calverton. "It's more than that. If he lied to Summer about being in Egypt, it means he knows that we're after him.''

Finding Desmond McKilroy proved to be easy. It was Christmas Eve, business was good in the West End and the Irishman wasn't far from it. Donaldson paid a taxi-driver fifty pounds to cruise the streets around Soho while he tracked the other man by doormen and club touts as McKilroy made the rounds of his clubs and shops. Annaliese slept, curled on the back seat of the car, grabbing the sleep that they needed after the flight from Egypt.

They stopped in Wardour Street, where McKilroy had a small film company. It imported pornography for his cinemas, cut it to taste and dubbed the English groans; all of this from a couple or so of first-floor rooms above a bookshop with an apartment thrown in above the offices.

"He keeps a woman there," said one of Donaldson's informants. "Beryl, they call her. And between her legs is what you might say is Denny's Christmas box. It wouldn't be like him to go without a bit of good cheer, not at this time of year. As soon as everything closes – say, two o'clock – then he'll be there like a rat up a drain, you can bet your money on it." Now it was two-thirty and Christmas Day.

There was a party going on. The street door was open and some of Denny's troops were drifting in after finishing their stints in the box-offices or from pulling punters off the pavements. Upstairs the throng was spilling out of the office and the cutting-room and on to the stairs. Warm bodies, interested in everyone like predatory cats.

Donaldson carried a bottle of gin.

"You're in the wrong place," said a girl who was sprawling on the wooden treads. "This is a bring-a-needle-party, know what I mean?" She caught the cold look in Donaldson's eyes and muttered: "And a Merry Christmas to you, too."

He went up to the second floor. Annaliese followed. Here it was different; there was carpeting, lace curtains over the fanlight, a jardinière with an ivy-leafed creeper that trailed to the floor. There was a brass bell-push on the apartment door, but Donaldson preferred to slip the lock with a credit card. He found himself in a narrow hall.

"Who the bloody hell are you and what in God's bloody name are you doing here!" The woman came bustling into the hall like a steam train, pulling a flowing black négligé around her and trailing a boa of white feathers. She was an ample female of about forty with blonde hair and a face that was normally friendly but prepared to make exceptions; and she was careful in her anger to close the door behind her as if it held in the family silver.

"I've come to see Denny," said Donaldson.

She guffawed. "You certainly pick your moments, dear!" Then: "No, but really I couldn't allow it. It wouldn't be decent."

"I promise not to look."

"Get away with you, can't a poor man have some relaxation?"

"Not tonight," said Donaldson. He brushed past her, and Annaliese pinioned her arms against the wall. From inside the room a gentle brogue complained: "What the hell's going on, Beryl? Can't you send the buggers away?" Donaldson opened the door and turned on the main light.

Desmond McKilroy blinked and sneezed at the brightness, but couldn't wipe his nose because he was stark naked and strapped by all four limbs to a metal rack. His penis was tied with a sprig of holly.

Helen Ainsworth returned home from the class at Woolwich with a feeling of deep bitterness inside her. She had listened while Ross spoke on the telephone to some man called Calverton and then to his explanations about John Donaldson and Kaster and his brother's death, and all the while he was telling her about betrayal as if it were the only human relationship that counted. Betrayal stood from the start between them; keeping them apart because anything else would involve a betrayal of David.

She found Tom Furnival's car parked outside the house. She remembered that the trade unionist had been at the dinner-party the night that David was murdered. Now he was in the drawing-room with her mother, drinking a glass of port.

"Hello, Uncle Tom, what brings you here?" she asked without thinking or caring much, or she would have noticed that the old man was still wearing his car-coat and staring at the glowing end of his cigarette as if it had suddenly become a wonderment to him.

He looked at her and shook an answer out brusquely, almost rudely. "That damned peerage," he said. "They've leaked the New Year's Honours List and I'm not to get it. They promised it to me but I'm not to get it." He stubbed out the cigarette. "You know," he added wistfully, "I've only just realized how important it was to me. I suppose it's been bloody obvious to everyone else that I wanted it; but I had in the back of my mind that I might refuse it on a point of principle – just fooling myself really."

"But why . . . ?" asked Helen.

Her mother answered. "It's the investigation after your friend Robert Marshall's death. They turned over all the stories about Tom's being a communist and a security risk." She looked at Furnival. "You ought to regard it as a matter of pride, you know: that your principles were once so strong and clear." Hortense Ainsworth spoke tenderly, and Helen realized that she had not heard her mother speak that way for years; probably because, with age, the people who needed her tenderness diminished. And now it suddenly struck her how her mother's softer, lively spirit had become frozen into grotesqueness for want of use.

All of this, she thought, what had happened to Uncle Tom included, was part of the same story, the spinning out of the consequences from David's original deception. She felt lonely and sickened by it. She couldn't stay at home with Uncle Tom as a reminder. It reinforced her intention, since meeting James Ross earlier that night, to go away now, tonight, rather than wait.

She packed a suitcase quickly and borrowed her mother's car for the long drive north to Northumberland and her cottage. At two-thirty on the morning of Christmas Day, she was in the vicinity of Darlington and it was snowing lightly.

"Mother of God," said Denny McKilroy with all the sang-froid he could muster. "So there's life after death after all. The last time I heard of you, you were bleeding to death in Selfridges."

"That was my brother," said Donaldson.

"Well, what do you know? Come on in, make yourself at home, help yourself to a drink and don't mind me if I'm a little tied up at the moment."

Donaldson took in the room. It was tricked out in Walt Disney dungeon style with lots of dark oak and protruding nails. There was a rack of whips and manacles on one wall, some unidentifiable leather gear, a sprinkling of mirrors and a well-stocked bar with the addition of a selection of dope-pipes and some gold accessories for the well-heeled coke-fancier. A brace of speakers was thumping out the "Horst Wessel Lied". The Nazi anthem was background for McKilroy's games of power and bondage and had nothing to do with Reinhardt Egger or Hitler's Last Judgement, but there the song was, like Fate's incidental music. Donaldson was struck how reality, which, taken as a whole, seemed to be random and pointless, was full of theatrical coincidences of detail; as if God couldn't handle the plot and was compensating with cheap special effects.

"What do you want with me?" McKilroy was asking. His body was smothered in oil, and leather thongs bound him to a gridiron which could be winched by iron chains to a beam on the ceiling or angled according to taste. His wrists writhed in their bindings as he tried to get free.

"You set my brother up to be killed."

McKilroy was stunned, though he couldn't have been expecting anything else. He collected himself and spoke. "Only in a manner of speaking. It was MI5. I'm just one of the victims."

"Why did they want him – or me?"

"Come on, Kaster!"

"Let's put it another way: why now of all times?"

"Can I have a smoke?" said McKilroy. Donaldson untied one of the other man's hands and lit him a cigarette.

"Don't drop it or you'll go up in flames."

"It's only baby-oil," said McKilroy. Perhaps he'd considered the point before.

The woman, Beryl, came in with Annaliese behind her. She went to the bar to fix herself a drink. She looked at the piece of holly tied with a ribbon to McKilroy's limp penis and commented: "It seemed like a good joke, what with Christmas and all."

"Why *now*?" Donaldson repeated the question.

"You should know," said McKilroy. He feared the reaction and quickly added, "I'm not trying to be tricky. It's this business in the newspapers – germ warfare – they want to station bombs in Europe. They thought you might be planning something for when the Americans come over here at New Year."

Annaliese looked sharply at Donaldson and asked: "Did he say 'germ warfare'?"

Donaldson didn't answer. He ignored the other man and sat down and laughed with a deep inward irony and despair. McKilroy cried out: "There's nothing bloody funny about germ warfare!" Donaldson nodded. "I know, I know." But he was thinking of the Last Judgement and that no enormity once invented by man ever goes away. The Last Judgement, whether it was the thing itself or the idea, still sat as a malignant force at the bottom of a Suffolk lake, untouched because in 1945 people still had the sense to be afraid of their own creation; and like savages they bowed down to the thing as a demonic idol fashioned by their own hands. *What to do with it? Can it be placated? Will it go away if we leave it?* Now men thought they knew better and they would make the thing afresh. But Donaldson knew they were wrong. The fear was still there, and it didn't matter whether their bomb or Hitler's bomb were effective for the fear to be real. Plague was the old enemy of mankind, the slayer of the firstborn of Egypt, and the mere threat of its resurrection would cause panic and paralysis. Donaldson knew this instinctively; and he knew what to do.

The oil on McKilroy's body, mixed with sweat, was starting to run. Fear was giving him an erection. The woman, from a curious sense of decency, covered his loins with a towel. No one stopped her. Donaldson was absorbed in his own thoughts, and the girl was watching him in her role as acolyte. They ignored the woman as she took the cigarette stub from the Irishman's hand and substituted a glass.

"I don't want fucking sherry!" McKilroy snapped. "Give me a real drink for once – Bushmills!" She replaced the glass and he tasted it, drinking his past. As the last drop dribbled down his chin he raised his head and asked: "What now?"

Donaldson broke off from his musings. "I want a gun and some explosives."

"Will you hear the man? I'm like an old whore getting fucked by whoever takes a fancy. The Boys, MI5, yourself – is there a queue down the bloody stairs?"

"You heard me."

"I know! I know!" McKilroy cried. He calmed down. "Listen," he said. "I've got this place in Stepney – it's a little builder's yard. There's an old boozer called Mike Hennessy who earns a few bob keeping an eye out for thieves."

"And?"

"There's a couple of guns in the safe and a pack of gelignite –

215

nothing big, just enough to blow up a bank on a fine day. Now, you're welcome to the lot if you'll just let me out of this rat-trap and then clear out of my life." He looked at Donaldson desperately and read his fate in the other man's cool stare. He shook his head. "You know, my mother wanted me to be a priest. I told her it was a dangerous profession. Too many of those fellas die of drink."

Chapter Twenty-Three

McKILROY's building business was in a backstreet running parallel to the Commercial Road and the river. It was a brick compound with a chicken-wire gate and a filthy-tempered dog who padded around restlessly and scratched his infested fur on any odd corner that looked attractive. There was a frame-building with corrugated-iron cladding, which kept the rain off the perishables, and a parked trailer with a smokestack and brown-paper-covered windows, which served as office and home for Mike Hennessy. At four in the morning of Christmas Day, it was in darkness and creeping with mists from the Thames.

A rattle at the gate set the dog barking and brought Hennessy out of the trailer in an army greatcoat and a pair of steel-toed boots. He carried a stick and a length of chain and his face looked as though both had been used on him.

"What do you want?" he asked in a breathless croak.

"Merry Christmas."

"Bugger off!"

"Denny sent me."

A pair of suspicious eyes peeped out from a thicket of eyebrows. "Sez who? How do I know who you are?" The dog came sidling up to him and he gave it a flick of the chain.

"I've got a note here." Donaldson pushed it through the mesh. It was in Denny McKilroy's hand.

"It says here I've got to co-operate with you," said Hennessy.

"That's right."

"Don't tell me he's got you robbing banks at Christmas? I only hope he's paying you double time." He opened the padlock and let them into the yard.

"Do you have a car here?" Donaldson asked as they crossed the beaten earth towards the trailer.

"A Ford Cortina – nothing much to look at."

"Does it go?"

"Oh, it goes OK, like hot shit off a wet shovel as the saying is. Full tank of petrol and everything in order except the road tax." He scratched his nose. "That's in the post."

"Start it up and prove that it works." Donaldson left the other man to demonstrate the car to Annaliese and went into the trailer.

The front of the trailer was an office. Hennessy kept it in a haphazard fashion, and the invoices and purchase-ledgers looked like a work of fiction. The back was cut off by a curtain, and it was there that Hennessy slept. Donaldson pulled the curtain aside and looked on a mess of torn-up newspapers and dirty bedding. The man was living like a drunken hamster.

"Where are the real books?" he asked as Hennessy came shambling through the door. The other man looked about to deny the fact and then thought better of it.

"It's a cold night out. A man could do with a drink."

"Where are the real books?"

Hennessy licked his lips. Donaldson reached into his pocket and threw across the half-bottle of brandy he had picked up at McKilroy's apartment.

"There's a floor-safe in the store." He indicated with his thumb, then took out a pencil stub and wrote the combination on a scrap of paper. "It's under a pallet of cement in the corner by the door." He handed over the keys.

Donaldson walked across the yard and let himself into the store. The place was much as expected: tiers of metal racks holding boxed stuff; bags of plaster and cement stacked on pallets; grey dust and the smell of resin from unpainted wood. The safe was where promised, under a wooden pallet and masked by a drains inspection-cover. It was a few seconds' work to open it.

Denny had told the truth: his armoury was as modest as befitted a man who had given up terrorism for a life of respectable crime. Two sawn-off shotguns wrapped in sacking and two bundles wrapped in oilskin. The first contained half a dozen sticks of gelignite with detonators. The second a box of shells, a Walther PPK and a Carswell silencer. Donaldson took the handgun, loaded the shells and fitted the silencer. He replaced the company books in the floor-safe. Accountancy was a wonderful profession.

On their arrival in Wardour Street, Ross and Calverton found the regular police already there. The road was full of cars with flashing lights mimicking the Christmas-trees. The party in the film-company offices was represented by a couple of girls in sequined dresses, the rest having vanished at the word "police", leaving behind them bottles and syringes like calling-cards. It was 5 a.m.

"Hello there, Williams. Have you met my man Ross?" Calverton introduced Ross to a fiery-faced man in a sports-jacket and slacks which covered a pair of pyjamas. "By the way, Williams, thank you for the card, a charming sentiment."

"Have you seen the corpse? Not a pretty sight, I can tell you."

"I'm sure," said Calverton. "Let's go inside, shall we? It's cold here, cold even for the time of the year, don't you think?" He took the Welshman by the arm and ushered him inside the door.

They went to the upstairs apartment. The murder-room was bright with lights, and Desmond McKilroy's naked and glistening body was centre-stage. He had been slit from pelvis to breastbone and laterally, and his guts by the yard were spilled on the floor. His face was set in a rictus of horror.

"This time Denny has really changed his image," said Ross. He felt sorry for the dead man. There were times when he felt sorry for the whole world. Neither emotion was of any use to anybody; so it was a case of suppress them or blow your brains out.

"What happened?" asked Calverton.

"We received a call forty minutes ago," said Williams. "One of the girls downstairs found the bodies. I've told all the tale to your man Elphinstone."

"Yes, he'll go far, will Elphinstone. But 'bodies' – you did say 'bodies'?"

"There's a woman in the bedroom – not mutilated, thank God – name of Beryl Stanley, a prostitute, otherwise Beryl the Peril."

Ross remembered a friendly-faced woman he had met at McKilroy's house. He supposed it was the same woman.

"You know, of course, that Kaster did this?" remarked Calverton, dragging up his dispute with Williams on that topic.

"It sounds like his style," said Williams blandly.

Elphinstone came up from the floor below. He had been showing photographs to the two witnesses. "It's Kaster all right, sir," he announced. "They recognized the pictures."

Williams said, without conviction: "Did you show them those? It'll ruin their identification evidence if it ever comes to a trial. You never show a witness photographs of just one suspect." No one commented that, whatever happened to Kaster, he would never be standing trial.

Ross had seen more than photographs. The computer at Wiesbaden – known as "the Kommissar" – as one of its tricks, had been programmed under a piece of research called Projekt Sprechererkennung to compile an image of the kind of face that normally produced a given type of voice. From the tapped conversation with Annaliese Schreiber, it had transmitted to London a picture of John Donaldson. It was a line-drawing – necessarily without hair-style or colouring – but recognizable. Another way of looking at Kaster.

"What's their story?"

"Well," said Elphinstone. "Kaster is with the girl as expected. They came to see McKilroy at two-thirty or thereabouts and left perhaps an hour later. No one suspected anything until four-twenty, when someone wondered why their host wasn't joining in the fun. They came upstairs to find McKilroy and instead found – well, all this."

"What does Kaster want?" Calverton asked of no one in particular. "Simple revenge on Denny for our shooting Anthony Donaldson? Not very stylish. In fact a bit over the top." No answer. Then: "What do you suppose he's going to do about weapons? I don't imagine he had any with him when he landed at Heathrow, and I fancy he won't get far sticking his finger into people's backs and shouting 'Hands up'. One wonders where Denny kept his?"

Williams stepped gingerly over a cord of the dead man's entrails, touched blood with his toe and wiped his shoes on the carpet. "It looks as though we have a regular manhunt on our hands. Have the Committee been informed of developments?"

Ross waited for the response. He had overheard Calverton calling Sir Lionel Sholto, fishing the head of intelligence out of his club as the news of the slaughter in Wardour Street broke. Sholto's immediate concern was not to be precipitate. "I rely on your judgement, Norman. It's a matter of balancing a merely potential risk to our American friends against the certainty of ruining Christmas."

Calverton said to Williams: "I've told Lionel, as you would expect. We concluded that Molly would only get excited: so we've left the Foreign Office to find out through the usual channels – steaming open our mail, or whatever they normally do – and naturally we haven't told the Americans."

"Naturally."

"Any delay can be blamed on the holiday."

For want of further information they continued to talk inconsequentially about Christmas, children, presents, the weather, while detectives from the Yard manoeuvred round them to take photographs and collect exhibits. Ross stood by the window and looked down into the street. The free show had collected its share of drunken spectators, and a group of them were standing on the opposite pavement and keeping warm by singing carols.

"For a manhunt we're going to need an incident-room," Williams was saying. "Most of the legwork will have to be done by the regular police, of course." He watched for reactions from Calverton and then proposed in a delicate Welsh lilt: "On purely practical grounds it seems to me that we'll have to pull the whole show back into Scotland Yard." He coughed. "We could provide you with a little office there."

Ross ignored the drift into detail. He stared into the darkness after Kaster as if he could pluck him out of the void into which he was fast disappearing. Where was he? What was he doing? There was so much blood in the room – why had Kaster done it this way?

Elphinstone, bobbing at the edge of things, interrupted. "One of the witnesses says she thinks McKilroy had a building and demolition business somewhere in the East End."

"And?"

"Well, it just occurs to me that it could be a front for procuring explosives."

"An interesting thought, that. You should look into it." Calverton passed round drinks from the bar, being careful not to tread on the bits of McKilroy lying about the floor. He coughed. "In view of its being Christmas, gentlemen, I believe we can relax the rule on drink." There were some muttered "thank yous" from the detectives and a silent toast to something or other. Calverton, pondering his drink, commented to Elphinstone: "Ask Williams's team to get on to the licensing people in Swansea to see whether any vehicle is listed against McKilroy or his companies. It occurs to me that Kaster may well be in need of transport."

"I'll try my best, sir – but the office at Swansea, and at this time. . . ."

"Do the Welsh celebrate Christmas?" ask Calverton. "Anyway, do your best." He turned to Williams. "Sorry to give orders to your chaps. I wouldn't want to step on your toes."

Chapter Twenty-Four

DONALDSON drove on through the night out of London towards Ipswich and the Suffolk coast. The roads were bare of traffic. Towards Chelmsford it began to rain, sheets of it blown off the sea across the flat landscape. Near Colchester they came across a police-car tucked up in a lay-by, but it was looking for drunks, not terrorists, and took no interest in the dull-grey Cortina heading north-east.

Six-thirty. Donaldson had been awake for twenty-six hours. He was fuelled on adrenalin his body feeling as if it was burning with the stuff. The girl was seizing another chance to sleep. She was curled up on the back seat; he could hear her soft breathing and, by angling the mirror, catch sight of her face, framed in fair hair and lit with calmness.

Why had she done that to McKilroy? There was another question which he didn't want to ask: *Why had he let her?* He could still see her, taking a knife to plunge it into McKilroy's abdomen and let his viscera tumble out and lie moist on the floor, still connected umbilically to the corpse. Then she turned and looked at him with a look of triumph and release that made "horror" and "ecstasy" pale words to describe what she had done and felt. And all the while he stood and watched and felt the dark people within him watching, too, and asking, for once, to be allowed to play.

Near Woodbridge he pulled off the road into a lane overhung by trees. It was too early to arrive in Disenham, a lone car in the empty streets. It would attract attention. In any case, he needed to rest, to plan, to sleep. He woke Annaliese and asked her to keep watch while he slept.

It was ten-thirty when he woke. Church bells were ringing in Christmas Day under the hollow sky, and the day was grey and cold. Through the trees the broad River Deben was visible winding slowly seawards. The wind whipped herringbone ripples across the water's surface.

"I didn't want to wake you," Annaliese said. He felt her hand on his shoulder. "I know that you need to rest, but it isn't safe. I was worried that someone would come along the road and find us. It would be . . . suspicious."

Donaldson squeezed her hand for whatever affection was in it.

Disenham was a discarded antique, an ancient seaport that had been picked up and handled by the Victorians as a possible resort and then put down again. There was a cobbled square called Thursday Marketplace, an old moot-hall and a heavily restored church. The main street held two banks that opened on Tuesdays and Thursdays, a newsagent's and a general grocer's that also sold beach-toys. The Victorian legacy was an oversized hotel.

The Marquis of Granby was granite-grey and stood on the seafront. The landward side was stitched together with a skein of gutters, pipes and fire-escapes. The side overlooking the sea was as grim as a funeral parlour, made worse by the addition of a sun-lounge with Spanish Riviera trappings and a flat mineral-felt roof. Next to the hotel was a floral clock and a nine-hole golf-course.

Donaldson approached the desk-clerk.

"Are you fully booked for lunch?"

The man looked at him out of indifferent eyes. "In this place?" His gaze drifted through a set of double doors to a dining-room of vast extent, divided by a makeshift partition. Out of twenty tables, a dozen or so were being set.

"Put me down for two." Donaldson watched the eyes come up from the desk again and pass from him to Annaliese with a dead-lizard look. "I was stranded on the road last night. I'd like to get cleaned up and on my way."

"Help yourself. The gents' is at the end of the corridor. Lunch is at twelve-thirty." The eyes went down again to a crossword he was filling in. Donaldson caught sight of the plastic name-tag: Tony – nothing more. Half a dozen words and it was first names already; it was a friendly hotel.

"Maybe I'll take a walk until lunch. Is there anything worth seeing around here?"

A smile.

"I heard there was a lake."

"Three of them, the Meres. Through Thursday Marketplace and along the lane. You a birdwatcher? There's nothing there but birds."

"Someone told me a German plane crashed there once."

"I wouldn't know – wasn't even born." The lack of interest oozed out of his pores. "There's an old bloke comes in here. Wing-Commander Benoist; you might ask him."

"I might," said Donaldson.

They followed the desk-clerk's instructions and found the lakes, a chain of three, each half a mile or so across, the water putty-coloured from a dark sky. The nearest had been civilized. A short jetty made of rail-ties jutted out from the bank and some red and cream rowing-boats were moored to it. There was a wooden hut where fares were taken and a little booth that sold ice-cream. Both were boarded up. A path led by the water margin to the other two meres. They were overhung by willows and bordered by stands of reeds except where here and there a narrow expanse of mud led to the water. A few birds rustled and flopped in the undergrowth, and the trail of a water vole cut a V across the flat surface.

"Which one is the plane in?" asked Annaliese. She clung to Donaldson's arm as the wind whipped through the trees and plucked at the bare, scraggy hedges.

"I don't know," said Donaldson. He stared out at the lake. The water, reflecting the flat colour of the sky, looked so shallow that he could have walked across it and picked the bomb up while barely wetting his feet. He saw himself striding back to the bank, bearing the Last Judgement in his arms.

PC Arthur Sullivan walked around the car-park of the Marquis of Granby, kicking the tyres of the cars and occasionally stooping to examine the depth of tread. He saw the grey Ford Cortina and thought it looked old and clapped-out enough that there had to be something wrong with it. He strolled by it and peered into the interior. He tugged at the boot-handle and kicked the exhaust to see if it was loose, then went to the front and checked the windscreen. The plastic cover for the road tax was there, and there was something in it. It was the label from a bottle of Guinness.

"Playing silly buggers, are we?" he murmured with satisfaction. He returned to the police station and, because he had nothing better to do, he started processing the complaint. It occurred to him vaguely that the vehicle might be stolen. In any case, he could ruin someone else's Christmas as well as his own.

*

They went back to the hotel. It was filling with people who had decided to give someone else the trouble of cooking their Christmas lunch. Retired ladies, permanent residents, fluttered palely about the foyer like end-of-season butterflies, stopping occasionally to peer into the dining-room. Old people's insecurity: someone was going to steal the dinners off twenty tables.

"This Wing-Commander Benoist," Donaldson asked the desk-clerk, "do you have an address?" The man had that elusive quality of all desk-clerks: that he could show some interest if you would only ask him a different question. This time he answered the one he was given.

"No need; he's in the bar. Just buy him a drink and he'll tell you anything you want to know. Liked the Meres, did you?"

The bar was in an open lounge. Two uncomfortable chesterfields, oak wainscoting and hunting prints. Over the bottles of spirits a row of wooden plaques held corny jokes burned into them: "You don't have to be mad to work here – but, if you are, it helps." A few family men had abandoned their broods in the dining-room and were conspiring to gulp pints of bitter, using the excuse of getting schooners of port and lemon for their spouses.

Their man was at the bar, his foot lodged on the brass rail. Age sixty or so, and well preserved in a florid way. He sported a trim moustache and a blue blazer with an RAF badge on the breast pocket. He saw them coming.

"Visitors?" He had a lively bass voice. "Tony said he had some new faces about the place. He knows I always like a bit of novelty and, believe me, there isn't much of that about here; at least, not now, not at this time of the year." He looked like a man who had lost something and then remembered that it was his name. "Sorry – should have introduced myself – Benoist." He spelled it out. "That's pronounced Benwar – Edmund Benoist. Wing-Commander" – a cough, discreet – "retired. And you?"

"Ross," said Donaldson. The name sprang to his lips as his memory searched for an alias. "John Ross."

"Pleased to meet you." A hand shot out. "And the mademoiselle?"

"May I introduce my wife?"

A murmur from Annaliese.

"Not English, though, eh?" suggested Benoist affably. "German, eh, am I am right? Not to worry, no prejudice on my side –

bygones, etcetera – don't you agree?"

Donaldson bought drinks. A large gin and tonic for the Wing-Commander.

"Are you dining?" asked Benoist. "Always do, myself – Sundays and holidays. I" – he leaned over confidingly – "don't have a wife. Died." He waited for a return token of intimacy.

"We are very happily married," said Annaliese.

They moved to the dining-room. The elderly ladies sat primly, expectantly. The family men, their conspiracy broken up, looked longingly at each other as they sat at table; then gradually focused on their wives and children with all the enthusiasm of inexperienced lion-tamers. A child took up the challenge and sang in an off-key soprano:

"Jingle Bells – Batman smells
Robin's gone away!"

Dinner came and went. Brown Windsor soup, turkey or roast beef, plum pudding.

"Will you pull a cracker with me?" Benoist asked Annaliese. They shared the prize; Benoist wore the paper hat, Annaliese took the lucky charm. "I count myself most fortunate," said the older man. "This promises to be one of the jollier Christmases for some years." He beamed on past them at the single ladies denied the delicacy of tasty company. "What brings you here by the way?"

"Our car broke down."

"The old Ford out front?"

"Yes."

"Funny. I didn't see you as a Ford man, myself. Salesman's car. Now, you I would have put you down for a Morgan. But there we are, I'm probably talking nonsense."

"No, I don't have a Morgan." But Donaldson once had and wished now that he had one, or something fast to outrun the police or his past or the Last Judgement, or whatever he called the manhunt that was forming somewhere out there against him. There was no time for talk. He had to move, act! But events had their own inertia. Nothing would move Benoist from smalltalk towards the answers he really wanted. The other man consumed his guests carefully and then suggested, as a *digestif*: "Would you like to return with me to my humble abode for an after-dinner potation – a drink?"

Donaldson checked his watch and stared out of the French windows into the garden. The sea wind was scouring the desolate

227

flowerbeds and a rose-bush sounded a persistent toc-toc against a pane of glass above the low murmur of conversation in the room. It was time for the Queen's Christmas speech on television.

"We should be delighted," he said.

The Wing-Commander lived in a small bungalow a mile outside the town. It was built of brick rendered with cement and sea-shells and had an attached garage and a sandy garden. Benoist had filled the place with aircraft memorabilia.

"Did I understand you to say that you had an interest in aeroplanes yourself?" He stood by the tiled fireplace of his living-room and fingered a twin-bladed propeller that hung on the chimney breast. It was centrepiece to a mosaic of squadron shields and other bric-à-brac.

"Strictly non-technical."

"What does that mean?"

"I like to hear stories about them."

"Ah! I can tell you those." Benoist picked up a brass model of a Spitfire and began a tale about the man who made it. Donaldson heard him out.

"I was told a story by the hotel receptionist—"

"Tony. Pardon me – do go on."

"Tony – that a German bomber once crashed near the town. Is that so?"

"It's true enough." Benoist looked at Donaldson narrowly; then resumed in the same cheerful voice: "I'm surprised, though, that Tony would know anything about it."

"Local interest, I suppose."

"I suppose so." He put the model down and looked around for other things, paused and began: "I say, would you like a walk? Too much food and drink a walk would settle the stomach."

"We got a glimpse of some lakes near here."

"The Meres," said Benoist. "Yes, we could go there."

The day had brightened up. The mud-coloured clouds were flying west before the wind leaving a brilliant sky over the empty streets of the town. As they walked, Benoist made conversation.

"Did you miss something?" he asked.

"Miss?"

"Your car breaking down like that – did it cause you to miss something – an appointment, a party?"

"No," said Donaldson. "Why do you ask?"

"You seem a bit on edge, if you don't mind my saying so. It happens to me when my arrangements go wrong; once I'm put out, it takes a lot to get me on an even keel again. I thought it might be the same with you. I noticed it back at the hotel."

Donaldson shook his head. "I've been running around too much lately. That's probably it."

"Probably. You should learn to relax." They turned into the lane by the Meres.

"Whereabouts in the area did the plane crash?" Donaldson asked.

"Didn't Tony tell you?"

"He said it was before his time."

"Yes, it would be." They were at the first lake. Benoist picked up a stone and threw it into the water. The changing weather had turned the colour blue, and the sun had tidied up the ragged look of the reedy banks. He went on. "There were a number of German aircraft brought down in this general area. Our chaps used to shoot at 'em as they came over the coast. The old airfield, RAF Disenham, is only a couple of miles away, not that there's anything much there now."

They paused, blinking in the sunlight, and stared at a moorhen scrabbling around in the reeds. Donaldson watched Benoist rocking on the heels of his heavy brown shoes and smiling at the sky with a dreamy air of well-being. *I am a hunted man!* Donaldson thought to himself, but couldn't feel the urgency; just a sense that the pace of the slowly elapsing afternoon was wrong.

"When I mentioned Tony's story," he said, "I got the impression that it brought a specific plane to mind." They had resumed their stroll along the bank and the second of the meres came into view, mirror-bright and streaked with the reflection of trees. Benoist stopped; he snapped the head off a dried reed, split the stalk and used it to pick his teeth. In the gesture Donaldson felt the other man's uncertainty quiver in the air. *He knows something.*

"There was a plane – a bomber – a Junkers in fact" – a flick and the toothpick spun off into the undergrowth – "came over one night, right at the end of the war, and got itself shot down – splash – right here in the Meres. Hell of a hullabaloo and all the town singing and dancing to have their very own German! No animosity, you understand, not by then: Jerry was beaten, so what was the point in hating him? There was only one survivor, and people couldn't buy him

229

drinks fast enough. They were quite put out when the Army arrived to take him away." He said something more but the words were lost in the scrunch of his shoes on the path.

"How deep are the Meres?"

"Twenty feet, give or take, at their deepest. Why?"

Donaldson saw himself again, walking out in the shallows towards the stricken aircraft.

"Which one did it land in?"

"Which lake?"

"Yes, which one?"

They stopped where the bank was crumbly and shelved gradually down to the water. There were tyre-tracks in the mud showing that someone made a habit of towing a boat there. A few coils of rusting wire, nailed to the trees, suggested that the second lake had once been fenced off.

"What is this?" Annaliese had found an old placard dumped in the scrub. It read:

MINISTRY OF DEFENCE PROPERTY
DANGER TO UNAUTHORIZED PERSONS
KEEP OUT

"It was here?" asked Donaldson.

Benoist nodded. "That's right. The War Department fenced the whole place off. Everything very *verboten* for a while until the fuss died down, as things will."

Donaldson looked again at the water – still, shallow and blue; and, below the surface, the plane, lying as a pregnant possibility on the muddy bottom. The calmness of the water invited a Pre-Raphaelite hand to break out of it, trailing bright droplets, and wave the sword Excalibur thrice in the air.

"Of course", said Benoist, "the plane isn't there any more."

Chapter Twenty-Five

Ross left the murder scene in Wardour Street for the office in Battersea High Street. It was Calverton's idea. "Why don't you get yourself some sleep?" he suggested to break the silence as Williams and the Yard detection team finished their drinks and stood about the room coughing politely and fingering their glasses. There was a tension in the air as if they were waiting for someone to start some cocktail-party conversation.

Calverton had turned to Williams and begun going into obsessive detail concerning the manhunt. He was unconcerned with McKilroy's death and yet something was troubling him. Ross overheard him say, "It's started, and Kaster's on the loose", and knew what frightened the other man: the threat that Kaster represented to the frail, imperfect order by which the likes of Calverton tried to structure the world.

The office was in darkness except for the night-desk and empty but for the cleaners and Bliss, who had been called out because of the emergency and then forgotten. The Scot had made a bed on a couple of chairs, placed his teeth in somebody's out-tray and was snoring loudly through his slack lips. Ross made up a bed of his own and tried to doze. Elphinstone minded the telephone, took messages and whiled away the time reading *Teach Yourself Accounting* in the pool of light from an anglepoise lamp.

Ross was wakened by the sound of the cleaners laughing. One of them had found a used condom in someone's wastepaper-basket among the empty bottles and Christmas cards. She noticed Ross, chuckled sympathetically and volunteered a cup of tea. Ross checked his watch: it was nine o'clock. He disturbed Bliss and suggested they freshen up and hunt out some breakfast. "Don't mind me, old man," said Elphinstone, "I'll mind the store."

The streets were grey and empty and the cafés closed. They found the Salvation Army serving tea and bacon sandwiches from a converted ice-cream van. They shuffled to the head of the queue and threw in a five-pound note each for some sandwiches and a "God bless you!"

"I thought you were Jewish?" said Ross.

"I am," said Bliss.

"That's bacon you're eating."

"You've never seen bacon being made; I've never seen bacon being made; in fact, I don't know anyone that's seen bacon being made. As far as I'm concerned, it's just a rumour that pigs have anything to do with it."

They walked back to the office and found Elphinstone looking bright and new-minted.

"We've found McKilroy's man, Hennessy. He went on a bender last night. Apparently Kaster visited him, plied him with booze and took his car."

"What sort?" asked Bliss.

"1975, grey Ford Cortina."

"Your problem's solved, then, isn't it?"

"Is it?"

"Sure. You'll find Kaster still pushing it."

"Do you . . . ?" The question died on Elphinstone's lips. "Ah, a joke!" He hadn't got used to the fact that the serious world is full of jokes.

Bliss relented slightly from baiting the younger man and suggested a game of cards to pass the time. Elphinstone proposed solo whist: they settled on three-card brag after teaching Elphinstone the rules. They played slowly for matches, without much concentration. Ross was reminded of the Army, of the SAS, of the long waits in the dark and stillness, whether it was to trap rebels in Oman or the IRA in South Armagh. The Army was fuelled on three-card brag. The idea that a manhunt was all movement was wrong, a cliché invented by film-makers to stop the punters from falling asleep in their seats. He wondered what Kaster was doing. Probably waiting for something, with time heavy on his hands.

Calverton made some routine calls; they took turns to answer the phone. In general there was nothing to report; the situation was out of Calverton's hands; only the regular police could be in enough places to keep an eye out for the car. It was understand that Special Branch was turning over all of Donaldson's known friends and acquaintances. Ross wished them luck: Kaster wouldn't be there.

The real call came at 3 p.m. A local bobby in a place called Disenham had seen Hennessy's car in a hotel car-park not two and a half hours before.

"I hope someone has had the sense to tell this local bloke to keep away from Kaster," was Bliss's laconic comment.

"It was there for quite a while, though," said Benoist. "The plane. Must have been until '51 at least." They were returning with slow paces to the Wing-Commander's house. The bright reprieve in the sky was passing and the sun moving towards the south-western horizon.

"Was it normal to leave a plane like that, without examining it?" asked Donaldson. "I've read the record: they were unable to check the bomb-load."

"I don't know about *normal*: there's nothing particularly normal about crashing your plane into a lake; though, I must say, if I'd been in the pilot's shoes, it's the sort of place I would have picked for a soft landing. From our side's point of view the usual procedure with these things was to recover the wreckage and have a look at it to see whether Jerry had dreamed up anything fancy."

"But in this case?"

"Well, obviously it wasn't done, though that's hardly surprising. When all's said and done, the aircraft was only a Junkers 88, and we'd been knocking them out of the air for five years so there wasn't much we didn't know about them; and, with the end of the war imminent, it wasn't so critical to discover what Jerry had been up to. I should think our people were more concerned with safety aspects. Unexploded bombs are a tricky thing to handle in the best of circumstances, and more so if they're lodged in a wreck under water. Unless you were forced to do otherwise, you would be well advised to leave them alone; and, if you absolutely had to deal with them, then you'd blow them up where they were were. Unless you knew what you were doing, you certainly wouldn't try to move them. Follow?"

Donaldson followed. He could see the British authorities paralysed into inaction by their uncertainty as to what exactly had been the bomb-load in Reinhardt Egger's aircraft. The risks in finding out had been unthinkable.

"What happened in 1951?"

"Oh, you know, the world was changing. People were starting to take holidays again and Disenham wanted its share of the trade. The boat business – you must have seen the jetty – started up round about then, and more people were taking to the water. There was talk of digging a channel between the Meres and opening the whole lot up – not that it ever happened – and in all this activity the locals were worried that someone would injure himself on the wreck."

"So the Ministry of Defence stepped in?"

"They sent a team of divers and spent a week going over the plane, but didn't find what they wanted. Then afterwards they brought a couple of tractors and simply dragged the whole thing out of the water and up on to the bank. They had to cut down trees to do that; and, in general, they made such a mess that people said that now the Meres were safe no one would want to see them. Which is more or less true: Disenham has stayed a pretty quiet sort of place, though whether on account of what the Army did I wouldn't like to say."

Donaldson felt there was something wrong in the other man's story but it remained elusive at the back of his mind as they walked back to the bungalow, where the car was parked. He felt that Benoist had been on the point of saying something else but couldn't. The Wing-Commander walked with his head slowly nodding so that he looked alternately at the sky or at his feet, but not at his guests.

"Why didn't the divers find what they were looking for?" asked Annaliese. The question caught Benoist with his hand on the garden gate.

"I expect they made a mistake. Perhaps their information was wrong. Perhaps the pilot dropped his bombs before crashing."

"But one of the crew was saved," she persisted. "He would know what was in the plane. He would know that the bombs had not been dropped."

"Was no investigation made at the time of the crash? Didn't they send down a diver to check the payload and decide whether it would be safe to leave it there?"

Benoist didn't answer. He pushed open the gate and walked up the path, between bare flowerbeds where, in summer, hollyhocks would grow. Donaldson remained at the gate with the girl. He felt the Last Judgement, with all its evanescent, illusory quality, slipping away from him again. The older man paused at the door of his home and turned.

"A cup of tea, I think," he said. "Don't you agree?"

At the other end of the little town, PC Arthur Sullivan put on his bicycle clips, unchained his machine and set off to do a quick tour to see whether the grey Ford Cortina was still somewhere around. He felt very excited.

"Are you a collector?" asked Benoist good-humouredly as they sat, nursing tea and slices of battenburg cake.

"I have some watercolours," said Donaldson, "and some contemporary oils."

"Then you'll understand the desire of the collector to show his collection."

"Yes."

Benoist suddenly felt a need to go around the room and wind the many clocks. He said he had made them himself in his garage-workshop. "I've often read in the newspapers about works of art that get stolen," he reverted to the subject.

Like Leonardo's *Last Judgement*, thought Donaldson, but he knew that Benoist was not alluding to that – indeed, had certainly never heard of the painting.

"I always wonder", the Wing-Commander went on, "what satisfaction the people who buy such things get. Eh? For some, I suppose, it must be a purely private joy, the possession of a secret, something that the rest of the world doesn't share. What do you think? Others, I imagine, must experience the gall of not being able to show their treasure to anyone. I wonder – it's by definition not the sort of thing one can discuss."

"I don't know."

"No, I suppose not. Well, there it is. Now, I know nothing about art – in my time it was left to the nancy-boys, if you'll pardon my French – but I do know something about collecting."

"Militaria."

"Exactly." Benoist searched around for something, found it on a table and lobbed it in the younger man's direction. Donaldson caught it. It was a grenade. The Wing-Commander noticed the speed of the younger man's reflex, the rapid check of the firing-pin, and grinned. "Well, is it live? What do you think?"

"I imagine you're not a madman; so I assume it isn't." He lobbed it back, and Benoist replaced it on the table.

"You're right of course. I disarmed it myself. It's all a matter of knowing what you're doing."

Donaldson understood. "You went down to the plane, didn't you?

That's why the army divers didn't find what they were looking for in 1951."

"It was partly the challenge of the thing," said Benoist as he led them into his garage. "I mean, one couldn't have this damned Jerry aircraft lying, so to speak, in one's own backyard – or should I say 'goldfish-pond'? – and not want, at the very least, to go take a look at it. It's against human nature! More to the point, it's against the nature of any collector worth his salt." He turned on the light. Donaldson looked around. Cars had been banished from the garage and the place had been turned over partly into a workshop and partly into a home for his collection. The floor was a maze of filing-cabinets and display-cases, and by the door was a workbench and a power lathe. Benoist pointed out the exhibits as they struggled through the clutter. The guidebook descriptions broke up his narration, but Donaldson gathered that as early as 1946 the demobbed airman had obtained some war-surplus diving equipment from a friend and had visited the wreck.

"Piece of cake, really; the Meres are very shallow and the Jerry pilot hadn't so much crashed into the water as belly-flopped and sunk as nice and gradual as you like with no mess or breaking up. I went inside her and found everything in apple-pie order."

"Had she jettisoned her bombs?" asked Donaldson.

"No. I'd say she was still carrying her full 900-kilogram load – about normal for the type – and there they were, all eighteen of them, looking like nothing so much as a basketful of eggs."

"A basketful of eggs?"

"Yes," said Benoist. He pulled back a dust-sheet from an object on the floor. "See for yourself. I took one."

Calverton now had to watch as Williams swung the whole of the police machine into action. He consoled himself with Lionel Sholto's last observation: "Give them enough rope, Norman, give them enough rope! They learn enough about tying knots in the police force – or am I thinking of the Boy Scouts?" Meanwhile he was isolated in the small office thoughtfully provided for him at the Yard, while Williams kept himself good-tempered by using the hunt for Kaster as an excuse to put the chief constables through the hoop. Calverton occupied himself with the total picture, filling out the pattern with snippets of information as they came in.

From Sebastian Summer: Donaldson had been a student of Russo-Byzantine art. He had been to the Soviet Union. No doubt, thought Calverton, at the time when, according to legend, Kaster had been educated by the KGB at their training-ground at Sokhodnaya.

Again from Sebastian Summer: his junior partner had made a study of Islamic art. This time he gave dates of a sabbatical in the Middle East which covered the period when Desmond McKilroy had met Kaster in Libya.

From the computer in Wiesbaden: Kaster's latest known contact, Reinhardt Egger, had a war record. Speculation: was he anti-Semitic and/or formerly involved with the Gestapo – either of which facts might interest a terrorist? The Bundeskriminamt would check and report again.

From the Bundeskriminamt: a check of the German military archives, the Bundesgeschichteforschung, in Freiburg revealed that Luftwaffe Major Reinhardt Egger had been a member of the staff of Reichsmarschall Hermann Goering. He had been taken prisoner by the British in April 1945.

From the Ministry of Defence in Whitehall: why did Calverton want to know? Could he call back on Monday?

Calverton wondered: where was Kaster now? Why had he been to Disenham? He thought of Ross, rushing by car to Suffolk. It was four o'clock, and Ross would be at Chelmsford.

At Benoist's bungalow the clock-chimes peeled in sequence through the house and garage. The Wing-Commander paused, still holding the dust-sheet like a magician producing a rabbit, and remarked complacently: "I set the clocks at just slightly different times. If they were all synchronized, then one wouldn't hear the separate chimes." He finished the action and let the cloth fall to the floor. "Well, what do you think? It does rather remind you of an egg, doesn't it?"

Donaldson did not immediately answer. He stared at the object lying in the wooden cradle that Benoist had made for it. He was right: its off-white, roundish casing made it approximately egglike. The aptness wasn't lost on him. The egg was pregnant with possibilities, the beginning and end of all things, a suitably cosmic dress for the Last Judgement.

"I thought you said that they found no bombs in the wreck in 1951." Annaliese broke the spell.

"I said they didn't find what they wanted," Benoist corrected her.

"They were looking for eighteen bombs and found only seventeen. There were quite a few enquiries at the time, I can tell you, though they didn't come right out with it and say what they wanted."

"But what possessed you . . . ?" Donaldson began, then paused: *possession* had become an emotive word.

"What possessed me to take a bomb from the wreck?" Benoist answered the question with a question. "What do you think is in that bomb?"

Did Benoist know?

"Propaganda!" The Wing-Commander beamed. "Propaganda pure and simple! Papers, leaflets and whatnot." He leaned over the eggshell casing and rubbed his hands over its smooth, bone-white surface. "Know what that is?" He tapped it. "Porcelain!"

"Porcelain?"

"Exactly! Now, why do you make bombs out of stuff as fragile as china?"

Donaldson realized that he knew the answer. "When you don't want the contents to be destroyed by being blown to bits."

"I say, you are sharp, aren't you? Quite right, of course. And, naturally, it follows that there isn't an explosive charge inside the thing, otherwise blow the contents to bits is exactly what it would do! All of which means that the thing is as safe as houses, follow?"

Donaldson followed.

"As a matter of fact, that isn't entirely true. There was a length of detonating cord and a small charge in a detachable cap – just enough to crack the case and chuck out the contents – but altogether not the regular sort of thing; and, believe me, in the matter of bombs of the exploding variety, I wot well that of which I speak, having personally dropped more than a few in my time."

"But propaganda?"

"It's how we started the war, dropping leaflets on each other, and it seems a reasonable way of finishing it. I expect it contains pleas for clemency for a defeated enemy and dire warnings against the Reds and that sort of thing – people will do any daft and desperate thing when they're losing. I thought more than once of trying to open it up to take a look, but it's been sealed up so tight that there's no obvious way of doing it without a lot of damage; and I wasn't prepared to do that. But one thing you can be sure of: propaganda is what's in there." He tapped the object again. "What else could there be?"

Donaldson felt like saying "Destiny!" It was appropriate, but too theatrical; and self-dramatization was something he knew he had to avoid: it meant the collapse of his cool self-control. He found himself unconsciously repeating in his head, "I must be rational and objective," until the words themselves became a meaningless mantra. He was brought back by Benoist speaking.

" . . . in the front garden. If you'll wait a moment, I'll find out who it is." Benoist turned his back on his visitors and went into the house. Donaldson heard it now, the sound of feet scuffling in the gravel. He followed the other man as far as the kitchen and out of the window caught sight of a middle-aged policeman ducking behind a forsythia bush and squatting there to observe the bungalow.

"The car must have been identified," said Annaliese calmly.

"He's on his own. There's his bicycle by the gate."

At that moment Benoist emerged at the front of the house, faintly bewildered and enquiring. "Is there anybody there?" in a singsong voice like a medium at a seance. "What are you doing there, man?" he asked as he spotted PC Arthur Sullivan. Donaldson didn't wait for the answer. He was already running.

As he came out of the front door, Sullivan was already straddling his bike and trying to frogmarch it through the gap in the half-closed gate. Benoist was in the middle of the path, torn both ways in a world that had suddenly gone crazy. Donaldson drew the Walther PPK and lined it up on the other man's forehead. Two saddened eyes looked back. "Don't do that. Play the white man, eh? We've broken bread and eaten salt together." Donaldson smacked him across the face with the gun butt and left him collapsed on the lawn. Sullivan was now ahead, pedalling hard along the beach road, three hundred yards from the bungalow and heading towards the town. Donaldson ran to the car, meaning to catch the other man easily in the open. But, even if he wasn't used to dealing with terrorists, Sullivan wasn't wholly stupid. As Donaldson got within fifty feet, pushing the car as hard as it would go, his opponent suddenly brought the bicycle to a dead halt at right angles across the road and set off on foot across the beach. Donaldson saw the bicycle but couldn't escape it. It whipped up, twisted and smashed into the windscreen. The car slewed from the road, did a half-circle on the beach, then came to a halt as the wheels bit trenches into the shingle. Donaldson got out of the car. He was covered in glass splinters but unharmed. The other man was nowhere to be seen.

He scanned the beach. The tide was out, a grey sea lapping at the small margin of sand. In both directions the flat expanse of pebbles stretched out for miles, broken only in a couple of places by the dark line of a wooden groin. There was no one about, only a dog rooting in the twilight. No houses within half a mile. No other signs of humanity than half a dozen dinghies pulled up on to the beach. They were roped down with green tarpaulins and the only sounds in the darkening day were the swish of the waves and the ping-ping of lanyards drumming against the masts.

Donaldson didn't want to shoot Sullivan. In the plans that were tumbling through his brain as he adjusted to the new phase of the game there was something he wanted of the policeman. But where was he?

He caught a movement among the boats. He guessed that Sullivan was hiding there because he knew that a middle-aged man was not going to outrun his younger opponent. Donaldson approached cautiously. A second dog appeared, saw him and squatted on its hindquarters with a curious look on its face. He smiled ironically, and only then did he glimpse Sullivan from the corner of his eye. The policeman was behind him and had a large stone which he was about to smash on Donaldson's head.

"You were hiding by the car," Donaldson said. He had turned before his enemy could strike and Sullivan, who was unused to violence, was for a split second mesmerized because the words reminded him that he was trying to kill a living man. His victim didn't give him another chance; his foot lashed out at Sullivan's abdomen and the policeman doubled up and dropped the stone. Donaldson seized it and brought it down on the other man's face. There was a groan and then no more struggling.

Donaldson stripped the body of its uniform. Next he went over to the boats, pulled back one of the covers, dragged the body over and tipped it into the dinghy. There was blood still leaking from the head wound, which meant that Sullivan was still alive. Finally he went back to the car, reversed it out of the rut and, feeling his way cautiously over the beach, drove down to the water's edge and abandoned it before the incoming tide. With luck the sea would cover it and for a few hours the grey Cortina would disappear from the world and give him time.

With the other man's clothing under his arm, Donaldson walked back to the bungalow.

Chapter Twenty-Six

Ross arrived at Disenham at 4.45, driven by the gloomy Scot, Bliss. They went straight to the police station, which turned out to be an ordinary red-brick house with a blue sign at the front. It was in darkness, but there was plenty of activity around two blue and white cars parked at the front. They held four uniformed policemen and two CID plain-clothes men from the skeleton holiday force at Ipswich. Bliss made the introductions.

"We've only been here twenty minutes ourselves," said the detective sergeant in charge. He was aged about thirty-five, with a hambone face and a Zapata moustache, and he looked out of condition.

"Road-blocks?" asked Ross.

"They've been set up. You should have come through one on the Ipswich road." They hadn't, and he knew they hadn't.

"What about the local man?"

"Sullivan? We haven't seen him. His last message was that the car had vanished from the hotel and he was going to get on his bike and look for it."

"Say your prayers he didn't find it," said Bliss.

Ross asked: "And what are you doing?"

"Waiting for him to come back – what else?"

The others, who had been sitting in the cars to stay warm, came over out of curiosity. Someone passed round a packet of cigarettes and they formed a circle, wreathed in the mist of their cold breath, their faces lit up in the flare of a match. Inside the house a telephone rang.

"Isn't anyone going to answer it?" asked Bliss.

"We can't get in. We don't have a key."

"For chrissake." Bliss didn't bother raising his voice. Ross broke the glass panel in the front door and released the catch. A burglar-alarm went off. "Now we'll have the fucking coppers down on us," said someone. Ross picked up the telephone receiver and took the call.

"One of the houses on the coast road," he reported to the others. "The woman says she saw two men fighting on the beach, not ten minutes ago!"

It took ten minutes to find the house. Blistered white paint and a view of the beach. A family of four were watching television with the volume turned up. The woman who made the call gave an incoherent account of the fight, broken with pauses as she tried to follow the programme.

"Whereabouts on the beach?" Ross pressed her. Outside it was dark: they would flounder for miles without directions.

"There, over there" – she stabbed vaguely with her finger – "about as far as here to the crossroads. It was near the boats." Ross worked out that the spot was half a mile or so north of the house. He went outside and told the others. They looked round at the dark expanse of pebbles and the sea, pale in the reflection of the moon. Someone sighed and remarked that he would probably break his neck on "that lot".

"They were watching TV," said Bliss as they crossed the road. "I could hear them, even outside. That's what I should be doing at Christmas, with a bottle of scotch by my side."

"You wouldn't have liked the programme."

"How do you know? I like Christmas variety shows. What was it?"

"*Hamlet on Ice*."

They fanned out in a line, eight men from the road to the sea's edge. They found the car first. The tide was turning and it was up to its wheel arches in water.

"Which way was it coming from, north or south?" Ross looked to the others, but no one could say. The angle at which it was left was inconclusive and there was no evidence on the pebbles.

"Over here!" someone shouted. They moved as a group towards the dinghies. Ross snapped at the others to keep up the search.

He didn't recognize the speaker, one of the uniformed men. Ross shone his torch into the boat and saw the naked form of a man. There was blood dried in a crust down the side of the head, but he was still alive – just.

Ross shouted to the others. "Forget everything else. Look for a bicycle! Someone check the road!" It took them five minutes to find the machine. It was twisted and lying on its side in a ditch. Ross stared at it, willing it to tell a story. From which direction had the car come? What had Kaster been doing there? He remembered that the windshield had been broken. "Is there glass on the road?"

"There's some a little further up," answered Bliss.

"Then Kaster must have been going south; he hit Sullivan's bicycle and carried it away from the glass.

"Heading back to London?"

"London is south-west. We're on the north side of the town here. Kaster must have driven through and out here to visit someone local. If he'd been just passing through, he'd have been heading north when he met Sullivan." He gazed northwards along the road and saw the lights of scattered houses and bungalows.

"I suppose we can make a few calls," said Bliss doubtfully.

Ross called the detective sergeant over. "Has anybody asked questions at the hotel where Sullivan spotted the car?"

"The Marquis of Granby? No. You think he may have met someone there?"

"It may be worthwhile finding out."

It was seven o'clock before they found Benoist gagged and trussed in his own house. He was too shaken to speak, even to give details of his missing car.

At 5 p.m. a blue Vauxhall saloon was stopped by the police road-block on the Lowestoft road two miles out of Disenham. There were half a dozen policemen, three of them armed, and two cars whose warning-lights lit up the surrounding bushes with irregular flashes.

"Can I ask you where you are going to, sir?" The sergeant wore an uncomfortable flak-jacket. He leaned down and shone a torch into the face of the driver. He glimpsed the other man's uniform and shouted back to his comrades: "It's one of ours." Then to the driver: "What brings you out here? Which force?"

"I'm Sullivan. Can you stop shining that bloody light in my eyes, Sarge?"

"Sorry." The flashlight was switched off. "The local man?"

"Yes."

"What's up, then?"

"The telephone lines are down; so I thought I'd better drive out here to make my report. I've been round the town looking for the

Cortina. Someone saw it heading for Bury St Edmunds, like a bat out of hell, about three o'clock. We're all wasting our time hanging around here."

"Wouldn't you know it!"

"Sorry, Sarge, but that's the way it is."

"I missed my lunch for this." The sergeant called back to the others: "Better radio in and tell them our man's buggered off!" To the driver: "About three o'clock? He could be anywhere. Sod it!" He fiddled with the flashlight, flicking it on and off. "Tell them three o'clock!" he yelled over his shoulder. "And what are you going to do?" he asked.

"Tea with my mum and then to a pantomime."

"This is a right bloody pantomime already!"

"Yeah. Can you let me through?"

A sigh. "I suppose so." He turned back and waved the car on so that the others could see. A gap between the police-cars opened up and the Vauxhall crawled through.

A mile further down the road, the Vauxhall stopped at a gap in the hedge where a farm gate opened on to a field. The driver got out, went to the rear of the vehicle and released the boot-catch. A female figure unwrapped itself from an object covered in sacking.

"Are you all right?" asked Donaldson.

Annaliese nodded. She climbed out of the boot and took a few paces to loosen her muscles. Donaldson examined her lithe beauty as, unconscious of him, she exercised her cramped limbs, arms and legs outstretched in the pale light. For a second she looked as though she were praying to the moon, but the impression passed and she came back to the car and sat in the passenger-seat.

"What now?" she asked. "Where do we go?"

"I know a place," Donaldson said. He found himself unable to say any more; waves of tiredness were sweeping over him but he knew they had to press on. He needed time to recuperate and to think. It was Christmas Day: and on New Year's Eve they were expecting him to deliver his verdict on them. Until then he would rest and plan.

It took Calverton until 5 p.m. to convince the Ministry of Defence that he needed urgent access to its archive material. Another hour was needed to bring in an archivist from Epsom to open up the files held by the Air Historical Branch at their drab offices in Theobalds Road and a further hour to retrieve the material, copy it, issue the necessary receipts and courier it to Curzon Street, where Calverton had established a temporary home. It was 7 p.m. by the time that he had sight of the interrogation of Luftwaffe Major Reinhardt Egger at the hands of the British and 7.30 before he received the report of the finding of Wing-Commander Edmund Benoist. They were two pieces of information that told him what John Donaldson had been looking for at Disenham and what he had probably found. At eight o'clock he began making telephone calls.

The emergency meeting at the Admiralty was attended by Lionel Sholto, Gervase Molineux and the two men from the Cabinet Office and Ministry of Defence, Rogers and Atherton. The rest of the Committee had been deliberately excluded. There was one other person present, a tall man of fifty with sleepy eyes and an even-tempered smile, whose name was Arbuthnot and who had been brought in a cloak of secrecy post-haste from Wiltshire. It was on his account that the meeting was unable to take place until 10.30.

Sholto and Molineux had been dragged out of separate diplomatic receptions: Sholto in dinner-suit and hair-oil, the Foreign Office mandarin in full tails with his chest covered in a spray of Ruritanian stars and sashes. Molly was short-tempered and several times snorted: "I hope this isn't going to take a long time, Norman." Rogers seemed tired, Atherton was slightly drunk and the stranger, Arbuthnot, looked frankly glad for something to do.

"A word to the wise," said Lionel Sholto, taking Calverton aside and treating him to a loud stage-whisper. Calverton waited: he knew that Sholto was going to say something facetious; Englishmen of his background always did when faced with a crisis – indeed, Calverton did so himself, which made him wonder if it was caused by the schools they went to. "You do know, Norman, that, while murder may no longer be a capital offence, there are one or two social blunders that are still hanging matters."

"I'll bear it in mind, Lionel. Now, can we get to business?"

They took their places.

"We have reason to believe", Calverton began quietly enough, "that Kaster has acquired a weapon containing biological agents, specifically anthrax and plague. In all probability he proposes to use it somewhere in London on New Year's Eve, that being the day when the Americans arrive and public interest becomes focused on the whole biological war issue." He waited for pandemonium to break out. Maybe one day it would.

"Could be a bit of a problem, that," said Rogers at last. Everyone agreed.

"Where did he get it from, this thing?" asked Molineux.

Arbuthnot chipped in briefly: "Old German bomb – aircraft in Suffolk – will happen if these things are left lying around."

"It seems that it's a leftover from the war, but none the less deadly for that," said Calverton. The others sat back and waited for more.

"I think you'd better tell us the tale, then," said Molineux grimly.

"This story goes back to the 1930s," Arbuthnot began. "The Japanese – God bless 'em – were heavily involved in research into the use of biological agents to use against the Chinese. They were at war, if you remember. Anyway, it's fair to say that at this time the Japanese were ahead in the game compared with any other of the Great Powers. In particular, a section of the Army in Manchuria, based at a place called Pingfan, were very active – very active – at the cost of many thousands of deaths to innocent civilians used in their experiments.

"The upshot of all this activity was a weapon known as the Uji bomb." Arbuthnot sucked on his pipe and went on: "Details a bit vague, I'm afraid. The Russians were the first to overrun Pingfan and, not unnaturally, they have proved to be a bit reticent about these matters. But there we are: to cut a long story short, we are talking about a bomb with an all-up weight of thirty-five kilos with a ten-litre payload, which was field-tested – apparently successfully – with *Yersinia pestis,* which is to say 'plague', and *Bacillus anthracis,* otherwise 'anthrax'. What do you know about plague?"

"Take it we know nothing," said Sholto.

Arbuthnot looked around for any contradiction and then picked up again. "Plague is transmitted in two forms. It survives in the wild in populations of rodents and other small mammals and passes around by means of their fleas: this form is known as *bubonic* plague. By and large, bubonic plague is not a problem unless humans come into contact with animal fleas, and this doesn't happen on a large scale unless there's a breakdown in urban sanitation. However, it happens that a person infected by plague can pass the disease on by coughing, and it is the inhalation of bacteria which causes the secondary form of the sickness known as *pneumonic* plague. Note that in this case there is no need for the agency of fleas: in principle it is capable of being passed in the sort of conditions applying in a Western city. Are we all clear? Good.

"Now, then, the Japanese are known to have had success with spreading bubonic plague. What that amounts to is that they put fleas in the bomb, dropped it and the fleas survived to pass on the disease. This is not so easy as it sounds since, in the ordinary way, the heat and stress of detonation would be enough to kill them. However, that may be by-the-by and what we are interested in is a rather different effect, because it seems that the Uji bomb was also capable of delivering a uniform aerosol-cloud over a distance of five hundred metres – say, the size of—"

"Trafalgar Square?" suggested Atherton.

"If you like. Now, if this is true, then it is quite possible that the bomb was also capable of delivering pneumonic plague, a much more nasty proposition." Arbuthnot paused and then resumed in his dry, conversational tone: "In other words, gentlemen, this weapon has beentestedwiththemostdeadlydiseaseknowntoman–anditworks."

Lionel Sholto asked: "Where do the Nazis appear in this story?"

"The Germans were rather late off the mark," said Arbuthnot. "It wasn't until 1943 that their principal establishment for biological warfare was set up by the SS at Posen. How far they got is a matter for conjecture. The official line is based on what the survivors had to say: the installation itself, as with Pingfan, was captured by the Russians. Since no one was likely to win any prizes for conspiring to wipe out humankind, you may form your own judgement as to whether to believe that the Germans had little success.

"The crucial question, to which there is no answer, is whether the Germans had access to the work that the Japanese had done. If they didn't, then they probably hadn't got far on their own in two years. But, if they were building on work that stretched back more than a decade and were applying some of the famous teutonic thorough-ness, well, then. . ." Arbuthnot left the rest unsaid. Calverton picked up the story.

"In April 1945 a lone German raider was shot down by the RAF over Suffolk, probably on its way to bomb London. The survivor from the crash was a Luftwaffe major, name of Reinhardt Egger, and he was duly interrogated by our people. I've just this evening read the records of that interrogation.

"Two things struck everyone from the very beginning. The first was that Egger wasn't a regular operational flyer. For want of a better word, he was a *salon* Nazi, very pally with Goering and on his staff. The second was that his aircraft had no damn business being over England at all; in April 1945 it was our turn, and to find the Germans having a go was, to say the least, annoying. These facts caused us to hang on to him and interrogate him for three years, on and off. You'll appreciate that at the start we had little to go on except gut feelings, and the picture only became clearer as there was time to analyse captured records.''

"We follow," said Molineux. "Go on, Norman."

"Egger's first tack was to behave the arrogant Nazi – Geneva Convention, name, rank and number and nothing more. When that didn't work, he became co-operative but ignorant: if it were up to him, says Egger, he would tell us, but the truth is he had no idea what the payload of his aircraft was except the usual high explosive and incendiaries.''

"Which might have been true," suggested Atherton.

"No – not on a mission so late in the war and with a high-class Nazi like Egger in charge. It didn't make sense, and Egger was told as much," said Calverton.

"How did he react?" asked Sholto.

"He conceded that it was a special mission with – perhaps – a new type of weapon. But he, Egger, was not a technical man and he couldn't say more.''

"Which, again, might be true," said Atherton, Calverton ignored him.

"By this time our people had discovered that the Germans had been developing nerve-gases. This was a worrying consideration. If the bombs lying in Disenham Mere contained nerve-gas, then disposing of them was going to prove a real problem. So they asked Egger: was his payload Sarin?''

"Sarin?" enquired Molineux.

Arbuthnot interrupted. "Isopropyl methylphosphonofluoridate. A by-product of pre-war German research into insecticides and very effective, too. The Nazis built a plant near Falkenhagen to make the stuff. The Americans used to have large stockpiles of it; maybe they still do.''

"Very interesting. Thank you, David – it is David, isn't it?" said Sholto. To Calverton he said: "What did our German friend have to say to that?"

"Oh, he agreed that it might well have been."

"Just like that? I mean, did he agree straight away?"

"Yes."

"Damned odd. Don't you think it's odd, Molly? You wouldn't think that anybody would be in a rush to admit that sort of thing."

"He could have been proud of the fact," answered Molineux. He invited the others to agree. "The Nazi mind – mightn't have seen anything nasty in it."

"Hardly," said Sholto. "Norman says he was cagey to start with. So what's he doing suddenly confessing? Hiding something worse?"

"That was the general opinion," resumed Calverton. "Our people were very suspicious. They suggested to Egger that maybe his load was Tabun – another nerve agent," he added to pre-empt Arbuthnot. "Egger was happy to agree that that was a possibility. Well, after that, the sky was the limit: Ricin, Botulinal Toxin, Saxitoxin and a host of fevers with rather colourful names. The interrogators put the lot to him. First he agreed; then he said he didn't know; then he asked people to stop asking him questions. Finally he broke down entirely and spent the next three years in various mental hospitals suffering from religious delusions. After that he was obviously of no use, so we let him go. He decamped to Egypt: the old family home, I understand."

"Anything in particular cause him to go off his head?", asked Atherton.

"Yes. Someone suggested that his plane might have been carrying plague."

"It seems to me", Gervase Molineux began after a break for coffee, "that we can't attach too much weight to Egger's testimony in this matter. Surely that's not all you have to go on, Norman?"

"No."

"Thought not. Wasn't there the plane? There must, one assumes, have been some wreckage. What about Porton Down? Didn't they get in on the act? All this questioning about weird and wonderful diseases doesn't sound as though it emanated from Aldershot. I suppose that this is your area, David?" He turned to Arbuthnot. "You did say it was *David*, didn't you?"

"Yes. David."

"Fire away, David," proposed Lionel Sholto.

"Right. OK. Well." Arbuthnot cleared his throat. "There was an investigation of the wreckage of the aircraft as early as 1945. That uncovered the fact that it had a payload in the 750- to 800-kilo range consisting of eighteen bombs in what appeared to be unusual ceramic casings."

"Ceramic?" interrupted Molineux. "Do you mean pottery?"

"Yes, more or less."

"I see. Carry on."

"Well, that was a bit of a teaser. No one knew what was in them, and opening them up or blowing them up promised to be a bit of a Pandora's box, so they were left strictly alone and the area was fenced off.

"There were plenty of theories, the front runner being nerve-gas. The argument was that since these things involve fluorine-containing organo-phosphorous compounds they might have proved a problem for the usual design of bomb. You see, we knew that the Germans had had a lot of problems in the final fluoridation process using hydrofluoric acid, which is very corrosive. Their pilot plants at Spandau and Munster-Lager had been bedevilled by corrosion troubles. So, putting two and two together, it seemed a pretty sound guess that the ceramic casings were an anti-corrosion device used by the Germans because they were worried about degradation of the nerve-gas during storage."

Sholto looked to Calverton and then to the others. "I think we all follow that. What changed everybody's mind?"

Arbuthnot answered more cautiously: "The truth is that after the war we – the Americans and so on – got into the act, making Tabun and Sarin and so on. And when we did it for ourselves we discovered that, once you had actually manufactured these chemicals, they were remarkably stable: in fact we could, and did, store them for years without too much difficulty. All of which tended to knock the nerve-gas theory on the head. Then someone noticed the similarity of the Disenham bombs to the Uji bomb."

Atherton explained the resemblance. Both the German bombs and the Uji bomb had a detonation cord cemented to the casing and a small charge placed in the nose, indicating that the contents were not themselves explosive and might be damaged by a large explosion. Then, too, both had ceramic cases, easily shattered without injury to the contents. "The only thing we needed to know was the biological agent being used."

"And you can guess the answer to that," said Calverton. They were reminded that Reinhardt Egger had gone literally mad at the mention of plague.

"In 1951 it was decided to dispose of the bombs," said Atherton. "Given that their content was problematical and their long-term stability uncertain, it was too dangerous to leave them where they were, in fairly shallow water near a populated area. It was also considered too dangerous to try to open one of them experimentally. It would have involved the risks of transporting the thing two hundred miles to Wiltshire, not to mention our ignorance of what exact precautions we should have to take in doing the deed. If there were an internal charge, for example, we could have blown ourselves to pieces and spread God knows what."

"So what was done?" asked Molineux.

Calverton answered sharply: "They dumped the whole lot unceremoniously into the North Sea, just as they had done with the chemical weapons! The point being that when they recovered the bombs in 1951 there was one missing. Kaster has found it."

"I see," said Molineux. Suddenly, under the electric light, his face looked grey and worn. "Tell me," he said to Arbuthnot. "In this day and age, what does plague mean?" Arbuthnot handed out copies of a report.

Chapter Twenty-Seven

THE SNOW started near Grantham. At first large snowflakes that flopped on to the windshield, tangible as pancakes, and by degrees vanished. The car was parked in a lay-by while Donaldson seized half an hour's sleep. A storm-drain gurgled and sucked up litter with the melting snow.

Near Newark he stole another car. It was from a hotel that advertised a late-night Christmas dinner-dance. It wasn't late, the dance had barely begun and the car would not be missed for hours.

The snowflakes became smaller, tighter. Stationary, they formed a veil, coloured tawny by the lights of the town. Driving through them was driving through a white funnel, a web of snow, an entrapment. There was no traffic worth the name. Other cars were grey spectres, smudges at the edge of vision.

He slept again, this time somewhere in the neighbourhood of Pontefract. The girl curled up with him, and they dozed in their own warmth until midnight came and went and they woke with a start at the chill that was eating into the car. Donaldson looked out on the snow. It was drifting. The car went into a wheelspin as he started it and only slowly did they get going again. He knew that if they had stayed another half-hour, then they would have been stuck. Was it fate or blind fortune that had woken them up in time? Forget about it. Cruise northwards slowly in the wake of a snow-plough.

From time to time he glanced at Annaliese. Sometimes she noticed him. Sometimes she gave him the feather of a smile. Otherwise she was self-absorbed; he didn't know what in. Her interior world was to him a magician's box – a complicated space full of nothing but corners to get lost in. As she lay down to sleep again, a touch of gentleness grazed her face and for a second he felt that he could love her. He touched the emotion, but it didn't feel authentic. Nothing about her, or about anything, felt authentic. Except, paradoxically, for the paintings and the symbols, which felt as if all the reality of the world had been distilled out of it and into them; and all the random material dross of creation took form from the framework they provided.

More driving. More miles seen through the persistent mist of condensation. Eating up miles. An accident on the road, marked by warning triangles and the amber lights of the AA service. A Little Chef diner, where they stopped for coffee and a sandwich. No one else there except a lorry-driver punching at a fruit machine and a man who came in, looking for something or other, went out, came back, unable to believe that what he was seeking wasn't there. Donaldson made a brief telephone call.

"Plague," said Arbuthnot's report, "is chiefly a parasite of rodents, which is transmitted from animal to animal and to humans primarily by fleas. Contrary to the common belief, the disease is not confined to rats but is harboured by more than eighty species of rodent.

"On the death of its host, its fleas will abandon the corpse to seek a new food-source. The fleas themselves, however, are affected by the disease, whose bacteria block the insect's alimentary canal. This has the result that the fleas cannot feed normally and will regurgitate the host's blood into the wound they have made, so contaminating it with the bacteria which are choking them. In due course the host will catch plague, die and be abandoned, and so continues the cycle.

"The symptoms of plague include swelling of the lymph nodes, massive internal haemorrhaging, coughing, fever, delirium and, almost invariably, death.

"In addition to transmission by the rodent/flea cycle, plague can also be transmitted by blood, sputum and lung exudate. The breathing in of contaminated droplets from the coughing or breathing of an infected person will pass the disease in this secondary form: pneumonic plague.

"Plague occurs in recurrent cycles, known as pandemics, with lulls in between. The underlying basis of this pattern is unknown, but at its peak a pandemic has repeatedly pushed human societies close to the point of collapse. Instances of near-disaster are the plague which virtually destroyed the Athenian Empire in the fifth century BC and that which crippled the Roman Empire under Justinian. The scale of these catastrophes is difficult to assess, but in the case of the Black Death of 1347 to 1349 a quarter to a half of humanity was wiped out in Europe with further enormous losses in Asia. In terms of individual cities, mortality rates are known for locations which were far less populous than they are today and which were visited by plague at a time when, it should be emphasized, the pandemic had passed its peak. Examples are: Milan in 1630 – 86,000 dead; the Venetian Republic in 1630 – 500,000 dead; Moscow in 1771 – 60,000 dead.

"Since 1894 there have been signs of a new cycle of plague having Canton in China as its focus. Since 1900 it has been endemic in North America amongst wildlife and is clearly spreading. The relative absence of a large-scale outbreak among humans is not fully explicable. It may on the one hand be attributable to good public-health measures, in particular the suppression of rat-populations in towns; but the low incidence in the countryside and in Third World countries, where these factors are not so significant, suggests that the explanation may merely be that the disease has not reached that point in the cycle where a major outbreak may be expected. If this is in fact the case, then plague of disaster proportions remains a possibility. In modern levels of population and in the worst case, deaths may be measured in billions."

Calverton finished his reading of the report first. He looked at the others' faces and detected not fear at what might happen, but embarrassment as if they felt that in some way they had failed or would fail. He felt it, too, but could not say why. He left them to it and went to another room to make some calls.

Williams wouldn't answer the phone; he was too busy. When finally forced, instead of his usual fiery self, he was almost languid with satisfaction. It was a loudspeaker phone, which picked up the background noise. The Scotland Yard second team – C13 and all – were there, as jolly as Scouts at a jamboree.

"Everything's under control here," said Williams. "The operation is developing nicely."

"Have you caught Kaster or not?"

"I didn't say that. As a matter of fact, he slipped the road-blocks at Disenham, and we believe he's heading north."

"Believe?" asked Calverton.

"We're using the local force. We haven't been twelve hours into this thing yet, and establishing reliable communications takes time. But, believe me, we're getting our organization into shape."

Organization. It occurred to Calverton that, if Williams ever caught Kaster, he would organize a commemorative tie and an annual dinner at some police social club in Cardiff. "You have the

254

roads out of Suffolk blocked?" he said.

"Not all. It takes time. The weather has turned to snow and we're having difficulty in getting men to turn out on a bank holiday."

He called Elphinstone. The younger man was excited. He had been trying to call Calverton at the Admiralty, he said, but the switchboard wasn't answering. He had sent a courier but the man had been involved in a collision with a drunk driver. What was wrong? Calverton asked. Elphinstone said that Ross wasn't responding to orders. He, Elphinstone, had told Ross to stay at Disenham to await further instructions. Ross had said he was returning to London. Elphinstone had insisted. Ross had told him to fuck off. There was clearly a crisis of authority, and in the circumstances Elphinstone had felt obliged to call the Admiralty and, when that failed, send a courier.

Calverton calmed the other man down and asked for a further report on the hour or more often as necessary. He called the switchboard but couldn't get an answer. He hunted out the duty officer and finally fixed for a direct line to be run to the conference-room. Next he returned to the meeting.

"So this is the Gospel According to Porton Down, is it?" said Lionel Sholto, putting down his copy of Arbuthnot's report.

"A bit short of that, I'm afraid. A summary. More of an Idiot's Guide – no offence, but that's what we call it."

"I see. Didn't I read somewhere that plague died out in England when the brown rat took over from the black rat as what you might call your standard British rat?"

"That's right. *Rattus rattus* – that's the black rat – carried a flea which was particularly suited to the transmission of plague: but since 1700 it has been successively displayed by *Rattus norvegicus*, which isn't as effective a host."

"Well, there you are, eh?"

"I'm sorry," said Arbuthnot, "but I'm afraid that, of recent years, *Rattus rattus* has been staging a comeback. It's now the most common rat in London again. Don't you be mistaken: if a plague breaks out, the rats are there to transmit it."

"Can't we vaccinate against it?" asked Rogers.

"Certainly. What scale would you like to vaccinate on?"

"I don't know."

"The vaccine takes two weeks to build up an immunity and, even then, isn't effective against pneumonic plague."

"If Kaster proposes to explode his bomb at New Year," said Calverton, "then we have six days."

"Streptomycin, aureomycin, tetracyclin and chloramphenicol are effective in the early stages – penicillin is no use except to treat secondary infections. 'Early stages' means within twenty-four hours, in the case of pneumonic plague."

"What about anthrax?" asked Atherton. "We haven't talked about that. Didn't I understand you to say that we might be dealing with a cocktail of bugs?"

"Yes. The inclusion of anthrax is a particularly nice idea."

"*Nice*?" enquired Sholto. "You have a *nice* choice of words."

"As well as being lethal on its own account, anthrax is quite astonishingly persistent. The spores can lie in the soil more or less indefinitely. It's pretty much an open secret that we did some experiments on the isle of Gruinard in 1941. And, to this day, we haven't been able to clean the place up. If the reports from Russia are correct, they recently had an outbreak of anthrax traced to a 400-year-old site disturbed by an archaeological dig. It doesn't take much imagination to see what would happen if one could create such a situation in, say, central London: bloody chaos, a no-go area and a perfect breeding-ground for rats."

"As you say," murmured Sholto, "*nice!*"

"I'm not sure", volunteered Atherton, "that this discussion is any longer within the remit of this committee. I feel that we should notify the Joint Intelligence Committee and drop the whole problem into the lap of the Cabinet and the Prime Minister."

"The Prime Minister is at Chequers for the holiday and has flu," said Rogers.

"What do we tell the Americans?"

"Let me understand this right," said Lionel Sholto. "This hellish little brew has been sitting at the bottom of a lake for upwards of forty years. Doesn't it ever degenerate, go bad, die off or whatever you want to call it? I mean, if the plague bacteria were being carried by fleas, as you say the Japanese managed on occasion, then they'd be getting hungry little beggars by now, wouldn't they?"

"Assuming it were carried by fleas," said Arbuthnot. "But you do have a point. I've got little doubt that Kaster's bomb contains live anthrax spores, but it is admittedly unlikely that *Yersinia pestis* – plague – has remained viable under those conditions over this span of time."

"You mean it is dead?"

"Another Christmas Day gone. Hours ago and I didn't even notice. Haven't you fellows ever noticed how they come around more quickly than ever – Christmasses, I mean?"

"Have you ever thought", said Arbuthnot, "of the secondary effects of plague? I'm talking now about effects which are quite independent of the disease itself."

Nobody had. They were tired. The badly lit room had dark corners where portraits of forgotten seamen, hatstands and dreams lurked in the shadows. There was a feeling that they ought to be doing something about something and a feeling that they weren't. Just talking.

"When the Black Death broke out in Europe," said Atherton, "people went crazy with fear. They whipped themselves to expunge their guilt. They burned Jews and witches." The others were looking at him. "I read about it in a book."

"It won't happen in London," said Molineux. "Not in Belgravia anyway. People will keep their heads."

"Not everybody," said Arbuthnot. "We will tell people that there is nothing to fear. And for a while they may believe us and sit at home, watching each other for symptoms. There may be some genuine cases of anthrax; in which event they won't believe what we tell them about plague. Some won't believe us anyway. There's a lot of flu about this winter. To an uninformed person, the symptoms will resemble what the media tell them about the early stages of plague. So will bronchitis, pneumonia – everything, if people worry enough.

"People will start to leave London. Only a few at first, but others will join in – they won't want to be last – there will be rumours. Everyone will know of a case of plague which the authorities are hushing up. People will stay out of central London. They'll start reporting sick so that they don't have to go to work – don't have to mix with other people. 'Why are so many sick?' others will ask. 'Is it plague?'

"The hospitals will be affected early. People will need assurance: 'Tell me that my symptoms aren't plague.' They will want injections, drugs, something to protect them. There won't be enough supplies – there never are. The hospitals will be short-staffed: too many potential patients: staff reporting sick. Perhaps the waiting public will riot? As the traffic heading out of the city builds up, there will be accidents, fighting and riots out of fear and frustration at the jammed roads. The casualties will flood back to overload the hospitals. As they become overloaded, people will say: 'Is it plague?'

"Public transport will run down. Too many people heading one way. Rolling-stock gets wrongly located. Staff stay away to avoid infection because they know that relatives of plague victims will be trying to escape, and they are particularly dangerous. The movement of supplies into London by rail will slow down and stop. The roads will be impossible in any event.

"The sewerage system will break down. Absenteeism among the workers will be high because they know all about rats, they see them every day; and rats carry plague. As the system collapses and impurities get into the drinking-water supplies there may be cases of typhoid and other diseases which will all feed through to the hospitals and be confused in the popular mind with plague. The contamination of the water-supply will pressure more people into leaving London and add one more turn to the mounting circle of panic.

"The police will try to cope. The traffic will be too much for them. There will be riots to control. Crime will be rife because of the opportunities given by the evacuation, and people will be aggressive, deluded and short of food perhaps. Every little liberation army and terrorist group will announce the downfall of capitalism. They'll let off bombs, shoot people, whatever takes their fancy. The police, like every other service, will be under strength.

"Fires will break out. In some places the traffic will stop the fire-engines. There may not be water. The fires will be left to burn themselves out. Factories and warehouses will be particularly vulnerable because they will be unguarded: no one is working.

"British shipping will be embargoed. No imports or exports. General disruption of manufacturing. Food-hoarding. The banks in the City will close fairly early in the crisis and sterling will fall like a stone. Central government may or may not continue in London, but it will have too much to do and few resources to do it apart from the Army.

"Of course," said Arbuthnot with a bland smile, "this is the worst case. The actual disaster could be smaller – probably would be – say, a few thousand dead, a few million pounds' worth of property destroyed. It's a test, really, of how good we are at controlling things, of managing a crisis."

"But there isn't any threat of plague," said Lionel Sholto. "You've said as much. The bomb is probably sterile."

"Oh, you don't need plague," said Arbuthnot. "These are secondary effects that have nothing to do with the disease. You only need the *illusion* of plague."

In Newcastle the snow would not lie, but ran off in black torrents down the gutters. The waters of the Tyne glimmered blackly under the High Level Bridge. In a side-street red Post Office vans were parked in a line, and wandering drunks waltzed in the roadway trying to find Christmas. Lone taxis swooped out of the dark like vampires.

Donaldson turned west, following the signs for Hexham and the Roman Wall. The snow had been light. It was white floss on the fields where the sheep were sullen and huddled together. He took the old military road which was built on the line of the Wall. Beyond the hedges, the broad, shallow ditches dug by the Romans formed waves in the white grass. The road was straight like the Wall, but avoided the exposed crags where the Wall had followed the high point of the bare hills and challenged the northern barbarians across an open landscape of moorland and small lakes. On the high ground the Romans had built their forts and garrison towns; the lines of stones still peeped out of the grass. The few trees were eternally bent by the wind.

The military road passed north of Hexham. The town was a glow on the horizon. Donaldson slowed the car and peered at the signs at every junction. Small finger-posts pointed at paths leading to the Roman remains: this pile of stones was a Mithraic temple, that one was a milecastle where half a dozen guards would play dice, rub their frozen hands and stare north across the cold wastes, trying to decipher shapes in the snow. Follow the paths to the green palings of the Department of the Environment fences with their lovers' gates that led on to the sites. In the Mithraic temple twin bearers-of-light had held torches before the altar, like Castor and Pollux. Mithras slew the magic bull and saved mankind through its blood.

The road ran on. Small stone farms hugged the ground, grew out of it. They advertised fresh eggs and bags of manure. Drive on, locked in the beam of the headlights, locked in the dark interior of the car. Farms named after the hills, blunt names in dead dialects. A broad track running off north between the fields.

Donaldson took the track, laying his own tracks in the thin film of snow. To the south the snow-clouds battered the moors of West Durham. Overhead a black sky was dotted with stars. The car rattled over the skin of dirt that overlay the stone. A ruined cottage with a tumbled-in roof stood off to the side, isolated on the moor like a menhir, black against a moonlit horizon. A sheep that had been dozing in the road danced in front of the headlights and then scuttled through a gap in the broken walls. They bumped over the ruts and across the bed of a shallow stream, and Annaliese nursed the pack of explosives in her arms as if it were a baby.

The track descended into a hollow in the hills, where a few stunted trees gave shelter to a small cottage. It had a walled-in garden full of frosted cabbages, an outside privy with a stone roof, a broken-down chicken-house, a shed. The house itself was squat and in darkness. Donaldson parked the car. He left Annaliese inside. She was shivering and complaining of the cold. Her voice sounded distant. Inside the shed he found the house-key hanging on a nail behind the door. There was a stack of wood and some cans and the place smelled of paraffin. He filled a storm-lamp, lit it and went over to the cottage where he tried the door. It gave easily and opened into a short hallway leading directly to the stairs. The floor held ranks of gumboots and there were heavy coats on the wallpegs and a smell of warming dampness. In the downstairs room the embers of a fire were collapsing in the grate. Upstairs feet creaked on the floorboards.

"Who is there?" The figure at the top of the stairs was curious, not fearful. It came down, clattering with loose shoes on bare feet, hidden by the halo of a torch.

"John, is that you?" said her voice.

"Hello, Helen," said Donaldson.

Chapter Twenty-Eight

THERE were police-cars parked on the heath outside Hortense Ainsworth's house. The old lady was in the drawing-room steadfastly offering cups of tea and refusing to answer questions. A detective inspector was on the telephone trying to explain the situation and ask for instructions.

Ross was there because Calverton had called his apartment. "James, why don't you visit the girl again? She may know things she doesn't even know she knows."

"What about Donaldson's other friends?"

"Oh, the Yard have laid claim to everyone who is known. Even as we speak, they are busy suffering accidental injuries and making full and frank confessions. Kaster is too shrewd to turn to any of them."

"Do you know yet what he wants?"

"Yes," said Calverton. "He has telephoned one of the national papers with his demands. He wants his brother released. Nothing more. Just his brother. I'm sure you'll understand that."

"I know you," said Hortense Ainsworth bluntly. "You're the Mormon." There was a twinkle in her eye. Ross looked past her into the fireplace, where there were the burned remains of a photograph. He remembered the one of Helen and John Donaldson.

"Has she gone?" he asked.

"Why not? Why should she wait around for the arrival of the police state? Who is your fascist friend?" She looked at Bliss.

"He's Jewish."

"Fascism is contagious. Now, *you'll* be a communist."

"No."

"With your background, you should be."

"With your background, not mine. I can't read the long words."

She laughed and took him by the arm.

"Where are you going?" asked the detective inspector. "No, not you. Her!" he said into the phone.

"I'm whisking her away from all this."

"Ha, ha, everyone's a comic."

"What do you want?" Ross asked Hortense. They stood outside the drawing-room door. The old lady pulled her dressing-gown around her. The heating was off and the morning was cold.

"I thought you were the one who wanted something. Would you like to see her room?"

The room was simply set out. Pale-washed walls brightened with a vase of cut flowers. Plain furniture and a single mirror in a small walnut frame. A davenport with an unfinished letter on it. Ross's name but no message. What had she wanted to say?

"Helen is in love with you." The words might have been spoken by Hortense Ainsworth.

I am in love with her. No, David is in love with her. Does it matter that David is dead?

He rummaged through the drawers of the davenport for letters, evidence of past loves. Had she been in love with Donaldson? Probably, but not with Kaster. Helen seemed fated to love people who were not there. There was nothing in the drawers but blank stationery and the scents of a life that he could not understand. He turned to the mother, wondering whether she had really spoken. She was fingering books on the shelf, examining titles in case they contained some secret she had missed. Ross took them one by one. To David with his education they might have meant something, but to him they meant nothing. They were merely possible containers for notes. He shook them but nothing fell out except for bookmarks. Cryptic notes were spy stuff. Helen's secret was herself.

"I haven't told the police where she is," said Hortense.

"Where is she?"

"I thought you knew."

"The cottage. Where exactly is it?"

She shook her head. "Helen needs . . . to consider."

There was no point in questioning her further. Ross left her still picking at the books in her own queer way and went downstairs to find the police gone and Bliss taking fragments of the photograph from the fireplace. He placed them on a table and pieced them together. They had been inexpertly burned and were almost complete. A cottage, but where was it?

They had breakfast together, Donaldson and Helen, sitting opposite

262

each other across a scrubbed deal table with a gingham cloth.
Annaliese was in bed, feverish, complaining of headaches.

"Your friend needs a doctor," said Helen.

"No."

"What's wrong with her?"

"Nothing – nothing serious." Donaldson had thought of the pale egg-shape sitting cocooned in sacking in the trunk of the car. It couldn't be that. Not that.

"Why did you come here?"

"The police are looking for me. I needed to stay out of London for a few days and thought that this place would be empty."

"What now?"

"I have to go out."

"And me? Can you trust me?"

"No!"

They looked round. Annaliese had come into the room, swathed in blankets, her face madonna-pale. She sat in a chair by the fire and shivered. "Let me have the gun," she asked Donaldson. "Find some rope and we can tie her."

"Will you do that?" asked Helen.

"Yes. Where are the keys to your car?"

"On the mantelshelf. Why do you need my car? What's wrong with yours?"

Donaldson didn't answer. He took the keys and went out into the shed to find a rope. He looked across the open hillside stretching for miles under its light covering of snow. Objects stood out on it crisp and naked.

"I don't like to do this to you," he said as he tied her.

"Why are you doing it, then?" Another question to be avoided. His fingers dancing over the knots. Anything to distract. Annaliese's voice saying something about Marxism, oppressed peoples and the victory of the proletariat. Helen asked: "Is what she says right? Am I a victim in the cause of World Revolution?"

A knot slipped. Donaldson tied it again, patiently. "Does it seem so ridiculous? Did you think I was some vapid dilettante with nothing else to do but sell high-class knick-knacks to pop stars and Arabs? Doesn't suffering and the solution to suffering mean anything to you?"

"And the solution is Karl Marx? I suppose it must be," she added thoughtfully.

"What did you think Marxism was, a quaint tradition of the Ainsworth family?" There was vehemence behind the words. Donaldson strained in tautening the last knot and threw the loose ends of the rope down. He was waiting for her to say "You have no real belief." Why did he expect that? For a second he was frightened by that strong independent intelligence.

Instead she said: "And terror?"

Why had he expected that other simple statement?

"And terror?"

Belief was the mind stretching out to clasp at a fleeing, fingertip reality outside of itself. *If he couldn't believe . . .*

Helen's quiet voice was repeating all the arguments he had rehearsed before. There had been nights when he had sat in the desert near Tripoli, discussing the classical theory of terrorism with a crowd of Gucci revolutionaries who drifted in and out, clutching their Kalashnikov rifles like membership cards. Helen said: "Polarize the situation; make people take sides; force the oppressing classes to reveal the instruments of their oppression so that the masses will see and know." The real revolutionaries, nationalists fuelled by thousand-year-old bigotries, didn't listen and didn't care: they had a clear goal, and terror was the only weapon to hand. Helen made no comment, but her mere recital of the arguments seemed to demolish them.

She asked: "Did you ever discuss the real significance of terror for the terrorist?"

Donaldson didn't seek any explanation of the question. Helen knew the real nature of terror. It was the use of force to break through the chaos of meaning that overlaid reality and impose the coherence of a simple idea. If he succeeded, the terrorist would at last understand the world.

"What have you been doing?" she asked when he next returned.

Daylight was fading. Outside, the sun threw the shadow of a van on to the window-glass. Why did he need a van? The radio was giving the results of the Boxing Day football matches. Her mother followed Charlton Athletic. She stood on the terraces in a fur coat and supporter's scarf.

That night he worked outside by the light of a hurricane lamp. She heard him beating metal and lugging a heavy object to the van. She watched Annaliese, trapped in the chair, still feverish but alive and watchful like an animal. The German girl tried to make conversation. She spoke about her trip to Ceylon and about Buddhism, but her voice was so low that Helen couldn't follow the words.

Donaldson retired to the bedroom. It was a simple room that held a bed, a washstand and a curtained-off alcove with a hanging-rail inside it. On the washstand he found the stub of a candle standing in a saucer. He struck a match to light it and by the guttering flame shadows raced around the room and the damp stains on the plastered walls formed a pattern of half-remembered things.

He took the painting out of his bag, unrolled it carefully and tacked it to the wall, driving pins through the unpainted strip at the edges of the canvas. He sat down on the bed and stared at it, willing it to explain what was happening. The face of Christ looked down on the damned with a pity that was terrible because it went with a capacity to prevent what it pitied. Such a paradox of pity destroyed Him and them.

Ross and the Scotsman arrived at Hexham as night was falling. "Near Hexham," Helen had said about the cottage. But how near? A circuit of twenty miles would give near sixteen hundred square miles to cover.

They routed out the desk-sergeant at the police station and secured his co-operation, but he didn't know the cottage from the photograph. He lent them some old Ordnance Survey maps. Was the cottage leased? he asked. If so, the local estate agents would be able to help, as soon as they opened, after the holiday. He could put them in touch with the local Ramblers Association; they knew the hills like the backs of their hands. There was a lot he could do as soon as the holiday was over.

They called Calverton. He told them that, twenty-four hours after it was stolen, the police had at last got the licence number and a description of Benoist's car from the vehicle-licensing computer at Swansea. Williams of Special Branch was cock-a-hoop with success. He had established a stolen-vehicles task force to monitor thefts nationally in case Kaster changed cars. Calverton thought the organization would break under the strain.

They pored over the photograph. It was taken in summer. The garden had sunflowers hanging on their stakes and leaning over the wall. Long shadows led off to the right; the unseen sun was from the left. Helen Ainsworth had a glass of wine in her hand. She and Donaldson and the unknown friend who had taken the picture had had dinner and gone out into the garden. It was an evening shot. The sun was in the west, and the hills, bathed in a bronze light, were to the north.

Ross stared at the pattern of the hills. With the information gleaned from the photograph, there had to be a way of locating them.

"What do we do?" asked Bliss. "Make a list? Visit every cottage in Northumberland?"

Ross took the Ordnance Survey map and a sheet of paper. He drew a pencil line through a hill shown on the map, four inches, four miles, and marked off where the brown contours showing the lie of the land intersected. At right angles to his base line he drew the vertical axis and scored it in tenths of an inch to represent fifty feet of height according to the contour-scale. Then at each point where he had marked the base line he pencilled a line to the correct vertical height and joined the tops of the verticals together before shading in everything below. The result was a profile of a line of hills viewed from the ground. He showed the result to Bliss.

"Where is it?"

"Near the Roman fort at Housesteads." Ross got up and took down a calendar from the charge-room wall. *Views of Northumberland.* "There."

Bliss looked at the picture and then at the sketch. "Bloody hell," he murmured. "It works!"

"Maybe." Ross replaced the calendar and took up the photograph again. "We need to estimate the distance of the background from the cottage and the length of the hill-line. If any of these hills are stacked behind the others, then our line on the map won't pick them up. In any case, we only have an approximation of their bearings. They appear to be north of the house and running east to west, but we're probably a few points wrong on the compass. If we get all that right, we still have a lot of cottages shown on the map."

"Bang goes a night's sleep," said Bliss.

266

Chapter Twenty-Nine

"I HAVE informed the Joint Intelligence Committee," said Lionel Sholto. "JIC informed the Prime Minister and the Prime Minister came back to London last night to chair a meeting of COBRA" – he smiled at all the familiar jokes about the acronym of the Cabinet crisis committee – "since when, COBRA has been spitting venom and putting the Ministry of Defence through hoops to produce its contingency plans for germ warfare."

They were in an Indian restaurant which Lionel Sholto favoured for anonymous meetings. Calverton ate an anonymous curry while his superior tucked into the house steak-and-kidney pie.

"And what is our position?" Since Williams had assumed operational control, Calverton was living on scraps from the Welshman's table.

"We – ah – we are in a generous mood." Sholto picked at a piece of gristle lodged between his teeth. "We are in what the Americans call a no-lose situation. Your persistence with the Kaster theme in the teeth of Special Branch's scepticism and your identification of Kaster's purpose have given us an intelligence *coup* that is quite unassailable, no matter how well Williams performs from now on. So why not let him run with the ball? More to the point, by generously passing over operational management to Special Branch, we scotch the malicious rumour that there is rivalry between the branches of the intelligence service. And, frankly, we exculpate ourselves should – ah – should things go wrong – should Special Branch fail to catch Kaster and he lets the thingummy off. The tricky thing is not to appear unco-operative and yet not to get too involved."

"We could all have a disaster on our hands," said Calverton.

"Possibly. By the way, what are your plans for the day? I was thinking that it might be a good idea if you were to see Anthony Donaldson."

"He's unconscious."

"But not for ever, I trust." He shrugged his shoulders. "It's merely a suggestion, Norman. I thought that it might be useful if you were out of the way for a few hours. It would help Williams to find his feet."

"Find his feet? If Williams fails, it will be calamity."

"Very likely. But in these matters one has to look for small satisfactions. Even come the end of the world there must be some pleasure in saying 'It wasn't my fault' and 'I told you so!' "

"Do you want to go for a walk?" asked Donaldson.

"Exercise for the prisoner? Why not?" Helen kept her eyes on Annaliese. The girl was in bed, smiling feebly, her face waxed with sweat. She held her hand out and Helen took it and kissed the fingers.

They took warm coats and boots from the racks in the hall and stepped out into the clear cold. They walked down the lane a while; then crossed the open fields to the crest of one of the hills. The wind battered their ears, breaking up their conversation. Donaldson felt his eyes filling with tears brought on by the wind and not the real thing. He paused to wipe them away and left Helen to gain fifty yards on him. She halted to wait.

"I'll catch you up."

She shook her head. "Any further and I'd have to chance a break for freedom."

"Would you, now? Would you?" he mused.

Neither of them was sure of the answer.

She changed the subject. "What's wrong with Annaliese? You know but you won't say."

"I don't know. That's the truth."

"Will she die of it?"

"Perhaps."

They walked down the far side of the hill. Here snow had drifted into a pocket of shadow where the sun couldn't reach it. They stood for a while, watching the shadows of clouds scudding across the grass.

"How long are you staying?"

"A few days. Maybe until New Year's Eve."

"The police could come here."

"Possibly, but not likely. Not many people know about this place."

"They might want to interview me. They could ask my mother where I was."

"I know your mother," said Donaldson. "She wouldn't tell them – a reflex action." He turned on his heels, and she followed him back up the hill. Then together they returned to the house and spent the short brooding day playing cards and listening to the radio. It had nothing to say about Kaster. Towards evening he went out and she saw him trailing a spool of wire by the garden wall.

Calverton went to see Anthony Donaldson. They held him in a secure private clinic near Haslemere. It was a quaint red-brick house with a croquet lawn and a tennis court where the net hung sadly with snow because no one had bothered to take it down. There was a picket of anti-abortionists outside, trudging in a black circle worn into the snow. They carried placards saying "Christ was Born at Christmas". Unless MI5 had gone into abortion as a sideline, they were labouring under a massive delusion.

"How is he?" Calverton asked.

The doctor was a fair-skinned Irishman. He studied his patient neutrally. Anthony Donaldson was wired and strung as if he had come unstitched. His sensitive face had a death-mask look. Calverton found himself staring at it and not thinking of the questions he wished to ask, but experiencing instead a hatred that leaked into every thought. He hated Anthony Donaldson because the ordered beauty of his face hid a chaos of unreason and evil and the contrast mocked Calverton and shouted out the fatal flaw in the world.

"If he comes to", said the doctor, "we can have our own fellows start the interrogation. They have a file on him. They can keep him on the boil until Curzon Street send someone."

"It isn't that," said Calverton.

The other man automatically disbelieved. He was programmed for scepticism.

"That makes a change. Most of the time you fellows want us to use the jump leads."

Calverton shook his head. He had seen the jump leads applied – drugs used to bring a patient suddenly out of a torpor like raising the dead, only to kill him again. And the last thing he wanted was Anthony Donaldson dead. He represented the final card in the hand. In the last resort they could always comply with Kaster's demand.

"—a 'friend', if you take my meaning," the doctor was saying. "He's in the next room."

"Who?"

269

"Calls himself Summer. A sugar-daddy to this one, I should think. Special Branch had him brought here – a closed-van job, so he doesn't know where he is. They have some idea that his voice will bring this one out of his dreams."

"Sleeping Beauty," said Calverton absently.

"Except that in this case the Queen kisses the sleeping Prince? Could be. We've tried most things in our time."

He showed Calverton out. They went past a waiting-room where Sebastian Summer sat on a couch amongst a scattering of old magazines, nursing his grief. Calverton allowed himself to feel for the other man: he sometimes did, spending portions of sorrow like his small bank-balance.

He handed back his pass, making small-talk. "You have demonstrators at the gate. They seem to have a mistaken idea about this place."

"The anti-abortionists?" asked his companion.

"Yes."

"It's not a mistake. It's a deliberate story we put about as part of our cover. Every week we have two deliveries of dead foetuses from London. It gives them something to find in the rubbish."

"How many cottages do we have?" asked James Ross.

Bliss counted the sheaf of sketches. "A dozen possibles, spread all over the place. You were right, this method is hit and miss. Without the fine detail these hills look pretty much alike."

They took their car and spent the day driving in turn to each of the identified locations. None of them was the cottage in the photograph. They stopped in villages and questioned the owners of grocery stores. No one could help them. They called Calverton and asked whether the Post Office had an address for them. No luck: people didn't have mail delivered at weekend cottages.

"This is bloody ridiculous!" said Bliss. "There's this old biddy dressed up like a wedding-cake who spends her weekends swanning around Northumberland spouting Marx and Mormonism and no one knows where her house is?"

"Northumberland is a big place."

"Too bloody true!"

They returned to Hexham in the evening and laid out the maps again. Somewhere they had gone wrong. What would happen if they changed their orientation? Say the hills ran south-west to north-east?

Chapter Thirty

THEY PARKED on the road and trekked down yet another half-mile lane of mud. A collie followed, head down, leery behind their heels. Bliss was full of fake smiles. "Good boy, nice dog, come any closer and I'll kick your teeth in." The morning's work was represented by another half-dozen bleak Northumberland farms crossed off the list, and Bliss was tiring of the whole idea. "What school do you say you went to that taught you all this daft stuff with maps, Jimmy? Do you have to fail a special exam to go there or is it enough to be dropped on your head?"

"I never said it would be easy," answered Ross. He looked about for clues, resemblances to the photograph, but there was only another bare hillside, a nondescript lane where the ditches were choked with plastic fertilizer-bags and, at the end, a stone farmhouse with a yard full of scrap metal. Not the place. The pattern of the hills was close, but not quite. . . .

There was a woman at home. Aged about forty, with speculative eyes, a smudge on her nose and upholstered in knitwear.

"Who are you?" she asked bluntly.

"Electricity Board," said Bliss. He thumbed through a sheaf of pasteboard identities and showed her one.

"It says 'double glazing'."

"My part-time job." He showed her another.

"It doesn't matter. We generate our own." She had her hands on her haunches and a game-cock air.

"That's right. We're the hit squad. We take out the competition."

"Is he always this mad, him, your mate?" she asked Ross. "Would you like a cuppa?"

"Yes."

"What do you really want, by the way?"

"Directions. We're lost. The trouble is: we don't know the address of the real place we're looking for."

"Really? Is it always like that – the Electricity Board?"

"More or less. They let us have photographs."

"Lying bugger," she said, but took the photograph. She looked like a woman who wanted to be lied to as long as it was the right lie. Her eyes scanned first the photograph, then Ross: big, brown eyes, youthful and pleasant and hurt somewhere or other. "Sorry, love," she said. "I don't know it."

Over cups of hot sweet tea, Bliss asked to make a telephone call. Calverton was out, and Elphinstone was manning the desk.

"Any messages?" asked Bliss.

"Everything's under control at this end," said Elphinstone brightly.

"It'll be the first time," answered Bliss and then gave his report. When he had finished he turned to the others. "Pillock," he said laconically.

"I'll drink to that," said the woman. So they took their cups and toasted the Electricity Board, might it rot in hell. "Would you like a bite to eat? A piece of cake? Some beans? I've got a tin somewhere."

They refused. She looked around the kitchen for something else to offer. The table held a bowl of water and a bicycle inner tube. There was a copy of the *Field* covered in potato peelings.

"Truth is," she said, "I do know that place – in the photo."

"Near here?" asked Ross.

She nodded. "I don't get much company. I thought you wouldn't stop if I told you straight away." She recognized the urgency in their eyes. "Please – stay for that bite to eat."

"My dear Norman", said Lionel Sholto, "you should have been there." They stood by a bank of lifts waiting to be taken to the conference-room where Williams had established a full-blown meeting of his operations committee. "Do you know," he went on impatiently, "I do believe that waiting for a lift is like waiting for the Second Coming: an act of faith that one is never certain is going to happen in one's lifetime. But where was I?" he asked as the lift arrived. He looked at his hands, which held the sheaf of directives handed down by COBRA that morning. "I remember. The PM asked for a list of Kaster's probable targets: the House of Commons, Buckingham Palace and so forth – you'd be surprised how many there are when the terrorist merely wants publicity. 'Can we defend them all equally?' comes the question. Well, no, of course not.

'Then, which ones shall we defend? Hadn't we better establish an order of priority?' This, naturally, was agreed to be a Good Thing – general agreement and praise of the Prime Minister's astuteness. 'Well', quoth the PM, 'let's have your priorities! Who is for defending the Americans?' Embarrassed silence; until, finally, the Foreign Secretary puts his hand up and suggests it would be a Good Idea. 'Wouldn't anyone like to reconsider?' asks the PM – this, of course being intended as an invitation to the others to fall in line with the Foreign Secretary. But what actually happens is that the latter promptly puts his hand down and says that, as a matter of fact, he didn't think that protecting the Americans *was* the first priority, but, for the record, he felt that he had to say it was, since the Yanks could be terribly touchy about that sort of thing. More embarrassed silence and then we are asked to leave the room and await instructions."

Calverton nodded. Sholto's story, of course, wasn't true – at least, not in the literal sense. It was truth glimpsed out of the corner of one's eye.

"Our instructions relate most strictly to the actual hunt for Kaster. Elsewhere there are wiser heads than ours, deciding what to do if our endeavours fail and the you know what goes bang. Probably we shall have to cover ourselves in brown paper and hide under the table." Sholto swept through a set of double doors and made a *grande dame* entrance into the conference-room where Williams and his cohorts were waiting.

"Lionel, glad you could join us!" The Welshman was playful in sports jacket and flannels and a shiny new Christmas pipe. He did a quick permutation of the names of those present. "Lionel, George – George, Lionel. Do you know Keith? Keith, this is Lionel and not forgetting Norman. Norman, this is Keith. You've met? Oh, you *have* met? Where was that? Peter, have you been introduced . . .?"

"Hello . . . hello . . . hello. We met at a seminar in Wigan."

A dozen or so men, mostly in police uniform. Calverton recognized the Scotland Yard second team, reinforced by Prescott of D11, otherwise the Blue Berets, a police unit whose training was modelled on the SAS. Prescott was a nail-biter, a compact man, tense and squat as if someone were forever sitting on him to stop him going off. Calverton reflected that the suspense must be killing him. D11 had no function until Kaster was found. Until then they were all dressed up with nowhere to go.

Sholto declined William's offer of the chair of the meeting. "Your show. Norman and I are merely here to help."

"Good, good. Looks like everybody's here, then."

"No one from the services or the Ministry of Defence coming?" asked Calverton. "I see Prescott – morning, Sidney! – but no one from the SAS."

Williams sucked air through the clean stem of his new pipe. "We thought we'd keep this matter an all-police affair. Not out of interdepartmental rivalry, mind you."

"Of course not," Sholto agreed. "Outsiders complicate the chain of command. Too many cooks spoil the whatnot, eh? We understand perfectly."

"Does that make our presence superfluous?" asked Calverton.

"No need to be touchy, Norman," said Sholto. "We are here merely to give suggestions – no executive responsibility. We are *with* but not *of* the police."

"*Homoiousian* not *homoousian*," commented Williams obscurely, but pleased to see dissent between the other two.

"Absolutely." Sholto didn't bat an eyelid. "Just to make it clear for Norman's sake, you might minute it that we are here, so to speak, as consultants."

Williams agreed, and thus the record showed that MI5 had no responsibility for whatever might follow. Calverton and Sholto settled to the rest of the meeting with a sense of satisfaction as to its probable outcome.

"I suppose we should start with a status report," said Williams. One of the others rattled it off quickly. It amounted to saying that none of Donaldson's friends and acquaintances could say anything useful about Kaster; that neither he nor the girl had been reliably sighted since their escape from Disenham on Christmas Day; and that the exercise in collating reports of stolen vehicles on a national basis was providing information which no one knew how to analyse.

"Our problem is lack of background, of in-depth background."

"You have what we have," said Sholto equably. "You have everything that Wiesbaden could give us and even what the Americans know – you can imagine with what delicacy we obtained the latter. Do you feel that we are holding something back?"

"This woman, Helen Ainsworth. We should like to interview her."

"Yes?"

"We think your man Ross knows where she is."

274

"He's not our man, merely a 'source'," said Calverton.

"Oh, we won't stick on a technical point, Norman," said Sholto. "Let's say he *were* our man: even so, does he know where this Helen Ainsworth is?"

"No," said Calverton. This was strictly true. The last report said only that Ross thought he might be able to locate her. The call was logged and recorded word for word.

"Well, there you have it," said Sholto.

Next point, thought Calverton. So far everything was going their way but he could not get rid of a gnawing feeling in his stomach. He had a recollection of having read somewhere that, when the *Titanic* was sinking, some of the guests continued to play cards. He supposed that, in that limited sense, one of the players must have counted as a winner.

Ross and Bliss left the farmhouse. The Scot had a grin on his ordinarily sour face.

"We were in with a chance there! She's not getting any, you can see that." He tugged Ross's sleeve. "If I'd told her I was a spy, she'd have fallen on her back with her legs wide open, did you know that? Spying is dead sexy. The only trouble is that all the women think I'm in double glazing."

They legged their way up the hillside, the rough turf uneven and springy beneath their feet. Ross looked back at the woman. She was standing in the yard amongst the piles of junk, waving at them as if they were soldiers leaving for the war.

She had held her portion of frustration like a charge of static waiting to discharge itself through whoever brushed against her. He had felt it as they sat for fifteen minutes talking evenly about nothing in particular, while the barriers against intimacy crumbled away with the pieces of cake they were holding, until, in the end, neither had wanted any more. So Ross had picked up his coat and they had said goodbye, each taking turns to glance at the workaday features of the other's face.

And there she was, gone back into the house never to be seen again, one not very attractive woman, briefly met. He was reminded of Helen, also briefly met: moments of poignant understanding passing between them in the short space of their encounter over David's corpse. That sort of intimacy didn't happen with friends. Friendship put a distance between people.

"Not a beauty", Bliss was saying, "but definitely a goer!"

"You want to go back?" Ross played him along out of male reflex.

"No. I don't want to be a sex slave, and that's what I'd become. It's her age that's the trouble: I'm sexually attracted to women who are old enough to be my wife." He peeped at Ross without expression. "I think I'm becoming perverted."

They crossed the top of the incline and the farm disappeared from view.

"I still say", muttered Bliss, "that we should have taken the car."

"For the sake of a couple of miles? We need the air." Ross had been cooped up too long with the other man. He wanted the exercise to crowd out his thoughts of Helen and Donaldson, wherever he was. Only a few days ago he thought he had killed Kaster: but the terrorist was still haunting him like the undead. Ross saw himself showing Kaster his reflection in a mirror and then driving a stake through his heart.

They looked down on the cottage; it was there as in the photograph but a little further away. What the picture hadn't shown was its loneliness in the hollow of the empty hills.

"Bleak," said Bliss, not feeling that anything more was necessary.

They started down the slope, scattering the few sheep, their heels plucked at by the tufts of grass.

"Is that her car?" Bliss asked. There was a green Volkswagen parked outside.

"Her mother's." Ross had seen it at her home.

"Doesn't she have her own?"

"A runabout, not good for any distance."

Bliss asked the make and model. His line in small-talk was the history of every car he had ever owned and car-magazine accounts of every one he hadn't. As a variation he could talk about cameras or power-boats. He was a catalogue of masculine consumer durables. This time most of it was blown away on the wind. Ross wasn't listening. He was preparing to meet Helen and that meant quelling memories of David.

They crossed the pebbled bottom of a stream and climbed the further bank past a line of stunted hawthorns. The house stood out sharp in the clear light. It had the rough beauty of an old woman's face, waiting for the smile of the sun to bring it out.

"A dump!" said Bliss. "It makes me wonder what people see in a place like this. Doesn't it make you wonder?"

It made Ross wonder. He wondered what it was like to own the roof over his head. He wondered what it was like to have a home. "Home" was a misleadingly familiar word from a foreign language: never quite translatable. He was still staring at the cottage when there was the sound of a window breaking, a shot and he found his left leg collapsing under him.

A second shot brought a yell from Bliss. Ross turned his head to see the Scot pegged out on the ground, legs akimbo. His arms were thrashing about but the legs were still, and Ross guessed that the bullet had gone through the abdomen and smashed the spinal cord. Bliss was crying quietly, "Oh, bloody hell, Jimmy, it hurts," as if it shouldn't; as if no one had told him the rules and he wanted to take his bat and ball home.

Ross looked to the house. The front of the building was only fifty feet away. He rolled over into the shadow of the garden wall and pulled out his own gun, a nine-millimetre Browning. He was certain that his enemy, too, had only a pistol; otherwise he would have taken them out at longer range where there was no cover and his second shot would have killed Bliss outright without the slow agony that was going on behind him in the grass.

He listened for a clue in the sounds but there was only the wind tugging at the grass, the flap-flap of an open door and the meaningless ululations coming from Bliss. A sheep came out of the garden and stood a few yards away, staring at him pointedly. Another one was watching Bliss. Between his groans Bliss cried out: "Fuck off! I'm not a lamb for the bloody slaughter yet!" He took out his gun and pumped the magazine into the sheep, which keeled over into the grass and kicked its legs for a few seconds before falling still. "I've killed Kaster!" he yelled out in a loud, clear voice and then broke into sobs which drifted around in the wind with nowhere to go.

Ross checked his leg. It was leaking blood through a tear in his trousers but he didn't think that the bone was broken. The bullet had taken a chunk out of the calf-muscle, but he would live if he didn't bleed to death. He pulled a strip from the torn part of his trousers and made a tourniquet. He fastened it clumsily, with his gun to hand and an eye out for any move by Donaldson. That it was Donaldson, he was certain.

What now? Donaldson had two options: to try to kill him or to cut and run. If Donaldson left him alive, then he ran the risk that Ross would raise the alarm. If he tried to kill Ross, then he ran the risk of being killed himself. Somewhere out of sight, Kaster was weighing the odds, and Ross knew which way they would fall: a professional would minimize his risk; and being killed was the biggest risk you could take. The only question was which route was Kaster's way out?

Ross crept along the line of the wall. The wound in his leg burned and blood was seeping through the tourniquet, but he ignored it. He reached the cover of a small shed and was able to stand. His eyes misted over for a second. Blood-loss – he tried to adjust the rough bandage. Still no sign of Kaster.

The wall ended in a right-angle towards the house. Parked in the shadow of the gable was a blue transit van with its nose towards him. Why the van? Ross asked himself. Surely to God the bomb wasn't that big? Where was Kaster? Was he really going to leave Ross to take pot shots at him? And then he saw movement.

A figure came from the back of the house – or rather, two figures, the first carrying the second swathed in blankets in a fireman's lift, staggering towards the van. Ross sighted the Browning and let his finger tighten on the trigger. He looked at Kaster's eyes, but instead they were Helen's.

"Be careful!" she yelled. "John has booby-trapped the whole place!"

"Where is he now?" Ross snapped back. But he knew already. Donaldson had also baited his trap with the vehicle. Ross whipped round on his heels and glimpsed his enemy sixty feet away, having come round the far side of the house. He dropped on his belly as the shots ricocheted off the grey stones. His hands splayed out to break his fall and his right hand caught the trip-wire in the grass which his foot by chance had missed.

He didn't hear the explosion which tore down a section of the wall.

Chapter Thirty-One

OUTSIDE the night was sitting black on the hills. Ross lay on a couch in the downstairs room of the cottage. The fire and the oil-lamps had been lit, and Helen was sitting at the fireside watching him and occasionally stirring the coals. The curtains were drawn but billowed as the wind slipped through a hole in the glass.

"How long have I been unconscious?" Ross's voice came out from somewhere deep, a train emerging from a tunnel.

"About two hours. It's five o'clock now."

"How is . . .?" he began. He could feel the shattered bits of himself being swept up and sorted. One of these days I must get my act together, he thought.

"The injury? Not too serious. Some mild concussion from the explosion and a bump on the head. The wound in your leg – is that what bullets do? – it's going to give you a bit of a limp."

"I meant, how is Bliss?"

"He's in the next room, just alive." She put a hand on his shoulder. "Leave him. It wouldn't help either of you to see him."

"Have you called an ambulance or the police?" he asked at last.

She shook her head. "We don't have a telephone, and John put the car out of action. I could have walked to the nearest farm, I suppose, but I couldn't leave your friend: not till you were in a state to watch over him. I thought he might lose more blood."

"You should have left us. It was more important to call the police." He looked up and saw that her eyes were bright with moisture and flickering in the firelight. "I'm sorry," he said. "But that's the way it is." There was something else he wanted to ask, something that he couldn't remember. "I need to stretch my legs, take a look outside." Maybe the cold would clear his head. "Then I'd better walk to the road, flag a car and get to a telephone."

She went to the kitchen and came back with a flashlight. Ross had got to his feet and checked the dressing on his leg. The leg hurt like hell but looked and felt serviceable. He took the flashlight, found his boots and coat and stepped out of the door into the solid blackness of the night.

First he found the gap in the wall where Donaldson had nearly succeeded in killing him. Two courses of stone remained; the charge had been placed above them. If he hadn't been belly on the ground when it went off, he would have been a corpse; but near the wall there had been a cone of dead ground and the stone fragments had passed over him. He traced two more trip-wires each linked to a charge buried in the masonry. They made a neat booby-trap that used the stonework to make shrapnel and maximize the effect of the explosive. Ross admired the economy of the idea.

He went into the shed. Amongst the wood and the tools he found two gas-bottles and a torch, some angle-irons and sheet-metal off-cuts. There was a tin of metal-primer and some white motor-vehicle paint. The place stank of acetone. The cutting and welding gear had been used in the open. He found the tracks where it had been dragged and, in the yard, near the spot where the van had been parked, there were bright spots of molten metal that had puddled and solidified.

"He went into Newcastle," said Helen.

Ross turned round. She was standing behind him against the shaft of light from the open door.

"That's where he got the van?"

"I imagine so."

"What was he doing here?" Ross indicated the signs of the cutting and welding. She shook her head.

"I was in the house. I heard the noise but he didn't talk about it. You haven't given me any clues to what he wanted. What did he have with him in his car?"

"He didn't say?"

"No."

Ross took the information in. He responded dully. The explosion had blown bits of him away and left only the phantoms behind in the way that an amputee still vaguely feels his missing limb.

"Why didn't he kill me?" he asked. They were standing where Bliss had been shot and wounded. There was blood on the snow. Ross thought, "I must do something to help Bliss," but couldn't get it to feel urgent. Instead he came out with, "Did he know that I tried to kill his brother?"

"Yes. I told him."

"Then why didn't he kill me? Don't tell me that he didn't check I was alive after the wall blew up."

"He doesn't blame you for what happened to Anthony."

"Doesn't blame? For God's sake, I wanted the bastard dead!"

"He understands. He knows that Anthony killed David."

She was speaking softly. Ross turned the flashlight to shine at her face. She raised her hand to mask her eyes and continued quietly, speaking through the pattern of her fingers. "John doesn't think in personal terms. He likes abstractions – beauty, truth, justice. He blames systems rather than individuals."

"He's killed a good few individuals!"

"No. The people he killed were just walking abstractions – tentacles of the system. He could slaughter the whole of humanity, but he couldn't kill a person he really knew." She shook her head and Ross saw the creeping remembrance of things past clouding her face. "Flesh-and-blood people are too real for him," she murmured.

"He doesn't know me."

"He thinks he does. You are the mirror of himself and Anthony. I'm sorry if that strikes you as funny, but that's the way he sees it."

"He doesn't know me," Ross repeated. But the idea made him hate Donaldson even more. Donaldson's understanding would reduce him to an object in the other man's mental landscape, a piece of property. He supposed that it was a matter of class. Donaldson was rich and assured enough to think that he owned the whole world. Ross was an orphan; and an orphan struggled even to own himself. He asked, "What do you think?"

She closed the fingers of her hand so that it shut out the flashlight and Ross's face. Now she could see John Donaldson, slender, dark, urbane, driven by a cold need to understand: now James Ross, square-built and fair, but having somehow missed out on his dead brother's good looks. What was driving him? A sort of anger with a world that had given him nothing?

"I can't explain it, but John has had a vision, even if he doesn't know it himself. And it's the most dangerous delusion there is."

"What's that?"

"He thinks the universe can make sense."

She let her hand fall and turned her face away. "Please – the light – my eyes. . . ."

Ross switched the flashlight off and saw only her after-image swimming in the dark. He held out a hand to take her arm and lead her back into the house, but found her waist. She slid into his embrace without asking. Their lips searched each other out, tentatively, like strangers brushing in a crowd, and then firmly, with recognition.

The question he had tried to remember came back to him.

"The girl – I saw you carrying the girl."

Helen pulled back from him.

"She's ill, feverish. I don't know what's wrong with her."

Ross stared at her, but she was invisible in the darkness, there and gone. "I have to get help," he said.

Donaldson drove south, forcing his vehicle by twisting backroads across the Durham moors. The snow still lay thick on the open fell, a white expanse under a white sky, empty and formless. He searched the road and the darkening horizon for shelter. Annaliese needed to rest, needed to be taken care of. She sat in the passenger seat cocooned in blankets, feverish and shivering, her thoughts turned inwards so that he had to repeat himself whenever he spoke to her. He had to tell himself, make himself believe, that her illness had nothing to do with the weapon he was carrying. It *couldn't* have; he had scoured the surface for cracks, and the bomb was still intact. There had to be another explanation, something obvious that he could not yet see but which had to be there.

"I liked her," Annaliese's voice came out of the darkness.

"Who?"

"Helen. She cared. . . ." There was no more; the girl was sobbing. Donaldson glanced at her and then at the road. There were lights ahead.

There was a hollow. A copse of trees grew on either side of the road and added to the shelter. The lights were sprinkled among the trees where there was no sign of a house. Donaldson pulled off the road and the van rocked over a gravelled path that led through a tunnel of overhanging branches to a clearing. It was a picnic-spot: rustic tables and benches and a no-litter sign. A fire was burning in the litter-bin and its flames showed half a dozen caravans parked around the circle.

"Where are we?" Painful words squeezed out of the blankets.

"I don't know." Donaldson watched a small group of people unfold from the fire and examine the van quietly. A dozen men and women, a scattering of children, all wrapped in winter clothes. A tall man in an RAF greatcoat advanced towards him.

"Who are you? What do you want here?" The tone was reserved but not hostile. Donaldson could see him now: a big man, somewhere in his forties, with a shock of greying hair and a hard face marked with heavy lines.

"I'm heading south, looking for work." Donaldson stayed in the cab. The engine was still running.

A nod. "You'll not be a travelling man?"

"No. I'm looking for work."

"Not a labouring man."

"No."

A couple of the women came over and peered through the window at Annaliese. Their breath misted the glass.

"Name?"

"She's sick," said one of the women.

"Donald – Donald Johnson."

"She's sick."

"Not a travelling man," the traveller told the others, looking for their reaction to the visitors.

"She's sick. What is she sick with?"

"She has flu – she needs to rest."

"Do you have your own food?" asked the man.

"Yes."

He nodded, then turned on his heels and shambled back to the fire. Donaldson got out of the cab and followed.

Chapter Thirty-Two

MORNING came, cold and pale. Helen Ainsworth woke to the unquiet sound, an insistent chop-chop beating on the wind. She looked out of the window at the grey mist hanging over the frosted grass and saw the sheep scurrying wildly over the hillside. She saw the helicopters.

There were three. They floated over the hills like hovering flies and beat circles around the cottage until they settled on the carcass of the ground. White ghosts came out of them, flickering shapes in the mist. She heard the crack of their rifles. They were slaughtering the sheep.

"Miss Ainsworth?"

The man stood in the doorway, mummified in stiff folds of white cloth. His voice crackled drily through a face-mask. A pair of dark eyes peered through the goggles.

"Yes?" Helen pulled her coat around her and stood on the entrance-step with the door closed behind her. She watched the men unload chemical-drums and bales of wire, the sheep dropping to the ground, legs kicking.

"Miss." He brought her back to listening to him.

"Yes."

"You have to leave with us." No expression through the mask. A panicky sheep blundered into the garden, bleating, looking for a way out. He took out a pistol and shot it in the head.

"You should have brought dogs to round them up," she said. "They'll scatter all over the hills."

"Yes. That could be a problem," he answered neutrally. Then: "You have to leave with us now."

"I'll get my things." She didn't know what else to say. This was obviously a dream.

"No."

"Oh." She searched her mind for reactions. "I'll come as I am."

284

"No."

"What do you want, then?"

"You must leave your clothes behind." He shouted to one of the others: "Carter, bring one of the suits over here!" To someone else: "Get a move on, man! We don't have all day! Get the samples back to the chopper!"

Men running about. Coils of barbed wire snaking in a perimeter around the house and garden. A man digging plugs of earth and bagging each one. Everywhere dead and wounded sheep writhing and bleating.

"Any rats around here?" He seemed to be fumbling for a cigarette but couldn't smoke.

"I don't know. We have fieldmice – sometimes."

"Fieldmice? How do you catch them?"

"I don't know. We don't bother. We see one or two perhaps, when the weather is cold."

"Do they carry fleas?"

"I don't know. I suppose they do. I don't know."

"Excuse me." Someone brushed past and went into the cottage by the front door.

"Please, Miss." He led her by the arm away from the entrance. One of his men rolled a large drum down the path and manœuvred it through the doorway. He returned with an armful of clothes and oddments and bundled them into a bag. Someone hosed the bag down.

"Where's that suit?" The suit came. "Please, Miss, take your clothes off and put this on." He nursed the package like a foundling child.

"Here?"

"Please."

"Do you have a blanket to cover me?"

"I'm sorry." He was sorry. "I'm sorry."

She nodded. She unbuttoned her coat showing the nightdress beneath. He turned away and saw his men pausing in what they were doing. "Don't watch, you bastards!" He was angry and ashamed. They put down whatever they held and all turned away. Helen looked at them, features invisible, anonymous backs, white as statues in the frost and mist. She pulled her nightdress over her head and stood for a moment pale and naked in the cold air; then, quickly, she struggled into the suit and fastened it.

"I'm ready," she said. She didn't put on the face-mask, and he didn't ask.

"Thank you." Even through the mask he sounded grateful. He took her by the arm again and ushered her towards the helicopter. They passed a man starting a small compressor; he shouted to one of his companions, who turned on a spray, and the house was suddenly veiled in a mist of fine droplets. She saw a man hammering a stake into the ground by the barbed-wire cordon. Others were carrying the sheep down from the hillside towards a funeral pyre like casualties from a battle. There was a placard nailed to the stake. It said: ANTHRAX INFECTED AREA – ENTRY STRICTLY PROHIBITED. The officer was muttering: "Fieldmice. How the hell do you catch fieldmice?"

"Fieldmice don't carry anthrax," she said.

"No? I suppose they don't – not anthrax." He led her to the helicopter and helped her into it. She looked back and saw the pile of dead sheep burning in a halo of flames.

"We'll bury them afterwards," said the officer, "and put quick-lime on the remains."

"Oh."

"We couldn't get a bulldozer up here, not in the time."

"I see."

She closed her eyes and felt rather than saw the explosion at the house. When she opened them, it was a level ruin that blazed brightly against the green of the hills.

The leader of the band of travellers was called Casimir Romaine. The others were all in varying degrees his family. It was one of these who came tapping at the frost-starred windshield to wake Donaldson up and invite him to breakfast in the chief's caravan.

Even indoors Romaine wore the RAF greatcoat of the previous night. He eyed Donaldson cautiously but asked him to sit down cordially enough. His wife cooked bacon and eggs, and they talked over the hiss and spit of her frying.

"Where are you heading for?" Donaldson asked.

Romaine turned up a pair of slow eyes and wiped the grease off his lips with a piece of bread. He had a wry, snaggle-toothed smile. "You mean to tag along with us, then?"

"It depends."

"Uh huh. Well, we're laying up here another day to rest and then heading south, maybe to London, maybe to the coast. Suit you?"

"Perhaps."

Romaine leaned over to turn on the radio and set it so that the announcer's voice mumbled in the background.

"You took a chance, camping with us last night."

"Did I?" said Donaldson evenly.

"Didn't you?" asked Romaine. He followed Donaldson's glance and looked over his shoulder at the framed Papal blessing hanging on the wall with a picture of a horse and a pair of baby's bootees. "The wife," he said. "Religious." His wife came over to present them with mugs of strong tea. Her husband sipped his and continued: "What would a stranger want, spending the night with a bunch of dangerous cut-throats like us?"

"Is that what you are?"

"Oh, we are, we are! We steel horses and kidnap children, everyone knows that; and no one wants us except to tell their fortunes. Or do they really believe we're like that? Could it all be kids' stories? Well, yes, it could and, anyway, nowadays no one believes them tales about the gypsy" – he stared at Donaldson with a grim humour in his face that looked dangerous for being unreliable – "except that people still look at us sideways out of the corner of their eyes." He masked his grizzled, unshaven face in his hands and dipped his beak of a nose into his mug of tea. Then, with a sigh: "All of this saving your presence, who decides to forget all these reasonable prejudices and accept our hospitality."

"I have a trusting nature."

"You have a bloody gun," the gypsy said quietly.

"Do I?"

"Do you think I can't look at a man and tell whether the bulge in his coat is on account of his big heart?"

More bacon and eggs came. As they ate, Romaine enquired about the girl.

"She's still sick," said Donaldson. "Do you . . .?"

"Have any medicines? Boiled hedgehog? Foxglove tea?" He shook his head. "That's all gypsy folklore crap: we use antibiotics like everybody else. What you need is a doctor."

The pips on the radio sounded the hour. Romaine turned up the volume. A newscaster gave the headlines. The police were looking for a dangerous prisoner who had escaped from Durham gaol. He was last seen with a girl accomplice and was driving a blue transit van.

"They broadcast that story an hour ago," said Romaine. "The registration number is the same as your vehicle."

"Well, now you know," answered Donaldson. He felt the muscles in his back tighten as the other man spoke.

Romaine continued calmly. "Bollocks. You never escaped from Durham. You were coming from the north – Northumberland or maybe Scotland, like you said."

"So I was. So perhaps I was telling the truth and it's the radio that's lying."

"What is it? Is it political? Are you Irish?"

"No."

"Nor me. No tinkers around here, follow? But I'm like all travelling people: anti-authoritarian. Do you like the sound of that? I got it out of a book. Nice word for a tough bastard." He picked at a piece of bacon fat and added: "It's the women, understand?"

Donaldson understood. He remembered them, clustering around the van, their concerned voices clucking as they examined Annaliese.

Romaine looked up through eyes that had grown hard. "They're not like us: they care. Last night they saw the girl. Me, it's not so important, and for them perhaps not for long – sentiment is a changeable thing."

"But for now?" asked Donaldson.

"But for now anyone the police are looking for can't be all bad."

Sebastian Summer kept his silent vigil at the bedside of the injured man. His being there was proof of what he had always suspected: that Anthony in some way consumed people. It didn't trouble him. Even being the victim of a love-object was better than the emptiness of being alone. And, then, he felt certain that, in his crippled fashion. Anthony had loved him: hours of his efforts had sometimes for a moment produced a flicker of transcendence in the younger man's pale, lovely face.

They had come for him in the night – he wasn't sure which one. He had been dragged off to some unspeakable cell and interviewed at length by patient interrogators who had been relieved only occasionally by a fierce little Welshman who spouted the Bible at him. They were insistent that he tell them about what they called Anthony's "other" life. They didn't grasp that he couldn't understand even that part of Anthony's life which he was in touch with. They told him that Anthony couldn't have hidden a part of his life. He told them that a man hides himself even as he reveals.

"I never could standing fucking intellectuals," said the first interrogator privately.

"He's not an intellectual, he's a poofter," said the second, who couldn't handle two ideas at the same time.

So they brought him out here to – wherever it was. He had a room next to Anthony's with a view over a yard full of wash-houses and kennels and an over-grown kitchen garden with old fruit-trees growing on espaliers. An Edwardian country house, he assumed: he had been brought up in something similar.

"Speak to him, bring him round," said a young doctor with the voice of an Irish priest. "You're his friend." Equivocal emphasis on the word "friend".

And here he still was – was it three days later or four? – talking to Anthony as he lay, alabaster-pale and strung up with tubes and bottles, being distilled into or out of them – Summer couldn't tell which. He sat for hours and fed the patient with the drip-drip of his words. Curiously, he didn't run out of things to say. Instead he filled the hours with the conversations they should have had but never actually managed. He told Anthony, with all the detail he could muster, his life and history as if he could somehow give them to him.

"This isn't going to work," said the doctor.

"Not for you; but maybe for me," answered Sebastian. Then: "May I have my shoes and socks back?" He had caught sight of his bare feet dark with veins. They had also taken his belt, so that when he walked he held the waistband of his trousers with one hand.

"They're afraid you'll try to run away."

"Ah," said Summer equably. "*They* – and aren't you part of *them*?"

The doctor thought this over. "Nobody is ever part of *them*," he said. There was nothing more on this occasion.

It was late afternoon and the light was failing. The doctor came into the room again. He had taken to watching Sebastian as Sebastian watched Anthony.

"Will he recover?" asked Sebastian.

"How should he recover? How does he get any better than he is now? From where he is it can only get worse. There are people who would like to invent eternity just so that they could lock him up for it." The doctor went over to the bed and looked at his patient and at the machines that supported him. He shook his head. "I take all that back," he said. "He is getting better." He left Sebastian Summer and went to his office where he telephoned London.

"We think that we may have an outbreak," said Lionel Sholto. "Anthrax or plague – we shan't be sure until the tests – but it looks as if the girl, Annaliese Schreiber, may have it."

The other men listened silently. Sholto's normally jocular boom was subdued as if explaining a joke that had fallen flat. He cleared his throat.

"Of course, this is for information only, and not strictly our problem. We have to get on with catching Kaster. But I thought you should have the – ah – overall picture; yes, the overall picture. The committee chaired by the Ministry of Defence made all the necessary arrangements. The Ministry of Agriculture provided technical advice. So it's all in hand, under control, so to speak. The impression will be created that this is a routine case of imported infection being dealt with in the normal manner."

"In the normal manner?" asked Williams. "With soldiers all over the place, I assume?"

"Well, as normal as can be managed in the circumstances."

They flicked distractedly through their papers.

Sholto began again. "This changes things, naturally. I mean that what before was hypothetical may now be actual. That makes a difference. The Prime Minister agrees. The Prime Minister may be prepared to consider departing from the normal rules about dealing with terrorists."

"What do you mean?" Williams interrupted. "There are no 'deals' with terrorists."

"No, that's true. That's certainly the general rule."

"So?"

"Let's say that we can mop up this present outbreak. It is, after all, limited to a fairly remote spot in Northumberland. What then? Can we run the risk that Kaster will explode his infernal machine in, say, central London?" He paused. "All the man wants is his brother released. Looked at afresh, taken in the light of all the circumstances, it doesn't seem so unreasonable, does it? If it could be arranged – flights to Libya and all that – the Prime Minister considers that, as a last resort, we might give him Anthony Donaldson."

There was general silence, then: "It's a matter of principle," said Williams.

"Principles are very dangerous abstractions," retorted Sholto.

Calverton raised his head from doodling on his scratch-pad and spoke. "The argument may have become a little academic."

"How is that, Norman?" asked Gervase Molineux.

"The call which I took outside a quarter of an hour ago. It was from our medical friends in Haslemere."

"And?"

"Anthony Donaldson is dead."

They drove to Durham in Romaine's ancient Vauxhall, creeping through the snow and darkness on the narrow backroads. Twice they were stopped by police road-blocks and released as a pair of "gypos", of no interest to them. The police were checking faces against a photograph of Donaldson but there was no resemblance. They hadn't worked out that photographs live a parallel life, similar to but not quite ours.

The Castle and the Cathedral had snow on every crevice and parapet. The river, pouring through the gorge beneath them, was muddy with water draining off the moors. In the market-place the bronze hussar on his pedestal was riding through snow like the French retreating from Moscow. There were telephone kiosks and telephone directories with the names of doctors inside them.

"Dr Havers?"

The figure in baggy trousers and carpet-slippers stood against the hall light. It had a stained-glass shade and threw lozenges of colour on the pastel walls. He was a comfortable, middle-aged man with the face of a friendly rabbit.

"Yes?" He was suspicious of Romaine, burly and unkempt, huddled in his greatcoat. Donaldson stood behind him, his hand in his pocket, gripping the Walther PPK.

The gypsy was polite. "We need a doctor – urgently."

"I'm not on call. Do you have an appointment?"

"No. It's urgent."

"Are you one of my patients?"

"No."

"The hospitals deals with emergency cases." Havers was speaking mechanically, peering out into the night.

"It's an emergency. You'll have to do."

"I—" He said no more as Donaldson came forward and pushed the gun into his ribs.

"That's enough. We want you now. Bring some medicines."

"Medicines? What medicines? I don't even know what's wrong with—"

"Tetracyclin!" said Donaldson. "Bring tetracyclin. Now! Let's move!" Havers retreated from the door and they followed him through into his surgery. A middle-aged woman appeared after them and flickered in the doorway.

"John?"

Donaldson turned around.

"It's all right, darling," said Havers. "Something's turned up, an emergency."

"I thought that Harold was on call?"

Havers spoke to her tenderly and calmed her nervousness. "Harold's under the weather. A bit too much of the Christmas spirit, I expect."

"That's very poor of him."

"Yes, I suppose it is. But, there's a dear, find the old black bag and check there's some tetracyclin in it, will you?"

Cautiously she did so while her husband found his shoes and coat. "I suppose I'd better put on my galoshes," he said. "The snow, you know." He threw a weak smile at Donaldson, trying to strike a spark of intimacy. Donaldson told him to hurry up. Two minutes later they bundled him into the car.

He acquiesced in being blindfolded, and they drove him in silence back to their encampment. Donaldson went immediately to the van and checked that the blankets covering the contents in the back were still undisturbed. They were. He had trusted Romaine, and his trust had been repaid. They were both aliens and they recognized each other.

Havers was ushered still blindfolded into the big caravan. Annaliese was lying in bed, with Romaine's wife and one of the other women comforting her. She was pale, but her face had a transfigured look and she held out a hand to Donaldson to clasp his, and murmured: "John." Havers was about to answer and then realized that it was not him that she was speaking to.

He examined her and administered the tetracyclin, then turned to Donaldson. "I don't know whether it will do any good. You seem to be the doctor around here and not me. I don't recognize the symptoms. She ought really to be in hospital." Thinking it might mean something, he added: "It'll be your responsibility if she . . . you know."

"Yes, my responsibility," said Donaldson quietly. He put the blindfold on the other man and led him back to the car. Romaine drove again. Snow and more snow. Donaldson sat in the back and emptied Havers's bag. He pocketed the supply of tetracyclin, meaning to give it to the gypsy. If Annaliese was really suffering from – no, put the thought out of mind. He would give the tetracyclin to Romaine in case his people needed it. Donaldson wondered where the gypsies would go after he left them. They would be untraceable wanderers. If they were infected, they could carry the disease anywhere.

"Here, take these." He held some tablets out to Havers.

"What are they?" The doctor couldn't see. His fingers tapped and felt their way around Donaldson's open palm reading his fortune.

"Sleeping-tablets."

The doctor counted them and mentally reckoned up their effect. Then, slowly, he swallowed them one by one and in a few minutes his head dropped forward and lolled on his chest. Donaldson pushed him into an easy position and then sat closed with his own thoughts until the lights of the city said they had arrived.

They left the sleeping man in the doorway of a public house and returned to the camp. The gypsies were asleep, and the clearing in the trees was white in the snow and moonlight. Donaldson took some cans of paint from the back of the van and, with Romaine's help, he repainted the vehicle a dull red and changed the plates. Tomorrow he would get something new.

The two men worked quietly, without speaking.

Chapter Thirty-Three

ALMOST FORGOTTEN in the excitement of the hunt for Kaster, the next meeting of the Operations Liaison Committee was scheduled for the morning of the twenty-ninth. The Americans attended, bright-eyed and energetic, with a punch-list of final points for resolution and a list of complaints from Washington.

"Believe me," said Grover Wagner, "I'm on your side in this. I've tried to explain to Langley and the State Department that there's no slackness on the British side. I've told them that it's just a difference in style. That's it, isn't it? A difference in style, not slackness."

"It's very kind of you to say so," replied Gervase Molineux.

That's right, thought Calverton. Give him the reassurance. Lord knows we could all do with it.

The Americans tabled their agenda and the British worked through it sluggishly until everything was wrapped up. Then they celebrated the conclusion with gin and tonic after being unable to satisfy the Americans' request for martinis. Molineux unlocked the drinks cupboard and, when they were finished, marked off the level on the bottle.

"Just between us girls," said the CIA man, sniffing the air, but probably only to assess the strength of his drink, "is there something going on that I should be aware of?"

"I don't know what you mean," said Lionel Sholto.

"You guys seem tired. Been burning the candle at both ends?"

"You know how it is – Christmas – merry wassailing in the English tradition." Sholto turned away and took another drink.

"We don't seem to have a full team here today," Wagner continued. "Where are the rest of Williams's boys?"

"Things to do, I expect. Why don't you ask Williams?"

"They have things to do," said Williams. The American nodded but examined him closely over the rim of his glass.

"I'm reminded of those dinner-parties where one's guests outstay their welcome," said Molineux when the Americans were gone. No one took this up. They resumed their places around the table while he went on in his best Foreign Office manner: "I suppose we'd better get on with the status report on the Kaster thing, yes? My position, of course, is just a watching brief." He looked around for anyone taking notes and suggested: "Let the minutes state that I am 'in attendance' rather than 'present'. I think that captures the right nuance."

"The Prime Minister", said Sholto, "is very distressed that our prisoner has died. Naturally I had to tell my Minister and he had to tell COBRA, and the news was not well received." He let his gaze turn to the window. "No, not well received. It cuts down our options – and you know politicians. I speak particularly of my Minister, though no disloyalty is intended, but they do love to keep their options open – and the effect is to put everything on to catching Kaster. Norman here" – he nodded at Calverton – "has brought along his man Ross, who had a brush with Kaster only recently. I suggest we bring him in. Let him be also shown as 'in attendance', if that's the expression."

Ross came in. He was still limping from his injury. Polite enquiries were made as to his health and he was offered a seat next to Calverton. Then he was ignored in case the facts confused everyone.

"We have had the laboratory reports from Porton Down on the samples we sent them – the ones from the cottage," began Atherton of the Ministry of Defence. "Thankfully they were negative, no trace of anthrax spores or of plague. We can—"

"Thank our lucky stars?" suggested Calverton.

"—congratulate ourselves that our handling of the Northumberland crisis was successful."

Williams broke off from humming a Wesleyan hymn and said impatiently: "I'm not so sure. We've received a report of a doctor who was kidnapped by Kaster last night to help the girl. It confirms Ross's report that she was ill. He treated her with tetracyclin, which indicates that she was suffering from plague."

"It means only that she *may* be suffering from plague," said Sholto judiciously, "or that Kaster *thinks* she has plague. Not at all the same thing. In any case, if Kaster is treating her with tetracyclin, then she should recover – that's right, isn't it?"

Gervase Molineux murmured: "It leaves the position somewhat inconclusive. But I don't see what we can do about it. I suggest we change the subject."

Williams unfolded a sheet of paper on the table. "We have a full print-out of break-ins and vehicles stolen in the Northumberland and Durham areas during the last four days." Everyone bent over to look, though no one but Williams was in a position to see. "We believe that we have identified the source of the metalworking equipment and paint that Kaster has been using."

"Does that help?" asked Calverton. "I mean, we all know what he has; but does it help us to know the source? It would be much more useful to know what he has been doing with it."

"He's been making a cradle for his bomb," said Ross. The others stared at him. He sensed their cautiousness about reaching any conclusions. "The bomb is too cumbersome, too immobile. If he has to change vehicles or move the thing about, then he needs something to help him."

"You could be right," admitted Williams. He passed copies of his print-out around. "We're not certain what vehicle Kaster is using at the moment. Ross reported a blue transit van; the doctor says a Vauxhall saloon. It ought to be something off this list."

"A hot-dog stand stolen from the vicinity of Newcastle football-ground?" quoted Sholto. "Your people are not very discriminating in their selection of which stolen vehicles to report, are they?"

"They generate information," Williams retorted sharply. "It is for us, for this committee, to exercise our judgement!"

"Ah!"

The meeting fell silent. Someone proposed coffee and a toilet break. Ross stayed in his seat and wondered about Helen and what had happened to her. When the discussion resumed, he didn't listen. He recognized the sound of men who were preparing themselves for failure.

The gypsies broke camp at noon and drove in slow convoy south. Donaldson's vehicle was tucked between two of the caravans. Romaine was in no hurry: they had been harassed in one place and would be harassed in another, and the travelling was the freedom in between. There was evidence of the police on the roads but no road-blocks. The police could not be certain what vehicle Kaster was driving or where in the country he was. They had no plausible public explanation for a full-scale manhunt. It was impossible to halt the thousands of vehicles moving every hour on the highways into London. Donaldson felt himself moving down an enchanted corridor past enemies frozen into inaction.

By late evening they had reached the outskirts of Peterborough. Romaine knew a barren spot by a rubbish-tip where they could camp undisturbed, make a fire from the wood lying about and collect some scrap to sell.

"You'll be leaving us now," Romaine murmured as he stared into the flames.

Donaldson didn't know whether this was a prophecy or a statement. He nodded agreement and threw some wood on to the fire.

"I need to change the van."

"That would be a good idea."

"It becomes more dangerous for your people, the longer I stay with you."

Romaine shrugged his shoulders. He took out a clasp-knife and applied himself to peeling the sheathing off a copper armature he had found amongst the rubbish. He threw the parings into the flames and watched them flash blue. "More snow," he said, glancing at the sky.

"Take these." Donaldson held something in his hand.

"What are they?"

"The tablets I got from the doctor."

"Oh? Is what the girl has contagious, then?"

"I don't know. It might be."

The gypsy grunted and put the bottle in his pocket. He stretched his legs, stood up and ambled off into the darkness. Donaldson followed and found the other man standing by a stunted elder, staring up at the stars beyond the snowclouds.

"Do you know anything about stars?"

Romaine gave a short laugh. "Where do you get your bloody ideas about gypsies from? Honest to God!" He kicked at something underfoot. "Look at all this bloody rubbish. The whole fucking world consists of rubbish when you're looking at it from where I am. If they dropped the H-Bomb, I wouldn't notice the difference." He touched Donaldson's wrist. "And don't start quoting that little gem as a piece of Romany wisdom. It's just me feeling pissed-off, understand?"

They walked back to the group and Donaldson checked out the van.

"This is it, then?" said Romaine.

"Yes." Donaldson held out his hand. Romaine smiled and shook his head, but grasped the hand all the same.

"Good luck."

"You, too." Donaldson opened the cab door and slipped into the driver's seat. He started the engine and in a moment the van was bumping down the track away from the camp-site. His last view was of the caravans in dark blocks against the crescent glow of the fire.

He found a patch of waste ground near some council houses. A couple of lorry-cabs were laid up minus their trailers. Donaldson parked the van in their anonymous shadow.

"I'm off to look for some more transport," he told Annaliese. "How are you feeling?"

"A little better." She was lying, and he knew it.

"Good – good." He kissed her gently then walked away. His feet crackled the patches of ice in the shallow potholes and disturbed a foraging rat, which glanced at him idly and waddled off. He wondered how many rats there were in Peterborough, or in any large town. A figure came to mind, something he had read somewhere, that the rat population exceeded that of humans. If plague ever took hold, it would be in the limitless reservoir of rats. They would become dark pilgrims, spreading the gospel of the Last Judgement.

The streets were more or less empty: a few people coming home from the pub; a group of youths in the bright doorway of a Chinese take-away. Melting snow had slid off the rooftops and was freezing again. There were numbers of empty cars but nothing suitable for his purpose. He trod the streets and the patches of open ground until the last pedestrians had gone home and there was no traffic but the occasional taxi.

He found a builder's yard with a high brick wall topped by glass and a wooden gate with metal spikes that wouldn't keep out an adventurous grandmother. There was probably a truck or a van left there for the night. And what else? A dog? Another nightwatch-man like Hennessy, but, this time, one who would have to be killed? He clambered the gate, scanned as much of the yard as he could see in the darkness, and slipped down the other side. This time there was nothing but stacks of materials and the usual debris of the business; and, tucked up in the shadows, an open wagon and a light van.

The van was a Bedford. Its doors were open but there were no keys in the ignition. He tore off the moulded plastic panels with the firm's name on, changed the plates for the set he had brought with him and hot-wired it to start. Then he drove out of the yard and back to where he had left Annaliese.

Chapter Thirty-Four

Ross stayed another night at the office in Battersea High Street. Calverton was locked up with Williams at the Yard's operations-room. Ross had sensed that they wanted him available, but not too close: like an old whore, a threat to the cosiness of their little family. Around breakfast-time Calverton called.

"The young Ainsworth woman, she's been released. Everyone is content that she hasn't been infected by whatever the Schreiber girl has." A pause. "I thought you'd like to know."

"Thanks." Ross put the phone down. He suspected that Calverton really cared; that was the joke. He telephoned the house in Black-heath. Hortense Ainsworth answered: Helen wasn't there. He wouldn't have been surprised if she were there all along but didn't want to know him. What had knowing him done for her except pull her world into bits? It occurred to him that Calverton was probably the only person who cared one way or the other whether he lived, and that was because Ross was going to save the Empire. The way he felt now, it didn't matter too much. What he needed was a shave and a change of clothes, and those were to be had at his flat.

He found her sitting by the window, looking over the crumbling asbestos garages into Eton Avenue. She was shivering, but the shivering had nothing to do with the cold. The last of her chicness had gone. Her face had been laid open to the bone of emotion.

"Helen."

She looked up and gave the remains of her confident smile.

"I slipped the lock with a credit card. You see, I have learned something."

Ross took off his jacket and slung it over a chair. He looked around the room. It was bleak and undisturbed, bigger and emptier than he remembered, with space enough for all the things that stood between them.

"They let you out of the hospital."

"Yes. They did their tests and found nothing; and, in the end, they had to let me go."

"Good."

"Good," she repeated dully. She fumbled in her pockets for something and nothing, and then said: "But they don't believe in me! They don't believe their own tests!"

"They wouldn't have discharged you if—"

"You don't understand! They had to release me because their tests told them there was nothing wrong. And they are scientific, rational men and they have to trust their tests. But it's in their eyes, James, the disbelief that they don't understand or admit themselves. They have made me into a leper. I've become guilty of something that can never be spoken of."

Ross held out his hand and touched her forearm, feeling the frisson of the soft down on her skin. Her eyes fixed on his – brown eyes flecked with other colours that would never fully be seen. Her lips were parted to ask questions that could never be adequately phrased or answered. He kissed her on the forehead, holding her face between his hands. She took his hands and let her lips pass over the fingers and her warm breath stir the skin.

She voiced her feelings without self-pity, out of a deep anger, confusion and suffering. Ross wondered if his brother had really loved her. He didn't doubt it: how could anyone know her and not love her? But in the end the question didn't matter: for good or ill, David had finally to be left to rot in his quiet grave; because it was James Ross who loved her now in the world of the living, which had in it all the reality that anyone was ever going to get.

Calverton sat back in his chair and listened to Williams bawling out a chief constable. The pale light indicated it was morning. They had worked through the night.

"I don't give a damn that your force isn't answerable to me!" Williams was yelling into the telephone. "If we have a disaster on our hands, no one is going to be interested in areas of authority and chains of command. They're going to see who cocked it up and then fall on him like the wrath of God! And at the moment the prime candidate is you!" He put down the receiver with a thump and looked around the operations-room at his subordinates. He rounded on them: "Work, you buggers, work!"

Calverton helped himself to a breakfast cup of coffee. His eyes were tired with too much reading. From all the reports he was still trying to derive a pattern of what Kaster was up to, instead of allowing himself to be run ragged, chasing Kaster's tail in Williams's fashion. But perhaps Williams was right? How could one tell?

"What's wrong?" he asked.

"Kaster was in Peterborough last night. We found his vehicle, the blue van he stole in Newcastle."

"And?"

"We don't know what he's driving now. Those clowns in Cambridgeshire have had six hours to trace every van that's been begged, borrowed or stolen in the county and they have come up with precisely nothing. According to them, there is nothing missing. Kaster has disappeared using some form of invisible transport!"

Calverton stood up to stretch his legs. Age was starting to affect his circulation; he stooped and scratched a persistent itchy spot on his left calf where he suspected a varicose vein was about to appear: one of the more ridiculous bits of entropy in the universe. Williams was lounging over his coffee and trying to relax by turning the conversation in a sociable direction. Their eyes drifted aimlessly along the walls of the room to read the road accident statistics and the police football-league fixtures.

"The Americans arrive tomorrow," said Williams casually.

"Yes, I suppose the Prime Minister will be terribly cross if we haven't sorted this business out by then."

"The PM would be," Williams answered. He leaned towards Calverton and unburdened himself. "Don't you ever feel, Norman, that it's impossible to control something this size; that everything is just too . . .?" His hands flapped about uselessly. Calverton noticed he had closely bitten fingernails. On his desk the Welshman kept a booklet with Scripture Union suggestions for Bible-readings, which he perused in his lunch-breaks. Calverton wanted to say something comforting but still couldn't remember the other man's first name.

"What are they relying on?" he asked.

"Relying on? Who?"

"The Peterborough force. What is their source of information as to stolen vehicles?"

"Owners' reports, what else? The owner finds his vehicle missing and informs the police. There's nothing else they can do: there's no such thing as a record of every vehicle that's supposed to be in a given area. They did put out a broadcast on the local radio, asking owners to check; but that didn't produce anything."

"Yet there has to be a vehicle. One that no one has noticed has gone missing."

"I don't see how. I mean, if you look out and your van isn't there, then you tend to notice."

"These are commercial vehicles."

"True."

Williams was hanging on to his reply. It occurred to Calverton that the other man's first name was Dai, but he couldn't be sure: sometimes they joked about the Welshman, calling him Taffy or Williams the Police. Thinking about it now was a distraction. He asked quickly: "Have they tried a street-to-street enquiry? You know, with loudspeaker vans and so forth? Asking all the people to make sure of their vehicles?"

"Yes, they've done that."

"Obviously without any luck." Calverton thought for a moment. "What would you do if you heard such a message?"

"Check that my car was all right; look in the garage, if I had one."

"What about the firm's car? I mean if it were left on the company's premises?"

"It would depend if it were my responsibility."

"Well, who *is* responsible for them? Let's say the business is closed for the weekend—"

"Or the holiday!" cried Williams. "If Kaster took a van from a small yard or a depot where there wasn't a security man, it could be another two days before anyone would know!" He grabbed the telephone and called Peterborough again. He ordered a check through the owners of all construction sites, builder's yards, warehouses and distribution depots. It took a further four hours to identify the vehicle that Kaster had taken.

Donaldson laid up for the day in a village west of Peterborough and then drove in a wide circuit to approach London from the south during the evening rush hour when it was impracticable for the police to set up any road-blocks. It was a slow drive through the suburbs past streets of ordered houses with gardens of flowering shrubs, now stripped of leaves; places where people imposed little pockets of intelligibility on the disorder around them. He hated them because they were false, private solutions, an avoidance of confronting the bleakness of a meaningless creation.

He headed for Chelsea. Would Sebastian be there? Would his home be watched? He guessed that even the police, with their stunning incompetence, would guard against his trying to get in touch with old friends. But that would be their weakness: they would watch Sebastian as a matter of routine, but in their hearts they wouldn't *believe* that Kaster would risk making contact with the art-dealer – and he would slip through that crack in their watchfulness into a little island of immunity where they would see him and not see him.

He had the keys to Sebastian's house. Trusting Sebastian, who always wanted friendship: "Use the place as you like. It's Liberty Hall, dear boy!" There was a uniformed policeman pacing up and down outside, bored into a stupor, stamping his feet, rubbing his hands and watching the swirls of his cold breath. Donaldson kept out of sight and returned to the street. There was a car parked half on the pavement, a hundred yards from the entrance to the mews.

He walked to King's Road and bought a newspaper. His picture was in it and a story about his supposed escape from Durham prison; the public was cautioned against approaching him. The photograph was of a suave art-dealer. Now he was unshaven and wearing an old jacket and overcoat he had picked up from Helen's cottage. He went back with the paper to the street where he had noticed the car. It was an old Hillman, and the cap to the petrol-tank had no lock. He rolled two sheets of the newspaper, removed the cap and inserted the makeshift fuse into the tank with the end trailing down to the wheel arches. He lit it and ran back to the van. His hand was on the driver's door when the car exploded.

The blast shattered windows, and a number of burglar-alarms went off. People seemed to spring out of the ground, suddenly visible in the pall of black smoke. The wreck of the car blazed fiercely, and subsidiary fires from its scattered parts flared here and there in the roadway. The policeman came dashing out of the mews, waving his arms at the bystanders and rattling a report into his pocket radio. Donaldson drove slowly forward through the dense smoke, slid through the archway into the mews, opened the garage doors beneath Sebastian's place and parked the van inside.

Sebastian Summer heard the explosion in the street and the sound of his garage being opened. He went downstairs and found Donaldson already there. The two men stared at each other. The shock took any other thought from Sebastian's head than that he was overjoyed to see the other man. "John!" He didn't know what to say, and then he remembered the dead brother and babbled out: "I'm so terribly sorry about Anthony. He was—"

Donaldson cut him off. "I need some help!" He was struggling to carry a prostrate figure from the back of the van.

"Whatever I can do." Sebastian forgot any other ideas and helped his partner to get Annaliese to the stairs and then support her whilst she climbed them. "Isn't this . . .?"

"Anthony's girlfriend. Yes."

"What's wrong with her?"

"I don't know. Something she caught whilst we were in Egypt or maybe when she was in Ceylon. I don't know."

They carried her to the bedroom and left her on Sebastian's bed. Donaldson returned to the sitting-room and poured a couple of stiff drinks from the bar. He handed one to Sebastian.

"I shan't ask you how you managed to get here – thank you" – Sebastian took a token sip from the glass – "but the whole world seems to be looking for you. I was arrested and kept in a cell for Lord knows how many days; and all the while the police kept asking me questions about Anthony and about you, as if you were about to do something terrible. I didn't know what to do, what to say! I wanted to help them – I wanted to help you – there was the matter of friendship . . ." The words trailed off into a look of hopelessness.

Donaldson examined the other man. His features were collapsing into confusion. Sebastian ran his fingers through his hair and found a smile someplace. Donaldson felt he owed him something – a release. "Friendship is all past," he said. "I've become someone else, a person you don't know; someone you don't have responsibility for."

"Don't say that, John! It sounds frightening. I prefer people to stay the same."

"They don't." He was reminded of Reinhardt Egger. The German had gone through life shedding personalities like the skins of a snake: liberal, Nazi, religious maniac. And, in a way, it didn't stop there. Donaldson knew he had become the old man's successor, carrying on where Egger left off, driven by the subliminal logic of the Last Judgement. His old personality had been a hologram, a trick of the light, three dimensions of nothingness.

A bell rang; someone at the door. Donaldson took out his gun.

"Do you really need that?"

"It's for your own good. Answer the door."

It was the policeman, his face smudged by oil smoke.

"Just checking that everything is OK, sir."

"Fine – everything is fine."

"Are you sure? You don't look—"

"It was the explosion – the shock – naturally. . . ."

"Naturally."

Sebastian stood in the doorway, rooted to the spot but mentally hopping from one foot to the other. He felt that something else was expected. "What caused the explosion?"

"Someone set fire to a car. The tank went up. I thought that it might have been. . . . Probably kids."

"Yes, probably."

"Then, if everything's OK, I'll say goodbye."

"Goodbye."

The policeman turned, then paused.

"I wonder if I might have a drink."

"Oh. . . ." Sebastian looked behind him. Donaldson had gone. "Please, come in." He opened the door fully. They went into the sitting-room.

"Whisky? Gin? I was just having one myself." His glass stood on the table. Donaldson had taken his.

"Just water. I'm on duty." The officer took a seat and looked about the room. He made some comment about the decoration and received a murmured reply from the kitchen. Sebastian came back with the drink. He sat down and stared at the table. There were two mats on the walnut surface, a ring of moisture on each of them. The after-image of John's drink was there, damp on the cork mat. Quickly he pushed it across. "Please, use this."

"Protect the table? OK." The visitor placed his glass on the mat and began to talk about Christmas. Outside the night had fallen. The rain had started and was rattling on the window-glass.

The unwelcome guest left, Donaldson came out of the bedroom.

"Thank you, Sebastian."

"What . . .?" The question remained unfinished. Is that it? Sebastian thought to himself. When did I decide? How did I commit myself? To Donaldson he said: "That's all right."

They poured more drinks and sat facing each other across the table.

"What is it you are trying to do, John?"

Donaldson didn't answer. Evidently Sebastian hadn't been told. He wasn't surprised.

"What were you saying earlier about Anthony?" he asked. He held out a hand to touch Sebastian's. The other man was shaking with tears and mumbling: "I'm sorry, I'm sorry!"

"Anthony is dead?"

Sebastian composed himself. "Yes."

"Aah!" Donaldson tried to remember whether that was important. Perhaps it was, and it was the pain that had anaesthetized his response. He recalled that he had demanded the release of Anthony as a condition of not using Last Judgement. He realized that he had not meant it: he had put a threat that was purely conventional, something they would understand. And, behind it, he wanted what? Peace? Happiness? Justice? Understanding? There had to be some counterpart to the guilt of being alive.

He cast his eyes about the room and saw one of Anthony's "Fenwick" paintings still on its easel. Anthony had left his trace behind him, and even that was a fake. He had never understood what his brother had been trying to accomplish with the "Fenwicks". It hadn't been simply the money: there was too much passion in them. There was something of the vampire in his attempt to bleed the essence out of a life that wasn't his. And now, in Anthony's typically ambiguous fashion, he had gone and not gone, and his spirit lived on in the ranks of the undead.

Chapter Thirty-Five

Ross woke early to the chime of milk-bottles being placed on the front doorstep and the cold dawn light creeping over the rooftops. Helen was still asleep, a breathing shadow in the bed. He washed and dressed and tried to reach Calverton on the phone but got only Elphinstone, diamond-bright and chatty. The latter was starting to ape the way Calverton spoke. "I don't think we'll be needing you, old chap. We've got the number of Kaster's vehicle and it's only a matter of time before we find him. Every policeman in London is on the lookout and all the likely targets are guarded. This is a disciplined operation and there's no scope for the freelance man. We don't want it all to end in the Gunfight at the OK Corral, do we?" Ross wondered whether Elphinstone still believed in fairy-stories.

He heard the sound of Helen awake. She was sitting up in bed with a sheet pulled to cover her breasts in the way he remembered from old Hollywood movies. It told him that in some ways they were still strangers, perhaps always would be: maybe there was something to the Hays Code after all. On reflection he decided that she was right to be guarded. He hadn't told her what Donaldson was trying to do.

"You're going out," she said. "When shall I see you again?"

"I don't know." That sounded too cruel. "Tonight – tomorrow – one way or another, everything will be finished by then."

"I should like to see the New Year in."

"Where will you be?"

"With all the others in Trafalgar Square, where else?"

He took in the information but promised nothing.

He went for a walk through the damp streets, aiming nowhere in particular, working off his thoughts on the pavements as the traffic struggled by in busloads of anonymous passengers and the shops opened one by one. His path took him down Baker Street. As he crossed Oxford Street he had to stop for an ambulance. He watched it on its way to collect Figgis, bleeding to death on a bed of cardboard boxes whilst Bliss gave him the last sacrament he was ever going to get. Then it turned up a side-street and vanished.

"Have you got ten pence for a cup of coffee?"

A drunk with a spray of beard and a young voice uncurled from his bed in a shop doorway and dodged around him with his hand out for money. Ross gave him a pound.

"Bloody hell!" The man ran off down the street, clutching his prize.

He reached Trafalgar Square without any intention of being there. In the shadow of the great Christmas-tree sent every year by the people of Oslo an old lady was feeding the pigeons. On the west side a woman was standing in front of the crib and telling the nativity story to two small children. On the stable was the legend: "The Word was made flesh and dwelt amongst us full of grace and truth"; but, in case that wasn't true, a team of police workmen was unloading sections of crush-barrier from the back of a wagon and assembling them in a perimeter fence. Ross sat on the edge of one of the fountains and stared into the water.

Kaster was here, somewhere in London. He had to be!

"What did you say?" A youth in denims, wearing dark glasses and stereo headphones was sitting next to him, rocking to the sounds in his head.

"Nothing." He was unaware he had spoken. The other man didn't hear the reply; he just smiled, finished a soft drink he was holding and threw the empty can into the fountain. Ross watched the ripples spread across the water's surface. Every action that Kaster took was causing ripples of effect that could be traced back to their source, his purpose and intent. They could detect the ripples. If only they could see the underlying pattern. If only they could see!

The National Gallery was open. Ross trailed across the square, crossed the road and mounted the steps to go in behind a small queue of American tourists. It was the first time that he had been into an art gallery and he didn't know why he went now except that this was the world that Helen and Donaldson shared. The paintings were part of the powerhouse of Kaster's imagination, the code that explained him.

The rooms were cooler and airier than he expected. Ross wandered through them in no particular order, staring blankly at the canvases. Why had the artist painted shepherds? Who was St Ambrose? He found himself in a room of French Impressionists and at last recognized something, a painting by Renoir. One Christmas he had received a present from a family who had fostered him. A calendar decorated with the picture by Renoir. It had hung by his bed with his birthday marked in red, but when his birthday came there was nothing more.

And that was art, a bundle of recollections. He had no business there. It wasn't telling him anything about Kaster. He left the gallery and on the pavement outside bought a hot-dog from a street vendor.

Calverton returned to Battersea High Street after lunch with Lionel Sholto at a self-service cafeteria at Heathrow. Sholto had been at his most morose. He picked at a pie, ambiguously described as "meat", and interrogated Calverton loosely on the status of the hunt for Kaster.

"What has happened?" Calverton asked.

"Our stock with the PM is falling. The Americans announced last night that their negotiating team had changed its route and was travelling to Brussels via Paris. Complete bloody chaos over there, with our ambassador dragged out of bed to turn up at Charles de Gaulle and make the best of it; while the French Foreign Minister was there in best bib and tucker with a horde of cronies sniggering on the side."

"Explanation?"

"Bland assertions from the Yanks that, since the meetings are taking place in Brussels on this Biological Thing, and the stopover in London was merely to change their socks, the alteration in programme had no diplomatic significance."

"What do they know of Kaster?"

"Oh," said Sholto airily, "I called Grover Wagner and asked him whether the CIA had doubts about our security arrangements – was that the reason for the change?"

"And what did he say?"

"I quote: 'You and me, Lionel, we're in the same business. Even if it were true, would I let them lay that one on you?' "

They sat in silence watching a sugar cube dissolve in a saucer of spilled tea among the debris of someone else's meal. Calverton took a small change-purse out of his pocket, counted the coins and checked his train ticket.

"You know," said Sholto, "it seems almost impossible to believe that one man could cause so much disruption. And why? I simply can't understand what motivates a man like Kaster. Is it ideology? I've never had an ideology, myself, at least not in that sense. Is it Marxism? Marxism, is that it?"

"I interviewed someone who knew Kaster when he was at university," said Calverton. "A man called Armitage. He runs a shop off Piccadilly Circus, sells games and things. Kaster saw him a little time ago and asked him some questions about German uniforms, but that is all by the by. The point is that Kaster was apparently an ardent Marxist in his student days: an intellectual, cold-hearted, bloody-handed type. His brother was even worse. Armitage said you could have knocked him over with a feather when Kaster reverted to the ancestral type, respectable figure in the art world and all that. Very good family, it seems. Uncle a bishop." He paused and stared around at the passengers waiting tensely over their hand-luggage. "I suppose that's it, the reason. If you asked Kaster why he is doing it, I expect that's what he'd tell you. Fervour for the revolution."

"You don't believe it?"

"Marxism? It's so old-fashioned. One might as well say he was doing it for Methodism. I mean – here in England. Maybe in South America Marx still makes a sort of sense. Anyway, people never tell you their real motives; I doubt that they even know them." He looked at Sholto, but Sholto wasn't listening.

"There was a time", the other man said distractedly, "when the CIA were decidedly less than value for money; when they were so obsessed with foliomancy that, whenever one asked them to do something, the answer was 'We'll do it on Thursday', for all the world like the bloody Gas Board. But the times change, Norman, the times change. In our heyday the Service was staffed with the likes of Kaster. Cambridge and communism – at least one knew where one stood, and even the traitors didn't do it for money. Now it seems to be full of proles like your man Ross, clocking on every day with their hands full of Thermos flasks and sandwich-tins. I'm not sure I don't prefer Kaster. At least he's a gentleman."

Calverton had nodded. He left some money for the meat pie and soon was back at the office, glad to see Elphinstone bouncing around with his puppy-dog welcome.

"Ross is here, sir!" was the greeting. "He barged in an hour ago saying that he had your permission. I didn't know what to do. He has a temporary pass, but his security clearance is, to say the least, uncertain."

"Yes, yes, I'm sure you locked up the teaspoons. What is he doing now?"

"He's got the vehicle print-outs and all the other material that Williams sent us and I've lent him a room. You'll find him there."

Ross was closeted in the nearest place Elphinstone could find to limbo, a junk-room where they used to make coffee in the days before the vending machine was invented. There was a rusted urn, a disconnected water-heater and a sluice. Ross had spread out his papers on the floor and was working from the old tea-trolley.

"You seem to be causing us administrative problems, James."

Ross looked up. "Your whole bloody system is falling apart," he said coolly.

Calverton winced. "I admit that it seems like that at times but there's an underlying rationality to it. Would you mind telling me what you're doing?" He looked over Ross's shoulder but at first made nothing of the papers. He wondered what the lassitude was that was coming over him.

"It's in here!" Ross picked up one of the files. "The answer's in here but we just can't see it."

Calverton nodded. Ross's anger bordered on enthusiasm. It was enthusiasm that Calverton had always admired in the other man's brother. The Victorians had had it when they built the Empire and its most tangible symbol, the railways. Sometimes he sat in his office and looked at the prints of trains which hung on the wall and heard its echo there, but faint, over the years. Where had that enthusiasm gone? He went over to the window and looked out into the courtyard. There was an ice-cream wrapper stuck to one of the ventilators, presumably left over from summer. Thinking of Lionel Sholto, he was inclined to agree now that it had been a shrewd move to shift operational responsibility to Special Branch. With all its imperfections, it was important to preserve the integrity and reputation of the organization against eventualities.

"Fortunately, we're safe until midnight," he said aloud.

"Why midnight?" asked Ross.

"End of the Old Year, beginning of the New – that sort of thing. I'm sure that Kaster won't have missed its apocalyptic resonances, the opportunity for self-dramatization. What other time would be more appropriate for the Last Judgement?"

"You think you understand him?" The question was hard, sceptical.

312

"Oh, our minds are never that far apart. Kaster is our twin, the dark side of our imaginings. At the last he is prepared to unleash all that irrational, unutterable violence which we know but cannot admit. He wants the catharsis of the soul which comes from speaking the unspeakable truth: from damning God to his face for the pain and incomprehensibility of the world." Calverton took out a handkerchief and blew his nose loudly. "Or something like that. I'm sorry, am I embarrassing you?"

"No." Ross looked back at his papers, Kaster's trail, a chaos of words spread across the page. "Let's look at what Kaster's done."

"If you wish." Calverton stood behind Ross and read his notes. What was the word that Lionel Sholto had used of the CIA? Foliomancy? Divination by paper, he supposed. Looking at the volume that had been produced by Special Branch, it seemed appropriate. They were trying to conjure Kaster out of words.

"In Newcastle he stole a van. Why a van, when he could have taken a car? A car would give him better performance and be less conspicuous. He took some metalworking equipment and some white and red paint. What has he used it for?"

"He repainted the van using the red paint," said Calverton. "Somewhat late in the day, Williams's people deduced from the report of the doctor that Kaster might have fallen in with a party of gypsies. You remember the doctor – the fellow from Durham who was called out to treat a patient in a caravan? This morning the police arrested a band of gypsies near Uxbridge. One of them admitted to helping Kaster repaint his vehicle."

"What about the white paint? He didn't use that to paint the van. The paint was used at the cottage: I found traces of it."

"I confess that's still something of a mystery. Presumably it is connected in some fashion with how he proposes to use the bomb."

"That's the point. Where would he explode it?"

"In an enclosed space, or somewhere where he could guarantee a crowd. There wouldn't be much effect otherwise. A theatre, a concert-hall, a public stadium? Williams has compiled a list of every New Year's Eve function in the capital, in so far as one can be comprehensive about these things – every little dance-hall and upper room seems to have been let for one party or another. Still he should have enough men; police leave has been cancelled." Calverton thought his voice sounded distant even as he spoke. He tried to put some force into it. "What do you think?"

"It would have to be somewhere important, somewhere that would give impact."

Calverton sighed. "Ah, yes, more drama! Our Kaster must have his moment in the spotlight. Terrorism as a mixture of mystery-religion and theatre of the absurd, eh?"

Ross turned away from the papers and looked at the other man. "What the hell are you talking about?" he asked. He felt a cold pity for Calverton. "Mystery-religion – theatre of the absurd – is that supposed to mean something?"

"Perhaps I shouldn't have used those expressions. I was trying to understand Kaster."

"And, if you understand him, does that mean you've won? It's a game between the pair of you, is that it? If you solve the mystery, then Kaster loses; and it doesn't matter that he blows the bomb up, because that doesn't count."

Meanwhile, in Chelsea, Donaldson spent the day watching television. The weariness of the old year infected the passing of the afternoon, and the media pundits explained the past and looked forward to the future with the voices of tired confidence tricksters seeking a last reprieve; but in all this he felt calm. There were poets who fell in love with death, and Donaldson knew that he had fallen in love with the Last Judgement; and the only tension was the urgency of a lover to consummate his passion.

"What has happened to you, John?" asked Sebastian Summer. Donaldson opened an eye to examine him. Poor Sebastian, wandering around the rooms clad in a silk dressing-gown and feeling the need to empty ashtrays and vacuum the floor. How to explain? How to convey what he experienced – an insane clarity of vision? Fra Angelico, Mabuse and a hundred other painters had captured it in the faces of their saints. It radiated from innumerable painted altar-panels, but until now he had stared with the fatuity of a critical eye. What did they call the saints? The Clowns of God? Men afflicted by their vision with a holy madness. Now he saw that his earlier mistake had been to cling to the power of reason, which had always been the glittering varnish over his perceptions. The act of the visionary was to step through it into the body of the painting and assume its substance as reality.

He looked at the clock. It was a pretty piece, Sèvres porcelain, powder-blue. Outside, the mews was folded in darkness. The television promised a Highland New Year. A faded Scottish singer would hoot and cavort just as he had done last year. Six hours to go.

"I should like a bath," he told Sebastian.

"Yes, of course." Sebastian went to draw it, and on his own initiative, he perfumed it. He stood over the tub, his senses absorbed in the splashing of the water and the bright droplets of scented oil puddled on the surface. Why had he allowed himself to be mesmerized by Donaldson? Why had every meeting and every parting become changed into a round of seduction and betrayal? Was it indeed possible really to know another person without being seduced, or was it that he demanded seduction and that it was not other people but his own inversion that betrayed him? He whistled a march tune to uplift his spirits. It was "The World Turned Upside Down". He stopped abruptly, having noticed the unconscious symbolism. The intertwining of life and art – he cheered himself up – like a bad book it got on one's bloody nerves!

When Donaldson had finished his bath, he dressed himself slowly. Taking it up carefully, he put on the vest that he had stitched together slowly one night at the cottage whilst Helen slept quietly upstairs and the wind slapped at the curtains and flickered the oil-lamps.

"What is that you're wearing?" Sebastian asked. He looked at the slender cylinders stitched to the material and the wires strung from them. "Dear God!" he exclaimed. "Those are explosives."

"Don't worry yourself," said Donaldson calmly. From the airline bag he had carried on his travels he took a white cotton overall and slipped it on. Next he took out the painting, scarcely needing to unroll it. With time its importance as an object diminished as the images impressed themselves upon the retina of his memory. Its existence had always been tenuous, the object of stories and stories about stories; and in the end the canvas rag would rot and it would become wholly abstract and, in a way, perfect.

Ross watched the evening lapse from a chair at Calverton's desk in the drifts of paper produced by the police and intelligence agencies. Calverton was more or less continuously on the telephone to Williams or to the Cabinet Office. There was a conference-line open to COBRA, and from the babble of voices he could pick out that of the Prime Minister demanding action. They were all hoping that the urgency in their voices sounded like action.

Ross was tired. His eyes burned in the dim light. It was almost ten o'clock and Kaster eluded him. The other man's mind worked to a different logic in a different world. They touched only through Helen, who at some time had loved them both.

Somewhere Kaster had a base within easy reach of central London, somewhere where he could hide the blue van. It had to be hidden otherwise the police would have found it. The question was where was the base when everyone associated with Donaldson's past life was watched?

He picked up the transcripts of the routine reports sent in by the watchers. There was nothing in them: the police had stayed at their posts and no one could have got past them. Only one man had reported any incident, an unspecified disturbance near the art-dealer's house which had taken him away for three minutes; but afterwards he had checked with Summer that everything was all right.

Ross called Williams. The Welshman was glad to talk, eager for new ideas.

"There was an incident near Summer's place," Ross said. "Yesterday at about seven in the evening."

Calverton left off his own call and came over to stand behind Ross.

Williams said: "You think it may mean something?"

"Just give me the details."

Williams had them to hand. His organization was reaching perfection.

"There was a fire in a nearby street. A car and some premises damaged."

"Fire? Are you sure it was fire? An explosion, maybe?"

A pause at the other end, a riffling of papers.

"Vandals put a torch to a motor-car petrol-tank. I suppose one would call that an explosion. I don't see that it means anything. The officer looked over Summer's place afterwards."

"Everywhere?"

"Everywhere."

"Including the garage?"

Williams read through the report again. "No," he answered, and his voice tailed away.

Ross turned to Calverton.

"We've just found Kaster," he said.

Chapter Thirty-Six

JOHN DONALDSON checked his watch. It was ten o'clock. He turned to Sebastian Summer.

"I suggest that you call our friend outside in for a drink. Wish him a happy New Year."

Sebastian struggled to his feet from the chair in which he had been brooding on his distress. Donaldson put a hand on his shoulder.

"Don't worry, Sebastian; it'll soon all be over."

The older man shuffled off the comforting hand. "First Anthony and then you, John. Between you, you have destroyed me." He pulled his dressing-gown close about him and went downstairs.

Donaldson went into the bedroom. It was in darkness. Annaliese was lying back feverishly in the bed, still awake. She smiled to see him and held out a hand, but he left it alone. What they had embarked upon left no room for sentiment. He moved a bottle of sleeping-tablets to within range of her fingers. There were voices at the front door.

He went down into the garage. Upstairs the floor creaked. He unlocked the rear of the van and dropped the makeshift ramp. Sebastian's gayest tones came through offering a drink and suggesting a cocktail "to my own little recipe". Donaldson focused on the van's contents, shapeless in the darkness under folds of sacking and blankets. Music, Delius, the piping of a cuckoo. He opened the garage door quietly, pulled back the coverings from the object in the van and wheeled it down the ramp. Beyond the doors the mews was spangled with globes of light from polished coach-lamps.

Helen Ainsworth put on the black raincoat she had worn on the day of David's funeral and locked the door of the Eton Avenue flat behind her. Upstairs the house was rumbling with the sounds of a party that had spread downstairs into the hallway in a rubble of bodies and bottles of cheap Italian wine. She negotiated her way through the press of jokes, invitations and outstretched hands and reached the front door. Outside, the cars and motorcycles were double-parked along the street under the lime-trees.

She walked steadily, directing her steps towards the West End, unknowingly following the path taken by James Ross that morning. In Baker Street two troop-carriers and an army staff-car cruised past in a drizzle of rain.

Ross and Calverton arrived in Chelsea to find Williams, Prescott of D11 and the Metropolitan Police Commissioner already there. A square bounded by King's Road and the Embankment, Oakley Street and Smith Street had been blocked off by police and troops, and closer to Summer's home the houses were being emptied. A line of party-goers flanked by police were dancing a conga on the pavement. Someone shouted: "Scotland Yard are throwing a party! Bring a bottle! Pass it on!"

There was a cordon of Blue Berets by the entrance to the mews and, parked in the street, a carrier full of Special Patrol Group all dressed up like war had broken out. In the mobile command-centre Prescott was lecturing on tactics.

"Has anyone telephoned Summer to find out what's going on?" Ross asked. The question went up and down the command chain. The police were still trying to patch in to the GPO telephone lines. Ross left them to it and went to one of the houses.

The door was standing open and there was a smell of cloves and punch still simmering somewhere in the kitchen. He found the telephone and the directory and looked up Sebastian Summer. The owner of the house came in from the street and disturbed him. The man was embarrassed in the presence of a guest, muttered "Excuse me," and helped himself to a bottle of rum from the cabinet before going into the kitchen to turn the gas off under the bowl of punch. "Forgot it," he said sheepishly. Sebastian Summer answered the telephone.

"Is John Donaldson with you?"

There was a gasp at the other end of the line. A voice. "Here, give me the phone." A crackle on the line. "This is the police here! Who the bloody hell are you? And why should Kaster be here?"

When they broke in on Sebastian Summer, they found the duty officer wiping the prints off his glass and straightening his tie.

*

318

Donaldson pushed his burden slowly through the rainy streets. His white overall was spattered by the rain and the passing cars. People glanced at him without interest. He struggled along Buckingham Palace Road and along Buckingham Gate. There were police-cars blocking the exits towards the Palace itself and the Mall. A mixed convoy of police and army was moving down Birdcage Walk towards Whitehall and Westminster. Let them! It didn't interest him. He turned back and headed towards Grosvenor Place. The rain blew in his face and streamed through the stubble of his beard.

Ross examined the empty vehicle in the art-dealer's garage. A detective was reading off the engine number against that of the van stolen in Peterborough.

"This is the one," he said and smiled. Something was solved.

Ross climbed in the back and found flecks of white paint where something had scraped as it had been dragged out. He scratched a sample with his fingernail and showed it to Calverton.

"Presumably he's stolen another vehicle," said the latter.

"How? Where would he find another van in Chelsea at this time of night? And, while he was looking, how did he move the bomb through the streets?"

They went back upstairs. In the sitting-room four detectives were shouting questions at Sebastian Summer and pushing him around in a bewildered circle. In his gaudy silk dressing gown he looked like an exotic doll. Williams of Special Branch was sitting thoughtfully in one of the armchairs, watching the action.

"Do you honestly think he knows what Kaster intends?" enquired Calverton.

"I doubt it," the Welshman sang over the bellowing of his men. "But how do we really know? All we can do is hurt him until he tells us where Kaster is – or until whatever happens happens."

Calverton regarded Summer again. He had seen him once before at the clinic in Haslemere. That time the dealer had been sitting like a statue; this time he was bobbing like a spinning top. Still the same look of suffering on his face. Perhaps he was someone who set up his life to be a victim, though doubtless he had nothing so physical in mind. And there was Williams with his chops open, rubbing his shirt-cuff on his over-shaved chin and watching the pain. Calverton supposed that afterwards – if there were an afterwards – they would revert to the unspectacular sadomasochism of everyday life, killing flies and hating foreigners or whatever form it took. It was a depressing thought, especially if it were inherent in the order of things.

Calverton fervently believed in order but sometimes he wondered whether he subscribed to a lie. Perhaps the rotation of the planets and the rigorous structure of the atom were just a parody of true order. How sad it would be, to look for moral order in creation and find that there was only physics!

There were times when he almost hoped that Kaster would succeed. There were times when he suspected that he hated the terrorist with a hatred born of envy: if only he, Calverton, could . . . what? He felt that there was some indefinable act he would like to commit, whose enormity would force the universe to reveal itself and cry "Stop!" And if it did not? Perhaps, after all, it would deserve what happened.

"Stop hitting him," Ross intervened suddenly in a low, calm voice. "He knows nothing, and you know it, too." Sebastian Summer stopped spinning and staggered to a halt. One of the detectives looked round.

"That does it! Now I've lost my fucking rhythm. Get *him*, the bleeding heart, out of here!"

Calverton took Ross out of the room. They found themselves in a bedroom with two policewomen standing around the bed. One of the women looked round, saw they were not in uniform and asked: "Doctors? Has the ambulance arrived yet?"

"Why?"

"This one here has taken a load of pills. Trying to kill herself, I suppose."

They looked at the girl on the bed. She was unconscious; her face was covered in sweat and her breathing was irregular.

"Stupid cow," said a policewoman without rancour. "No man is worthing killing yourself for."

Ross turned to Calverton. "What happens next? Is Williams going to bring his torturers in?"

"Torturers? That's a little harsh, isn't it?"

"Is it?"

Calverton didn't answer. He picked up a book from the table by the bed and flipped it open. He put it down. Next to it an ivory figure of the Buddha together with a card: "*Existence is suffering – love, Anthony*."

"Which Christmas cracker did that one come out of?" said Ross. He placed the figure back on the table. "The answer isn't here. It's in the pattern of everything: the cutting gear, the white paint, the vans – they all mean something."

"Then tell me what it all means, James!" Calverton sounded as if he were pleading. Ross shook his head and moved towards the door. The two policewomen watched the men leave.

In the main room Sebastian Summer was being given a cup of tea. A detective in suede coat and check trousers was haranguing Williams. "Now, look here, Taffy . . . !"

"Bernard."

"OK, *Bernard* . . ."

"But I prefer to be addressed by my rank."

"Bugger that, *Bernard*, I'm supposed to be on leave and nothing you can do to me can compare with my old lady. This is no time for a bloody Scout meeting. Do you want me to tear the wings from this bloke or not?"

"I'm leaving," Ross told Calverton.

"Where are you going?"

"I don't know."

"You can't just leave. What about Kaster?"

"I'm not sure I care about Kaster. I don't even care about David."

At the head of the stairs Calverton took him by the arm and said: "I wish that you had joined us at the beginning. It might have been different. David – everything – it might all have been different."

Ross nodded. All along Calverton had been trying to enlist someone who didn't exist, but this wasn't the time to tell him. For a moment he felt sorry for the other man with his bedraggled ginger moustache and his bereaved look. "Yeah, it would have been a great idea."

"Good, good." There was nothing more. They were driven apart by a doctor and a brace of ambulancemen pushing their way up the staircase; then Ross found himself out in the street, caught in drifts of rain and light.

He returned to the house with the telephone and called his flat. There was no answer. Helen had gone. He called her home. Hortense Ainsworth answered snappishly that her daughter wasn't there. He remembered that she had said something about seeing the Old Year out in the crowd of revellers in Trafalgar Square. They weren't the only revellers. Through the window he could see soldiers and Blue Berets, strung out on adrenalin, pouncing on shadows and whispering coded endearments into their radios. It was a terrific party, as sexy and aggressive as the best ones.

In Piccadilly Donaldson passed the Royal Academy. In the drab darkness he didn't at first recognize Burlington House, and when it registered he was fifty yards beyond. He stopped and thought of going back; but what he wanted to go back to were the Summer Exhibitions, strawberries and the sight of new canvases that still smelled faintly of linseed oil. He tried to think about the last exhibition he had seen, but when he conjured the recollection of one of the pictures the tenebrous image of the Last Judgement came instead with a suddenness that made him start.

"You all right, mate?"

Donaldson turned round.

"Saw you wince. Got a stitch? Bit of indigestion, eh? Not the heart, bit too young for the heart, eh? Not surprised, pushing that sodding great thing around. I hope you're working for yourself; I wouldn't work for any other bugger what had me out on a night like this."

Donaldson shook out a few words. "I'm all right." But he was not. The elation he had felt earlier was ebbing away in the cold; his hands were clenched and the sweat freezing on the back of them. If only . . . if only. . . . The past was littered with other people he might have been, with other directions he might have taken, all lying around like derelict cars abandoned in a chase. If he closed his eyes, part of him could walk away into a different future where the Last Judgement would stay confined within its frame, just a painting.

The stranger padded along behind him muttering a step at a time between puffs of white breath. He wore a herringbone overcoat, the trousers from a business-suit and a pair of red sneakers with the toes kicked out.

"It must be heavy, that thing. Don't they have a gas-cannister inside them – calor gas, butane, propane? Heavy, those are. I used to hump them around. We had them, for cooking. Last time I had a job I was living in a caravan. That was in Rotherham. Ever been to Rotherham? I wouldn't like to push a gas-bottle about, but I suppose it must be part of your job."

"Yes."

"Thought it would be. Got a light?"

"I don't smoke."

"I suppose not. Not with the food. Unhygienic. And there's the gas. Dangerous, eh? Might go off like a bomb – hey, there's a laugh!"

Donaldson stopped and faced the other man. He had frank, hurt eyes that couldn't focus on anything for long and a nervous mouth with lips that flickered over unsaid things and picked out words at random.

"What do you want?"

The man was surprised. He thought for a moment. "I don't suppose you can spare a bite to eat? A sausage? I suppose they'll still be cold until you reach your pitch. How about a bread roll?"

"I haven't got any with me."

"Oh."

They stared at each other in silence for a second.

"What's Rotherham like?"

The man cheered up. "Oh, it's a dump, much like everywhere else."

Donaldson nodded. He reached into his pocket and fingered some change. He took it out and gave it to the stranger. "Go to a pub. Get a drink and a bite to eat."

"I'll do that." The man accepted the money and smiled. He stood on the pavement and watched Donaldson draw away into the darkness. "I'll think of you!" he shouted, too loud so that the drivers of passing cars looked round. He waved his hands then rubbed them together for warmth before slotting them into his pockets.

"No sausages or bread rolls on a hot-dog stand," he murmured to himself, then hummed a tune for comfort.

Chapter Thirty-Seven

HELEN reached Oxford Street. Passing by New Bond Street she had a sudden desire to go to the Summer Gallery; maybe, because this New Year's Eve, to look at the pictures he had chosen would help to lay the ghost of John Donaldson. She let herself in and turned on the light. After a moment's thought, she adjusted the dimmer so that bare shapes were visible to act as cues to her recollections. Then she stalked the paintings one by one, testing each in her memory, where they made less impact than the scent of wax from the floor and the bowls of pot-pourri which Sebastian kept by the entrance to each room. John, she remembered, could justify each one by some rational canon of beauty.

She left the gallery and walked into Piccadilly. People were seeping through in a current, forming eddies in the Circus, only to be sucked out through Coventry Street and the Haymarket towards Trafalgar Square, their faces set with an eagerness to bury the past and hope for the future. "Speak no ill of the dead." Helen suspected they were right: there was a shared need to erect a tombstone over the past so that it could be reinterpreted; and Trafalgar Square was the place where people could bring their dead and inter them to the bells that closed the Old Year.

James Ross was caught on foot by the crowd blocked against entering Parliament Square. The police had erected barricades in Victoria Street and Great George Street and backed them with a line of troop-carriers. A BBC reporter was trying to force his way through and film the floodlit emptiness of the square. Ross could hear him shouting to someone: "This isn't supposed to be happening. There was nothing about it in the briefing issued by the Met. Have you seen the Mall? The whole place is closed with troops end to end. What the hell is going on?"

Ross managed to reach the barricade. A few people had succeeded in climbing over it and were being chased around the square like hares. He was pressed up against the breast-high barrier, his face pushed into the face of the policeman on the other side. He produced the identification Calverton had given him.

"Let me through."

"What's that, your credit card?"

"Forget it. Who's in charge?"

The constable snorted as the barrier was pushed against his chest. "Don't make me laugh!" He linked arms with his comrades, and with a grunt they all pushed back. An officer on horseback was moving along the rear of the line, tapping the backs of his men with his stick and snapping encouragement. "Maintain that line there! That's it, keep 'em back!" Ross caught his eye and threw his card over the heads of the others.

"My ID!" he shouted. "Let me through!"

The officer caught it, glanced at it, and shouted back: "OK, that one! Him! Let him through!" A hand was extended and Ross was helped over the barricade.

"Important business?" The officer was leaning over, soothing the neck of his horse. The rain was streaming off the animal's twitching flanks. He repeated the question.

"Yes." For the moment Ross thought that meeting Helen was the most important thing in his life. Loving her was the only thing that seemed to make sense. "I'm trying to get to Trafalgar Square."

"No problem, it's only blocked off on this side, so that no one can get at Whitehall or the Palace. Come with me and I'll get you through on to the Embankment." He turned his mount's head and went at a smart clip across the square. Ross caught up with him at the barriers on the far side where the crowd was smaller. "Stick to the Embankment and then up Northumberland Avenue. You shouldn't have any trouble." He called to his men to let Ross pass.

Donaldson came at Trafalgar Square from the north side. The place was seething with people. Laughter, yells, plastic horns braying, all coming from no one in particular. The centre of the square was a press of humanity around the column and the lions, throwing off streamers like sparks of light. The noise was deafening.

He halted on the pavement in front of the National Gallery. He had arrived yet he felt lost. In the crowd milling around him he was more alone than he had ever felt in his life. The intense, almost religious exaltation that he had experienced earlier had gone and, instead, it seemed he could hear his own footsteps as he hunted in the hollow places of his heart for some last scrap of emotion to find only that terrible pity which had transfixed him in front of the painting: the burning sorrow for the inevitability of suffering and damnation.

He was cold. He pulled the flimsy white coat around him and felt the bulge of the explosives stitched underneath and the crackle of the canvas wrapped around his body. In the end, everything would come down to them.

He moved on. He pushed through the revellers and reached the sheltered angle where the steps from the gallery came down to the pavement. There he waited, glancing only now and then at his watch, sensing the approaching hour in the growing tension of the crowd. It was eleven forty-five.

In Northumberland Avenue the last streams of people were making their way towards the square; Ross was caught up with them. In the long walk from Chelsea his injured leg had started to give him pain and he was limping badly. He stepped out of the crowd into a doorway where another man was sheltering from the rain. As he stooped to massage the calf-muscle he could hear the man whistling and see his white reflection on the wet paving-stones.

"Look at them go," said the stranger. "Like bloody lemmings!" He lit a cigarette and the match spun past Ross's eyes to fizzle out in the rain. Somewhere a bottle was broken and a cheer went up. "As soon as it's midnight, they'll all be coming back this way, drunk as skunks and wanting a bite to eat." Ross looked up and saw the hot-dog stand parked in the gutter and leaking steam into the cold air.

"Want one?"

"No."

"What are you staring at, then?"

"I'm not sure." Ross shook his head. It was swimming with pictures: Helen's cottage in Northumberland; Donaldson working under the black night-sky on an object whose shape was hidden by the searing light of a burning torch. White paint falling in white droplets on the melting snow. Lionel Sholto scornfully quoting a police report: "A hot-dog stand stolen from the vicinity of Newcastle football-ground?"

"What's inside that thing?" Ross asked urgently.

"Who wants to know?"

Ross grabbed the stranger by the shoulders. "For God's sake, man!"

"Keep your hair on, mate!" The street vendor was still shaking when Ross let him go. "There's nothing inside except a few tins of frankfurters, some buns and a bottle of gas to keep everything on the boil." The man brushed invisible flecks from his coat. He mumbled: "You want to watch your step, mate. I know a thing or two about karate."

"Sure you do," said Ross. He stared at the other man and saw a pair of scared eyes staring back. He let the man go. "Sure you do," he repeated. The aggression had been burned out of him. In all his ignorance there were times when he understood too much. That sort of attitude, Figgis had said, can get you killed. "What other pitches are being worked tonight?" he asked.

The vendor laughed. "You're kidding me! Where else outdoors are you going to find a crowd near midnight on New Year's Eve?" He didn't get an answer. He was looking at Ross's back disappearing into the rain.

Helen stood on the pavement opposite the National Gallery, pressed against the stone balustrade which cut off the central section of the square where the crowd was at its densest and the fountains were alive with people dancing in the water. She watched them and saw wishing-wells and crowds of believers descending steps to immerse themselves in the Ganges, washing away the past and hoping for the future; feeling that they were accomplishing something by going through the rituals. And perhaps they were.

Something cold and soft touched her hand. She glanced down and saw a snowflake melting at the warmth of her skin. She looked at the sky, chopped into sections by the interplay of lights, and the clouds with their smoky reflection through a hanging veil of snow. From the square came an audible "Aah!" as faces by the thousand were turned upwards.

"Helen." A hand gripped her firmly by the wrist. She turned and saw Donaldson, his pale face close to hers as the crowd on the pavement pressed into them. The exclamation was frozen on her lips by the bleak emptiness in his eyes. "Where are the others?" he asked.

"There are no others."

"Then why are you here?"

"Where else should I be on New Year's Eve?"

He staggered slightly as someone pushed past him, and Helen found herself holding him with her lips pressed up against the lobe of his ear and the susurration of his breath audible above the roar and songs of the crowd. She heard him say, "Help me, Helen – I'm suffering!" but when they moved apart again she saw only the same impassive face resisting her.

"You must come with me." He spoke calmly. He was looking across to the gallery, which was a shadow in the confusion of snow and lights.

"John, let me help you!"

"It really isn't possible."

"At least let me try?"

He didn't answer. She was being pulled by him, and the jostling crowd, all blind eyes, blind smile, blind laughter, made way for them to cross the road. A group of youths charged past chanting "Torremolinos! Torremolinos!" They danced across the roadway and climbed the stone plinth under the statue of George IV. "Mind his horse doesn't shit on you!" Cheers and a shower of streamers floating upwards to meet the snow. It was 11.55.

Ross reached the square at a run. His head was spinning. A hot-dog stand, for chrissake! Kaster had stolen it, taken out the gas-bottle, enlarged the space and strengthened the base to take the load; then he had sprayed the result white. The theft had even been reported, but they had dismissed it despite the evidence that Donaldson had been working on something other than the stolen vans. Yet it was perfect: mobile, untraceable by any registration mark, a bland piece of hardware that was inconspicuous in a crowd.

The square was dammed with people moving in slow rotation about the column, its top lost in the drifting snow. The rise and fall of their voices was the sea sucking through a shingled beach. The emergency services were grouped near the exit into Whitehall: a couple of ambulances, some trucks in army drab, a control-centre with its doors open to the night and a little tableau of lights and figures inside like a nativity scene.

He pushed through the crowd on the eastern pavement. The Army had placed a picket outside South Africa House, just in case, and some embassy guards, built in concrete, were set around the entrance to wish any strangers a Happy New Year. Well, this time they were not the target. Kaster didn't think in narrow political terms; Ross had guessed the meaning behind Calverton's words, and even briefly felt it when he hunted down Donaldson's brother. Tonight was going to see art and myth turn into reality.

He was stuck in the crowd; any relaxation and he seemed to be driven backwards in a sea of bodies. There was a skin of melting snow on the ground, and his shoes slid over it, giving a sensation of being adrift in a flotsam of warm flesh, lapped by the limps that fended him off. At the edge of vision the National Gallery was a dim shade, viewed through a gauze of light and snow.

It had to be the gallery! Where else in the square was a stage for Kaster's final performance? A cast of thousands and the television crews to take the pictures to an audience of millions – and, if the bomb went off, to scatter and carry with them plague and anthrax to . . . anywhere.

People, jammed with barely room to breathe, swaying to a rhythm that was no individual's rhythm. Faces, jammed against each other with smiles pressed out of bared teeth by the weight of other people. Warm breath, smelling of wine and beer. Ross was racing but unable to race, his body pushing him into a resisting wall of bodies, every step forward having to be fought for. A dream chase through dark corridors where the heart bursts to reach a goal that never comes closer. Another step won or lost. His face burning the flakes of snow from his skin. Then suddenly he was on the north side of the square and the curtain wall of the gallery was there to be touched.

Abruptly the pressure of the crowd relaxed. People were moving in a slow surge as those on the pavement and in the road tried to reach the hallowed ground in the centre of the square. Ross held to the wall and clawed his way towards the steps to the gallery entrance, looking for signs of Kaster's presence. He checked his watch: it showed two minutes to midnight. Then he saw it, a white shape tight against the wall. And, next to it, John Donaldson and Helen.

Donaldson turned and saw Ross. His face showed no surprise. Ross didn't expect it would: in a drama surprise becomes the stuff of normality, and Donaldson was living a drama. Instead, his instincts reacted to their training and he drew a gun. Ross heard Helen shout, "John! No!" and then a shot that flattened against the wall and a ricochet like a kick in the guts which threw him to the ground.

There was an animal roar from the crowd and a chaos of movement as people stampeded away. The pavement between the two men was cleared and they saw each other unopposed across the white box containing the bomb. Donaldson's gun was on the ground where Helen had knocked it from his hand. The roadway was a complete bedlam. In the centre of the square the crowd had sensed the disturbance and were cheering wildly. Then the pavement was empty. Donaldson was running across the road.

The crowd divided. People were running but not moving. Bodies went down under the crushing of feet. Screams blended into the cacophony of cheering and songs. Donaldson reached the far side of the roadway and leaped on to the granite balustrade. On the other side the ground dropped away fifteen feet into the packed centre of the square. Faces looked up at the lone figure framed against the dappled web of snow. Shouts – laughter – cries of "Jump! Jump!" Donaldson jumped.

Ross was hard on the other man's heels, reaching the balustrade a second after Donaldson had gone. He looked down and saw his enemy borne up on the outstretched hands of the people below, spreadeagled, arms laid open, crucified for an instant against the upturned faces: then the image was gone and Donaldson was on his feet driving a wedge through the spectators towards the shadow of the giant fir-tree flickering in its Christmas baubles. Ross levered himself over the stonework and dropped on to the paving.

A few hands came out to receive him, but he landed heavily. He felt the jolt and his injured leg give way. A bolt of pain shot through the nerve and a soundless scream burned out of his lungs as his hands dropped to the calf-muscle and came up with blood from the reopened wound. A chant went up of "Blood! Blood!" and a space cleared itself around him. Then from Parliament Square the sound of Big Ben chiming midnight drifted in with the snow, and the noise in the square dropped to a hush of expectancy.

Ross struggled to his feet, half-blinded with pain. He could see Donaldson at the end of a long tunnel flanked by the faces of corpses. The vision resolved itself into the struggles of the crowd fighting to get clear and Donaldson in the shadow of the tree's overhanging branches, his face radiating an unearthly calmness.

Ross staggered forward, dragging his wounded leg, leaving a trail of blood-spatters in the dirt and slush. He stumbled twice and got to his feet again. His head was pounding with the rush of blood; his ears echoed with the beat of the distant chimes and the sighing of the mass of humanity. From his jacket he took his gun. Donaldson remained motionless, detached.

He felt Helen by his side, heard her voice. Her arm was around him, supporting him, taking his weight as he forced each step forward. Somewhere impossibly distant, voices were groaning, words forming, a rising chorus counting the sounding of the hour. Nine! Ten! Eleven! Ross took the gun in his shaking hands and sighted it on the other man's still figure. Donaldson's face was divided by the foresight. It was strangely peaceful. The piercing eyes were looking through Ross into – Ross couldn't guess. He let the gun fall. Suddenly he felt an overwhelming pity for the other man, trapped in the darkness of his own fantasies. He wanted to shout out, offer him a lifeline back to reality.

Twelve!

A cry of release went up from the thousands of voices. Ross felt Helen's grip relax and he slipped to the ground. She was holding a gun, the one that she had struck from Donaldson's hand. She aimed it and fired once. The noise was drowned in the deafening joy and agony of the crowd. Donaldson was staring at her, trying to say something. Then he clutched at his breast where petals of blood were spreading across it and fell to the ground, his fingers scrabbling after something inside his coat, bound close to his body, a painted rag of canvas torn by the bullet and speckled with blood. There was a blast of light and noise, an explosion that wiped out all other light and noise. The heat-wave struck Ross in the face and was gone. He opened his eyes and saw the fire licking at the lower branches of the tree, and then, as the resin caught, a tower of flame blazed up its full height until it formed an incandescent candle to the blackness of the sky.

Chapter Thirty-Eight

Ross came to in darkness relieved only by a faint orange reflection sweeping regularly across a low ceiling. For background noises there were sirens and the crackle of radio voices.

"Hello, James. How are you feeling?"

Ross opened his eyes. It was Calverton, leaning over him, his face too close out of the same poor sense of other people's need for space.

"We'll get an ambulance for you as soon as we can. There's a bit of a rush on at the moment."

"Why do I need an ambulance?"

"You've been injured. A bit of concussion, a little blood-loss."

"In fact the story of my life?" Ross sat up slowly. He was on a narrow bunk inside some sort of stationary vehicle. The orange light came from a police car parked next to it. The radio traffic was still going on in strangulated snatches. "Where is this?"

"Trafalgar Square. One of the first-aid centres."

"What happened?"

"Would you believe that Kaster blew himself up?"

Ross shook his head between his hands until the recollections fell back into place. Donaldson had caused the explosion. Why? What had that look on the dead man's face meant? What had he seen in those last seconds? Calverton was saying "—bodies all over the place. All hell broke loose as people tried to get clear. Total chaos. It seems that Kaster was wearing explosives around his body; so his friend Summer told us, and he seems to have been proved right." He glanced at Ross. "Hope you're going to be all right, James?"

"I'll survive."

"An ambulance will be free soon, I'm sure."

"Forget it." He tested his legs. His trousers had been torn and a clean dressing put over the wound. "Where is Helen?" he asked.

"Helen? Ah, the Ainsworth girl. You don't mean she was here?"

"I just want to know where she is now."

"But she was here?"

Ross shook his head. "No."

"Tea?" enquired a voice from the door. "Hot, sweet and doctor's orders."

"Would you like a cup of tea, James?" Calverton asked solicitously.

"Where is the bomb?"

Calverton seemed taken aback.

"It's in our good hands, no need to excite yourself over that."

"Why didn't Donaldson blow it up? He saw me coming; he should have had time. Why didn't he blow the damn thing?"

Calverton looked away. "I don't know whether I can answer that – not the 'whys' of it all. But it seems that there was no detonating charge to the thing. I suppose that is rather odd, isn't it? It suggests that he never intended to explode the bomb: that it was all a gesture, a . . . sacrifice?"

"He killed himself and left us to see what he might have done."

"Yes, something like that. One can't tell: not being able to see the problem through his eyes."

"I suppose not." Suddenly Ross had had enough. "Where's my coat?"

"You're leaving? Are you fit enough? I really think you should stay."

"Is that a threat?"

"Good Lord, no! I mean – I could make it one, James. There will be enquiries, a lot of enquiries."

"Don't worry. I'll be around." Ross found his coat. He felt weak but able to get by. He found his way to the door and looked out into the night.

The square was full of light. Vehicles all over the place with headlights on and emergency roof-lights beating time to each other. Spotlights thrown up in the backs of army wagons, pouring their glare over the pavements, bleaching the square of colour. There was debris everywhere and the wounded still being taken away from the scene. The Army, like looters, were fingering over the wreckage.

"The operation has been a success," Calverton commented from somewhere behind him. "Taken as a whole, I mean. A qualified success, but a success none the less."

"Sure it has." Ross descended a couple of steps to the ground. There was thin snow underfoot and light snow still falling. The air was bitter and resinous from the burned-out tree. A pall of steam was hanging over its embers in one corner of the square.

"I can get you a car," said Calverton. "Take you where you want to go."

"Thanks." Ross didn't look at the other man. He heard him snapping orders to someone; bring a car. Then Calverton was hanging close by him.

"It's difficult to take it all in, isn't it, James – all . . . this? I mean, that one man should be able – it doesn't make sense. The way that events can line up behind one individual, it seems so – what's the word? – contrived? But take Hitler—"

Ross cut him short: "It's like winning a lottery. Somebody has to. It doesn't mean a damn thing."

Ross accepted the car and had it take him to Blackheath. There was a light in the hallway showing through a fanlight and a television set flickering black and white in a darkened room. Did anyone still have a black-and-white set? Maybe Hortense Ainsworth did.

Helen came to the door. Her face, never particularly beautiful, was engraved with grief. She invited him in in a matter-of-fact manner and made small-talk in a low voice while she took his coat and offered him a drink. She walked ahead of him down the passageway.

"My mother is asleep. Try to keep your voice down in case she wakes. Are you sure you won't have a drink? You look—"

"A mess," Ross extended a hand to grip her arm. She froze, her back still turned to him.

"You can clean up here, if you want. Or stay the night. We have a spare room, more than one. Uncle Tom—"

"Why did you shoot John Donaldson?"

She turned at last and faced him. He remembered that first time he had seen her at David's funeral, the same suppressed tears. They seemed to stare at each other across rows of graves.

"He was suffering," she said. "I still loved him enough to help him that far."

"So now he's dead, like David."

"Like David," she said. Ross could see the tears forming in her eyes, but, quickly, she stepped forward so that his arms embraced her and her head was against his, her hair grazing his cheek, so that the tears, if they finally came, were invisible. So, even now, with her trembling body held close to his, he knew that he would never know her and that there would always be that core of secrecy that would always be hers. In time it could make her precious to him.

Calverton called the following morning. Ross asked how the other man had found him.

"Mere shrewdness, James, when I telephoned and found that you were not at home."

"What do you want?"

Calverton dropped all pretence at facetiousness. Ross could hear him caring for him down the phone: in everything Calverton stood too close. But it was well enough meant. "Some information for you, James. I thought that we owed you that, at least."

"What is it?"

"We discovered what was wrong with the Schreiber girl. It was malaria. It seems she picked it up in Ceylon." He hazarded a laugh. "For a time it made us a bit panicky."

"Go on."

"The bomb," said Calverton. "Our people have opened it up. Remarkable speed, eh?"

"And?"

"There was nothing inside it. Absolutely nothing."